Also by Sandra Gulland
The Many Lives & Secret Sorrows of Josephine B.

Tales of Passion, Tales of Woe

SANDRA GULLAND

SCRIBNER PAPERBACK FICTION
Published by Simon & Schuster

SCRIBNER PAPERBACK FICTION
Simon & Schuster, Inc.
Rockefeller Center
1230 Avenue of the Americas
New York, NY 10020

First Scribner Paperback Fiction edition 1999
Originally published in Canada in 1998
by HarperCollins Publishers Ltd.

SCRIBNER PAPERBACK FICTION and design are trademarks of
Macmillan Library Reference USA, Inc., used under license by
Simon & Schuster, the publisher of this work.

Manufactured in the United States of America

3 5 7 9 10 8 6 4

Library of Congress Cataloging-in-Publication Data
Gulland, Sandra.
Tales of passion, tales of woe / Sandra Gulland.
—1st Scribner Pbk. Fiction ed.
p.   cm.
Includes bibliographical references.
1. Josephine, Empress, consort of Napoleon I, Emperor of the French,
1763–1814—Fiction. 2. France—History—Consulate and First Empire,
1799–1815—Fiction. 3. Empresses—France—Fiction. I. Title.
PR9199.3.G7915T35   1999
813'.54—dc21   99-21531
CIP

ISBN 0-684-85607-7

For my father,
who loves stories,
and my mother,
who loves books.

In a dark time, the eye begins to see.
—*Theodore Roethke*

Tales of Passion,
Tales of Woe

Prologue: Marie Antoinette (spirit)

He calls her Josephine.

I approach her with caution. I do not want to startle her, only observe her, writing at her escritoire. It is an old piece of furniture, made in the Islands—a crude design but of sentimental value. She remembers her father sitting at it, cursing over the bills, as she often does herself.

She pauses, looks up, her hand suspended over the page of her journal.

She's not what one would call a beauty, yet he worships her with a passion that verges on madness! Big hazel eyes, I grant you, and yes, long curling lashes, a slender, graceful form, artful dress, etc., etc.—but are these qualities that bewitch? Perhaps it is the caress of her musical voice that has cast a spell. (I know about spells.) No, it's her maddening gentleness that drives him to despair. He wants to consume her, possess her, enchain her! And she . . . well, I see that puzzled look in her eyes.

She glances over her shoulder. There is no one, I assure her. She listens, and hears: the steady ticking of the pendulum clock, the crackling of the fire in the bedchamber. She dips the raven's tail quill in the ink.

I only want to help! History was cruel where I was concerned. They made me into a monster, took my husband, my children, my head.

Beware! I want to warn her. Small deceits, one upon another, destroy faith. You will not miss it until it's gone. Betrayed, one becomes the betrayer. The Devil lights the path. Say what you will, there is no return.

She puts down the quill. A tear? Such thoughts oppress, no doubt. Loyalty defines her; she lives to please.

Such is the luxury of commoners—a conceit, if you will.

She pulls her shawl about her shoulders; I've chilled her, I know. It can't be helped. She knows not the future. I do.

I

Our Lady of Victories

How many lands, how many frontiers separate us!
—*Napoleon, in a letter to Josephine.*

In which my new life begins

March 10, 1796—Paris, early morning, grey skies.
I am writing this in my jasmine-scented dressing room, where I might not be discovered by Bonaparte, my husband of one day.

Husband. The word feels foreign on my tongue, as foreign as the maps spread over the dining room table, the sword propped in the corner of my drawing room. As foreign as the man himself.

My face in the glass looks harsh, etched by shadow, reflecting the dark thoughts in my heart.

How unlike me to be melancholy. I'm tempted to black out the words I've just written, tempted to write, instead: I've married, I am happy, all is well. But I've promised myself one thing—to be honest on these pages. However much I am required to dissemble, to flatter and cajole, here I may speak my heart truly. And my heart, in truth, is troubled. I fear I've made a mistake.

[Undated]
Josephine Rose Beauharnais Bonaparte
Josephine Rose Bonaparte
Josephine Tascher Beauharnais Bonaparte
Josephine Beauharnais Bonaparte
Josephine Bonaparte
Citoyenne Josephine Bonaparte
Madame Josephine Bonaparte

Josephine
Josephine
Josephine

We've just returned from Saint-Germain. Bonaparte is in a meeting in the study, and I'm back in my dressing room, seeking solace. It seems that everything is going wrong. Where to begin?

This morning, as I was dusting my face with rice powder, preparing to leave, I saw Bonaparte standing in the door. "The coach is ready." He had a riding crop in his hands and was twisting it, bending it. He was anxious, I knew, about going out to Saint-Germain to see my children at their schools. Certainly, I was uneasy myself. I wasn't sure how Hortense was going to take the news.

"You're not wearing your new jacket?" I asked, putting on a pair of dangling sapphire earrings. I'd changed into a long-sleeved violet gown over a dotted gauze skirt. It was a new ensemble and I was pleased with the effect, but I couldn't decide which shoes to wear—my lace-up boots or my silk slippers, which went so nicely. It had stopped raining but was damp out. The boots would be more practical. "The boots," I told my scullery maid, who pushed one roughly onto my foot. I made a mental note to begin looking for a lady's maid as soon as Bonaparte left for the south.

As soon as Bonaparte left for the south, and life returned to normal.

Today, tonight and then tomorrow, I thought—twenty-eight hours. Twenty-eight hours of frenetic activity, soldiers coming and going, couriers cantering into the courtyard. Twenty-eight hours of chaos. Every surface of my little house is covered with maps, journals, reports, scraps of paper with lists on them of provisions, names, numbers, schedules. Books are stacked on the dining room table, on the escritoire, by my bed. Twenty-eight more hours of his fumbling caresses and embraces. Bonaparte works and reads with intense concentration—oblivious to me, to the servants—and then falls upon me with a ravenous need. Twenty-eight more hours of dazed bewilderment. Who is this man I have married? Will life ever be "normal" again?

"What's wrong with this jacket?" he demanded.

"It needs mending," I said, smoothing the shoulder. The worn grey wool was pulling at the seams and the edges of the cuffs were frayed. I would have it mended, if I could ever get him out of it. If I could ever get him out of it, I might burn it, I thought, kissing his smooth cheek. "And you look so handsome in the new one." The knee-length tails helped detract from his thin legs and gave the impression of height.

He kissed me and grinned. "I'm not changing," he said, tweaking my ear.

It was a slow journey to Saint-Germain—the rain had made the roads muddy—so it was early afternoon by the time our carriage pulled into the courtyard of Hortense's school. I spotted her on the playing field and waved. As soon as she saw us, she dropped the ball and spun on her heels, covering her face with her hands. Was she crying? I touched Bonaparte's arm to distract him, but it was too late—he'd already seen my daughter's reaction. He gazed across the playing field with a sad expression in his grey eyes.

"Something's wrong," I said. I feared what the problem might be.

"I'll wait for you inside." Bonaparte pulled down on the rim of his new general's hat. The felt was rigid yet and it sat high on his big head.

I squeezed his hand, as lovers do. "I won't be long," I promised.

The ground was soft under my feet. I could feel the damp soaking into my thin-soled boots. A spring breeze carried the scent of ploughed fields. I picked my way around the wet spots, reminding myself that Hortense was young. Reminding myself that it was normal for a girl of twelve (almost thirteen) to have a delicate sensibility, especially considering . . .

Especially considering what she's had to endure. It has been almost two years since the Terror, yet even now my daughter sometimes wakes screaming in the night. Even now she cannot pass the place where her father died without bursting into tears.*

* Joephine's first husband, Alexandre Beauharnais, the father of her two children— Hortense (twelve) and Eugène (fourteen)—was beheaded on July 23, 1794, at the height of the Terror, the violent phase of the French Revolution in which thousands of aristocrats were guillotined.

My niece Émilie ran to embrace me. "Is Hortense hurt?" I asked. "What's wrong?" My daughter looked so alone, hunched over by the goal post, her back to us.

"She's crying, Auntie," Émilie said, shivering, her hands pushed into the pockets of her plain woollen smock. "It's the hysterics!"

Hysterics? I'd been warned that girls of fourteen were subject to frightful convulsions, but Hortense was not yet of that age. I lifted the hem of my gown and headed toward my weeping daughter.

"Hortense?" I called out, approaching. I could see her shoulders shaking. "Darling—" I reached out and touched her shoulder. Even through my gloves I could feel her bones—the bones of a girl still, not yet the bones of a woman. I considered turning her, but I knew her stubborn strength. Instead, I walked around to face her.

I was startled by the haunted look in her eyes. Pink blotches covered her freckled cheeks, making her eyes seem abnormally blue—her father's eyes. Her father's critical eyes, following me still. I took her cold, bare hand and pressed it to my heart. "What is it, darling?" Thinking how she'd grown in the last year, thinking that she was tall for her age, and that soon she would be as tall as I am, taller perhaps.

"I'm afraid, Maman." A sob welled up in her.

A gust of wind rustled the leaves. My straw hat flew off my head and dangled down my back by a ribbon. It was not the answer I'd expected. "Of what?"

"That you'll marry him!"

Him: Bonaparte. I tried to speak, but could not. The words stuck in my throat. How could I tell her that the deed had been done, the vows spoken, the contract signed: Bonaparte and I were man and wife. How could I tell her that this man was now her father—for better or for worse, for ever and ever. "Hortense, General Bonaparte is a kind man," I said, reprimanding her gently. "He cares for you sincerely."

"I don't care! I don't care for *him*." Then she hung her head, seeing the stricken look in my eyes. "I'm sorry, Maman!" She took a big breath and exhaled, blowing her cheeks out like a balloon.

I folded her in my arms. "I have to go back. Are you going to be all right?" I felt her nod against my chest. I stroked her soft golden curls. She would need time. We all would. "I'd like you and Eugène to come to Fontainebleau with me next weekend, to see Aunt Désirée and the Marquis," I said, swaying like a mother with an infant in her arms again, lulling her baby to sleep. I felt a thickening in my throat as I recalled the feel of her at birth, her tiny skull, her piercing cry. It *is* going to be all right, I wanted to tell her. (I want to believe it myself.) "Can you come next weekend?" Bonaparte would be gone by then.

The weathered door to the school creaked on its hinges, startling a maid who was perched on a stepladder washing the crystal candelabra. I heard Bonaparte's voice, his lecturing tone. I knocked on the door to the headmistress's study.

Madame Campan was seated behind her enormous pedestal desk covered with books and stacks of paper. The small room was furnished in the style of the Ancien Régime, ornate, musty and dark. A vase of silk lilies had been placed under the portrait of Queen Marie Antoinette. Two years ago Madame Campan would have lost her life for showing sympathy for the Queen.*

The prim headmistress motioned me in without taking her eyes off her guest. Bonaparte was perched on the edge of a puce Louis XV armchair, holding a teacup and expounding on the uselessness of girls learning Latin. His saucer was swamped—with coffee, I guessed, to judge by the aroma.

When he paused to take a breath, Madame Campan stood to greet me, smoothing the skirt of her gown. Dressed in black, she could have been taken for a maid but for the intricate beaded trim of the head scarf she wore, as if in perpetual mourning. "Forgive me for interrupting," I said, taking the chair beside Bonaparte. He searched my eyes for a clue. This was an awkward situation for him, I knew, a difficult situation for us both. Things were not going according to plan.

"General Bonaparte and I have been discussing education in a Republican

* *Madame Campan had been lady-in-waiting to Queen Marie Antoinette, who had been beheaded two-and-a-half years earlier during the Terror, when the monarchy had been abolished and a democratic Republic installed in its place.*

society," Madame Campan said, pulling her head scarf forward. "It isn't often one meets a man who has given this matter thought."

I removed my gloves, tugging on each fingertip. My new gold betrothal ring caught the light. I put my hand over it and said, "General Bonaparte is a philosopher at heart, Madame Campan. He gives all matters thought." I offered Bonaparte a conciliatory little smile.

Bonaparte emptied his teacup and put the cup and saucer on the side table between us. I reached out to keep the table from tipping. "It's late," he told me, pulling out his pocket-watch. "Aren't you going to tell her?"

"Yes," I said, flushing, seeing him through a stranger's eyes: a short, thin man with a sallow complexion, lank hair, shabby attire. A coarse-spoken man with poor manners. An intense, humourless man with fiery eyes—a Corsican, a Revolutionary, an opportunist. My husband. "We have an announcement to make," I told Madame Campan.

Only my closest friends knew that we'd married. I wasn't looking forward to informing my family—nor my acquaintances, for that matter, many of whom would be condescending, I feared, in spite of Bonaparte's recent promotion to General-in-Chief of the Army of Italy. The genteel world would silently judge that I had married beneath me. It would be said that as a widow with two children to educate and place in the world, as an aristocrat without fortune, and indeed, as a woman over the age of thirty, I was desperate. "I—that is, General Bonaparte and I—have married." I took my husband's hand; it was as damp as my own.

Madame Campan sat back abruptly, as if pushed. "Why . . . that's marvellous," she said, with the appearance of sincerity. "What a surprise. But that's marvellous," she repeated. "When?"

"Twenty after ten last night," Bonaparte said, drumming his nails on the arm of his chair. "Twenty-two minutes after, to be exact."

"Well." Madame Campan made a small, dry cough into her fist. "Your children have been very good at keeping this secret, Madame . . . Bonaparte, is it now?" I nodded, grieved to hear my new name spoken, grieved to be giving up the lovely and distinguished name of Beauharnais. "No doubt Hortense and Eugène are . . . ?" She held out her hands, palms up.

I felt my cheeks becoming heated. "That seems to be the problem. General Bonaparte and I came out to Saint-Germain today with the intention of telling my children, but . . ." I tried to swallow.

Madame Campan leaned forward over her desk, her hands tightly clasped. "Hortense does not know?"

"We were going to tell her just now, but she was upset, so I didn't think it wise."

"She was crying," Bonaparte said, shifting his weight.

"How curious," Madame Campan said. "She was so cheerful this morning at breakfast. Do you know why?"

How could I explain without offending Bonaparte? "Perhaps she didn't like seeing me on a man's arm," I said, stretching the truth only a little. "She's so attached to the memory of her father, as you know."

"Oh dear, yes, I see. Your daughter is . . . sensitive." She spoke the word with deliberate care, pressing her hands to her chin in an attitude of prayer. "She feels everything so strongly! Which is why she is gifted in the theatrical arts, I believe, and in the arts in general. She is, as I have often told you, my favourite student." She paused. "May I make a suggestion?"

"Please do! I confess I'm at a loss."

"Perhaps if I told her? Sometimes it's better that way. I could talk to both Hortense and Eugène together."

I glanced at Bonaparte. It was a coward's solution, I knew, but a solution nonetheless. "Good," Bonaparte said, standing.

After, Bonaparte and I stood silently on the bottom stone step of the school, waiting for my coach. "I guess, under the circumstances, we should consider whether or not to visit Eugène now," I said finally, looking out over the fields to Eugène's school next door. On the one hand, I hated not to see him; on the other, I owed four months' tuition. "He's not expecting us," I said, as my carriage creaked to a stop in front of us.

"Back to Paris," Bonaparte told my coachman, opening the carriage door himself. "I approve of Campan's approach," he said, climbing in after me. "She's educated, but she's not a bluestocking. And she's not proud either. I thought she was lady-in-waiting to the Queen."

The carriage pulled through the school gates. I nodded apologetically to the beggarwoman sitting in the dirt with her infant at her breast;

usually I had something for her. "She was," I said, tightening my hat strings. Madame Campan had practically been raised at court. "She was in the Tuileries Palace with the royal family when it was ransacked. A man from Marseille grabbed her and was going to kill her, but someone yelled that they didn't kill women and that saved her."

"She was lucky. I approve that the girls learn to make soup and have to tidy their rooms themselves. I'll enrol my younger sisters."

Bonaparte has four brothers and three sisters—my family now. "Your sisters who are living in Marseille with your mother?" In town now, we were passing the castle, a ruin, like so many.

"I'm going to move them all to Paris."

"That would be lovely," I said, smiling in spite of a pain in my side.

"How much does Campan charge?"

"For the year? Three thousand francs."

"That's ridiculous," he said, opening a book he'd been reading on the way down, the life of Alexandre the Great.

"Eugène's school is even more." And I was paying for my niece Émilie's tuition as well—or trying to. It had been a long time since I'd had any income from home.* My coachman cracked his whip. I let my head fall back against the tufted upholstered seat and closed my eyes, the memory of Hortense's tears coming back to me.

"Not feeling well?"

"I'm fine," I lied.

Now, in the quiet of my little dressing room, I give way to despair. What *am* I going to do? Not long ago I'd promised my daughter that I wouldn't marry Bonaparte. Now she will think I've betrayed her. She is too young to understand what is truly best for her, too young to understand the complexities of love, and of need. Too young to understand that promises made with love may also with love be broken.

* *Josephine's mother, a widow, lived on the family sugar plantation in the Caribbean island of Martinique ("Martinico"), where Josephine had been born and raised. A small percentage of the plantation's earnings constituted Josephine's main source of income—when she received it, that is, which was rarely. Formerly under French rule, the island was now controlled by England.*

Late evening, I'm not sure how late. Still raining.

More meetings, visitors. Bonaparte is downstairs still with two of his aides. The smell of cigar smoke fills the air. I'm bathed and dressed for bed, awaiting my husband. This is our last night together before he leaves.

After a fast evening meal (he eats so quickly!), Bonaparte read out loud the letter he'd written to the Directors announcing our marriage. Satisfied, he folded the paper, shoved it into an envelope, dripped wax on it and thumped it with his seal. Then he put the envelope to one side and rummaged through the drawer where the papers were kept, pulling out a sheet of rag bond. He stood and motioned for me to take the seat at the escritoire. "I need a letter to my mother from you."

Of course! I put my lacework aside. He would be seeing his mother in Marseille, informing her of our union—his mother who, according to Corsican custom, should have been asked for permission first. His mother, who would have refused permission had she been asked. His mother, who was opposed to her son's marrying a widow with two children, a woman without a dowry, a woman six years older than her son.

Bonaparte paced, dictating what he thought the letter should say: that she was now my honoured mother, that I was looking forward to meeting her, that I would visit her on my way to Italy to join my husband, that—

There was a sudden rush of pouring rain. I held the raven's tail quill suspended. I was to go to Italy? "But Bonaparte—"

"In six weeks, after I run the Austrians out."

I smiled. Was he joking? I was saved from my dilemma by the sound of a man calling out from the garden, "Open the damned door!"

"Was that Director Barras?" I asked Bonaparte, going to the door to the garden. "It is you!" I kissed my friend's wet cheeks.

"And good evening to you, General Bonaparte, Commander-in-Chief of the Army of Italy," Barras proclaimed in a mock official voice, balancing his gold-tipped walking stick against the wall. "My heartfelt congratulations on your recent appointment." Bonaparte looked sullen, even as the Director shook his hand.*

---

* The executive authority of the Republic was vested in a council of five directors— "five Majesties." Director Paul Barras was considered the most powerful of the five, and hence the most politically powerful man in the French Republic.

"Thanks to *you*, Père Barras," I said, draping his military greatcoat over a chair by the fire to dry. Less than a year ago Bonaparte had been unemployed. Barras had been instrumental in getting him a series of promotions, but this last, to General-in-Chief, had taken considerable persuasion on Barras's part. The Directors had been reluctant to grant the command of an army to a Corsican.

"Not bad, not bad," Barras said, turning Bonaparte like a mannequin, examining his new uniform. "A little big at the shoulders perhaps?" His own jacket seemed a little tight on him, I noticed; the tails split open at the back. "But why these frayed epaulettes?"

"What were you doing out in the garden, Paul?" I asked, changing the subject. I'd brought up the matter of the epaulettes earlier, but without success. (Bonaparte is so stubborn!)

"I knocked and no one answered. How you can manage on such a small staff, Rose, is beyond me," Barras said, running his hand through his thinning hair. (Dyed black?)

"I'm looking for a lady's maid, in fact." On learning that I was going to marry a Revolutionary, my former maid had quit. "If you hear of one—"

"Her name is Josephine now," Bonaparte said.

"You're changing your Christian name as well?" Barras frowned, considering. "*Josephine*—yes, I like that, Rose, it rather suits you. As does your gown, I must say. Don't you look lovely. I do know of a maid though. My aunt was telling me of a girl. But only one? You need at least three more. Enough of this Republican simplicity. Republican romanticism, I call it. And speaking of romance, how *are* my lovebirds this miserable evening?"

"Just fine," I said with more enthusiasm than I felt.

"The Directory can only provide me with eight thousand francs," Bonaparte said.

Barras flung back his tails and sat down. (Was he wearing a corset? Barras, at forty, was becoming vain.) "I know, it's not enough, but at least it's not the counterfeit stuff England is flooding us with in an effort to ruin our economy." Raising his hands to heaven. "As if our economy weren't already ruined."

Bonaparte wasn't humoured. "How am I supposed to feed and equip an army on only eight thousand?" He drummed the chessboard with his fingers, sending two pieces tumbling to the floor.

"Prayer?" Barras caught my eye and smiled, his beguiling lopsided grin. "After all, it's legal now—well, almost."

"Barras, you do amuse," I said, offering him a glass of the Clos-Vougeot burgundy I knew he favoured.

"No, thank you—I just came by to drop off the list you asked for, General," he said, handing a folded-up sheet of paper to Bonaparte.

"But these are only the names of the generals," Bonaparte said, scanning the list. "I asked for the names of all the officers in the Army of Italy."

"Even the captains?" Barras stood, reaching for his walking stick.

"Even their aides."

"You're leaving tomorrow evening? I'll get my secretary to bring it over to you in the morning." He punched Bonaparte's shoulder in a soldierly fashion. "Best of luck liberating the Italians from the Austrians, General, as you so nobly put it. Don't neglect to liberate their paintings and sculptures while you're at it, as well as all that gold in the Church coffers. That's where you'll find the money to feed your soldiers." He threw his walking stick into the air and caught it, looking to see whether I had noticed.

Have to go—I hear Bonaparte's footsteps on the stairs.

March 11, morning, a light rain.
Sleepy this morning, but smiling. Bonaparte approaches conjugal relations with the fervour of a religious convert and the curiosity of a scientist. He's intent on trying every position described in a book he found at a stall by the river. There are over a hundred, he claims, and we're only on position nine.

Indeed, I'm learning never to predict how things might be with him. He can be imperious and insensitive one minute, tender and devoted the next. Last night we talked and talked . . .

"Like foam on the wave," he told me, caressing my breast.

"I like that," I said, watching the watery undulations that the firelight was making on the wall, thinking of the sea.

"The poetry or this . . . ?"

"That was poetry? *And* that." His hands are soft, his touch surprisingly gentle.

"It's a line from *Carthon* by Ossian. *Her breasts were like foam on the wave, and her eyes like stars of light.*"

It took me a moment to realize who he meant. Bonaparte pronounced the Scottish bard's name like "ocean."

"Alexandre the Great chose Homer as his poet, Julius Caesar chose Virgil—and I have chosen Ossian."

"Bonaparte, you disturb me when you talk like that."

"Why? Don't you like that progression: Alexandre, Caesar . . . *Napoleon?*"

"I'm serious. Can't you be a normal man?"

"Aren't I a 'normal' man?" He pressed against me.

"Well, in that respect, yes." In that respect, absolutely. Except that Bonaparte was insatiable.

"Can I tell you something?"

"Of course!" I was enjoying the quiet intimacy of our talk, this late-night pillow confession.

"Sometimes I think I'm the reincarnation of Alexandre the Great." He glanced at me. "Now you'll think me mad."

"I notice you read about Alexandre the Great a lot," I said, not knowing exactly how to respond to such a statement. It was true—there were things about Bonaparte that seemed strange to me.

"You don't believe in that sort of thing?"

"Sometimes. But not always. When I was a girl, a fortune-teller predicted I would be unhappily married and then widowed."

"So you see? The prediction came true."

"Yes." My first marriage had certainly been an unhappy one. "But she also predicted that I would become Queen."

He propped himself up on one elbow. "That's interesting."

"More than a queen, she said." But not for very long. "So *you* see, predictions are often just foolishness."

"Let's be foolish now."

"*Again?*" I smiled, wrapping my legs around him.

"You have no idea, do you, how beautiful you are. You are the most beautiful woman in Paris."

"Bonaparte, don't be silly."

"I'm serious! Everything about you enchants me. Don't laugh. Sometimes, watching you, I think I'm in the presence of an angel come down to earth."

I stroked his fine, thin hair, looked into his great grey eyes. I felt confused by the intensity of his feeling. I have never been so loved before. My first husband scorned me; Bonaparte worships me. It makes me want to weep. The truth, the terrible truth, is that I feel lonely in my husband's arms. If I am an angel, then why does my heart not open?

Throughout the night, I heard the clock chime one, two, three o'clock. At four bells, Bonaparte wasn't there. I listened for the sound of his footsteps, watched for a flicker of candlelight, but the house was dark, silent. I tried to go back to sleep, but could not, night thoughts haunting me. Night doubts, night fears. Finally I put on my dressing gown, my slippers, and with a candle walked the rooms. From the half-storey landing I saw a light below. I slipped down the stairs and went to the open door of the study. Bonaparte was there, leaning over the octagonal table, holding a lantern above a map. I watched him like a thief. What did he see, looking over that map? He looked so intent. What were his thoughts, his dreams?

"Bonaparte?" I called out, finally.

He looked up, startled. "Josephine," he whispered wondrously, as if he had found me.

Early afternoon.

What commotion! I have only a minute. Tonight Bonaparte leaves for the south, to take command of the Army of Italy. The entire household is engaged in frantic activity. My scullery maid is taking in his breeches (he balked at the expense of a tailor). I asked my manservant to put a proper polish on his riding boots and the cook to prepare a basket of travelling provisions—hardtack, hard-cooked eggs, pickled pork brawn, beets. I sent my coachman to the wine merchant for a case of Chambertine—an undrinkable wine, in my estimation, but the one Bonaparte insists on (it's cheap)—and to a parfumerie for the almond meal and rose soap he likes to use on his face. I must remember to boil elecampane root in springwater for his rash. And what else? What have I forgotten? Oh, the—

A half-hour later—if that!

Bonaparte burst into the upstairs drawing room and took a seat. I knew what his little smile meant. I told my scullery maid, "Agathe, perhaps I could have a word with my husband—alone."

Bonaparte's rumpled linen shirt was off even before we got to my bedchamber. "Junot and Murat will be here in fifteen minutes."

"That doesn't give much time."

"I can be quick," he said, as if this were an accomplishment.

I turned my back to him so that he could unfasten the buttons on my gown. He ran his cold hands over my breasts, pressed against me. I turned to him and kissed him. He is a small man, but vigorous. And quick, as he said.

"I'd like you to wash," he said, disentangling his pantaloons.

"I was going to." I was taken aback by his soldier bluntness.

Naked (small body, big head), he climbed into the bed and pulled the bed sheet up over him, looking at me expectantly. I went into my dressing room and re-emerged in a gauze nightgown trimmed with violet ribbons. "Take it off," he told me.

I did so reluctantly (Bonaparte is six years my junior) and lay down beside him. "Position ten?" I asked, teasing.

"Twenty-three." He ran his hand over my breast, my belly. "I've jumped ahead."

I smiled. Was he joking? (It is so hard to know with him.)

Then he sat up, said, "Close your eyes. You just lie there." I did as instructed. I felt him crawl down to the end of the bed, felt his hands part my legs, felt the warmth of his breath, his . . .

Mon *Dieu.* I swallowed, took a sharp breath.

Bonaparte was curiously unrushed. A voluptuous warmth came over me. I curled my fingers through his hair as waves of pleasure rose in my blood.

After, I lay for a moment, catching my breath, drying my cheeks on the covering sheet. Bonaparte was sitting on his haunches, regarding me with an awed expression. Then he grinned. "Well, that's the best one so far," he said, swinging his feet onto the floor.

"Come back here," I said, grabbing his hand.

9:00 P.M.

A kiss and he is gone.

I hear the crackling of the fire, my scullery maid singing tunelessly in the bath chamber, the heavy tread of my old manservant's wooden shoes on the narrow stairs, carrying up buckets of hot water for my bath. My pug dog Fortuné sniffs in all the corners, looking for "the intruder." I listen to the busy clicking of his little nails on the parquet floor.

The sounds of normal life, I realize. But for the battered tin snuffbox forgotten on the window ledge, the dog-eared volume of Ossian's *Carthon* on the mantel, one would not know that Bonaparte had ever been here. This man, who has come into my life like a whirlwind, has just as suddenly gone, leaving me breathless, dazed . . . and confused, I confess.

In which I break the news to my family & friends

March 17, 1796—Paris. A bright spring day.
I've a new maid. She curtsied at the door, lifting the hem of her linen shift. Her long chestnut locks were pulled into a tight braid that hung down her back. She is young, not yet of an age to pin up her hair. "Louise Compoint, Madame," she said, taking in the furnishings. "But I am called Lisette."

I slipped a finger through Fortuné's collar and asked her to come forward. Her mother had been a maid-of-the-wardrobe, she informed me, her father unknown. She'd been "adopted" by the aristocratic family her mother worked for and educated in a convent. Now her mother was dead and the aristocrats had fled during the Revolution. "I can wick lanterns, Madame, as well as dress hair. I understand clear starch and my needlework is good. My mother taught me well."

"This is a small household," I told her. "My lady's maid must serve also as a parlour maid and even as a kitchen maid, should the need arise."

"Yes, Madame. I've churned butter and blackleaded grates. I can also let blood. My mistress was often ailing," she explained, in answer to my startled look.

She is only seventeen, but I liked her forthright spirit. She had a natural grace. "We are a Republican family, Lisette. I will treat you with respect; I expect the same in kind. I permit no followers, and if any man makes advances, I expect you to inform me. You are allowed a half-day off a week to do as you please. Your room is in the basement. It is small, but it has a window and it will be your own."

"Yes, Madame!" Her teeth are excellent.

March 20, just past noon—still in Paris.
It was early, not yet ten in the morning, when I heard the children in the foyer. I stood and prepared to face them, clasping my hands to hide my betrothal ring. Nothing has changed, I was going to tell them; marrying Bonaparte did not mean I loved them less.

". . . and then my horse *jumped* the cart." Eugène lumbered into the drawing room with the grace of a heifer. Hortense followed, frowning, pulling at her hat strings.

My daughter greeted me with reserve, stiffening as I embraced her. "My hat, Maman," she said, pulling off her crêpe bonnet, leaving on the white lace cap underneath. I knew by her manner, her averted eyes, that she was angry with me.

"I jumped the grey mare." Eugène smelled of soap and perspiration. I pushed a curl out of his eyes. At fourteen, he would soon disdain his mother's touch, I knew.

"But what's this about jumping carts?" I reproached him.

My new maid came to the door. She looked comely in my cast-off gown of peach chintz. "You rang, Madame Bonaparte?"

Bonaparte. Hortense and Eugène exchanged glances. I motioned to Lisette to come forward in order to introduce her. She curtsied to them both. A flush coloured my son's cheeks. Hortense dipped her head, but it was clear her thoughts were elsewhere, her eyes darting about the room—looking for evidence, I realized, of Bonaparte.

"Thank you, Lisette. If you could bring us some hot chocolate? And the comfits." Hortense has a weakness for sweets.

"Maman, it was safe. The mare can jump five feet easily," Eugène said, falling into the down armchair, his legs sprawling.

Hortense lowered herself onto the chair with the horsehair seat, her shoulders back, her posture faultless (for once). I took a seat by the harp. "I understand that Madame Campan has talked to you both about my marriage to General Bonaparte," I said—too bluntly, I thought. Not the way I'd rehearsed this speech in my mind!

"Four days ago," Hortense answered, enunciating precisely.

"Yes, she told us. We know all about it," Eugène said, squirming.

"I want you to know that General Bonaparte cares deeply about both of you." I felt I'd handled things poorly, that I'd let them down. I wanted to reassure them.

"Maman?"

I sat forward eagerly. "Yes, Eugène?"

"Can I go to the Luxembourg Palace this morning, before we leave for Fontainebleau? Director Barras told me I could ride his horses any time I wanted."

I sat back, stupefied. Horses? Was that all my son could think of? How confusing this situation was! "No, Eugène," I said, making an effort to sound calm. "I have another plan. Today is Palm Sunday. I was thinking we would go to mass together."

Hortense looked surprised. (And pleased, I observed with relief.)

"Church?" Eugène groaned, sliding down into the depths of his chair.

"We'll walk," I insisted, standing.

I was surprised by the number of people standing in front of Église Saint-Pierre, enjoying the spring sun before going inside. Not only was it a Décadi* *and* a Sunday (a rare concurrence), but Palm Sunday as well. For once everyone could enjoy a feast-day together—Catholics and Atheists, Royalists and Republicans alike. I put my arms around my children as we climbed the steps. If there could be peace in the nation, then surely there could be peace in my little family.

*A new calendar had been established during the Revolution. The ten-day week ended in Décadi, the official day of rest. The names of the months were changed as well: Vendémiaire (the month of vintage), Brumaire (the month of fog), Frimaire (the month of frost) and so forth. Nevertheless, many continued to observe the old calendar, causing considerable confusion.

Fontainebleau.

We weren't able to leave for Fontainebleau until shortly after two, so it was quite late by the time we pulled into the courtyard of the Beauharnais home in Fontainebleau. "I expected you earlier, Rose," Aunt Désirée said, patting at her powdered hair, which was dressed in fat sausage rolls. Her immaculate house smelled of beeswax and turpentine.

"We got off to a late start," I explained, keeping an eye on the children to make sure they took off their muddy boots before walking on the carpet. "We went to church." I knew that this explanation would please.

"Is Grandpapa awake?" Hortense asked.

"Go! Go, my pets! He's been waiting for you both." The children raced up the stairs, pushing and pulling at each other. I did not attempt to quiet them; I was relieved to hear them laughing.

"I've been most anxious for your arrival, Rose," my aunt said, gesturing to me to take a seat. "I have excellent news." She perched on the edge of the green brocade sofa, nervously jiggling an enormous ring of iron keys.

"Oh?" A sick feeling passed through me. I'd come with news myself, and I feared my aunt would not consider it in the least bit excellent.

"My husband died!" she said, crossing herself.

"Monsieur Renaudin?" I had no reason to regret the man's passing. He and my aunt had separated before I'd even been born. Stories of the evil Monsieur Renaudin had excited my imagination as a child—stories of the man who had tried to poison my aunt, and who had (it was later discovered) been imprisoned for trying to poison his own father.

"And so the Marquis has asked for my hand in marriage." Aunt Désirée made this announcement with a girlish flutter of her eyelids.

"That's wonderful!" I said, repressing a smile. The Marquis was over eighty years old—my aunt, a quarter century younger—and I doubted that marriage was much on his mind. "And I take it you've consented?" My religious, proper and socially sensitive aunt had suffered, I knew, from living with the Marquis all these years without the Church's blessing.

"But Father Renard insists we wait a year—out of respect. I'm terrified the Marquis will die before he makes an honest woman of me," she said, picking up the loose sofa pillows one by one, as if looking for something.

She found a coin under one of the pillows and, frowning, put it back. (A test of her servants, I realized.) "So I told Father Renard I'd donate a new candelabra to the church and he finally agreed to six months. I know where I can get a used one for a fraction of what I'd pay in Paris. A good washing down with vinegar will make it like new." The cushions back in place, she pulled a tangle of crumpled handkerchiefs from the depths of her bosom and set to work smoothing them out one at a time on her lap. "And so, Rose, tell me: how are you?"

"Fine! I have news as well." The words came out louder than I'd intended, and far bolder than I felt.

"Has your cow calved, dear?" She put a pastel green handkerchief aside and stuffed the remaining ones back into the crevice of her ample bosom.

"No," I said, taken aback. "At least, not yet. No, I've . . ." My heart was pounding against my ribs! "I've married, Aunt Désirée," I said finally.

Aunt Désirée was holding the green handkerchief to the light, examining it for stains. "Did you say *married*, Rose?" she asked, turning toward me.

I nodded, disquieted by her calm manner.

"Why . . . that's wonderful," she said, crossing herself, "but to whom?"

"To a military man by the name of Napoleon Bonaparte. He's—"

"What type of name is that?" my aunt demanded, frowning suspiciously.

"It's a Corsican name, Aunt Désirée, and—"

"You married a *Corsican*?" She reached for a brass bell and rang it vigorously. "But Rose, Corsicans are . . . they're barbarians, they live like Gypsies. They steal, murder, *lie*—they have no morals whatsoever! And they don't speak a proper language, you can't understand a thing they say."

Fortunately, a parlour maid in a frilled cap appeared just then at the door. "Salts!" my aunt commanded.

"We're out of salts, Madame," the maid stuttered, wiping her palms on her white bibbed apron. "But we do have hysteric water, Madame."* Aunt Désirée snorted with impatience.

* Hysteric water: a mixture that was said to cure uterine disorders—"an excellent water to prevent fits, or to be taken in faintings." It was made of a mixture of roots of zedoary (similar to ginger), lovage and peony, parsnip seeds, mistletoe, myrrh, castor oil and dried millipedes steeped in mugwort tea and brandy.

"Aunt Désirée, he's not like that at all," I said, as soon as the maid disappeared. "His family is old nobility, and he was educated at the best military schools in France. He's very fond of me, and *especially* fond of the children," I added with feeling.

"Monied nobility, Rose?" With a squinty-eyed look.

"He has a good position as a commanding general," I said, avoiding her question. Not only did Bonaparte have no money, but our marriage contract stipulated that we contribute equally to all our household expenses. "He will be able to help Eugène in his military career." This was my trump card. I was depending on it.

"They made a Corsican a general?" Aunt Désirée demanded, attempting to fan herself with the limp green handkerchief. "A general of *what?*"

"Monsieur Bonaparte is General-in-Chief of the Army of Italy," I said, using "monsieur" in a shameless attempt to appease.

"I've never heard of an Army of Italy. Is it French even?"

"Yes, of course!" I exclaimed—although everything I'd learned about the Army of Italy had led me to believe that it could hardly be called an army at all, more a ragtag collection of drifters and petty criminals, hungry and without uniforms, much less muskets. "He left to take command two days after the ceremony." The wedding seemed like a dream to me now, like something that might not have happened.

"A church ceremony, Rose?" she asked, pulling and twisting the green handkerchief, worrying it.

"No," I admitted. Bonaparte was anti-Church, but I wasn't going to tell her that.

I heard a sniff. Oh dear! Was she weeping? Dismayed, I reached out to comfort her, but she turned on me like a hawk. "Rose, how could you?" she wept, dabbing her cheeks. "How could you have married a man with such a horrible name!"

I'm writing this now in Aunt Désirée's guest room in Fontainebleau. I talked to her at length, trying to calm her. I finally persuaded her to take a glass of hysteric water and lie down. (I had a glass as well.) I regret the way I've handled things, but at the same time, in coming to Bonaparte's defence, in trying to persuade my aunt of the wisdom of what I've done, I began to convince myself. Bonaparte had the words "To Destiny" engraved on the inside of my betrothal ring, for he believes in fate, believes that we are fated. Are we? I wonder. I can only hope that somehow, someday, fate will prove that I have done the right thing. For my family's sake, I dearly hope so.

March 21—Paris. Almost noon.
I received my first letter from Bonaparte this morning. So soon! It took me a long time to make out the words, and there are still parts I can't read. Bonaparte's handwriting is as impassioned as his words, which are ardent and tender.

The letter was addressed to Citoyenne Bonaparte in care of Citoyenne Beauharnais, as if Citoyenne Bonaparte were a guest in my house, someone separate from me—which is how I feel yet.

March 25, sunny, a beautiful day.
A good (and productive) visit with Thérèse, followed by an amusing few hours with my delightfully eccentric friends.

Thérèse arrived early in her elegant little barouche which she drove *herself* (practising, she explained, to enter the races that would be starting up again in the Bois de Boulogne). "And so how is Madame Bonaparte this fine afternoon?" was the first thing she said. The exotic scent of neroli oil filled my antechamber. She bent her knees to make it easier for Lisette to take her fur-lined cape.

"You're wearing a wig?" I asked, regarding my friend with astonishment. Under a jaunty hat adorned with a heron feather was a mass of blonde ringlets.

"Only twenty francs." She turned her head from side to side to make the curls bounce. "So I bought twenty-seven—and all of them blonde." She pulled both her hat and her wig off, and dug her nails into her scalp. Her own black hair was tightly braided and coiled. "You haven't answered my question," she said, holding up a finger.

"Madame *Bonaparte* is just fine, thank you. I already got a letter from my husband, in fact," I told her. "But there are parts I can't make out." I pulled the letter out of a desk cubby and showed it to her, pointing out the indecipherable passage.

"Mon Dieu, I see what you mean. What a mess," she said, squinting. "I think it's 'perpetual.' 'You are the *perpetual* object of my thoughts.' He signs himself B.P.?"

"For Buona Parte . . . I think."

"Oh la la," she said, reading on. "He's *madly* in love with you."

"That's just the way Corsicans are," I said (flushing), taking the letter back.

"No doubt," Thérèse said with a teasing look. "And your children?" she asked, helping herself to an aniseed-zested licorice comfit. "What do they think of their new papa?"

I made a face. "Hortense burst into tears."

"Because you married?"

"Just because she saw me *with* Bonaparte!"

"If you like, I could have a word with your daughter."

"Madame Campan already did," I quickly assured her. My oh-so-proper daughter disapproved of my friend Thérèse, separated from her husband. *And* Barras. *And* any number of others, for that matter, including her own godmother!*

"Speaking of your daughter, I had a brilliant idea. What about Director Reubell's eldest son?"

I looked at her blankly.

"As a husband—for Hortense."

"But she's not yet even thirteen, Thérèse. And since when have you become a matchmaker?"

"Since I suggested you to the Corsican. Seriously," she said, "the Reubells may be a merchant family, but they're wealthy. And, of course, Reubell being a Director . . . that counts for something, I suppose? They'd likely be willing. Hortense has a noble bloodline, after all."

---

* *Fanny Beauharnais, a bohemian poet, is related to Josephine through her first husband. She is Émilie's grandmother and Hortense's godmother. She is being sued at this time by a young woman claiming to be her illegitmate daughter.*

"Director Reubell is a radical Jacobin," I said, checking to see whether we had everything we needed: quills, ink, a folio of paper, the files. "An aristocratic genealogy wouldn't make any difference to him one way or—"

Thérèse laughed. "You're joking?"

"Well, in any case she's going to need a dowry."

"How much do you have?"

"Five."

"Five thousand? That's *all*?"

Five thousand in debts was more like it.

"But what about the Island property?"

I shrugged. "With Martinico in British hands, I don't stand to inherit a sou."

Thérèse pinched her cheeks together, considering. "Mind you, anyone can make a million these days. Why don't you get into military supplies? If the Revolutionaries can do it, anybody can." She looked at me. "You find that amusing?"

"Making the small deal now and then is one thing; supplying the military is on another scale altogether."

"The concept is the same—all you need is nerve. I noticed that you beat those two bankers at billiards the other night—the wealthiest men in the French Republic and you humbled them. *That's* nerve, if you ask me."

I smiled. *Well.*

"And look at your Masonic connections, your government connections, your financial connections."

"Those are *social* connections."

"I think you're underrating yourself. You're in an ideal position to make a small fortune, if not a large one. And face it, a fortune is not such a terrible thing. The Revolutionaries are raking it in as fast as they can. They figure it's time for a feast after such a long famine, and you have to admit, they've got a point. Barras says anyone who doesn't get into military supplies is a fool. It's fast money, it's big money, and there's virtually no gamble involved."

"So long as one has the contacts and the money to invest."

"Really, Rose—Josephine! Sorry!—I doubt very much that that would be a problem. After all, you have dear Père Barras, don't you? King of the Profiteers."

I raised my eyebrows. King of the Rotten was what most people called him. "Very well, Mama Tallita, I'll consider." I opened the file marked "Active" and looked at the clock. "We have only one hour."

A review of our projects proved discouraging. We have yet to succeed in getting Citoyen Mérode erased, even though he was put on the List* due to his cousin's emigration. We *have* succeeded, at last, in getting Citoyenne Daco and her son released from prison, but Citoyens Mercier and Pacout remain. Citoyen Pinson, sadly, died. We'll see what we can do to help his widow and five children. In addition to our charities, eleven men and women have approached us for help getting their names taken off the List, getting jobs, getting released from jail. In light of the growing number of requests we decided to meet every week, before the ladies gather to play cards.

"Speaking of whom," I said, hearing a carriage pull into the courtyard.

"Ah, it's the Glories." Glories? "You haven't heard that? That's what Barras calls us," Thérèse explained. "Because we dress for the glory of the Lord."

Glories indeed!** Before I could tell Lisette to please show them in, they'd entered, filling the dining room with their exotic scents, their fluttering fans and bobbing plumes, their silken ruffles swirling with all the erotic sensuality of a harem.

---

* *The List was a listing of émigrés and relations of émigrés forbidden from entering France. Having left the country because of the Revolution, émigrés and even their families were considered enemies of the Republic. Those listed lost all civil rights, had their property confiscated and risked execution if discovered on French soil. The names numbered over a hundred thousand. To be "erased" meant to have your name taken off the List.*

** *In addition to Josephine and Thérèse, the group included Fortunée Hamelin, Madame de Châteaurenaud (called Minerva), and Madame de Crény. Fortunée Hamelin (nineteen) is a créole like Josephine. She is famous for her wit, her daring (un)dress and her dancing. Minerva (thirty-six) is a voluptuous woman known for a mild, sweet manner and an interest in the occult. Madame de Crény (thirty-five), met Josephine when Josephine's first husband, Alexandre, forced her to live in a convent. Thérèse Tallien (twenty-three) is one of the famous beauties of the day. A wonderful teller of stories, she describes herself as a comedian.*

"Ah, it appears we've interrupted a charity meeting," tiny Madame de Crény said, the ends of an enormous red and yellow striped bow flopping down into her eyes like rabbit ears.

"We were just finishing," I said, gathering up the papers.

"Is it true you married the Corsican?" Minerva asked, trying to keep her pug dog from sniffing at my pug dog, who was growling menacingly.

I gave Thérèse an accusing look. "I didn't tell them," she protested. "I'm innocent."

"Hardly!" Fortunée Hamelin was half-naked in spite of the chill spring day; her gown of India gauze shot with silver revealed more than it concealed. (She boasted that her entire ensemble could fit into her embroidered pocket of Irish linen.)

"You must not blame Thérèse," Madame de Crény said, following me into the drawing room where the game table had been set up. "Director Barras is the guilty party."

"As usual." Fortunée propped her mule-heeled slippers on a footstool, displaying to advantage what are generally considered well-turned ankles. (She was wearing drawers!*)

"He has no willpower, the poor dear," Minerva lisped softly.

"And to think he's running this country."

"He *is* running this country." Madame de Crény perched on a chair, swinging her feet.

"Do you think he is dyeing his hair?"

"It must be that opera singer I've seen at his receptions."

"More likely it's her younger brother." (Laughter.)

"*And* he's wearing a corset."

"Just when we ladies have taken ours off."

"*That's* liberation."

"So, Rose, where exactly *is* this husband of yours?" Minerva asked, peering into the study.

"Her husband who loves her *madly.*"

"Thérèse!"

"How romantic."

* Drawers—or pantaloons—were considered men's wear, worn only by women of ill-repute.

"How inconvenient."

"He's in Nice, taking command of the Army of Italy," I explained with pride.

"So are we in an interesting condition yet?"

"It's a little early, don't you think? He left two days after we were married."

"It only takes me one minute," Thérèse groaned.

"And look at me, twelve babies," Minerva boasted. "My husband only has to smile at me and I'm in an interesting condition."

"We've noticed."

"*I've* noticed that most of the women of Paris are in an interesting condition these days."

"It's the style—even virgins are stuffing their gowns with pillows."

"Did you hear? Even Madame Lebon is in an interesting condition."

"No."

"Yes. *Finally.* After five years of marriage, she went to a German doctor. He told her that barrenness is cured by the presence of immoderate heat in a woman accompanied by turgescence."

"Pardon?"

"I think what it means is that a woman must . . . you know, *spasm.*"

"In order to have a child?"

"Apparently, this is a common German belief."

"I've never 'spasmed' with my husband, and believe me, I've had quite a few children by him."

"What's a spasm?"

"The doctor told Madame Lebon that if she were . . ." Fortunée rubbed her fingers together. "Then that proved a spasm had occurred."

"Hardly!"

"What is this, Rose? It is a wig?" Minerva picked up the mass of ringlets.

"Rose is now Josephine," Thérèse said, slipping on the golden curls.

"You're changing your first name?"

"Bonaparte wants me to."

"I thought his name was *Buona*parte."

"He's changing it." Everything was changing!

"Oh, a wig could be handy. No one would recognize you," Fortunée said.

"I bought twenty-seven of them. Only twenty francs each, so I should be able to make a nice profit on them."

"Real hair. Nice! But why so cheap?"

"Well . . ." Thérèse grimaced. "That's the thing."

"Oh no," Minerva whispered.

"The . . . guillotine?" Madame de Crény squeaked.

"Hair is hair, isn't it?" Fortunée Hamelin said with a shrug. "I'll take three."

Lisette entered the room with a tray of clattering glasses and an open bottle of champagne. She placed it on the side table and stood, smoothing the folds of her ruffled tulle apron.

"Speculation? Loo?" We settled on Speculation, Fortunée insisting on an ante of fifty francs to begin with, "to get the blood racing."

"Oh, I feel lucky today!" Madame de Crény said, wiggling her silver-painted fingernails before shuffling the cards.

Thérèse raised her glass, her ringlets bouncing. "To Josephine Bonaparte."

In which the past continues to haunt me

Mid-afternoon, March 28, 1796.
Good news: thanks to Barras, the sequester has finally been lifted on
Alexandre's property.*

March 31.
The Department of Confiscated Goods SW 24 is located in a former convent on Rue de Grenelle, not far from the Invalides. I presented my letter
of authorization to the man at the gate, and then again inside to a man sitting at a desk playing solitaire. He held my document to the eight lit candles in a silver candelabra, squinting at the seals and stamps before pulling
a ring of keys from a desk drawer (lying next to a pistol) and barking at a
man with a matted beard snoring on a sofa: "Gaspard, you dolt!" Taking
up a tin lantern, the yawning Gaspard gestured for me to follow him up a
set of narrow, dark stairs and through a series of rooms, each one filled
from floor to ceiling with crates labelled Comte this, Marquise that—
the boxed remnants of lives lost, lives taken.

In the last of the rooms, Gaspard unlatched unpainted wooden shutters over a small window, illuminating a harpsichord, several (lovely)
harps, statues, large oil portraits of men on horseback, women with their
children . . . I turned away from their staring eyes. It was only by chance
that I had survived.

* *Josephine's first husband had been convicted (falsely) of conspiring to get out of
prison. He was executed, and his property confiscated.*

"316, 317, 318 . . . 322." Gaspard indicated a line of rough-hewn wooden crates on the floor, each labelled Vicomte A. de Beauharnais.

"Is this all there is?" I asked. Seven crates.

April 1.
I am overcome with the vapours. I asked Lisette to go for Dr. Cucé, to bleed me, but she offered to do it herself, from my foot. I owed the doctor money, and so I took the chance. Lisette made the cut quickly and with confidence; the bright blood flowed into the chipped porcelain bowl. I feel faint, but pure.

Late afternoon.
Stronger now. What happened:

I had risen early in order to help clear a spot in the study for the crates to go. But shortly after eleven, Lisette announced a caller: Louis Bonaparte.

"A young man, heavy-lidded eyes. Italian, I think." Lisette has become forthright in her descriptions.

I was puzzled. I'd never heard of a Louis Bonaparte.

I ran my hand over my hair. I'd dressed in a gown of washed-out blue gauze, the flounce in need of mending—appropriate for a day of going through the musty crates, which I expected to be delivered at any time. "Tell him I'll be a moment," I said, pulling on a pair of silk stockings. I slipped a blue velvet pelisse on over my chemise and rouged my cheeks. An embroidered muslin veil thrown over my shaggy hair gave me a fashionably Roman look. *Bien.*

The young man stood to greet me, slipping a green leather book into the inside pocket of his tailcoat. It was Luigi, Bonaparte's young brother, the brother he regarded as a son! "Napoleon told me to change my name to Louis," he explained. He looked to be Eugène's age, although I understand him to be a year or two older. "I beg you to forgive my calling at such an early hour, Citoyenne Bonaparte," he said respectfully and with a melancholy air. He'd been at a spa in Châtillon and was now on his way to Nice, he explained, to join his brother's staff, as aide-de-camp.

I welcomed him warmly and asked if he would care for a coffee, tea or small beer. He confessed to a longing for my Island coffee, which his brother had told him about. "Alas, the last of my Martinico beans are gone—but my cook, who is himself from the Islands, has discovered an excellent substitute bean from the southern Americas." I rang for Lisette, requesting coffee, chocolate liqueur and a basket of the biscuits my cook had made this morning.

We talked of the spa he had been at, his coming voyage, the danger of ruffians on the roads, the performance of Voltaire's *Brutus* he'd seen at the Théâtre de la Republique the night before. We agreed that the great actor Talma was "diverting beyond moderation" (his words). I told him Talma was an acquaintance of mine, and that he had even once lived in this very house, which astonished him—perhaps because it is so modest an abode. In short, a pleasant conversation.

It was just as Lisette appeared with the coffee that I heard Fortuné barking out on the verandah. "I'm having some things delivered," I explained, standing. "No, please, *stay,* finish your coffee."

Louis downed his coffee and stood, taking a biscuit. "I must be going in any case," he said, accompanying me to the front steps. Two carters were unloading one of the crates—a heavy one, I gathered, from their strained expressions.

"You've made a purchase of a National Property?" Louis asked, observing the seals.

"In a manner of speaking," I said, not wishing to explain that these crates contained my first husband's effects.

The crates practically filled the tiny study. My manservant shifted a few so I could squeeze between them. Then he got a crowbar and began prying off the tops.

The first crate contained household items: china, linens, musty bed curtains. There were surprisingly few personal possessions: an inkstand, an oak box with mother-of-pearl inlay, a blue glass jar of metal military buttons. Some clothing: a pair of riding boots that Eugène might be able to use. Four riding crops, one with a gold handle. But no pistols or swords—stolen, no doubt. And no silver, either. A leather portfolio contained financial records, letters of correspondence. I put these aside for Aunt Désirée and the Marquis. (I did not wish to read them.) And, as I feared, a velvet bag of small linens, garters, a mother-of-pearl hair ornament: Alexandre's "trophies." I threw these away, but then perversely retrieved the hair ornament, which I fancied.

And then there were the books: four large crates. Water had damaged one of them: the pages of the texts were swollen and dusty with mildew. I instructed my manservant to burn these in the garden.

In the remaining crates were a number of valuable texts:
-a complete set of Diderot's encyclopedia, the pages uncut
-the complete works of Voltaire
-a lovely edition of Cicero's *Treatise on Laws* with an embossed morocco cover and hand-stitched spine
-a folio Bible, much thumbed (surprisingly)
-Rousseau's *Discourse on the Origin of Inequality among Men*

There were a number of books about Freemasonry, the natural world, art and architecture. At the bottom of the last crate were a few novels (including, in plain wrapper, *The Life of Frétillon the Wriggler*). And at the last, a sheaf of music and an oak box of artist's supplies. These would be for Hortense.

But other than that, little of value. My children's inheritance.

Dear Rose,
I will be coming to Paris to purchase fabric for my wedding dress on the 4th of April. Will you be in? Perhaps I could pick up the correspondence you mentioned. I was heartbroken to learn that all that lovely silver was missing. Ruffians! It was in the Beauharnais family for six generations.
Your loving Aunt Désirée

April 4, late afternoon.
Aunt Désirée hadn't even taken her gloves off before she began to lecture. "Your scullery maid should have disappeared when I came into

the room," she said, running her fingers over my shelves to see if they'd been properly dusted. "She should avert her eyes. And your lady's maid is wearing silk. It makes a rustling sound that is suggestive to men. There will be trouble, I guarantee it. Servants should wear only linen of a dull colour, and certainly no powder. My priest gave me an excellent book on service. I'm reading it out loud to my servants after our evening prayers. You do say a prayer with them all at the end of the day?"

"Things have changed, Aunt Désirée," I said weakly.

She gave me a scathing look. "Rose, my dear child, I had hoped that by now you would have realized that this foolishness about equality has nothing whatsoever to do with servants. It is God's will that they serve us."

She stayed for one hour. I've collapsed, exhausted. At least she didn't get onto the subject of my Corsican husband, "the barbarian."

Nice, 10 Germinal

I haven't spent a day without loving you; not a night has gone by without my taking you in my arms. I haven't even taken a cup of tea without cursing the glory and ambition that separate me from the soul of my life. As I attend to business, at the head of the troops, while touring the camps, you alone are in my heart.

And yet you address me formally! How could you write such a letter? And from the 23rd to the 26th, four days passed. What were you doing that you could not write your husband? My spirit is sad; my heart is enslaved; my imagination frightens me.

Forgive me! My spirit is occupied with vast projects, yet my heart is tormented by fears. —B.P.

April 9.
"I can't tell you what I suffer the moment I take up a quill," I confessed to the Glories. "My first husband detested my letters, and now Bonaparte." It seemed to be my fate—my curse.

"He's angry because you addressed him formally, as *vous?*"

"But that's how a wife is *supposed* to address her husband." The crown of Madame de Crény's hat was garlanded with tulips secured by a wide bow of black and white striped satin.

"Unless you're the baker's wife."

"How egalitarian do we have to become?"

"He's ardent, I suppose," I said with a disheartened sigh.

Fortunée Hamelin scoffed. "That usually means quick."

April 10.
I'm nineteen days late.

April 11.
I'm exhausted and have a pain in my side that the motion of a carriage seems to inflame. Troubling conversations at both schools about the children. Too fatigued to explain. For now, fifteen drops of laudanum* and to bed.

April 12, 1:00 P.M., still in my flannels.
I feel rested, restored (although that pain persists). What happened—

When we let Hortense down at her school, I was told Madame Campan wished a word with me. I asked Eugène to wait and went inside.

"My purpose in summoning you, Madame Bonaparte," Madame Campan informed me, "is to discuss the possible establishment of the flux. Now that your daughter has turned thirteen, things will begin to move quickly. It is best to think ahead."

It took me a moment to understand what she was referring to. "In my family, we called it the flowers," I said, feeling a bit silly.

"Many do." The headmistress's leather chair creaked as she leaned back. "Or the ordinaries. Our dear departed Queen called it the *general*. The general has come, she would say, or the general is late, or early,

* *Laudanum: a solution containing opium, used widely in the eighteenth century for pain, particularly for "women's complaints."*

depending on his whim." Her voice betrayed a quaver. The stoic head-mistress would invariably weaken recalling her years as lady-in-waiting to Queen Marie Antoinette. She cleared her throat. "What I wish to ask you is this: would you like me to send a courier when the time comes? I flatter myself on the importance of my role in the hearts and minds—the souls!—of my charges, but when the general calls to escort a girl into the realm of womanhood, it is her mother who should be at her side."

"Of . . . of course," I stuttered.

Madame Campan smiled and leaned forward. "No doubt you have given thought to the matter of corsets."

I nodded, but this time the schoolmistress frowned. "I must advise you to refrain from corsetting your daughter. Such a practice might damage her organs. Your daughter is approaching the age of womb disease—one can't be too careful. Madame Bonaparte, you look concerned. Have I alarmed you?"

At Eugène's school the pattern was repeated: my presence was requested by Citoyen Muestro, the headmaster. Eugène groaned, which gave me fair warning that the news would not be good—and it wasn't. Eugène was failing all his subjects, I was informed—all but horsemanship. And furthermore, he'd participated in a prank on the cook, causing a "ghost" to rise up in the henhouse, very nearly giving the man apoplexy. I left the schoolmaster's office shaken, his threat ringing in my ears: "If your son does not begin to apply himself, we will have to ask you to withdraw him from this institution."

Eugène thrust out his chin. "I don't care! I hate school," he said, putting away the scrapbook he was working on.

"You're only fourteen, Eugène. You have to go to school." I made a place for myself on his narrow bed. "You will never get to be an officer if you don't get an education."

"What about General Hoche? He's General-in-Chief and he never went to school."

Hoche? It startled me to hear my son speak Lazare's name. Startled me and weakened me. Eugène had only been twelve when his father had died. Throughout that terrible first year he'd been sullen, moody, angry. It had been angels, surely, who had sent us Lazare Hoche, a man with a heart so generous that he could heal even the most shattered soul—my own, Eugène's. He'd taken Eugène into his care, into the army as his aide and apprentice, cared for him like a son. But General Lazare Hoche has a wife and a child of his own—and Eugène now has a father.

April 13.

I've been all this morning looking through a book Madame Campan has loaned me, *A Treatise on All the Diseases Incident to Women.* It was written by a physician to King Louis XV. Madame Campan told me Queen Marie Antoinette herself consulted it. There is a great deal in it on all manner of complaints. For example, on the subject of the flowers (the morbid flux, the author calls it):

The menstruous Purgation is a Flux of Blood issuing monthly from the Uterus. Galen, in his Book of Bleeding, *attributes the Origin of the Menses to a Plethora. Does not, says he, Nature herself cause an Evacuation in all Women, by throwing forth every Month the superfluous Blood? I imagine that the Female Sex, inasmuch as they heap up a great quantity of Humours by living continually at Home, and not being used to hard Labour or exposed to the Sun, should receive a Discharge of this Fulness, as a Remedy given by Nature.*

1. The first Fact of this morbid Flux is that it has a stated Time wherein it appears, and this ordinarily from the Age of thirteen to sixteen Years.

2. It is known by Experience that the Menses generally cease betwixt forty-five and fifty Years of Age.

So, it is indeed possible that Hortense, having turned thirteen, might soon begin her periodical sickness. The author cautions against exposing girls of this age to spicy foods or to music in an immoral key. If only I knew which musical keys were immoral!

April 15.
A persistent pain in my side and a feverish feeling. And still no sign of the flowers.

April 17.
The pendulum clock had just struck two when I heard a horse cantering down the laneway. I went to the front steps. It was Eugène, dismounting a grey gelding covered in lather. He threw the reins around the stone lion statue and bounded up the steps two at a time. "You're riding alone?" I asked, embracing him. The road between Paris and Saint-Germain was isolated, known to be dangerous. "Aren't you supposed to be in school?" His eyes were red-rimmed. Why? "Has something happened?"

"Maman, it's about General Hoche," he said, catching his breath. He pulled a torn sheet out of his vest pocket, a page from *Les Nouvelles.* The newsprint shook in his hand. I squinted to make out the small type: *General Lazare Hoche has been killed in the Vendée.*

"Eugène, it can't be true." Barras would have notified me immediately. But my son was not convinced. "If you like, I'll go to the palace," I assured him. "Director Barras will know for sure."

It was cold in the Luxembourg Palace in spite of the enormous fires burning, the carpets, the hangings, the drapes of crimson damask. And strangely quiet but for the rhythmic swish of the porters' brooms, cleaning up after the daily mêlée of petitioners. I followed the footman through the cavernous reception rooms, my thoughts on that scrap of newsprint folded into the palm of my glove.

Four workmen regilding the wainscotting in the Grande Galérie fell silent as I went by. Only five months before the once-elegant palace had been fit only for vermin and bats. Slowly Barras was having it entirely restored. Slowly it was beginning to look like a palace again—and every bit as intimidating. I glanced in a looking glass, adjusting the tilt of my hat. I was calling on the most powerful man in the French Republic, I reminded myself. It was hard to believe. My dear, eccentric friend, Paul

Barras, was now ruler of the land. "Père Barras," Thérèse and I called him, because of his big-hearted generosity.

"Is Director Barras taking callers?" the footman asked Barras's elderly doorkeeper, who motioned me in with a flourish.

"Entrez!" I heard something shriek from within.

"Bruno, was that a parrot?"

The doorkeeper grinned, his three front teeth missing. I stepped into the room. It took a moment for my eyes to adjust. Barras preferred rooms dark, draped in velvet—a gaming-room ambience.

"Pretty lady!"

"Well said!" Barras was stretched out in his favourite chair, a multi-coloured bird perched on his white-gloved hand. "Meet Igor, a gift of the Sultan of Turkey—along with a tiger. But I sent the tiger over to the Jardin des Plantes and kept this clever fellow. It's a little frightening how quickly he learns."

"Ha, ha, ha." The parrot imitated Barras's soft chuckle perfectly.

"Look—Toto's gone into hiding," Barras said with a grin. Only the nose of the miniature greyhound could be seen peeking out from under his desk.

"I had a parrot in Martinico." A vile creature. Cautiously, with one eye on the bird, I kissed my friend's cheek. Barras was wearing a Florentine purple taffeta jacket I'd not seen before. It was pulled in at the waist; he looked as if he might burst. Yes, a corset was likely, I thought. And it was true, I decided: he *had* died his hair black.

Barras eased himself up and nudged the bird onto the perch of a cage set in the window alcove, disentangling a claw from his lace cuffs.

"Damn the Royalists," the bird shrieked.

Barras threw a gold-fringed velvet cover over the cage. "Brandy?" he offered, pouring himself a tumbler. I declined, taking the chair he indicated with a wave of his glass. He sat down across from me, cross-ing his legs at the ankle. Toto made a mad dash across the room and bounded onto his master's lap. "And to what do I owe the pleasure of this call?" he asked, stroking the dog's head. "I rather expected you at my salon this evening. You'll return tonight? The Sultan will be here and I wish to give the impression of a harem." A roguish grin.

I pulled the article from inside my glove, unfolded it and handed it to him. "Eugène saw a report in *Les Nouvelles* that concerned him." My voice was not as calm as I had hoped.

Barras patted the pockets of his waistcoat, withdrew a gold-rimmed lorgnon and pushed it into his eye socket. "Lazare . . . killed?" He let out a laugh.

I felt a tingling sensation in my chest. "So, it's not true?" I said, sitting forward. Eugène would be anxiously awaiting my return.

"Certainly not. Wishful thinking on the part of some Royalist, no doubt. You can't believe journalists. Haven't I taught you anything? Lazare is unkillable—you know that."

He put Toto down and accompanied me to the door, leaning on my shoulder. "But one question, my dear, before you go." Smiling his charmingly crooked grin. "Why such a fret over Lazare Hoche?" Tweaking my chin. "Madame *Bonaparte.*"

In which I learn the Facts of Life

April 20, 1796.

I've been to see a doctor about the cessation of my monthly illness. "You've recently married, Madame?" he asked.

"My husband is in Italy now."

"He left—?"

"Twenty-one Ventôse."

Then he asked a number of questions. Are my breasts knotty? (No!) Have I experienced a feeling of fearfulness? Anxiety? (Yes, yes.) Do I suffer from toothache? (All my adult life.) Do I desire to eat loathsome and unwholesome foods such as carrots, raw turnips, roast pig? (I confessed I loved carrots.) Do I fear dying? Do I have forebodings and gloom? Am I overtaken by a fear of undefined evil? Do I suffer from heartburn?

"Excellent, you will carry to term," he said, apparently satisfied with my answers.

"Do you mean, Dr. Cucé, that I am with child?"

"I confirm it."

"But Dr. Cucé—"

"No need to be fearful, Madame," he said, polishing his spectacles with the corner of his jacket. "Although it is not advisable for a woman to procreate after the age of thirty, you need not be concerned about consequences of a fatal nature. You have, as you informed me, already produced two children by your first husband, a procedure that has effectively opened up the channels."

"Dr. Cucé, it's just that I do not feel that I am . . ." My breasts are in no way tender and my belly is not distended. "And what of the pain I am suffering? What of the fever?"

"The pain is . . . ?" He poked his manicured finger in my side.

"Sometimes quite bad," I said, "and at other times only an ache." At that moment, a steady, throbbing, painful ache.

"A minor inflammation of the stomach." He wrote out a recipe for a purging diet-drink and an herbal tea to soak my feet in.

Twenty livres—on account.

Thérèse kissed me on both cheeks and on my forehead, as if bestowing a blessing. "That's wonderful news! Bonaparte is so efficient."

"I just wished I believed it. I'm not in the least bit tender, and this pain is so . . ." Worrisome.

"Did you take the hartshorn, nutmeg and cinnamon powder I sent you? Did you boil it in springwater, as I told you?"

I nodded. "And then I tried a remedy my Aunt Désirée sent me, along with her special prayer. And then another my scullery maid swore on the head of Brutus would curb a morbid condition."

"And nothing helped?"

I shook my head. Something was wrong.

April 21.

An amusing caller this afternoon—he helped chase away the vapours.

"Captain Charles." He introduced himself with a theatrical bow. He is young, in his early twenties I would guess, with an alert pixie look. A pretty man, exceptionally well made and with good features, excellent teeth. His thick black hair was pulled back into a braid. His sky blue hussar uniform brought out the extraordinary colour of his eyes—a light aquamarine blue. (Who *is* it he reminds me of?) "I've just arrived from Marseille," he explained, "where I was entrusted with a letter for you." As if by magic, he pulled a document from behind the marble bust of Socrates.

I smiled behind my fan.* A trickster!

The letter was in a woman's hand, the script ill-formed, like that of a child. "It's from General Bonaparte's mother?" *My son has told me of his happy marriage, and henceforth you have my esteem and approval.* "How kind of her to write," I said, suspecting, however, that Bonaparte had dictated her letter as well.

"Yes, the General's mother is so very kind," he echoed, but with a curious long-suffering look that made me wonder if he meant the opposite.

I heard the businesslike clicking of my pug dog's nails on the parquet floor. Fortuné entered the room with the air of a master. "What a charming little dog!" Captain Charles stooped down, holding out his hand.

Charming? Most people consider my surly pug ugly. "I beg you to be cautious, Captain. My dog has been known to bite."

Fortuné approached the captain's hand and sniffed it. The captain picked Fortuné up and, with a playful growling sound, rubbed his face in Fortuné's fur. "He's never allowed a stranger to touch him," I said, astonished as much by Fortuné's response as by the captain's.

April 27.

"My protégé has done it!" Barras slid off his horse. I came to the garden gate, wiping my hands on my apron. He stepped over the little fence and folded me in his arms, twirling me. "I told them he could do it, but this—this is a miracle." He was in his directorial robes still; one end of the scarlet cape caught on a rosebush.

"Paul, wait." I disentangled him from the thorn. My scullery maid stood frozen in the process of hanging a carpet over the stone wall, her head craned over her shoulder.

"It's unbelievable. Even I never expected . . . !" He was short of breath from such a show of youthful vigour, and dangerously flushed.

"Now, Père Barras," I said, motioning him toward the garden bench, "perhaps I could persuade you to take a seat? And then—at your leisure! I wouldn't want to rush you!—if you could tell me, what is this miracle?" I

---

* *Josephine had bad teeth and was in the habit of smiling with her lips closed behind a fan.*

removed my apron and used it to brush off the stone bench. "And which protégé?" For Barras had many.

He paced back and forth on the narrow path, kicking up stones. "Your husband. Who else?"

"Bonaparte?" I sat back, tilting my straw hat so that it blocked out the sun in my eyes.

Barras clapped his hands. "He's had a victory!"

I smiled, incredulous. *Already?*

"Yes—at Montenotte." He waved his hands in the air as if deranged. "And with that starved, pathetic little Army of Italy that the Directors were so reluctant to grant him." Pacing again, flinging his cape over his shoulder. "Haven't I always said I have an eye for talent? I told them he could do it. And now they'll have to admit that I was right. *Ha!*"

April 29.
Another victory! This one at Millesimo. I've pinned a map to the wall in the study and have tagged it with flagged pins, just as Bonaparte did when planning his campaign.

April 30.
And yet another at Dego! "I can't take all this celebrating!" Barras groaned, holding his aching head.

17 Floréal, Luxembourg Palace
My friend,

Please forgive this letter—I'm tied up in meetings with the Directors all day. I wanted you to be the first to know: your husband has had four more victories, and in only four days! Twenty-one Austrian flags captured! I'm ordering a fire-rocket show over the river—hang the expense. At this rate, Bonaparte will be opening the Pope's treasure chest soon.

I advise you not to grant any interviews to journalists, who will be pressing, I warn you. All information must come from the Directory.

Are you unwell? Thérèse mentioned that you've been in bed with a fever. This news will cure, I'm sure. Gather your strength—there will be ceremonies on end.

Père Barras

Note—I'm negotiating to buy Grosbois. Imagine, the previous residents were the royal family. With luck and a little persuasion (of the gold variety), the royal estate will be mine for a song. It would take millions to make it habitable again, however.

May 4.

Fever, pain again, quite sharp this morning. Dr. Cucé coming soon.

3:00 P.M.

Dr. Cucé actually bowed before me. "Madame Bonaparte!" he exclaimed, pronouncing it "Bonne à Pare Té." "All of Paris is delirious! Four more victories and in only four days. My wife was beside herself when I informed her that my honoured patient is Our Lady of Victories. And when she learned that I would be coming to attend to your health today, she practically fainted dead away. If I may be so bold, might you have a small token, something the Hero of Italy has touched? A handkerchief would be excellent, but better—perhaps one of General Bonne à Part Té's hairs? I'd happily waive my fee. No! I insist, don't get up. I'll look myself. In this drawer? This brush?" I nodded, too fatigued to protest and chagrined that the brush had not been cleaned. "Ah, oui!" the doctor exclaimed, extracting a long, dark hair and holding it to the light. He turned to me, his eyes gleaming. "For my wife, of course. You know how women are?"

May 5.

Confined to bed still. Thérèse was just here with herbals and good cheer. She showed me an account in the journal *Ami des Lois*. Apparently, someone had sent in verses written in my honour—unsigned, however.

"But I think I know who wrote them," she said. "Wide-Awake."

Captain Charles? (Thérèse has dubbed the amusing trickster Wide-Awake because he's always so bright.) "Don't be silly, Thérèse," I said, pulling the coverlet under my chin. "He's a decade my junior." And in any case, I suspected that the pretty captain might be the type of man who only coquetted with women—nothing more.

"Young men adore you. Look at Bonaparte—he's six years younger than you. And what about Lazare? How many years younger is he?"

"Five," I said, blushing.

[Undated]
Slowly, I begin to get better. I detest being sick.

May 6.
It was late morning—I'd just had a bath—when I was informed that there were two men downstairs wishing to see me. I considered telling them I wasn't receiving, for I'm not yet fully recovered. "I think one might be your husband's brother," Lisette told me.

Bonaparte's older brother Giuseppe tipped his bicorne hat and bowed from the waist. "I'm called Joseph now," he informed me, displaying the tips of his even teeth. "Charmed to meet you at last." He is both taller and older than Bonaparte, a soft-spoken man with an indolent look. He was expensively if curiously turned out in a yellow tailcoat and matching knee breeches, a little cut-and-thrust sabre covered with gems dangling from his hip. Colonel Junot, one of Bonaparte's aides, stood beside him, cracking his knuckles.

"What a surprise!" I greeted my brother-in-law. "I can't tell you the pleasure this gives me," I said again, aware that I was exclaiming too much. Should I address Bonaparte's brother by his Christian name? Should I offer my condolences on his wife's being delivered of a stillborn? What were the customs in Corsica?

Joseph pulled my hand to his lips and kissed it theatrically with his eyes closed, as if overwhelmed with feeling. I waited for him to finish. "My brother desires me to tell you of his overwhelming love," he said.

"Bonaparte has often told me of his love for *you*," I answered, wondering how I might dry his spittle from my hand. I motioned to Lisette to serve cordials, swiping my hand against my skirt and through the air as I did so, as if I were an exuberant sort of woman. "When did you arrive in Paris? I long for news of Bonaparte. Four victories in four days—it is impossible to imagine!"

"General Bonaparte rode five horses to death," Colonel Junot said, cracking his knuckles again.

Mon Dieu, I thought. "Your journey, how was it?" I asked, my voice thin.

"We came the long way, by sea," Joseph said. "But you will be happy to know, kind sister, that the return shouldn't take longer than one week now that the passage over the Alps has been secured by treaty. Comfortable lodgings have been prepared for you."

Lodgings? I closed my fan. I didn't understand.

"You are to join my brother in Italy, kind sister."

I pulled my train to one side and sat down on the chair next to the harp. "Forgive me, but I'm not sure if I am able to—" Would it be improper to inform him of my interesting condition?

"You do not understand, kind sister," Joseph said softly, the muscles in his jaw twitching. "My brother, the General, he—"

"The General must not be disobeyed," Junot said, twisting his fingers but failing, this time, to crack them.

They left soon after. I've ordered my coach-man to harness the horses—I must talk to Barras.

5:00 P.M., or shortly after.

Barras frowned. "But that's impossible. The Directors must first give their consent."

"They seem to be unaware of this."

"The fact is, the Directors wouldn't permit you to go, we wouldn't grant you a passport. It's simply not safe yet. And besides—" He propped his chin in the palm of one hand, regarding me with his puppy-dog eyes.

"I doubt that it would be in our best interest, frankly. You'd distract the Liberator of Italy from his military duties." He made a lecherous grin.

"So the Directors wouldn't allow me to go to Italy?"

He shook his head, the feather in his cap bobbing.

I left shortly after, but not until I'd promised Barras I would attend the first weekend gathering at his new country château. "It will be wonderfully restful," he promised me.

May 19—Grosbois!

I am sitting in a chair that was likely sat in by Louis XIV, the Sun King. I am writing at a desk where treaties have been drafted, staying in a château where the great men of history have slept.

I am, frankly, stunned by the magnitude of Grosbois, now Barras's country estate. *This* is a castle.

"What it is, is a headache," Barras said, pointing out all the repairs that are needed to the roof, the foundation, the windows. For it has fallen, to be sure, into neglect. It took two manservants eight full days just to capture and kill the vermin, he told us. (*All* the vermin.)

We are a small party: Thérèse and Tallien (recently reconciled but already bickering, alas), Julie and Talma* (also together again), a Deputy Dolivier (who is also a banker), Fortunée Hamelin (thankfully, her pompous husband stayed at home), Ouvrard and his wife, Lucile Beaucarnot, a singer with the Opéra (Barras's current favourite) and her comely young brother. They are all out walking now, in search of views. I did not feel robust, so I declined.

In any case, it was an excuse to enjoy a short but delicious sleep under silk sheets—under the purple,** Aunt Désirée would say. Soon I'll ring for Lisette and begin dressing for dinner. The water in the basin has been scented with rose petals; a crystal bottle of the finest claret has been placed on the table in front of a flower-filled fireplace. I can smell bread baking.

*Julie Careau and the great actor François Talma had lived in Josephine's house when previously married.

** Under the purple: royal life.

Three cooks are at work preparing what will no doubt be yet another of Barras's sumptuous feasts. (The menu is before me now.) Barras has arranged for a string ensemble to play as we dine. And then after, sated no doubt, we will retire to a golden salon where Talma will read, I will play the harp while Lucile Beaucarnot sings and—eventually, inevitably!—Thérèse will have us aching with laughter over her hilarious imitations. "And *then* the game room," Barras warned us with a wicked grin, flinging his scarlet cape over his shoulder. He is clearly happy in this role, the grand master, orchestrating our pleasures. I am only too willing to oblige.

Late (I'm not sure of the time).
We gathered for dinner at five in full dress. (My new cream-coloured muslin gown embroidered with gold thread was perfect for the occasion.) "May I have the honour?" Barras offered me his arm. We led the small procession into the ancient dining room.

"A fresco by Abraham Bosse?" Thérèse inquired. The walls were painted with a medieval scene.

Barras shrugged. "I just live here."

"How old *is* this place?" Ouvrard said, examining the massive fireplace that dominated one end of the room. He is a tall man, young (in his mid-twenties), exceptionally well-made. The wealthiest man in the French Republic, it is said.

"It has been a royal domain since the thirteenth century. Le Monsieur was the last resident," Barras said. Le Monsieur, the Pretender, the brother of King Louis XVI—and, according to Royalists, King. "We walk in the footsteps of history."

"*You* walk," I corrected him.

We were seated, we ate, each attended by a silent valet. We drank, we got noisy: I took in the news. The deficit was a concern: two hundred and fifty million. The government was going to sell a number of National Properties in an effort to raise money.* The Directors were considering

---

* With the Revolution, the government had seized Church property, as well as the estates of émigrés and arrested aristocrats. From time to time, in order to raise money, the Republic put these properties up for sale—usually at a very good price.

❧ *Dinner Menu* ❧

1 soup
1 appetizer
6 main dishes
2 roast dishes
6 side-dishes
1 salad
24 dessert dishes

Soup
Monk small onion soup

Appetizer
Sturgeon broiled on a spit

Main dishes
Confidence man sautéed turbot fillets
Eel tartare
Cucumbers stuffed with marrow
Chicken-breast in a puff pastry shell with Béchamel sauce
John Dory fish in a caper sauce
Partridge fillets in rings

Roast dishes
Local gudgeon
Carp in a court-bouillion

Side-dishes
Snow eggs
White beetroot sautéed with ham
Madeira wine jelly
Orange blossom cream fritters
Marie Antoinette lentils in a cream of concentrated veal broth
Artichoke hearts in a shallot vinaigrette

Salad
Shredded celery in a herb-mustard mayonnaise

Twenty-four desserts

introducing new taxes: a patents tax, a stamp duty, land tax. There was talk of a tax on doors and windows, which led to a heated debate.

"The peasants will be forced to live in the dark," Thérèse objected.

"The English do it," Ouvrard observed. "They've done it for years."

"And look at the state of their peasantry."

"The English are taxed for living," Tallien said. "For breathing."

"But they don't have a deficit," Deputy Dolivier said.

"And they don't have every Royalist country in Europe waging war on them for daring to embrace democratic ideals. The fact is," Barras said, assuming his Director's tone, "it costs us a great deal to keep our men in arms. Over half our revenues go to the Ministry of War. A standing army of five hundred thousand requires . . . How much would you guess a day, simply in sacks of wheat? Over six hundred," he said, not waiting for us to guess.

"Six hundred and fifty," Ouvrard corrected. "Seven hundred head of cattle, seventy thousand sacks of oats—a *day*. The horses alone require two million bales a day."

"Spoken as an army supplier," I said.

"Yes, and proud of it," Ouvrard said earnestly. "Although I'm afraid that the title would not be considered worthy in most gatherings."

"Everyone's quick to accuse army suppliers of corruption," Barras said, "but the fact is that the French Republic would have collapsed long ago without them." He made a signal with his hand; the twelve valets moved in unison, filling our glasses with Madeira, taking away the dishes. Then he pulled a deck of cards from out of the side table, threw a sack of coins on the table. "Shall we have a quick game before dessert? How about five hundred to start?" He leaned toward me. "I'll advance you," he whispered, tossing out a second sack. "That's for Madame Bonaparte, lads, but be careful." He winked at his guests, "She plays to win."

(I did: fifteen hundred.)

May 21—back home in Paris.
Indisposed again—fever, terrible pain. It was a mistake to go to Grosbois.

I hardly have the strength to hold this quill! I've been examined by three doctors—Thérèse's, Barras's and my own Dr. Cucé. They stood about my bed scratching their heads. Last night the pain was so violent, I feared I would not see the dawn.

May 24.
The flowers came on suddenly and frightfully. And with such pain! I feared I was going to die. I felt light, as if I could float. I felt myself flying. Lisette covered me with a bed sheet. "I'm sorry about the mess," I said, closing my eyes.

Later.
"Madame Bonaparte, you are healing, the morbid condition of the uterus has improved, but I regret to inform you that you are not . . ."
Not with child, alas. "Was I before, Dr. Cucé?"
He scratched his chin. "A mole, perhaps?"
A mole?

[Undated]
From Madame Campan's book:
A Mole is a Mass generated in the Uterus, which may be mistaken for an Infant in the Womb. Physicians affirm that all Moles are real Conceptions which cannot happen unless there has been some Intercourse between the two Sexes. Nor do they believe that a Woman can become pregnant through Imagination. Hence as often as we meet Moles, we may assure that there has been Co-habitation with Man.

May 28.
I started a letter to Bonaparte, to tell him, but couldn't.

Headquarters at Milan, 20 Prairial
Every day death leaps around me: is life worth so much fuss? Farewell,
Josephine. Stay in Paris, do not write; at least respect my solitude. A thousand
knives stab my heart; do not plunge them in deeper. —B.P.

23 Prairial
Josephine, where will you be when you get this letter? If in Paris, my misery is
certain! I have nothing left but to die. —B.P.

Late afternoon, around 4:00.
Thérèse saw the distress in my eyes. "What is it?"

I confessed to her my fears. I told her how disturbing Bonaparte's
letters were. "I don't know what to think. He says things that frighten
me. It's as if he's in a fever. I'll get a letter telling me to be careful, to
take care of my health, not to come to Italy—and then a few days later
I get a letter saying that he's going to kill himself because I haven't
arrived!"

"Do you think he might be a little . . . ?" She made a twirling motion
at her temple.

Tears spilled down my cheeks. "No, of course not." Although, in fact,
that was my deepest fear. "It's just that he becomes so upset, I fear he
might . . ."

"Step in front of a cannon?"

I nodded, staring down at my hands. They were the hands of an older
woman—not my hands, surely. "He wants me with him."

"So go."

"Thérèse! A battlefield is no place for a woman. And what about
Hortense and Eugène?"

"Your Aunt Désirée will look after them."

"But my health—"

"Is improving."

I sat back. "You really think I should?" I felt as if I'd been condemned.

She took my hand. "Remember how it was during the Terror, how we were fighting for something bigger than we were?"

I nodded impatiently. What did that have to do with it?

"It's not over yet," she said. "I know, we like to *think* it is. We dance, we play cards, we go to the theatre. I admit it! I'm the first one at a fête and the last one to leave. And why not? We're the survivors. Death tapped us on the shoulder and we escaped. Life is short, so why not enjoy it? But we're fooling ourselves. The Republic is faltering. Everything our loved ones died for is at stake. Our beloved Republic is falling and yet we dance on, trying to ignore it."

"But Thérèse, what does this have to do with whether or not I should go to Italy? Saving the Republic has nothing to do with me," I said, a feeling of anger rising up in me.

"Would you concede that it might have something to do with your husband?"

Yes, I did believe it possible, that much depended on Bonaparte—*why*, I could not say. In my most secret heart, I believed he could save us—and worse, that we needed to be saved.

Noon, 27 Prairial
My life is a perpetual nightmare. A deathly premonition stops me from breathing. I no longer live. I have lost more than life, more than happiness, more than repose. I am almost without hope. If your illness is dangerous, I warn you, I will leave immediately for Paris. —B.P.

In which I finally depart

June 19, 1796, early, not yet noon.

Barras was resistant at first. "It's victory nerves, that's all," he insisted.

"Paul, this is serious. It's more than nerves." I dared not tell him the full extent of my fears, that Bonaparte might be mad.

"Look, it's simply unreasonable of him to expect you to join him."

"Please, listen to me!" Barras looked at me, startled. I'd never raised my voice to him. "If . . . if I don't go to Italy," I said, more calmly this time, "Bonaparte will come here." This was the one argument that was likely to persuade him, I knew.

"To Paris? He would leave his troops in the middle of a campaign?"

Yes, I nodded. He would. He *will.*

"That would get him court-martialled."

I nodded. Ruined! Shot!

"That's strange. He didn't mention any of this in his last letter to me." He looked over the stacks of paper covering his desk. "Here it is," he said, holding a letter up and squinting at it. "Just the usual business—his conditions for the armistice agreement with the Pope."

"Bonaparte is dealing with the Pope?"

Barras smirked. "Getting a little high and mighty, one could say?"

"It's the Republic he represents that is high and mighty."

"That's the problem—that's what's getting the Directors so upset. Bonaparte doesn't represent the Republic, and yet he's acting as if he does. Ah, here's the part." Barras cleared his throat and read out loud. "'I hate women. I am in despair. My wife does not come—she must have a lover who is holding her in Paris.'" Barras looked at me, amused. "So who is this lover?"

"The only man who has been admitted to my bedchamber of late is my doctor, I'm afraid. Fevers are not conducive to romance."

"I must say, you do look frail. Are you even well enough to travel?"

Early evening—Fontainebleau.

"Oh!" Aunt Désirée cried out when she saw us. "I wasn't expecting you. Hortense, look at you, a little lady in that bonnet. And you, Eugène, such a handsome lad. You're growing like a cabbage."

Hortense jabbed her brother in the ribs. Eugene grabbed her wrist and tried to pin her arm behind her back.

"Children!" I stooped to give my aunt a kiss, glaring at Eugène. "Why don't you two go out to the stable to make sure the horses are taken care of."

"My groom will look after your horses," Aunt Désirée said, tightening the sash of her squirrel-lined dressing gown.

"The children need to be outside," I whispered as they raced for the door. "It's a long ride from Saint-Germain." The walls shook as the front door slammed shut. "And besides, there is something I need to talk to you about, Aunt Désirée—privately." I settled into the armchair next to the sofa.

My aunt gave me a baleful look over the top of her thick spectacles. "I warn you, Rose, I'm out of salts."

"Still?" I paused. "I have to go to Milan."

"To Italy? But isn't that where the fighting is?"

"I know, Aunt Désirée, it's just that—"

"How would you get there? The roads are so perilous. Even between Fontainebleau and Paris, one risks getting robbed. And what about your health? Just look at how pale you are."

"I'm needed there, Aunt Désirée, my husband—"

"A woman belongs with her *children*. And what about our wedding? The Marquis and I can't get married without you." Sniffing.

I was dismayed. My aunt never used to cry, and now it seemed she was crying all the time. "I have a suggestion to make. Perhaps the priest could marry you and the Marquis before I leave."

"When will that be?"

"Possibly next week," I said, my voice faint.

"Next week!" my aunt shrieked. "Father Renard was reluctant to marry us next month even."

"Perhaps I could explain the problem to him." Pay him a goodly sum. Or promise to.

"But Rose, my gown isn't finished. It isn't even begun."

I heard the children's voices in the foyer. I put my finger to my lips, *shush!*

"The children don't know?"

"What don't we know?" Hortense asked, pulling off her hat.

Eugène grinned at his sister. "A mystery," he hissed.

"You're going to have to tell them sometime," Aunt Désirée said angrily, taking up an embroidery hoop and jabbing a needle into the tautly pulled fabric.

Not now! But it seemed I had no choice. "I'm going to be making a trip," I told them reluctantly.

"Oh?" Hortense looked apprehensive.

"To Milan," I said, with an apologetic dip of my head.

"Where's Milan?" Hortense asked Eugène.

"To the war?" Eugène spoke the word with reverence.

"You're leaving us, Maman?" Hortense's straw hat fell to the floor and rolled for several feet before falling over with a soft *poof.* She backed out the door.

"Hortense!"

I was breathless when I got to the park. "Hortense!" I stopped, catching my breath, one hand pressed against the pain in my side. It was growing dark, the shadows disappearing.

I heard a sob from behind a stone wall. Hortense looked so small sitting in the dirt. I gathered her in my arms. "Sweetheart." I stroked her hair. She was shaking. "Oh, my big girl," I whispered, swallowing hard.

I heard the creaking of wagon wheels, the lazy clip-clop of a horse's hooves on the cobblestones on the other side of the wall. Hortense took a jagged breath. Then, between sobs, it all came out. I would not see her in the year-end play. All the other parents would come, but who would be there to see her? And, at year end, when all the girls went home, where would she go?

"But I'll come back," I promised her.

"I don't believe you!" she sobbed.

June 20—back home (exhausted). A balmy summer day.

Aunt Désirée and the dear old Marquis are married at last. ("Kiss me," she yelled, making the sign of the cross over him, "I'm your wife!") Now I must attend to the passports, the financing, a wardrobe. I'll try to see my doctor today, and the apothecary. I'll leave instructions with my manservant to look after the beggar families that come to our gate. I should talk to my lawyer to make sure that my will is in order. I must talk to Joseph Bonaparte soon too—today, if possible. He and Junot will be travelling with us. I must find someone to take my horses; they should be exercised daily. I can't decide what to do about my cow.

Oh—the post-woman just arrived with the mail. Please, let there not be another awful letter from Bonaparte!

May 4, 1796, La Pagerie, Martinico
Madame Bonaparte,

Your mother has asked me to write on her behalf. She can no longer hold a quill for the Rheumatism has greatly inflamed her joints.

Your mother wishes you well in your marriage. She prays that your husband is a Christian man and that he is of the King's party.

However, she declines your offer to come live in France with you. She has used the money you sent to purchase the slave Mimi's freedom, as you specified. We will send her to you as soon as we receive money for passage.

I regret to say that there was no income from the plantation last year.

Your mother has asked me to pray for you and your children.

In the service of the Eternal Lord, Father Droppet

I've read Father Droppet's letter many times over. It has been a very long time since I've had news of home, and this small token only makes me miserable. I'll send word not to send Mimi until I've returned from Italy. What a blessing it would be to have her with me once again! I'm so relieved she is willing to come.

June 21.

"So is it true, darling?" Madame de Crény asked, playing a card. "Are you really going to Italy?"

"Over the Alps," Thérèse informed the Glories, rolling her eyes. (She'd been upset initially—she didn't think I'd actually do it.)

"The Alps? Mon Dieu."

"It's faster than going around," I explained.

"I didn't think it was even possible."

"Bonaparte opened up the route."

"Route de Josephine they're calling it," Thérèse said.

"My husband said he'd move mountains for me, but your husband has actually done it." Minerva looked pleased with her jest.

"Just the thought of those towering precipices makes me sick."

"Not to mention the banditti."

"Did you hear about—"

"Don't tell her!"

"Tell me what?"

"Nothing, darling. *Nothing!* You'll be fine."

Evening.

"Bonaparte's brother Joseph can't leave for six days," I informed Barras.

"Did he tell you why?" he smirked, rummaging around in his papers. "He's taking a mercury cure."

I raised my eyebrows. Mercury is used to cure syphilis.

"Having a bit too much fun in town—research for the romantic novel he claims to be writing, no doubt. But can *you* manage it in six days? You'll need to put together a wardrobe—hoops and the rest of it. The Italians are quite provincial."

"Hoops? You can't be serious."

"Servile, tradition-bound, ignorant, superstitious. Dig out your old corsets. *And* a bustle."

I groaned. I'd had my bustles made into pillows long ago.

"And don't forget, Madame Bonaparte, *ma belle merveilleuse*,"* he lectured, pointing a letter opener at me, "always put your handkerchief in your wineglass—only juice for the ladies." I made a face. "And no playing billiards with the men, either, no talking with them about finance and politics." He opened a drawer, riffled through it and then sat back with a puzzled expression. "What am I looking for?"

"Something to do with Italy?"

"Ah, yes!" He took out a file. "I'm to get passports for you, Joseph Bonaparte, Colonel Junot and . . . who else? Oh, that aide-de-camp, the funny little fellow Thérèse calls Wide-Awake. The financial agent—you know who I mean. All the ladies are mad about him."

"Captain Charles?" I was hoping the captain would be able to join us. "He's a financial agent?"

"Oh dear, you didn't know? I wonder if it's supposed to be confidential. I can't remember who told me. He's affiliated with the Bodin Company, apparently. It's hard to imagine—he's so young . . . and so very, very *drôle*."

Drôle, indeed! "At least Fortuné won't bite him. Even my dog finds him amusing."

"You're taking the dog? Mon Dieu, but this is short notice. Why is it I'm always rushing around doing something for Bonaparte? Ah, *here's* what I was looking for. It's a letter from the most beautiful man in the French Republic, our very own General Lazare Hoche. He requests permission to come to Paris." Barras held the letter up with a gloating expression. "Pity you won't be in town."

"You'll see to the passports?" I said, standing.

---

* *Merveilleuse: an extravagantly (and wildly) dressed woman of the period, typically of the newly rich class of profiteers, bankers and financiers.*

"You're flushed! Forgive me?" He kissed my cheeks. "Ah, but you forgive anything, all my little sins."

"I wouldn't be so sure," I said, tying my hat strings. Remembering to smile.

June 23.

"Madame, it's . . . it's . . . !" My maid was actually tongue-tied. "It's the famous General Hoche. Himself!"

"Here? That's impossible," I said, throwing off the down coverlet. It was almost noon, but Dr. Cucé had insisted I get constant rest in preparation for the journey. "General Hoche is in the south. He won't be in Paris until the end of the month."

"I'll go tell him he's not here." The excitement had made Lisette giddy.

"Perhaps there has been a mistake." *Surely* there had been a mistake. "Is this gentleman in his late twenties, tall, with a scar?"

"Broad shoulders, dark eyes," she said, her hands clutched to her heart.

"Lisette, please!" I laughed. "Is my morning gown pressed? Can you find my lace shawl—the one with the silk fringe? Oh, mon Dieu, my hair."

"Rose," Lazare said, turning to face me, taking off his hat. He was bronzed from the sun, his scar white in contrast, snaking down from his forehead onto his right cheek.

"General Hoche." I extended my hand. Lazare. *Lazarro.* He seemed taller than I remembered him. Hercules, Barras called him. "What a pleasant surprise." Joy flooded my heart. "I congratulate you on your recent victories."* A man of peace, people are hailing him.

"There is no glory but that of the Republic for which I fight."

---

* *General Lazare Hoche had taken on the difficult task of quelling the uprisings (fuelled by émigrés and England) against the Revolution in the south of France.*

"Of course." I smiled. Lazare believed in the Revolution as if it were a religion—and with good cause. Under the Ancien Régime, he had been nothing more than a dog keeper. Under the Republic, he'd risen to become one of the greatest generals in the land—*the* greatest general, Barras claimed.

I pushed forward a chair. "Care for a cognac?" There was a pitcher of orange juice from breakfast. "Or a pétépié?"

"A pétépié would suit the hour," he said, with a knowing smile.

I poured out a tall glass of juice and added a good measure of rum and absinthe. "You haven't forgotten the pleasures of Martinico," I said, handing him the glass. My hand was trembling slightly; I feared I might spill a drop, feared he might notice.

"Indeed, they haunt me." His fingers touched mine.

The clock on the mantelpiece chimed the hour, echoed a moment later by the clock in my bedchamber. "You have come early to Paris," I said, my voice quavering slightly.

"Just as you, I gather, are departing." He nodded at the open shipping trunk by the door to my bedchamber.

"Yes, I'm leaving for Milan in three days."

"*You're* going to northern Italy?" He sat back. "Is that not risky?"

"I have confidence in my husband, General Hoche."

"As you should," he said, meeting my eyes.

Oh, Lazare, my precious Lazarro. Memories flooded my heart—memories of the fever heat of passion, of love. I stood, went to the window to the left of the fireplace, pushed it open. I still loved him, I realized. Loved him and respected him, for the honour he lived by, his Republican zeal, his passionate commitment to *la liberté*.

"Today is the day of your birth," I heard him say.

"And yours is tomorrow, if I remember correctly." I remembered perfectly.

Lazare came up behind me. I felt the warmth of his hand on my bare shoulder. "My doctor will be calling shortly," I said, turning, my heart pounding violently.

"Are you not well?" he asked with that familiar tenderness that made me weak.

"I'm getting better," I whispered, swallowing. Could he not hear my heart?

"Do you think General Bonaparte would mind if I gave his wife a birthday kiss?" he asked, with a bold and teasing look.

"Yes, General Hoche," I said, looking up at him. I touched the tip of my finger to the cleft of his chin. "I do believe he would mind."

Lazare leaned toward me. I felt his tongue, his heart—my own.

Later, almost ten in the evening.

Tonight, after a bowl of broth, I went out to the garden and sat on the bench under the lime tree, my arms wrapped around my knees like a child. The moon bathed the landscape in an eerie light. Lazare's visit had filled me with melancholy. I thought of my mother, so very far away. Was she looking up at the same moon? Did she even think of me? I wondered what had become of them all, my family, the slaves I'd grown up with—my nanny, Da Gertrude and my maid, Mimi. Dear old Sylvester was probably dead. I thought of the graves of my father, my two sisters. I thought of the mound of dirt by the river—the grave of the voodoo priestess. I remembered her terrible words: You will be widowed. You will be Queen.

Overwhelmed by memory, by feelings of longing and loss, I took the Saint Michael medal that Lazare had given me on parting out of my pocket. Saint Michael the Archangel, sword in hand. Saint Michael the warrior saint, standing victorious over the forces of evil.

"I want you to have it," he told me. It had been his mother's, he said. His mother who had died giving birth to him. His peasant mother who could neither read nor write. He told me it would give me courage.

"Truly?" Yes, he said, the courage to do the right thing. I puzzled over some words on the back: *la liberté ou la mort.* "I had it etched on," he explained, somewhat shyly. I told him I would treasure the medal always.

Later, turning from the door, he said, "We never really said goodbye."

"Is this goodbye then?" I asked him.

He never answered, I realize now.

June 26.

Lisette woke me gently, touching my shoulder. "There are two big coaches out in the courtyard, Madame."

I went to the window, pulled back the curtain. One of the men on horseback was Bonaparte's courier, Moustache—so named for his enormous appendage. He dismounted and said something to Captain Charles and Junot. Bonaparte's brother Joseph was standing to one side, writing something down in a little book.

A horse whinnied. At the gate a number of mounted guards appeared—nine? ten? "We have an escort?"

"It's a parade!" Lisette said.

Evening (9:00?)—at Aunt Désirée's in Fontainebleau.

"Finally!" Aunt Désirée exclaimed when I arrived. She peered out the window. "Where are all the others?"

"They're staying at the inn in town." I felt gritty from the dusty trip down from Paris.

"A man has been waiting over an hour for you to get here. I've been trying to entertain him, but between the lace man coming and then the water carriers . . ." Aunt Désirée led the way into her dark drawing room, the heavy brocade drapes pulled against the afternoon sun. "He doesn't even play trictrac, only piquet, and he says 'tyrant' when he should say 'king.' A gentleman, by his dress, but with plain manners." She made a face. "He blinks."

"Is his name Hamelin?" I asked, pulling off my gloves.

"You *do* know him."

"I'm afraid so." I had hoped Fortunée Hamelin's husband would journey to Italy on his own.

"He's been most impatient for your arrival. I think he might be a Freemason from the way he stands with his feet stuck out at an angle."

"Citoyen Hamelin is the husband of a friend of mine, and yes, a member of Loge Olympique. He's begged leave to come to Italy with us on business." The making-money business. The recovering-from-the-devastation-of-the-Revolution business. The recovering-from-a-weakness-for-horse-racing business, I had reason to suspect.

"I see," Aunt Désirée said with unconcealed contempt, as if the very word business were beneath her. "He has consumed five small beers," she hissed in a créole patois, opening the door to the music room.

"Madame Bonaparte!" Citoyen Hamelin jumped to his feet, blinking rapidly. He was wearing a cutaway tailcoat that stuck out at the back like the wings of a beetle. He took my gloved hand and kissed it, leaving a faint smear of pink rouge. "I was, I confess, beginning to give way to doubt and deliberation. The road is heavy, and one knows the dangers one can encounter, the brigands, the *chauffe-pieds!*"*

"Citoyen Hamelin, you understand, there is no room in our carriages—"

"I will lease a post chaise."

I lowered myself into a chair. "What a good idea," I said weakly.

After Citoyen Hamelin had *finally* departed, I followed my aunt up the narrow stairs to see the dear old Marquis.

At the first-floor landing Aunt Désirée said, "Wait here," in her hushed, sickroom voice. The air was thick with the smell of mothballs. Through the half-closed door I heard her say, "Wake up, Marquis! Rose wants to have a word with you. She's going away, to Italy. No, not me, *Rose.*" Then the door opened wide. Sunken into the feather bed was the withered Marquis, a full-bottomed court wig stuck crookedly on his head. "Be quick," my aunt hissed, stepping aside. "He might fall asleep."

Holding onto a bedpost, I leaned over to kiss the dear old man on the forehead. His wig smelled of pomade. "You are looking well, Marquis," I said, marvelling at the dry furrows of his skin.

"Louder," Aunt Désirée said. "He didn't hear you." She was going through the books on the shelves, blowing dust off the spines.

"I am going away, Marquis," I said, loudly this time. "To Italy."

He frowned. "Are the boys downstairs?"

---

* *Chauffe-pieds: literally "hot feet," the term given to the criminals who would extort what they wished by burning the feet of their victims.*

I glanced at Aunt Désirée: oh no. *The boys*—his two sons, Alexandre and François. Alexandre had been dead for almost two years, and François was as much as dead. An émigré, he would be arrested and executed were he even to set foot in the French Republic.

"Forgive me, Rose," the Marquis said tremulously, suddenly clear. "At my age . . ." I took his hand, skin and bones, bones and skin. His new betrothal ring was loose on his finger; it had to be large in order to slip over his big knuckle. He swallowed, his Adam's apple bobbing up and down like a mechanical lever. "I pray for Alexandre every day," he said, his voice raspy. "I prayed for him when he was alive, but it didn't help much. And as for François . . ." He covered his eyes, cursed.

I stroked his hand, my throat tight. Aunt Désirée gave me a warning look.

"So, you remarried," he said finally, recovering himself. "Eugène told me your husband is going after the Austrians."

"Yes." We'd had this conversation several times before.

"Tell him . . ." The old man fought for breath. "Tell him we must get back Mayence."*

June 27, close to 11:00 A.M., I think—still in Fontainebleau.
At eight this morning everyone descended on Aunt Désirée's modest town house. I stood on the front steps holding onto a wiggling Fortuné. The small courtyard was a chaos of men, carriages and horses, preparing for departure. Everywhere there was yelling and confusion. Junot was yelling at a postillion who was trying to untangle some harness. Hamelin—"the blinker" I think of him—was yelling at a footman who was trying to cram an enormous sea-trunk into his small post chaise. And everywhere, servants were rushing to and fro, yelling at each other. Only Bonaparte's brother Joseph was silent, standing by the gate writing something in a book.

---

* *The Marquis's son Alexandre, Josephine's first husband, had been arrested for "allowing" the Austrians to invade Mayence (Mainz, in German), on the west bank of the Rhine River. The French traditionally believed that the Rhine River was their natural boundary.*

"I can hold the dog if you wish, Madame Bonaparte," I heard a voice behind me say.

It was funny Captain Charles in his red-tassled boots. He looked shining, his brass buttons gleaming. Gladly I handed Fortuné over. The captain stroked Fortuné's ears and then even kissed the top of my dog's head! "Could I have the honour of showing Madame Bonaparte to her carriage?" He shifted the dog under one arm and offered me the other.

"But what about—?" I looked back over my shoulder. Was everything taken care of?

"I insist, Madame. We must look after you." He opened our carriage door, pulling at the step until it came clattering down. Then, with a twirl of his white gloved hand, he motioned me in.

"We?" My travelling kit was already on the seat: my medications, my Tarot cards, the novel *Clarissa* by an English author, my writing journal (which I'm writing in now).

"The saints and I."

I smiled. He was so sweet. "Who provided the cushions?" There hadn't been cushions on the way down from Paris.

"I did. I recommend that you sit on the side facing away from the horses." Captain Charles jiggled the door to get it to shut. I touched my hand on the windowsill. "Oh, I wouldn't put my hand *there*," he said. I looked at my white glove—it was streaked with grime.

Captain Charles slipped off his gloves. "They will fit you, Madame. I have very small hands. See?" He held up his hand—it was the size of a child's.

I slipped on his glove. It did fit. "You are a gentle and kind man, Captain Charles." I took several deep breaths, laid my head back against the hard, cracked leather. Be strong, I told myself. It wouldn't do to faint. Not now, not at the start of such a long and perilous journey.

II

La Regina

Ogni talento matta.
(Every talented man is a madman.)
—*Italian proverb*

In which I join the Liberator of Italy

June 29, 1796—Briare.

Only two days travelling and already we are miserable. Citoyen Hamelin is distraught over fleas in his coach. Colonel Junot is made cross by the slow pace. My brother-in-law Joseph is not in good health (due to the effects of his mercury cure), and is disinclined to suffer silently. Thank God, Captain Charles is of our party—he alone is cheerful.

July 5—Roanne.

Today we followed the river road along the Loire to Roanne, a bustling town of merchants and carters. Passing through the market I heard foreign tongues. Roguish men with long black hair and rusty swords observed our entourage with hungry interest.

It was dusk by the time we pulled into the courtyard of this humble inn, the best in the vicinity. The innkeeper ran out to meet us, waving a leg of chicken in one hand. His beard glistened with grease. He threw the bone to a dog and started gesticulating wildly to Joseph about a courier who had been murdered.

"It happened not far from here, to the south," Joseph explained as we climbed the stone steps to the inn. "The courier was carrying promissory notes intended for my brother."

"How awful!" I wondered if it was the same courier who had so often brought me Bonaparte's letters.

"Yes, it was a goodly sum," Joseph said, opening the door to the inn for me.

Inside, the air was sweet with the smell of quince roasting on cinders. I sat down on a bench by the stairs. I had a fever, I feared, and that pain again. "I'll wait here for Lisette," I told my brother-in-law, who wished to examine the accommodations. He put his journal and writing kit on the bench and went upstairs. The journal slipped onto the floor, and as I picked it up I couldn't help but notice an entry that said, "10:15 A.M. J and CC play string game."

Citoyen Hamelin clattered in. Quickly I put Joseph's journal back on top of his writing kit. *Josephine and Captain Charles play string game,* he had written. Cat's cradle, he meant—but why note it down? It was child's play. "Do you realize that the murderer stayed in this very inn?" Hamelin demanded, blinking rapidly. "In the very room I have been assigned?"

Then Lisette entered, followed by Colonel Junot, his nose pink at the tip. She was wearing her travelling gown without the lace insert, I noticed. The innkeeper's wife ran to take her basket.

"*Queen* Lisette, is it now?" Captain Charles said.

She glared at him. "If it gets any hotter, I will die," she said, fluttering her fan.

"It will be even hotter in Milan," Colonel Junot said, cracking his knuckles. "But there are ways to cool off. Vigorous exercise is recommended, the type that works up a sweat."

"How unladylike," Lisette said, glancing up to meet Junot's gaze.

"Is Colonel Junot married?" Lisette asked me later, admiring my necklace before putting it away in its case.

"Colonel Junot has yet to find a woman with a sufficiently large dowry," I said, and then added, "He has a mind to coquet with you, I've noticed."

"You think he fancies me?"

I detected a hopeful tone in her voice. "Colonel Junot is the type of man who will always fancy an attractive young woman." I turned from the looking glass to face her. "Lisette, I hope you understand that it would be unpardonable for you to allow the attentions of an officer."

"I do not encourage Colonel Junot, Madame," she said, helping me into my walking gown.

"You don't neglect to wear your lace insert?"

She flushed. "It needs mending, Madame."

"My sweet Lisette," I said, "you are so young and so very pretty. You must learn to be careful. That's all I'm saying."

Shortly after 4:00 P.M.

We've just returned from a refreshing stroll. Feeling weak yet, I leaned on Captain Charles's arm as we walked along the river, the other members of our party going on ahead. We talked like old friends: of fashion (the charming high-crowned leghorn hats that women are wearing now, how they look best with hair loose and flowing); of his birthday (he's twenty-three today, so young); my children (how I miss them already); of novels (he recommended *The Sorrows of Young Werther* by the German writer Goethe). Then we talked of more serious, financial concerns—the shocking depreciation of our currency, the soaring inflation.

"I understand you are a financial agent," I dared to say.

"That is not the sort of thing a soldier would wisely admit to, Madame." The captain brushed a black curl out of his eyes—his blue, blue eyes. "Especially to the wife of his commanding general."

"I assure you, Captain, I will not mention it to anyone." Bonaparte, specifically.

"Then yes, I confess I am an agent—for the Bodin Company, an investment firm based in Lyons. The brothers Bodin—there are two—are from Romans originally. We grew up together."

"I once did business with a speculator in Lyons. I recall he mentioned the name Bodin." I'd made an exceptional profit on a shipment of salt-petre, and then again on an order of lace. "That surprises you?" I asked, perceiving his astonishment.

"Well, it's just that—"

"Women are perfectly capable of doing business, Captain," I chided him.

"Yes, Madame, but you would hardly seem to . . ." He flushed.

I would hardly seem to *need* money, he'd started to say. "I won't bore you with stories of how my children and I went without bread during the Terror, Captain."

"It wouldn't be boring in the least."

"It's really a rather familiar tale by now. Like so many, we lost everything. My husband lost his life; his property was confiscated. I had two children to support, feed and educate. One does what one must in such circumstances." It sounded noble, but the truth was that I enjoyed making deals. Learning to do business had given me an exhilarating feeling of independence.

"And now, Our Lady of Victories, you have everything."

"Everything including debts." As wife of the Liberator of Italy, my expenses had more than doubled. As wife of the Liberator of Italy, I'd been appealed to for any number of charities—charities that it was not in my nature to turn down.

"Perhaps, Madame, I could be of help in that respect." He paused. "I'm sorry, have I offended you?"

"No, not in the least," I stammered, my cheeks blazing, for I'd suddenly realized who the captain reminded me of: William, a boy I had loved in my youth.

Late now, almost midnight, an evening of tales and tricks.

The talk at table this evening was much concerned with the murderer, whom the innkeeper, his wife, three daughters, two sons, the innkeeper's sister and her two sons were only too happy to describe in great detail. With each account the villain became more and more sinister. So it didn't help when, just after ten, we were suddenly apprehended by a man in a mask, who jumped into the room with a violent shout.

Junot leapt to his feet, his hand on the pommel of his sword. We gasped, Lisette screamed, but Junot seemed unable to pull his sabre from its scabbard. He cursed crudely, so preoccupied with his dilemma that he failed to notice our laughter—for the man in the mask was none other than Captain Charles.

Junot stood at his place, his blond hair sticking out like a haystack. "What did you do to my sword, Captain?" he demanded, cracking his knuckles.

Captain Charles made what sounded like a frightened duck call and sat down beside me. "How tragic to be murdered on one's birthday," he whispered, cowering as the giant Junot approached. (We saved him!)

July 10 (Sunday)—Lanslebourg.
The ascent to the Pass was perilous. We followed a narrow road through thick fir woods, the glaciers glittering above us.

I exchanged a concerned look with Joseph. "Are we actually going to go over?"

"It will be my first time too." He had been writing all morning—notes for his novel, he claimed. "How does this sound? 'The pretty young woman cast a glance upon the handsome soldier, trembling as if she had seen the vault of heaven open.'"

"I like that," I lied.

"I'm not sure about the word handsome," Joseph said. "Virile might be better."

Captain Charles put down the book he was reading (Voltaire's *Lettres philosophiques*). "Are we staying in Lanslebourg?"

"That's where our mules and porters will be," Joseph said.

"We are crossing the mountains on mules?" I asked, alarmed.

"Perhaps you would prefer to be dragged over on a litter. My heroine is going to do it that way, packed in straw."

"Your heroine is going to cross the Alps?"

"The poor girl." Joseph looked up at a towering precipice. "She is exceedingly frightened."

Entering the tiny village of Lanslebourg, I felt we had come upon a new species of human. Everyone seemed deformed in appearance, enormous wens protruding from their necks. The growths are called goiters, I am told, caused by the water.

July 11, dawn.

We depart in a half hour. We've been given bear-fur blankets to wrap ourselves in, beaver-skin masks to go over our heads, taffeta eye-shades to protect our eyes from the blinding glare.

The mountains tower above us like giants. A trembling has come over me that has little to do with fever. I've put my miniatures of Hortense and Eugène in the little velvet jewel bag sewn to my petticoat, for heart. Lazare's Saint Michael medal I've tucked into my bodice, for courage.

Benedictine Abbazia di Novalesa.

We're over. We were carried in chairs across perilous cliffs by ancient little men. It was even more terrifying than I thought it would be.

July 12—Turin.

We were late departing this morning due to a problem with the way our carriage had been reassembled. (It had been carried over the Pass in pieces, on the backs of mules shod with spiked shoes.) Consequently Junot forbade any stops, so by the time we rolled into the tiny but stately city of Turin, I was rather desperate for relief. My heart sank when I saw a regiment of French cavaliers led by a young man in the uniform of an aide-de-camp.

"August!" Junot jumped out of our carriage while it was yet in motion. "What's all this about?"

"The General sent me to escort Madame Bonaparte to Milan." The aide glanced at me, tipped his hat. "But first the King of Sardinia has requested an audience."

Junot cracked his knuckles, grinning. "The King of the Dormice is learning to bow, is he? To us Republicans? That's a good one. Well, I wonder if I should be kind enough to grant his Highness the honour?"

"Perhaps I didn't make myself clear," the young aide stuttered. "His Highness has requested an audience with the General's *wife*."

Lisette has mended the train on my ivory silk gown and unstitched my pearls, which we'd sewn into the hem of a petticoat for security. I've bathed, my hair has been dressed, I've been rouged and powdered. "There," Lisette said, adjusting a pearl-studded ornament in my hair. "You look beautiful." I studied my face in the looking glass, pulling at a curl so that it fell forward. Lisette had plucked my brows into a graceful arc. Yes, by candlelight the King of Sardinia might find me pleasing.

If I didn't melt first, I thought, wiping the perspiration from my brow. Already my gown was damp. I opened the double-sash doors onto the balcony overlooking the piazza. I could see the treetops of the ramparts beyond, and beyond that, in the blue horizon, the icy peaks of Mont Cenis, glittering like an enormous diamond in the sun.

Church bells rang for afternoon vespers. I'd forgotten how lovely bells sound. I watched as a veiled woman in black made her way to church, her eyes fixed on the ground. What will they think of me, these women? Me, the Parisian merveilleuse in her revealing Parisian gown, enjoying her Parisian pleasures . . . her Parisian freedom, I was beginning to understand.

Fortuné yelped at a rapping on the door. "Oh, it's you," Lisette said.

"Please, Mademoiselle," Captain Charles said, "refrain from such an unseemly expression of unrestrained joy." He scooped up Fortuné and rubbed his face in the dog's fur. Then, releasing the delighted dog, he informed me that we would not be going to the palace for another hour.

"An hour!" I'd been waiting forever, it seemed. Waiting to be taken to the palace, waiting to be presented to the king of this realm. Waiting for the laudanum I took for pain to take effect. "Forgive me, Captain Charles. I'm nervous, I confess." I'd never met a king before.

"Why should *you* be nervous?" The captain brushed off a footstool, flipped up his tails and sat down. "I should think it would be the King who has reason to be uneasy. After all, your husband rather badly trounced him."

What was it I feared? That I might do something foolish. That I might become faint, with pain and with fever. That I might embarrass Bonaparte, the Republic. "It's just that I never expected . . ."

"La Gloire?"

La Gloire, indeed! Fame was the last thing I'd expected from marriage to Bonaparte. Strange, intense little Napoleon, the ill-mannered Corsican—a hero now, the Liberator of Italy. The man to whom kings bowed.

Lisette held out a glass of orange water. "I put a little ether in it, Madame. You look pale."

Late, I'm not sure of the time.
I survived. It was horrible. (The King fell asleep on his throne!) Barras was right—I should have brought a hoop.

July 13—Milan.
Approaching Milan I could hear cheering—it sounded like a lot of people. Bonaparte's brother Joseph stuck his head out the window, holding onto his tricorne hat. A band struck up the *Marseillaise. Amour sacrée de la patrie*, I hummed along, a lump rising in my throat. I wanted to look out, but I didn't think it would be ladylike to be seen hanging out a carriage window. "We should wake Colonel Junot," I said, waving to a gang of urchin boys who were racing beside us.

"What?" Junot sputtered, running his fingers through his hair. "We're in Milan? Already?"

"Is my plume straight?" Joseph asked, adjusting the tilt of his hat. "How do I look?"

"Fine," I said, popping an aniseed comfit into my mouth to sweeten my breath. In fact, all of us looked as if we'd been travelling in rough circumstances for two weeks: rumpled, worn and irritable. It had been a gruelling trip.

The crowd was chanting *Evviva la Francia! Evviva la libertà!* I caught sight of an immense Roman arch festooned with bright banners. "Nervous?" Captain Charles whispered. I answered by widening my eyes. Yes!

There *was* a crowd—men in powdered wigs and old-fashioned court-style jackets, women (the few I could see) in wide-hooped gowns, their heads covered with black scarves. Behind the aristocrats were the peasants in rags, quite a number, a sea of faces. A column of gendarmes stood at attention, the sun glittering off their muskets. I thought of my children, Aunt Désirée. They would have thrilled to see such a crowd.

I recognized Bonaparte's young brother Louis on horseback with the aides. But where was Bonaparte? My stomach felt queasy. I must not be sick, I told myself. Not now.

We came to an abrupt halt. "We're here," Joseph said, with his annoying giggle.

"Finally," Junot said, cracking his knuckles.

A footman in lilac livery opened the carriage door. A breeze blew dust in. I did my best to ignore it—to blink and to smile—for there, standing before me, was my husband, Napoleon Bonaparte.

His face was bronzed by the sun. Backed by the cheering crowd, his soldiers at attention all around him, he had a regal air. "Welcome," he said without smiling. "What took you so long?" he barked at Junot, stepping back so that the footman could let down the step.

Evviva la libertà! a man yelled. Fortuné, in his travelling basket, whimpered to be let out.

"Your wife has not been well," Joseph told his brother contritely, his hands pressed between his knees. "We had to make stops."

Bonaparte looked at me, his big grey eyes sombre. The footman was having trouble getting the step down. I felt I was in a dream. The man standing before me seemed a stranger—this man, my husband, the Liberator of Italy.

"May I help?" Captain Charles asked the footman, for the step mechanism had jammed again. "I have had to wrestle that latch many times over the last weeks," he rushed on, aware of his presumption, "and consequently have come to have an intimate knowledge of its perverse ways."

Bonaparte stared at the captain. "You must be Charles, the aide-de-camp."

"General Bonaparte, sir!" The captain saluted.

Evviva la Francia! a child cried out.

"Be quick then, Captain—I wish to embrace my wife."

The footman stood back. Captain Charles pressed down on the left side of the step and it gave way with a clatter. Bonaparte took my hand. "Careful!" he said—as if, I realized (heart heavy), I were a woman with child. I stepped down onto the dusty road. He put his hand under my chin. "I have been starved for you."

I smiled, speechless, overcome by the dust, the bright sun, the crowd. Overcome by the intensity of Bonaparte's eyes. "Bonaparte, I—"

He placed his right hand at the nape of my neck, his thumb pressing against my skull. Then he kissed me—without modesty, without restraint, as if, man and woman, husband and wife, we were the only two people on earth. For a moment I resisted, the roar of the crowd in my ears. And then I gave way to him.

My hat slipped off. I grabbed for it, then I stood back, pressing Bonaparte's hand to my heart. Distantly I heard people cheering. He stared at me, his eyes glistening. "We came as quickly as we could," I assured him, but my voice was drowned out by a trumpet blare. "I'm feeling a bit faint." Everything looked bleached. The crowd seemed to shimmer in the heat. I took hold of his arm. The other carriages in our caravan pulled into view: Hamelin's wreck of a hired fiacre, the servants' carriage, the baggage wagon.

A man in yellow-striped rags ran through the line of soldiers. "*Evviva Napoleone!*" he cried out as they pulled him away. "*Evviva la libertà!*"

Bonaparte led me to a carriage harnessed to four grey horses, their brass bells jingling. The ornate berlin was festooned with red, white and blue ribbons; it looked like a feast-day cake. "To cover the Austrian royal insignias," Bonaparte said, lifting a bow to reveal a royal emblem underneath.

"Aren't the others coming with us?" I asked as he handed me in. The upholstery was a pale cream-coloured brocade. I sat down uneasily. My periodic sickness had become unpredictable. I could never be sure what to expect—or when. "What about your brother?" And Junot, for that matter?

"This reception is in *your* honour," Bonaparte said, settling himself beside me and taking my hand. He was thinking of kissing me again, I knew. I opened my fan and fluttered it, leaning my head against the tufted upholstery. The heat was oppressive.

"Perhaps a little air," Bonaparte said, letting down the glass. A bouquet came flying through. He put the glass back up. The crowd was chanting *Evviva la Francia! Evviva Napoleone!* Their fervour frightened me—frightened and amazed me.

I heard the postillion cry out something in Italian. Our carriage swung gently as the team of horses pulled it forward. I put my hand to my side, against the pain.

Crowds cheered as we wound our way through narrow, rutted streets, along waterways and canals thick with barges. The air was filled with the pungent smell of potatoes, chestnuts, aubergines cooking, fish frying. "This is a beautiful city," Bonaparte said, stroking my hand. "You will love it here."

"Yes," I said, although I felt disappointed, in truth. Milan was smaller than I'd expected, and it seemed curiously vacant in spite of the crowds. The few women I saw on the street were dressed entirely in black. The shops had no windows; even the residences were shuttered.

Bonaparte pointed to a sign in the shape of a cardinal's red hat: "A hatter." A pair of scissors signified a tailor; a snake, a chemist; a bleeding foot, leeches. "But the water is unclean," he went on as we crossed over a stinking canal. "We have much to do installing a new sanitation system." A man in a banditti hat, defecating by the side of the road, raised his hand in salute. "And educating the inhabitants," he added.

At one intersection we were obliged to wait for the passage of a cart loaded with an enormous barrel of water. Chained prisoners followed behind, swinging long leather tubes out of which water came, dampening the dust.

We came upon a great square where five goats were grazing. "This must be the famous cathedral," I said, astonished by its grandeur. The church looked even bigger than Notre Dame and far more ornate.

"Three murderers live in there and I can't do a thing about it."* Masons stopped their work on one of the turrets to cheer as we passed. I smiled at them and waved. (Like a queen, I thought.) "The façade has been under construction for five centuries," Bonaparte said. "I intend to finish it." His statements surprised me. This wasn't a soldier speaking— this was a ruler.

We pulled through a broad portico into the courtyard of a villa of glittering pink granite. In the centre was a fountain, spurting brown water. The footman opened our carriage door, his lilac jacket stained from running ahead of our carriage. I stepped down, lifting my skirt up out of the dust. An enormous number of servants dressed in black bowed at our approach.

I hung on Bonaparte's arm as he strode up the steps and through two majestic colonnades into a vast marble hall. I glanced back over my shoulder. We were being followed by a crowd of noisy, clattering "help." Everywhere I looked there were men in uniform, standing at attention. "This is your home," Bonaparte said proudly, sweeping his arm aloft.

Lisette blew dust from her hands. "Our trunks will be brought up soon, Madame—or so they say." She rolled her eyes. The rigours of travel had brought out a feisty humour in my maid.

A clock chimed nine bells. Nine? "Do you know the time?" I guessed it to be around three in the afternoon.

"I think it *is* nine, Madame, but the day begins a half hour after sunset, I am told, so the time is always changing, depending on the time of year." She blew out her cheeks in exasperation.

I smiled. She reminded me of Hortense, and a wave of longing came over me. "I'll be needing a bath," I told her. I had taken laudanum and was feeling more at ease, enveloped in a rosy glow.

"I don't think they know about baths here," she said, crinkling her nose.

---

* *Churches were official sanctuaries. Any criminal who took refuge in a church could not be arrested.*

Lisette reappeared some time later. "I give up, Madame! I tried French, I tried Latin, I even tried Greek. I told them water, they fetched a mirror—a cracked one. I told them a bath, they brought me a melon rolling around stupidly on a tray."

"We need Bonaparte."

"The General is in a meeting with his officers, Madame," Lisette said, reappearing. "He said he would only be a moment."

But it was over an hour before Bonaparte appeared. A frowning child in a blue smock followed behind him, carrying a vase of flowers.

"I want a bath," I told him, accepting the girl's solemn offering.

Bonaparte raised his eyebrows in expectation.

"But we can't make ourselves understood!" I gave the girl a coin and she ran away giggling.

A copper tub in the shape of a coffin was carried into a little room outside my bedchamber. An endless stream of maids with steaming jugs ran in and out. At last the tub was full. I told them thanks (*grazie*—the only word I know), and indicated that they could go, but they just stood there. "Could you ask them to leave, Bonaparte?" He barked something in Italian and the maids scurried away like a flock of birds, murmuring *prego, prego, prego*.

Lisette helped me off with my gown. I slipped into the soapy water. The ceiling of the little room was painted with cherubs. Lisette's fingers were strong. She massaged my scalp, my neck. My headache dimmed. She helped me into my best nightdress—a cool diaphanous blue silk. I was going to have to tell him.

Bonaparte threw back the bed sheet. I blew out one of the candles and stretched out beside him on the musty feather bed. The laudanum and the bath had brought on a feeling of tenderness in me.

He kissed my cheek innocently, as one kisses a child. I could feel the heat coming off him. "There's something I have to tell you, Bonaparte." I took his hand and pressed it to my cheek. "I'm not with child. Not any more—at least that's what my doctor said." I could not bring myself to tell him that the doctor thought it might only have been a mole. There were things men preferred not to know.

Bonaparte sat up, his arms encircling his knees. "When did this happen?" he asked, staring into the shadows.

"About a month ago." I put my hand on his back. I could feel him rocking slightly. "I was going to write, but then I thought it best to tell you in person."

"This happens," he said, turning back to me with tears in his eyes.

"Oh Bonaparte!" I took him in my arms, my heart aching. If only I could give him what he wanted, what he needed. If only I could return his love.

Bastille Day, some time after 10:00 P.M. (maybe later).
We've just returned from a dismal Bastille Day ball. I now understand the meaning of the expression "bored to tears." Bored to *death*.

As we entered the vast, dark ballroom, Bonaparte was hailed. Then we were escorted to a podium where he was hailed yet again. "What do we do now?" I asked him, trying to make myself comfortable on the lumpy chair. Women in the corners whispered behind their fans, regarding me with disapproval. My gown was much more revealing than what the other women were wearing. I regretted not bringing a shawl.

Bonaparte drummed his fingers. "We're the guests of honour. We're required to sit."

All night? I felt like a prisoner of the podium.

We were hours, it seemed, listening to lofty addresses as every noble in Milan was introduced. (One man bowed so low he practically touched his nose to the floor.) My cheeks ached from smiling.

After the introductions Bonaparte was called away for an emergency meeting concerning some military matter. I sat on display, looking out over the dance floor. Thin red, white and blue ribbons had been strung from the rafters. They gave a dismal impression. The air reeked of pomade, garlic and perspiration. A haze of rice powder from the thickly powdered wigs filled the air like a fog. The only laughter came from a cluster of valets standing by an empty marble fireplace. It was a joyless occasion, and I feared it did not bode well for the months to come.

"Is the *bellissima regina** permitted to dance with a commoner?" Captain Charles hissed from one side of the podium. He was wearing a charming Chinese ensemble of green silk trimmed with gold, and green slippers to match. "The musicians, although lacking in what a Parisian would call finesse, are, at the least, vigorous." He removed a plume from his velvet toque to fan himself with.

I smiled behind my fan. "First of all, Captain Wide-Awake, let us be clear: I am not a queen."

"You just happen to be seated on a throne?"

"Which is where I'm required to stay, alas."

"How . . . thrilling." With a comical expression.

"Don't make me laugh," I said, laughing.

"Why not?"

"I'm not allowed to enjoy myself. This is a serious position." I sat up straight.

"So, you won't even join us for a cotillion? I thought all Parisian women had a passion for dance."

"In Paris there is only one true passion, Captain," I said, "and that, I fear to say, is the pursuit of wealth."

The captain held up his green-gloved hands and made an expression of mock surprise. "Cynicism in a woman surprises me."

"Forgive me, Captain, I was trying to be clever—a mistake on my part, for I am not a clever woman."

"Yet I believe it fair to say there is truth in your observation. I personally have a passion for the pursuit of wealth, as you put it—or rather, a passion for beautiful things, the one necessitating the other."

"I suffer that weakness myself," I said, smiling ruefully.

"I prefer to think of it as a virtuous flaw, for is not the worship of beautiful things a religion of sorts?"

"You jest and speak of holiness at the same time, Captain. You are a daring man."

* *Bellissima regina: Italian for "beautiful queen."*

"It is all one, I believe: the holy, the beautiful and the bold—with respect to men, in any case. I cannot speak for women, who, in my observation, regard daring with alarm, and certainly not reverence."

"We all enjoy daring, Captain, men and women alike. Men are driven to be daring on horseback, for example, or on the fields of war. Women, on the other hand, are dealt few wild cards. The few we get we tend to play somewhat innocently, at the dressmaker's, or at the hatter's."

"Or perhaps at . . . ?" He tilted his head in the direction of the gaming room.

"I enjoy games of chance, Captain Charles, but one wouldn't call my approach daring by any means. I am by nature cautious."

"Yet you are said to win."

"I greatly dislike losing," I confessed.

"In that case, I have a wild card to suggest for you," he said. "*Speculation*. It is, after all, the most thrilling of the games of chance, but"—he paused, regarding me seriously—"in the right hands, entails little risk. Just the thing for a woman who is, by nature, cautious."

A portly man dressed in an old-fashioned long velvet coat was heading in my direction. "Excuse me, Captain, but I believe I am about to be accosted."

"Do you require my protection, Madame? I could be your *cavaliere servente*."

"And pray, Captain Charles, what might that be?" I was relieved to see that the man in the long velvet coat had been detained by another.

"The cavaliere servente is one of the few charming customs of this country. When a woman's husband is absent, she requires the attention of a substitute: her cavaliere, who waits upon her hand and foot, who fulfills her every need."

"Her *every* need?" I gave the captain a teasing look. He was the type of man one could coquet with safely.

"Well, excepting, of course, the marital obligations, to which only the husband has a right. It is due to the rigour of this understanding that jealousy rarely arises between a husband and his wife's cavaliere servente."

"Interesting." Both men were advancing toward me now. "Speaking of husbands, Captain Charles, might you know where General Bonaparte is?"

"I believe he is conferring with his officers in the antechamber, Madame."

"Would you do me a favour, Captain?" He jackknifed from the waist. "Would you tell him to come here?"

The captain looked aghast. "Moi?"

"Yes, please."

"You want *me* to tell General Bonaparte what to do?" He mimed a nervous Nellie.

"Yes, my cavaliere servente, I would like you to inform my husband that his wife needs him—*now*."

"I'm afraid I'm not very good at this," I told Bonaparte later, in the privacy of our room. There was a cooling breeze coming from the canal, carrying with it the pungent scent of sewage. "What were all your meetings about?" I asked, closing the shutters.

"The Austrians are advancing again." He took his sword out of its sheath and ran his finger along the edge, examining it. "I think I'll take your horse with me when I go."

"You are leaving, Bonaparte?" *Already?*

"In a few days."

My heart sank. Could I manage in Milan without him? "But why are you taking my horse?"

"You will be coming to join me."

"On campaign? But Bonaparte, won't that be—?"

"You don't think I can live without you, do you?" he grinned, tugging my ear.

July 16, early morning.

It seems Bonaparte and I are always parting. The soldiers whistled as we embraced. "For luck," he said, kissing me. He slipped a ribbon from my hair and put it in the pocket next to his heart. "I'll send for you," he said, swinging onto his horse. Then he galloped out the gate, his men scrambling to catch up with him.

In which I learn about war

Shortly after 5:00 P.M.—still very hot.

A small afternoon gathering this afternoon. It was impossible! The men stood around the fireplace at one end of the cavernous salon to talk about horses and tell battle stories, while the women sat in the window alcove at the other end of the room discussing fashion, children and dogs. I was relieved when Captain Charles joined in, but shortly a footman came to inform the captain that his horse was ready.

"But you just got here," I said, dismayed. He was the only bright spark in the conversation, frankly.

"General Leclerc expects me in Verona tonight, Madame."

I excused myself from my difficult guests and accompanied the captain to the entryway. "I thought you were my cavaliere servente," I teased him, "and yet already you are abandoning me."

He bowed, a graceful melting movement that a girl might make. "Will you forgive me?" He took my hand and kissed it, his breath warm. "No doubt you will require proof of my attachment. Perhaps there are other ways I could be of service?"

Oh, but he was a naughty boy, I thought, and oh but I was finding it an amusing charade. "What might my cavaliere suggest?"

He took a coin from out of his pocket; before my eyes it became a handful! "My talent, if one could call it that, is an instinct for increase. I guarantee a return of thirty percent." He took his cloak from the maid, his hat, and gave her the coins.

"That's a bold promise, Captain." Was he serious?

"I am said to be bold," he replied, examining his hat in the looking glass, creasing the brim.

Bold, indeed. I adjusted his plume so that it stood straight up. "There," I said, feeling now rather hennish.

"In addition to all the other requirements, I might add," he said, buckling his sword sheath.

"Such as?" I asked, stepping outside where a groom was waiting, holding his horse.

"Discretion." Captain Charles took a fistful of mane and leapt gracefully into the saddle. "Ten thousand, Madame, for starters?" His horse tossed its head, pawing at the cobblestones.

I put up two fingers, twenty. Double or nothing: my game.

July 23.

Hidden under an enormous black shawl (like all the women here), I went to church this morning to light a candle for Alexandre. Two years ago today he died.

If I've learned one thing, it is that life is precious and fleeting. I weep to be separated from my children. And I dislike being separated from Bonaparte as well. I prayed to Saint Michael that he would be victorious. Already I want to go home.

July 17, Saint-Germain
Chère Maman,

Yesterday General Hoche sent me a letter. Since he makes mention of you, I copy part of it here:

"It is with the greatest pleasure that I grant your request for a leave of absence for your friends. Perhaps they will help you forget the losses you have suffered. I will not leave Paris without seeing my dear Eugène. It would have been preferable if his mother had not taken him away from me; I would have made every effort to fulfill my duty toward an unlucky friend."

And now, just this afternoon, General Hoche fulfilled his promise and came to see me. Everyone at school was excited, even the teachers! I showed him my scrapbook, which he liked. Then we fenced. He taught me some excellent new moves. He agreed it was time I had a horse of my own.

I am improving in my studies. The headmaster does not scowl at me quite so much. I've been riding every day. I saw Hortense twice this week—she is busy with her projects.

Your loving son, Eugène

H.Q., Castiglione, 4 Thermidor
My brothers Louis and Joseph have arrived and assure me your health is restored. It is terribly hot; my soul is burning for you. —B.P.

July 24.
Suddenly there is such a flurry of activity. I'm to meet Bonaparte in Brescia. From there we will go to Verona together.

In the midst of all the packing and preparations, the hapless Citoyen Hamelin ("the blinker") came to call. "Please forgive me, Citoyen, for being distracted," I told him, "but I'm preparing to join my husband in Brescia." I was trying to decide whether I should take my pug dog with me. And what about my medications? Did I have sufficient laudanum? How long would we be gone? "We're leaving tonight and we only found out last—"

Hamelin blinked several times before exclaiming, "Brescia! Madame, the road to Brescia is infested with ruffians. I shall come with you. I will be honoured to risk my life in order that the wife of the General should enjoy a safe voyage." Immediately he headed for the door. "Forgive me, but I must rush off! I must have my muskets cleaned, obtain grease for the carriage wheels. There is nothing more tempting to a rogue than a broken-down vehicle. No, no, Madame—I *insist*."

Evening—Brescia.
Bonaparte met us on the road. I joined him in his carriage. "You are well? You look well," he said, regarding me hungrily. "Close the curtains."

July 29—Peschiera.

The dawn was breaking as our carriages pulled into the courtyard of a villa on the outskirts of Verona.

"Is this where the Pretender lived?" I asked Bonaparte, yawning. I felt exhausted. We'd travelled from Brescia at night, but the road had been jolting and what sleep I'd managed to get had been fitful, disturbed by Bonaparte's ardent caresses.

"It's not as grand as I expected it to be," Bonaparte said, jumping out before our carriage had come to a full stop.

We sat out on the verandah overlooking rolling hills dotted with mulberry trees, drinking coffee and eating fresh figs from a tree in the garden. The air smelled sweetly of cut grass. Bonaparte became animated as he told us stories about the Pretender. "He led a simple life. The people here knew him as Comte de Lille. No one realized he was King Louis XVI's brother. Only his servants knew he was the Pretender to the throne of France."

"How do you know all this, Bonaparte?" I had had three cups of strong coffee and was beginning to feel alert.

"I have spies following him. He's in the north now, in Germany —my men never let him out of their sight. His daily rituals are very regular. He is dressed by eight each morning, a simple ensemble decorated with an insignia, a short sword. Then he sees his chancellor. And then he sits in his study and writes. At midday he stops for a meal—he keeps a frugal table. Then he shuts himself up in his closet and paces back and forth in a state of agitation for a little under one hour. This pattern is repeated every day."

"To think that he sat in this very chair," Citoyen Hamelin said, blinking. He wiggled the arm. "It needs fixing."

"It must be a lonely life," I said, gazing out over the mountains. I thought I saw movement in a dark crevice. Did they have mountain goats in this country? I wondered. I stood and went to the stone balustrade. "What's that moving on the mountain?"

But Bonaparte was occupied telling Hamelin about the last report he had had on the Pretender, the book the Pretender had been reading. "And it's still in the library," he said, "with a marker on page 231. He was on page 204 several months ago, so he can't be a very fast reader."

"Perhaps he did not read from it every day," Hamelin said, blinking. "Perhaps he only read a few days a week. If so, then one could say that he—"

I turned to Bonaparte. "Austrian soldiers wear white uniforms, do they not?"

He came to my side. "I don't see anything."

"Over to the left—see that line of white dots?"

Bonaparte pulled a collapsed glass from out of his pocket, shook it to open it and held it to his eye. "You must leave immediately," he said, letting the glass drop.

We were hours on the road, Lisette, Hamelin and I in the carriage, four dragoons following on horseback. At the fort in Peschiera a portly general with whiskers like sausages rushed out to meet us. "You can't stay here— the Austrians are closing in."

Hamelin and Lisette regarded me with alarm. "My husband instructed us to stay here," I told the general. The air smelled strongly of fish.

"But Madame, what if . . . ?" Hamelin exclaimed.

"Madame Bonaparte," General Guillaume stuttered, "I beg you to consider. If anything were to happen to you, I—"

"I appreciate your concern, General, but we will not move unless ordered to do so by my husband," I repeated, with a firmness that astonished even me. Bonaparte was the only rock I had to hold on to.

I am writing this now in a small stone cell in the basement of the fortress. At least it is cool. An hour ago we had a meal of lake trout washed down with watered Montferrat. We ate in silence. "Leave the horses hitched," I instructed the groom. Lisette and I will share a room. Our valises packed, we will sleep in our clothes. If we sleep.

A numbing fear has enveloped me. That, and anger I confess. How could Bonaparte have put us into this position! Put *me*. For the sake of his lust, he has endangered my life.

July 31, Sunday—Parma.

I was woken at dawn by a clatter of horses in the courtyard, the sound of metal clanking against stones.

I touched Lisette's arm. "I think someone has arrived," I whispered. She moaned and turned back into her pillow. "We might have to leave soon. Best to rise," I said, releasing the pedal of the chipped washbasin and splashing my face.

I tied a red scarf around my head créole-style and creamed my cheeks with rouge, blind without a glass. I heard a voice. "It's Junot, I think."

Lisette opened her eyes. "Colonel Junot?"

"It doesn't look good," I overheard Junot saying to General Guillaume as I came down the stone steps into the courtyard. "The Austrians outnumber us three to one."

"Colonel Junot, what has happened?" I asked anxiously.

"We had quite a battle last night." His breath smelled of liquor. "General Bonaparte has set up a command post at Castelnuovo. I'm to take you there, but we must leave immediately."

Hamelin, blinking against the morning sun, appeared at the entrance to the fort, followed by a servant lugging his heavy valise. And then Lisette appeared, carrying a wicker basket.

Junot jumped to the door of our carriage. "Allow me," he said, gesturing us in.

"I'm so sleepy!" Lisette yawned, climbing in after Hamelin. "Did you sleep, Madame?" she asked, smiling with her eyes at Junot.

"A little." I was anxious to join Bonaparte, but anxious as well about leaving the protection of the fort. Nowhere seemed safe.

Junot headed out the open gate on horseback, the dragoons falling in behind. A young dragoon with a pink face jumped onto his horse and trotted to catch up with them. He smiled and tipped his hat at me as he raced by.

"The young men always like *you*, Madame," Lisette teased, handing me a warm roll lined with a sausage.

"Did I miss something?" Hamelin asked, looking up from his book of Italian phrases.

"I remind them of their mothers," I told my maid. The freshly baked bread lifted my spirits, restored faith. We'd not had time to eat.

"Would you be offended if I told you that you remind me of my mother?" she asked.

"Not at all. In fact, you remind me of my daughter." We exchanged an affectionate look.

Our carriage lurched forward. I waved to General Guillaume as we pulled through the gate. He turned away, his hand over his heart. He was frightened for us, I realized, a cold feeling of fear coming over me.

It was cooler along the shores of Lake Garda, the vast water calm, the blue hills in the distance misty. I was relieved not to hear sniper fire.

Lisette and I were playing cat's cradle when we were startled by the ominous boom of a cannon. The carriage halted abruptly; I put out a hand to keep from falling forward. I saw a flash of light, heard musket fire, cannon again. But it was the sound of a horse's scream that chilled me—that, and the violent jolting of our carriage. I realized we might tip. I heard Junot yelling, "Get down, get down, dismount, you idiot!"

"What's happened?" Hamelin hiccupped, pulling down on his hat.

The door to the carriage was thrown open. "Jump!" Junot grabbed Hamelin and yanked him out. A crack of gunfire sent him scrambling.

Lisette leapt into Junot's arms. He let her down and pushed her toward the ditch. I gathered my skirts. I felt strangely calm; even so, I tasted tears. A sudden jolt threw me off balance. I heard a thunderous boom. "Get out!" Junot yelled.

I jumped, scrambling after Hamelin and Lisette, my petticoat tearing. I rolled down an embankment, coming to rest in marshy reeds. I crawled through the mud to the others. Lisette looked deathly pale. I put my arm around her. She was trembling. Or was I?

"My hiccups are gone," Hamelin said, blinking.

I heard the sound of a man crying out. "It must be one of the soldiers." I climbed back up to the top of the embankment.

"Madame, don't! Be careful," Lisette hissed. "Come back!"

I peered through the tall grass. Junot was crouched beside a fallen horse, a big chestnut. It was thrashing, bleeding from a wound in its neck. The other horses were rearing and kicking, trying to free themselves of the entangled harness. It was all the postillion could do to hold onto them while a dragoon cut the traces. And then I saw the young dragoon . . .

I ducked down, my breath shaky. My hand was covered in mud. I wiped it on the grass slowly, as if in a dream, then slid back down the embankment, trembling.

"What's going on?" Hamelin asked, holding a limp Lisette in his arms. Had she fainted? I tried to answer, but I could not, for I had seen the young dragoon, fallen from his horse, his foot caught in the stirrup, his face . . .

"What's wrong with Lisette?" I said finally, gasping.

Hamelin shook her. "I can't get her to wake up."

"Do you have a flask?"

"Oh!" He felt in his pocket, pulled out a leather-covered bottle and handed it to me. "Whisky. There's a little left."

I opened it and held it under Lisette's nose. Her eyelids flickered. I poured some of the liquor over my fingers, wiped it on her forehead, her lips, her nostrils. She moaned. "Sit her up more." I feared she might retch.

Hamelin slumped her forward. Lisette shook her head, looked up at me. "I feel sick, Madame!"

"Have a sip," I said, handing her the flask. "But just a little," I cautioned her, watching her tip back her head. We had to be ready to run.

I heard Junot yell, the crack of a whip, the carriage clattering, horses. We were showered with loose stones. Then Junot came tumbling down the embankment. He cursed when he hit the mud. He crawled over to us, his face frightful with mud and blood. Lisette handed him her handkerchief out of her bodice. "Are you all right?" he asked, pressing her kerchief to his lips.

"It's uncomfortable here," Hamelin said, slapping at a mosquito. They were everywhere now. "This pestilent air—"

"Colonel Junot, we heard the carriage."

"I whipped it on." He cracked his knuckles.

"We're stranded?" Hamelin exclaimed.

"The Austrians will assume you're in it and stop firing. But we've got to get into the woods without their seeing us." Junot started crawling along the ditch. "Can you follow?" I nodded. "Stay down," he hissed.

Once in a more secluded area, not far, we were able to get up out of the mud. Lisette's teeth were chattering, in spite of the heat. "Do you know where we are?" I asked Junot. I put my arm around Lisette, to steady her, steady myself.

"Near Desenzano," Junot said, slapping at a mosquito.

I remembered Desenzano, a village of narrow little streets opening onto the lake. Bonaparte and I had passed through it two nights before on the way to Verona.

I sensed the beat of a horse's hooves. Cocking his musket, Junot went to the edge of the woods. "A carter," he said, returning. "He's stopped to look at the dead horse."

A creaking wagon pulled by a fat red horse came into view. Loaded on the back were crates of chickens. The carter was wearing a black scarf around his head, like a peasant woman. He pulled to a stop when he saw us, said something in Italian. "Can you understand him?" I asked Junot.

"Just get in," Junot said, aiming his musket at the peasant. We climbed onto the wagon, sitting down uneasily on top of the chicken crates. "Go!" Junot said to the driver, climbing up beside him, but the carter just sat there.

"Do you have your little book?" I asked Hamelin.

Hamelin felt around in his pockets, put on his spectacles, ruffled through the pages of his book of Italian phrases. "Nohn sahp-pee-AH-mon DOH-veh chee troh-vee-AH-moh," he said (or something like that).

"What did you say?" Junot demanded.

"We are lost," Hamelin said, blinking. "I think that's what I said."

"We're not lost!" Junot grabbed the peasant's whip and cracked it, flicking the horse's rump. The mare bolted forward, setting the chickens to squawking.

We smelled Desenzano before we saw it. The mare balked, tossing her big head, refusing to go forward. "It's the smell," I said. I put a handkerchief to my nose, my eyes watering.

"There was a battle here last night," Junot said, cracking the whip again. But the mare wasn't budging. Then the driver yelled something at the horse and it pulled forward at last, swishing its plaited tail.

"He said *stupido*, didn't he? I think he told the horse it was stupid." Hamelin leafed through his book of phrases.

"*Stufato*, I thought he said." A feeling of faintness had come over me.

"Stewed meat?" Hamelin read.

Junot glanced back at me. "Cover her eyes."

I tried not to look as we went through the town, but I could not keep out the smell of gunpowder, burned flesh, faint whiffs of a sweet odour. The soft bump of the wagon over a body. The whimpering sounds, like those of a child. "I heard someone call out. Can't we stop?" Then I made the mistake of opening my eyes. Everywhere there were bloated bodies. The cobblestones were awash with blood, drying in the morning sun. Two peasant women were pulling a coat off a dead soldier, a boy with a grey pallor to his skin, vacant eyes. The pickers looked up at us and one of them grinned, toothless as a baby. I pressed Lisette to me, my trembling fingers entangled in her sweat-damp hair.

As we approached Castelnuovo there were herds of cavalry horses tethered, loaded munitions wagons, tents pitched, soldiers everywhere. The smoke of numerous campfires gave the landscape an ethereal look. Tears came to my eyes at the sight of the flag of the French Republic hanging from the thatched roof of a peasant's hut—the temporary headquarters of the Army of Italy.

"What took you so long?" Bonaparte demanded, emerging. "Your escort arrived back well over an hour ago."

"It was rough going," Junot said, saluting, red in the face. He glanced at Lisette. She was staring out over the maize fields.

"It was a good thing I was there," Hamelin said as Bonaparte lifted me down from the wagon.

I fought back tears. "I think I should sit down." And then the sobs came, overwhelming me.

"Get ether," Bonaparte commanded an orderly. He grasped me by the shoulder. "Fight it, don't give in to it." But I had been fighting it for too long. "The Austrians are going to pay dearly for this," I heard him say under his breath.

I drank the ether water the aide brought, coughed. It tasted brackish. That smell was with me still. "Give some to Lisette." She was sitting in the wagon, watching us with a dazed look. Even the chickens in the crates were silent.

"The driver wants a reward," Junot told Bonaparte, cracking his knuckles. "At least, I think he does. Maybe you should talk to him."

"Give him whatever he wants," Bonaparte said, squeezing my hand.

"Are our trunks here? Can we change?" Lisette asked, standing.

Junot put out his hand to help her down. "Careful, she might fall," I told him, my voice tremulous.

"You should eat—it will give you strength." Bonaparte led me into the little cottage with a thatched roof.

Inside, it was dark. The floor was just dirt. The hut was hot, airless, smelling of goats. A table in front of an empty fireplace was covered with reports, illuminated by a tin lantern. An enormous map was nailed to the rough plank wall. Bonaparte led me to a straw pallet. He said something in Italian to a peasant boy with a dirty face. "And salami?" Bonaparte asked, looking back at me. I shook my head, no. I didn't think I could eat.

"The coach will be ready in thirty minutes, General," Junot said, looking in.

"The harness is mended?"

Junot nodded, cracking his knuckles.

"We're leaving you, Bonaparte?" I began to tremble.

Nearing Toscane, we were met by a courier mounted on a black horse slick with lather. "Turn back!" he yelled. "The Austrians are on ahead. They've taken Brescia!"

Mon Dieu, I thought, *Brescia?* Brescia was so close to Milan.

"What are we going to do now?" Hamelin asked, taking out his travel book. "We can't go north, east or west."

"South," Bonaparte said, pacing.

"I want to stay with you!"

He regarded me with an expression I couldn't identify. This man, my husband, wasn't the man I had known in Paris. Here, in the rough-and-tumble atmosphere of the camp, surrounded by men who regarded him with devoted loyalty, he seemed transformed. Confident, expansive, there was a certain nobility to his movements. Like his men I believed in him, felt an aura of security when I was in his presence. "*Please,* Bonaparte."

He knelt down beside me, taking my hands in his. His touch calmed me. "You must understand—the Austrians are closing in. We're anticipating quite a battle. You will be safe in the south."

His eyes told me I must, that it was for the best. I sniffed and nodded. He kissed me with great tenderness. "You were brave this morning," he said with a smile.

"Oh, Bonaparte!" I pressed his fingers to my lips. There was strength in him. I could understand why his men followed him with such absolute devotion—he ennobled them, just as he ennobled me.

He stood and addressed his courier, who was standing in the door, twisting the ends of his massive moustache. "Cross the Po river at Cremona," he told him, tracing the route on the map with a paper knife. "It's less risky there." He scratched something on a paper. "My Uncle Fesch is in Parma. He will give you shelter for the night. Then take him with you south. Tell him that's an order. Head down into Lucques—they are a peaceful people. I'll send word when it's safe to return."

"A kiss?" I said, standing.

"For luck," he smiled, taking me in his arms.

It is past midnight now. We are in Parma, in the home of Bonaparte's Uncle Fesch, a jolly sort of man with a ruddy complexion. A maid just came for my tray, the pastries untouched. "I cannot eat," I told her slowly, in simple French. *Scusatemi.* "I am ill," I added, not untruthfully.

And terrified, still.

And haunted: by the image of a boy's face, his thin body on the dusty road, the smell of Desenzano, the cries of the wounded left to die.

Tears, tears. I begin to tremble. *Mon Dieu.* I am the daughter of a soldier, the widow of a soldier, the wife of a soldier. But until today, I never knew what war was.

In which I am surrounded by Bonapartes

October 2, 1796—Milan, sweltering hot afternoon.
It has been some time, I see, since I've written here. So much has happened, and yet so much remains the same. Bonaparte is victorious, against all odds. Yet the enemy is a many-headed Hydra. How many armies can the Austrians raise? Every time Bonaparte vanquishes one, yet another rises up in its place. I fear there will never be peace.

Oh, it is the vapours again, surely. I am overcome with malaise. I feel another attack coming on, a strange shimmering at the edges. Migraine, the doctor told me the last time it happened, a paroxysmal pain in the temple. Pain, certainly, for even laudanum could not touch it. The last time I had an attack, I stayed in a darkened room for three days, daring not move or even speak. This land will be my grave, I fear.

November 23.
Victory! (Relief.) Once again the Austrians have retreated behind the walls of Mantua.

December 9.
Bonaparte is back, his health weakened by a plunge into a swamp. (I pray it is not mal-aria.*) The quiet domestic life we are finally enjoying now

* *Mal-aria: malaria, translated in Italian as "bad air," which people believed to be the cause of the disease.*

will help, I hope. How little time we have had together! He's having his portrait painted, we're planning a ball—and, I should add, attending nightly to what Bonaparte refers to as "our project." Maybe now, with time together, we'll succeed.

December 24, Christmas Eve.
"Madame?" Lisette curtsied when she realized Bonaparte was sitting in the alcove by the window. "Your sister, General, she is—"

"Maria-Paola? My sister is here?" Bonaparte jumped up. "Already?"

Lisette glanced at me. Oh la la, her eyes said.

"Uff. The boat was disgusting!" Bonaparte's sixteen-year-old sister is a striking girl with curly black hair and sapphire blue eyes—even more beautiful than I'd expected from all I'd heard. "I threw up on the deck, over the side, in the dining hall, in my bunk." She'd plucked her eyebrows into a thin line, like the servant girls. "You're mussing my hair," she protested in bad French, when Bonaparte embraced her. She has a shrill voice. "*This* is where you live? Magnifico!"

Bonaparte turned toward me, his arm around his little sister. "Paganetta," he said proudly.

I nodded, smiling stupidly. *Pagan*etta, indeed. She is only sixteen, yet so womanly. And a spirited girl, it was easy to see, well aware of her charms—*la beauté du diable.** "Welcome, Maria-Paola, to—"

"I'm not Maria-Paola any more, I'm Pauline."

"Welcome, Pauline, to—"

She swept by me without listening. "Remember, Napoleone, you promised! I get my own suite."

December 27.
A constant stream of maids and footmen has been running up and down the hall doing Pauline's bidding. The bed sheets are not sufficiently soft,

* *La beauté du diable: beauty of the devil, or bloom of youth, the sexual appeal of a girl.*

the mirror not sufficiently ornate, the china sugar dish does not match the silver tea equipage and the tapestries hanging on her walls are frayed. I watch this flurry of activity with irritation. I have a reception to prepare for and nothing is getting done.

December 29.
I caught Pauline in my wardrobe, hiding in my ball gowns. "I'm playing!" she insisted. (Playing? She's sixteen!) In the reflection of the looking glass I saw her stick her tongue out at me.

"I'd prefer if you didn't 'play' in my suite, Pauline," I said, smiling with all the sweetness I could muster.

January 7, 1797.
At the opera last night four young men arrived at our box insisting that they had been invited. Pauline, it turned out, had looked at each of them through the large end of her opera glass (which in this country means, *Come see me*).

Bonaparte only laughed when I told him. "You find that amusing?" I demanded. Frankly, I feel like killing his little sister.

30 Ventôse, Luxembourg Palace
Chère amie,

Terrible news—Thérèse sued Tallien for divorce yesterday. She and the baby and the nanny and three house servants are with me now. Apparently Tallien threatened her with a pistol. I told her I'd do what I could to keep it out of the journals.

And speaking of journals, according to the Républican *I'm unable even to write this letter because I've been put in prison for making false bank notes. Ha!*

I'm apprehensive regarding the upcoming election. The Royalist faction is gaining strength. Our Minister of Police claims one hundred deputies have made oaths of allegiance to the Pretender. One deputy even had the gall to stroll in the Tuileries gardens in red-heeled boots. *

Director Letourneur assures us that we need not fear, that all will be under control because he will be patrolling the streets of Paris on horseback. (The dolt!) And as for Director La Réveillière, he is taken up with matters pertaining to a cult he has founded. I advised him that every good religion needed a martyr, and that to make his a success he should get himself hanged. He failed to see the humour.

Père Barras

May 9—Milan.

We're back in Milan after a difficult three months of travel. In January Bonaparte defeated yet another Austrian army—the *fifth*—and then turned his attention south, to Rome, forcing the Papal states to succumb. Then, with the south secure, he chased the Austrians into the north, until finally, two weeks ago, they agreed to a preliminary peace.

And so, at last, the Austrians are defeated and Bonaparte is victorious. His wife, however, is not. I wage a losing battle with his spirited sister Pauline. This morning I discovered her in the pantry with a footman. "I think you should consider getting your sister married," I told Bonaparte. *Fast.* "General Leclerc is in love with her," I suggested. Victor Leclerc was an absolute fool for the girl. "Everyone calls him the blond Bonaparte because he imitates you." Short, serious, with thin lips and big eyes, Victor Leclerc even looked like Bonaparte, but for his fair colouring.

"His father is a merchant." Bonaparte stood and went to the window, his hands clasped behind his back. "Wealthy, though."

Pauline yawned. "Perhaps you would like to sit down." Bonaparte glanced at me, suddenly unsure. Matters to do with his family flummoxed him completely.

"Perhaps I should go," I said, standing.

"Stay!"

* *Before the Revolution, aristocrats wore boots with high red heels.*

"What's this all about?" Pauline demanded.

"You must have a husband," Bonaparte said.

"I'm already betrothed." Pauline glared. (At me!) "You *might* recall."

"Deputy Fréron is a middle-aged drunk with three illegitimate children by an actress—a bad one."

"He was going to leave her!"

"She claims he married her!"

"Bonaparte?" I touched his hand. He and his sister would only end up brawling at each other. And if anyone was a match for Bonaparte, it was Pauline.

Bonaparte sat down, scowling. "What about General Leclerc?"

Pauline looked from me to her brother and back again. "Little Victor?"

"Marriage would bring many benefits, Pauline," I said. "General Leclerc comes from a wealthy family."

"Flour merchants!"

"He was educated in Paris," I persevered. "The family has a country seat—the château of Montgobert." For all I knew it was a pile of stones.

"What about a trousseau?" she demanded.

"Whatever you like."

"The gowns must be by Signora Tandello."

Bonaparte coughed. Signora Tandello was the most expensive dressmaker in Milan. Yes, I nodded, of course, *anything*.

"How much of a dowry would I get?"

"Joseph and I will have to talk about that," Bonaparte said.

"No doubt a great deal," I added.

Pauline pursed her lips. "Bien."

May 15, La Chaumière
Darling,

It is just as well you are in the Land of Antiquity, for the situation in Paris has become worrisome. The election was a disaster. The Royalists have taken control of the legislative councils! Even General Pichegru, who everyone knows is in the pay of the Pretender, was elected President of the Five

Hundred. I was at a dinner last night where the guests talked quite openly of putting the Pretender on the throne. The Royalists' agents—of whom there are rumoured to be a number in Paris—are throwing gold around quite freely.

My home life is worrisome as well—a disaster, some might say. I was mad to have reconciled with Tallien. I love him with a passion, you know I do, but I simply can't live with his drinking, his wenching and fits of jealous rage. And now it's too late, alas. Every woman in Paris is in an interesting condition, it seems, myself now included.

> Your loving and dearest
> (and yes, somewhat miserable) friend, Thérèse

Note—I heard that your friend Aimée* died. My sympathy, darling.

*May 22—Mombello.***

It's a lovely spring evening. Fireflies dance outside the open windows. I am writing this by moonlight. How late is it? I'm not sure. Thérèse's letter disturbed me terribly. I am filled with sorrow, grief. How many lives have been sacrificed for this Revolution of ours, our precious *liberté*? I think of Aimée, all my loved ones who have died. I think of Alexandre. *La liberté ou la mort.* Will their sacrifice be for naught? Will the Royalists be victorious, put a king back on the throne, abolish all that so many have died for?

I kept Lazare's Saint Michael medal close to my heart today—Saint Michael with his sword, Saint Michael fighting tirelessly against the forces of evil. I think of Bonaparte facing the enemy, over and over again. I think, with admiration and pride, of his astonishing victories. But to what end, I can't help but wonder, is he chasing the Royalists out of Italy, establishing a democracy here? What would it matter if Paris were to fall to the enemy?

---

* *Aimée Hosten, a créole friend of Josephine's with whom she was imprisoned.*

** *A country villa north of Milan that Josephine and Bonaparte leased for the hot summer months.*

May 30.

It took a moment for Lieutenant Lavalette to catch his breath. He is not a young man. He took off his hat and straightened his wig, which failed to cover his bald spot. "I arrived in Genoa in the early afternoon, General," he began, standing at attention. "After refreshing myself at my inn, I made straight away for the Assembly and as—"

"Get to the point." Bonaparte drummed his fingers.

"I was informed that your mother was on a vessel in the harbour, General."

"And where is she now?"

"In Genoa, General, I—"

"You left her there? Lieutenant, Genoa is on the verge of an uprising!"

"She insisted," Lavalette stammered. "She said, 'My son is here, I have nothing to fear.' " (Bonaparte smiled.) "I ordered a detachment of cavalry to escort her, General. They will be arriving tomorrow."

"They?"

"Your mother and a man—she didn't give his name. And a boy—her son, I think she said. Your brother, General?"

"Girolamo?"

"And two daughters."

"Mon Dieu, Bonaparte," I said, standing abruptly. "That's almost your entire family!"

June 1.

We set out to meet them on the road, Bonaparte and I and the two "youngsters"—Pauline and Louis. South of Milan, a carriage came into view escorted by soldiers on horseback. Bonaparte let down the glass. "It's them."

"Put up the glass," Pauline protested.

"Don't screech." Louis covered his ears. He is two years older than Pauline and the two constantly bicker.

"Oh, I feel a fright," I said to Bonaparte. I was fatigued from the heat and parched with thirst.

Bonaparte ran his fingers through his hair. "Maria-Anna has changed her name to Elisa and Maria-Anunziata is now Caroline. But Girolamo's only thirteen. I can still call him Fifi."

"How should I address your mother?" I felt a sick headache coming on. Why had I not thought to take laudanum?

"As Signora Letizia." Bonaparte clasped and unclasped his hands, then wiped his palms on his thighs. "She gave birth to thirteen children; eight survived."

"Remarkable." I didn't know what else to say.

"She is famous for her tiny hands and feet," Pauline said.

"She's from Corsica's Sartène district, well known for bandits and blood vendettas." Bonaparte adjusted his sash. "As a child, I thought my mother was a warrior."

One of our horses whinnied. Bonaparte pounded on the ceiling. I fell forward as the carriage came to a sudden halt. Bonaparte pushed the door open and jumped to the ground.

"Aspetta un momento," Pauline yelled, tying her hat strings. "Napoleone, aspetta!"

The footman let down the step and helped Pauline out of the carriage. I heard shrieks: my Corsican family. I pulled my shawl modestly around my shoulders.

"Madame?" Louis held out a white-gloved hand. "May I offer my protection? The Bonapartes are known to be rowdy."

"How is it you are so gentle, Louis? Are you sure you are a Bonaparte?" I was relieved to see him smile. No more risky remarks, I told myself.

We approached the noisy group. A boy was tumbling in the dust, laughing. Girolamo, no doubt. Bonaparte punched him on the shoulder and the boy punched him back, feigning to box.

"I wonder who that fat man is," Louis said.

An older man with a pudding face was standing by the coach, his mouth hanging open as he watched the Liberator of Italy clasp his young brother in a headlock, the boy cursing like a sailor. "You don't know him?"

A plump girl of about fourteen—Bonaparte's youngest sister Caroline, I expected—was making excited hops in front of Pauline. Regarding everyone with a look of disapproval was a thin, mannish woman with heavy features: Elisa. And at the centre of the commotion was Signora Letizia, a tiny woman clothed in a black linen gown set off rather incongruously by yellow fluted neck-ruches. "You are killing yourself, Napoleone." At least, that is what I thought she said, for her heavy Corsican accent made her difficult to understand.

"Ah, there you are." Bonaparte released his hold on young Girolamo, who went tumbling. He took my arm and turned to face his mother. "Maman, allow me to present my wife, Josephine."

I made a respectful curtsy. "At last I meet my honoured mother," I said, kissing her on both cheeks. She was smaller than I'd expected, but a great deal more frightening.

She frowned, looking me over, and said something to Bonaparte in Italian. Then she turned to her eldest daughter. "Get your husband."

"Now?" Elisa let out a hiccup.

Bonaparte looked from Elisa to the man standing by the coach. "Elisa got married? But I didn't give permission!"

"You are not the head of this family," Signora Letizia informed her son.

"Félix!" Elisa yelled. "Get over here."

"I'm going to get married too!" Pauline displayed her ring.

Bonaparte's mother fixed a baleful look on me, as if I were to blame. A whirlwind of dust stung my eyes. I squeezed Bonaparte's arm. "It's too hot in the sun."

"He's an idiot," Bonaparte fumed in the privacy of our room. "How can Elisa stand him?"

"I don't believe she cares for him in the least." Elisa, it would appear, cared for no one.

"She's not going to get a sou."

No dowry? I could just imagine the maelstrom such a pronouncement would provoke. With the Bonapartes, I was beginning to understand, even the smallest slight was cause for battle. "Do you think your mother will allow Pauline to marry General Leclerc if you don't grant Elisa a dowry?"

Bonaparte scowled.

I covered his hand with my own. "I believe you are right, Bonaparte. I believe your mother is a warrior."

June 3.

Bonaparte's Uncle Fesch, his brother Joseph and Joseph's timid wife Julie have arrived, so now all the Bonapartes are here—all but Bonaparte's brother Lucciano, that is, who I'm told refused to come to Italy because of me. (Or rather, I should say *Lucien*, for apparently he has changed his name as well.)

"His wife miscarried," Lisette told me, "and he claims it's your fault." Lisette has become an invaluable informant.

"How could I have had anything to do with it?"

"It's because you prevented Pauline from marrying Deputy Fréron."

"I wasn't the one to forbid it! And in any case, what would that have to do with Lucien's wife's miscarriage?"

"Lucien Bonaparte and Deputy Fréron are friends."

"They are?"

"And that's why General Bonaparte got his brother Lucien assigned to the Army of the North—to get him away from Deputy Fréron. Or rather, you got the General to do it."

"Bonaparte will do something just because I ask him to?" I smiled at the thought.

"And so Lucien Bonaparte and his wife had to move north and then she miscarried—"

"I was so sorry to hear that."

"And so the mishap was your fault."

I frowned, puzzled.

"Because of you, they had to move. When they moved, it happened." Lisette shrugged. "Bonaparte logic."

June 4 (Pentecost Sunday).

Our first big family dinner. I am chagrined to discover that the preferred subjects of conversation among the Bonapartes at table are infertility and money.

"Why is there no bambino, Napoleone?" Signora Letizia tapped her knife for emphasis. She had taken the position of honour at the head of the table.

Bonaparte ignored his mother's pointed stare. He was sitting with his arms crossed, glowering. His brother Joseph, as the eldest, had claimed the chair to the right of their mother and it bothered my husband, I knew. (The Bonapartes take any indication of rank very seriously.)

"As the French Ambassador to Rome, I will be making sixty thousand francs a year," Joseph told Uncle Fesch. "As General-in-Chief of the Army of Italy, Napoleone is paid only forty thousand." He picked up a fork, examined it with interest and passed it to his wife, who likewise examined it, turning it over to read the inscription.

"*Magnifico!*" Elisa's husband Félix said, wiping the perspiration from his brow.

"Joseph, you can get some very good deals on sculptures in Rome," Uncle Fesch said, leaning back in his chair.

"Lei e troppo vecchia, Napoleone," Signora Letizia told Bonaparte.

I coughed on a chunk of chipolata sausage in the rice. *Troppo vecchia:* too old. I am too old, she'd told him—too old to have children.

"O primavera, gioventù dell'anno. O gioventù, primavera della vita!"* Pauline sang off-tune.

"Maybe she's barren," Elisa said. (Hiccup.)

"Plombières is an excellent health spa for that problem," Joseph's wife hissed across the table at me. "It's expensive, however." The daughter of a silk merchant, Julie Bonaparte had a straightforward view of the world: profit, loss, supply, demand. Mark-up. And now and again: quality goods.

"What does barren mean?" Girolamo had pressed the bread into dough and formed a moustache with it.

"I'll explain when you're older, Girolamo," Elisa told him.

"I'm thirteen. And I'm changing my name to Jérôme."

"Liar. You're only twelve." Caroline grabbed a chunk of his dough moustache and threw it across the table.

"Maman had thirteen babies, five died," Pauline said.

* *Oh spring, youth of the year! Oh youth, springtime of life!*

"*Magnifico!*" Félix said solemnly.

"Salute. To Maman!"

"Cin-cin!" (Hiccup.)

"Cin-cin, cin-cin." Uncle Fesch raised his glass, oblivious to the chunk of bread dough in his wine.

"Salute." I raised my glass to my new family.

[Undated]

Joseph, Elisa, Lucien (not here), Louis, Pauline, Caroline, Jérôme.

Joseph, Elisa, Lucien, Louis, Pauline, Caroline, Jérôme.

I'm getting it.

June 8.

"Forty thousand francs," Bonaparte announced to Elisa. "Each."

Bonaparte and Joseph had just returned from a meeting with a notary in Milan to arrange dowries for Elisa and Pauline.

"I'm getting forty thousand?" For a moment I thought Elisa might even smile.

"Well, actually, for you, thirty-five plus three Corsican properties—Vecchia and the two vineyards." Bonaparte shrugged. "It amounts to the same thing."

"Vecchia is damp." Elisa made a face. "What did Pauline get?"

"Forty thousand—in gold." Pauline stuck out her tongue.

5:15 P.M.

"Napoleone!"

Bonaparte looked up. "Was that my mother?"

"Napoleone!"

It sounded as if Signora Letizia was outside the door to our suite. "She wishes to speak to you, I believe."

Bonaparte went to the door. "Your footman is asleep," I heard his mother say. "Is l'anziana inside?"

L'anziana: the old woman. A surge of anger went through me. This morning, Lisette had heard my mother-in-law refer to me as la puttana, Italian for whore! I'd been doing everything in my power to gain my mother-in-law's favour, but nothing seemed to please her. Indeed, even my acts of kindness were viewed as an affront. I made her look like a peasant, she'd told Bonaparte. When I won at reversi, I made her look stupid. (I'd intentionally only won one game out of four.) I was too trusting of my servants—I should sleep with the silver at the foot of my bed. I shouldn't be giving the beggars so much. I laughed too much—I should be silent, like Joseph's wife Julie. And didn't I realize I was too old to wear flowers in my hair? In short, she was determined to detest me.

Bonaparte stepped outside. I could hear his mother talking to him in Italian. Then he burst back into our room, his mother close behind. "*Zitto! Basta!*" Bonaparte stomped his feet.

Signora Letizia crossed her hands over her chest. "Then I refuse consent. Pauline will not marry."

Bonaparte sat down on a chair, his legs stretched out in front of him. He hit the arm of the chair with his fist. "You're telling *me*—the man who waged war on the Pope and won!—you're telling me to arrange a Catholic ceremony for my sisters?"

"Please, Signora Letizia, do sit down." I pulled out a chair for her. She stood ramrod stiff. I searched for a possible compromise. "Could a religious service be performed without anyone knowing?" I asked Bonaparte.

Bonaparte snorted. "Banns would have to be read . . ." He made a circling motion with his hand to mean, and on and on.

Signora Letizia moved toward the door.

"Un momento, Signora Letizia. Per piacere." I turned to Bonaparte. "A dispensation could be granted from having banns read, surely." For a price. "And the ceremony could be performed here, in the little chapel." We could air it out, get rid of the bats. "No one need know. And the civic ceremony could come after."

Silence.

"The civil ceremony must come first," Bonaparte said finally.

"Would that satisfy you, Signora Letizia?" I asked, as gently as I could. Her lower lip stuck out in a pout. "Elisa too."

"Elisa's already married!"

"Not by the Church."

I touched Bonaparte's arm. What did it matter, one ceremony or two? "They could be at the same time." I didn't dare suggest that our own marriage might also be blessed.

He grunted. I looked over at Signora Letizia. She tipped her head slightly. Did that mean yes? I wasn't sure. "Very well then," I said with more confidence than I felt. I opened the door for Signora Letizia. "We will work out the details this afternoon," I whispered to her. She stomped woodenly out of the room.

I closed the door behind me, but was startled by an explosion of laughter.

"Well done!" Bonaparte embraced me.

June 14.

"There's a strange little man to see you." In honour of the festivities Lisette had put on her best gown—a muslin chemise banded by violet shirring that she'd done herself.

"The priest from the village?"

"I . . . I think *not.*"

A little man entered the room, his boots in his hand. His socks were dirty and full of holes. He bowed before me. "Signora Bonaparte?"

"Father Brioschi?" It *was* the priest. But his clothes! "Lisette, ask him if he brought his vestments."

"Habetisne vestimenta?" she asked him in Latin.

"Si." But he just stood there.

"I'll get someone who speaks Italian," Lisette said, heading out the door.

I nudged a wooden chair toward Father Brioschi. "Peccato," he said. *What a shame?* I wondered what he meant. I was saved from the discomfort of this "dialogue" by Lisette returning with Caroline Bonaparte, her plump young body squeezed into a pink taffeta gown covered with a froth of ruffles.

"Caroline, this is Father Brioschi. Could you—?"

"*This* is the priest?"

"Could you ask him whether he has brought his robes?"

"Ha portato i suoi abiti?" The little man said something in Italian and shrugged. "He didn't bring anything," Caroline said.

"Perhaps your uncle has something he could borrow." Uncle Fesch travelled with an elaborate wardrobe, much of it gleaned from the coffers of vanquished Italian nobility and clergy.

Shortly, Lisette returned, staggering under the weight of a jewel-encrusted white wool cape. I displayed it for the humble priest. "Per voi."

He ran his fingers over the glittering surface, whispering something reverent in Italian. "He said it's as lumpy as a diseased sow," Caroline said.

The oratory smelled mouldy in spite of all the flower bouquets. Pauline emerged in a gown so revealing that Father Brioschi was rendered speechless. Victor Leclerc looked on blissfully, his hat cocked sideways, wearing a grey overcoat very much like that of Bonaparte. He could not take his eyes off the wonder of this beauty, his bride. (His bride could not take her eyes off her own reflection in the polished brass.) Then a frowning Elisa and a trembling Félix joined them at the altar—thankfully, no hiccups—and Father Brioschi was finally able to squawk out the lines.

So, now that the ceremonies are over, it's time to prepare for a feast, a reception and a ball. Already, the Bonapartes are bickering over the seating arrangements at table tonight. Already, I'm exhausted.

[Undated]

"Is something going on?" Lisette asked, biting off a thread. "Signora Letizia changed her gown."

"Likely it has to do with the viewing today."

"The viewing?" Lisette licked the thread to knot it.

"During the Ancien Régime, the public thronged to Versailles every weekend to watch King Louis XV eat an egg. So, the Bonapartes thought that the public should be allowed to watch Bonaparte eat."

She looked astonished. I put up my hands as if to say, Don't ask me, I have nothing to do with it!

June 19.

"They're gone, Madame!" Lisette poured me a glass of champagne.

"Pour a glass for yourself, Lisette," I offered. I was in a celebratory mood. Jérôme had been sent back to school in Paris. Joseph, his wife Julie and young Caroline Bonaparte had departed for Rome. Louis had been sent to Brescia with dispatches. And now, just this morning, Signora Letizia, Elisa and her hapless husband had left for Corsica.

Leaving only Pauline.

I heard a door slam, a shrill voice.

I clinked my glass against Lisette's and smiled ruefully. *Only* Pauline?

In which I receive shocking news

June 21, 1797—Mombello.

"Is this all the mail there is from Paris?" I put down the small stack.

"That's what Moustache said," Lisette said, staring out the window.

"Nothing from my daughter?" Nothing from Eugène, either.

"Just what's there." She burst out laughing. "The footman is drunk! You should see him."

I went through the stack for the third time, more slowly: a letter from my banker; two letters from Barras; three from Aunt Désirée; two from Thérèse; a number from people whose names I did not recognize, the usual requests for favours. And bills, of course. Quite a few.

I tore open a notice from Madame Campan. It was only an announcement about an upcoming recital—a recital I would miss. Attached was a little note: "I thought you would like to know that 'the general' called on your daughter. All is well. She has become a beautiful young woman. She was brilliant in the part of Cassandra in *Agamemnon*."

Lisette was laughing again at the scene outside the window. "Madame, come here—quickly." She turned, puzzled by my silence. "Madame, what is it? Is it bad news?"

"Oh—no." I smoothed out Madame Campan's note. The perspiration from my hand had caused the ink to smear.

Lisette stood up. "Would you like me to get you some orange water?"

I shook my head. How could I explain? I handed her the note. I felt foolish, so suddenly overcome. Somehow, I hadn't realized—had not been prepared.

"That's nice." Lisette turned the note over in her hands, mystified. *A beautiful young woman.* "Yes," I said, blinking back tears.

June 22.

"Madame Bonaparte is in the garden," I heard our footman say. I saw a white plume bobbing above the boxwood hedge, heard a young man's voice. A *familiar* voice! I picked up my skirts, hurried down the narrow path, my heart racing.

We very nearly collided. Eugène lifted me in his arms, twirling me clumsily. "I can't believe it, it's actually you," I cried out, my eyes stinging.

He wiggled his hands behind his ears. "Yes, Maman, it's me—truly. Just in time for your birthday."

I took his hands in mine, blinking and sniffing. He remembered! "You didn't write. I wasn't expecting you for another month." It was such a joy to see him.

Sheepishly, he pulled his hands away. "I know, I'm neglecting to wear my riding gloves, I'm neglecting to clip my nails." Imitating my voice, grinning.

"I wasn't thinking that," I protested, laughing. "When did you grow so tall?" Yet still, that boyish face: dimples, freckles across his nose. "How was your journey?"

But before he could answer, he was startled by my new dog sniffing at his boots. "What's this?" he exclaimed, jumping back.

"His name is Pugdog." The tiny black creature sat down by the side of the path, panting like an old dog, his lame leg sticking out to one side.

"What does Fortuné have to say about that?" Eugène bent down to stroke Pugdog's head.

I made a sad face. "Fortuné was killed, Eugène."

"Fortuné!"

"Not long ago. He challenged the cook's mastiff and . . ." My eyes welled up remembering.

"*Fortuné* took on a mastiff?" He scoffed at the thought.

"Come," I said, pulling on his arm, "Bonaparte's in the stable."

My son stopped abruptly on the path. "General Bonaparte?" he stammered.

"He'll be so pleased that you've arrived." I tugged at him again, but he was too big to budge. And then I understood. The stepfather he hardly knew was now a hero, hailed Liberator of Italy. The stepfather he hardly knew was now his commanding general.

June 23.

Immediately, Eugène's training has begun. "A superior war is won without fighting," I overheard Bonaparte instructing him this evening, after our meal. "One can use the forces of nature to good effect, but knowledge is the key. Battles are won here." Bonaparte tapped his forehead. "Not here." He put his hand on the pommel of his sword. "Am I understood?"

"Yes, General!" Eugène said eagerly.

Bonaparte caught my eye and grinned.

June 29, 8:00 P.M. or so. Stiff!

Eugène, Junot and Captain Charles spurred their horses, raced ahead. Lisette did her best to keep up (she's bold on a horse). I was content to follow at a more leisurely pace, taking a path that edged a pond, relishing the solitude, the vistas. It was a glorious summer day.

Before long I realized I was lost. I was beginning to worry when I saw a man on horseback on the horizon: Captain Charles. I kicked my horse into a gallop. "I was lost!" Laughing, I pulled to a halt beside him, doubling my reins to hold my horse back. The burst of freedom had excited him.

Captain Charles struck a heroic pose. "I returned to rescue a damsel in distress."

"So this is East Wind," I said, looking at the captain's mount. There'd been talk about the horse Captain Charles had recently bought, outrageous speculation about how much he'd paid for her. (The one-hundred-louis ride, Pauline called the mare.) Well built, a glistening black, she radiated both power and beauty.

"Like her?" He stroked his horse's neck. The silver ornaments on her headband sparkled in the light.

The horse was magnificent, without a doubt. And the captain cut an exceptionally handsome figure, I thought, noting the unusual stitching around the cuff of his riding jacket, the square bone buttons. "My father once had the good fortune to own such a horse," I said. "A gambling win. Lady Luck, he called her."

"Mine was luck of a different sort."

Our horses were walking side by side now, in pace. "Oh?"

"I did rather well on a business contract." He swiped a fly off East Wind's ear.

"Through the Bodin brothers?"

"Yes, and as a result they've invited me to join their company. They have profited from buying and selling National Properties, but now they wish to expand into the area of military supplies, specializing in horses."

"For the Army of Italy?"

"I guess it is foolish of me to reveal such a thing." Or simply very trusting, I thought. "May I tell you something in confidence, Madame? As soon as peace is signed, I intend to resign the army. Not every man is meant to be a soldier."

Certainly, it was hard to imagine the captain with a sabre in his hand—hard to imagine him using it. "Military suppliers do very well." Military suppliers became outrageously wealthy overnight.

"With the right connections, yes, but without—" He made a clucking sound that caused his mare to spurt forward. "So far the Bodins have been unsuccessful in their efforts to get a government contract."

"They've applied to the Minister of War?"

"Yes, but without the consent of a certain director, it's useless." He glanced at me.

"Director Barras, by any chance?"

"I understand you are on intimate terms with him."

"Director Barras and I are friends."

"That puts you in a powerful position."

I laughed. "Not really."

"Madame, may I ask you something?" We headed down a steep incline. I leaned to keep my sidesaddle from slipping.

"Certainly," I said. No doubt he wanted me to recommend the Bodin Company to Barras. I am so often appealed to for favours, I've come to recognize the clues.

"Might you consider joining our company? I hope I haven't offended you by suggesting such a thing, Madame."

I pressed my calf against my horse's side, to move her over. "On the contrary." Indeed, it was a most interesting proposition.

"With the right contacts, one could make millions."

Millions. My horse pricked her ears. I heard the pounding of hooves. Lisette (in the lead!), followed by Junot and Eugène, appeared at the edge of the woods. They raced toward us at a gallop, yelling and laughing.

"It appears we've been discovered, Captain," I said.

"And now there will be rumours." Captain Charles spurred East Wind. She bucked into a gallop. My horse pulled at the bit, eager to follow. I grabbed her mane and gave her her head, my heart pounding, the wind in my face.

July 3.
The Austrian delegates will arrive in one week—representatives of the most ancient royal court of Europe. I'm in a panic! If only I'd had my tooth attended to earlier.

July 4, late afternoon. (Hot!)
Dr. Rossi, the dental surgeon, is a little man with bushy red whiskers that he constantly pulls on. He told me a new tooth would successfully root—for a price, nine hundred francs, and this without a guarantee. I explained to him the urgency of my situation; I'm to return in the morning.

July 5.
I'm ill! It was *ghastly.*

Evening, almost midnight (can't sleep from pain).
What happened:

There was a peasant girl in Dr. Rossi's antechamber when I arrived. She grinned, displaying yellow teeth. Dr. Rossi's maid showed me to a small room, in the middle of which was a leather chair. I was asked to sit and (apologetically) asked to remove my hat, which I did. The doctor entered after a moment, pulling on his whiskers. He peered into my mouth and probed at my bad tooth with a pointed metal object. He seemed pleased by the pain this caused me: "Excellent, excellent."

After his maid gave me morphine for nerves, he excused himself, explaining that he would only be a moment. I heard cries—the peasant girl?—and then he rushed into the room with a bloody tooth pinched in a vise-like tool, two assistants dashing in after him. Involuntarily I shrank back, but the assistants laid hold of me, and the doctor yanked my tooth out and pushed the new tooth into its place. Then one of the assistants held my jaw closed while the other wound my head with a strong strip of linen so that I might not open my mouth.

And so here I am, mute and dazed, bandaged and sedated, with a peasant girl's tooth in my mouth. I dare not get sick.

July 7.
My tooth came out—an infection had set in. I'm taking generous doses of laudanum. God meant me to have bad teeth, and to receive the Austrian diplomats thus. Or so I tell myself.

July 9.
The Austrian delegates will be here tomorrow. I've been all day in the hands of beauticians: I've been waxed, massaged, pounded and polished. Lisette painted my nails as Eugène quizzed me on the name and title of each diplomat (Cobenzl, Gallo, Merfeld, Ficquelmont), their children, parents, aunts and uncles even, the year each was born, the town. "You know all this, Maman," Eugène said, throwing down the lists.

July 10, 4:00 P.M. or so.

They'll be arriving in an hour. "You've never looked more beautiful," Bonaparte told me reverently, taking in the details of my gown, a muslin draped in the style of the ancient Romans. A filigree laurel of gold held back my loose curls.

"It's not too modern?" I studied the effect in the looking glass.

"That's the point. The old world meets the new. Old world *bows* to the new."

New world, indeed. I smiled, for Bonaparte refused to lace his boots with silk ribbons. I knew aristocrats. I feared they would laugh at his laces and round hat.

"Uff! They'll be wearing plebeian shoelaces soon enough," Bonaparte said, giving me a careful kiss before disappearing back into his study to his maps and documents, texts and correspondence—the work that keeps him up all day and all night, day after day. Winning battles had only been a step; the important work was establishing democracy in Italy.

"Kings never worked so hard," I said to Lisette, turning to view myself from the side. I'd become slender in Italy, due to ill health. I was pleased with the effect—it made me look younger.

Captain Charles and Eugène appeared at the door wearing tablecloths for capes and lampshades for hats. "Vee must 'av peace!" they barked in unison, imitating an Austrian accent.

"Don't make me laugh," I pleaded. "I'll ruin my make-up!"

11:20 P.M.

It went well! I am pleased. Bonaparte, however, is *not*. I'm having a bath prepared to calm him.

On the whole I found the diplomats to be pleasant—especially the Comte de Cobenzl, the head of the delegation, who speaks elegant French. "I look forward to many pleasant evenings," I told him as they left, adding, daringly, "Citoyens." The Comte de Cobenzl, who heard me distinctly, smiled and embraced me fraternally.

He is an ugly but genial older man with the aristocratic talent of putting everyone at ease. We talked of Corneille's *Le Cid* (parts of which I was surprised to discover Bonaparte had committed to memory); Goethe's new epic *Hermann und Dorothea;* the corresponding theories of electricity and animal magnetism; Mozart's opera *The Marriage of Figaro.* Bonaparte praised his beloved Ossian, which surprised and impressed the Austrians, I could see—they hadn't expected a Republican general to read poetry.

"The charming bastards," Bonaparte cursed as soon as the door closed behind them. "They have no intention whatsoever of negotiating a peace agreement."

July 14.

This evening as I was preparing for bed, Bonaparte burst into my dressing room. "They're balking," he said, pacing in front of the wardrobe with his hands behind his back. "They refuse to come to an agreement." He sat down on a little stool. "And why should they? As long as the Royalists are gaining strength in Paris—" He clenched his fists.

July 16.

The trouble began before the midday meal. Lisette and I were meeting with two of the cooks, discussing the menu for a reception in honour of the Austrian delegates.

"Solo—" I turned to Lisette. "What is the word for chicken?"

"Pollo."

"Solo pollo." Only chicken. The words rolled off my tongue like a song, as if I were in an opera. A comic opera. Opéra bouffe.

The cooks could not comprehend. No pasta? No salami?

"Lisette, explain to them that that is what the General wishes—" I was interrupted by the sound of someone shouting. It was Bonaparte, yelling in Italian. He only spoke Italian when he was angry. Or amorous.

The two cooks began to laugh.

"What did he say?" I asked Lisette. Bonaparte had been quite explosive of late. The peace talks had not been progressing. The Austrians were not taking him seriously. They were biding their time in the belief that soon the Royalists would be back in power in France.

"He said asswipe, Madame." Lisette flushed.

Asswipe? It was unlike Bonaparte to be crude. "Are you sure?" Lisette has been studying Italian, but how would she know a word like that?

"And blazes. And devil."

"The General is savage as . . ." The head chef held up a meat axe, grinned. "Meat. Axe." Enunciating slowly, proudly, in French.

There was another angry outburst. "That haughty, demanding prick!" Napoleon shouted, in French this time. My cheeks burned.

The cook with the wen on his neck snorted. That word he knew.

I stood. "No, you stay," I told Lisette.

Bonaparte was standing with his back to the door. His grey wool waist-coat was stained with perspiration. The scene was one of disorder, the carpet strewn with journals from Paris. I recognized one—the *Mémorial*, a Royalist publication. Berthier, Bonaparte's chief of staff, was sitting at the desk in the corner, staring at the General, a quill in one hand. They seemed frozen in an antique tableau, shadow silhouettes against the light. The very air felt dangerous, like gunpowder, as if it might explode. "The lives of good men have been sacrificed," Bonaparte yelled, breaking the spell. "And for what? Without a peace agreement, what have we accomplished? Nothing!"

"Un momento," I whispered to the hall porter, positioning myself beside the door out of sight, standing purposefully, as if spying on one's husband was the normal thing to do.

"The enemy isn't here, the enemy is in Paris! The Royalists have taken over. The traitors should be arrested, banished! All of them! *Veni, vidi, fugi,* my ass.* The journals should be repressed! They're in the pay of England, of Austria, of every damned Royalist nation in Europe—why should they be tolerated? And the Church fomenting trouble again. *Basta!*

---

*Veni, vidi, fugi—*Latin for "I came, I saw, I fled"*—was attributed to Napoleon in a Royalist journal in Paris. It plays on the famous line by Caesar,* Veni, vidi, vici, *meaning, "I came, I saw, I conquered."*

Berthier, take this down. Address this to the Emperor. Yes, of course, the Emperor of Austria. Tell him this. Tell him if a peace agreement is not signed by the first of September— No, don't put that. Put . . . what is it? Yes. Put fifteen Fructidor. Let him figure it out. If the peace negotiations are not concluded by fifteen Fructidor, we go to war. You heard me: war!"

I stepped into the doorway. Bonaparte turned to me, his eyes bulging. He looked feverish, emanating a manic energy.

"Has something happened?" I crossed the room and took his hand. He is shortsighted; it is a mistake to address him from a distance. "What's all the shouting about?"

"Shouting?"

"We could hear you in the kitchen."

Bonaparte glanced at his chief of staff, puzzled. "We weren't shouting."

La Chaumière
Darling!

A quick note: I've heard rumours that Lazare is being considered for Minister of War. Your husband is to take orders from your former lover? Nom de Dieu!

Your most loving, etc., Thérèse

July 18, past midnight (can't sleep).
"May I ask you something?" Bonaparte's hand on my shoulder was cold.

"Of course." I kissed his hand, as if to warm it—warm him.

"How . . . close were you with General Hoche?"

"We were friends."

He snorted. "You were lovers. Everyone knew that."

I pulled the covering sheet up over me. "In prison, yes." A partial truth.

"General Hoche is said to appeal to women. He's a chevalier of the bedchamber, it is said."

"Bonaparte, please, don't be like this." I pressed myself into his arms, pushing through the thicket of elbows and hands he put up as obstacles, pressing against him, knowing his need.

August 1.

"What does *res non verba* mean?" Eugène asked, looking up from reading the *Moniteur.*

Res non verba was Lazare's motto. I looked over my son's shoulder. The article quoted a speech Lazare had made to his troops. "It means, the thing, not the word—that what you do is more important than what you say," I told Eugène, disconcerted by my son's inability to translate a simple Latin phrase. I heard the sound of spurs jingling outside the door. Hastily, I folded the journal. "Eugène, don't speak of General Hoche around Bonaparte," I said under my breath, standing to greet my husband.

July 22, Luxembourg Palace, Paris
Chère amie,

It is almost midnight as I write this. I am in a state, I confess. Forgive my hasty pen. Regrettably, things did not work out with respect to Lazare. It is too complex a matter to explain here. Nobly, he retreated. Whatever you might hear, he did this of his own accord.

Director Reubell has gone mad with fear. His delirium recalled to my mind an ancient Oriental proverb: that one should not confuse the sound of the beating of one's heart with the hooves of approaching horses. It is the beating of my own heart that causes me pain. I begin to see that my life has been spent not as a conquering knight, but as a rather pathetic courtier, sitting, ever hopeful, in the antechamber to the boudoir of the Goddess of Love. In all my groping encounters, was it not simply Love I sought? (I recall a little lecture from you, my friend, to this effect.) And yet, having at last been blessed, I submitted not to the light, but to the darkness within.

I hear the hooves of approaching horses. By the time you receive this, it will all be over. It is said that the guilty are victorious. If so, I need not fear.

Père Barras

July 23, Fontainebleau
Dear Rose,

Imagine General Hoche behaving in such a shameful way! He had nine thousand soldiers quartered at La Ferte-Alais and he as much as admitted that he was going to take over by force. And to think that our Eugène served on his staff.

Your godmother, Aunt Désirée

Note—I saw Marie-Adélaïde d'Antigny this morning when I stopped by with the money for her education and keep.* She has just turned eleven, a pretty little thing. I almost wept to see her—she looks just like Alexandre! Please don't forget to send money.

July 27, La Chaumière
Darling,

Lazare was forced to leave Paris under a cloud of suspicion, accused of being a traitor. I am sick with apprehension. Barras refuses to talk about it. If you can shed any light on this mystery, please let me know.

Your loving and very dearest friend, Thérèse

Wetzlar
Rose,

Forgive me for writing. I have a courier I can trust—otherwise, I would not compromise you in this fashion.

You will have accounts of my disgrace in the journals. I beg you to believe me when I say I did not behave dishonourably. Although clear in conscience, I carry the burden of shame. It is not a mantle I wear willingly. Assure your son that I honoured my vows to the Republic.

Should anything happen to me, please, I beg you, help my wife and child.

I love you still.

Burn this letter.

Your soldier, always, Lazare

---

* Josephine's husband Alexandre had at least three known illegitimate children, one of whom was Marie-Adélaïde d'Antigny. Josephine and Désirée jointly contributed to her support.

[Undated]
Oh, Lazare, Lazarro . . .

August 4.
Something happened in Paris—but what? Today, when Bonaparte was meeting with the Austrian delegates, I went through the journals in his office. Apparently, Lazare was named Minister of War, and then there was an outcry due to his youth and he resigned. And then his troops were discovered close to Paris, within a forbidden zone. (From what I can make out, the constitution forbids troops within twelve leagues of the building in which the Legislative Councils meet.) And then he was publicly accused of being a traitor to the Republic.

I cannot make sense of this. There is no greater patriot than Lazare, no man more honourable. It sickens me to think of him publicly reviled, branded with the one word he most deeply loathed: *traitor.*

September 8—Passariano. *
We've arrived in Passariano, at last. We are staying in the palace of the last doge of Venice. The courtyard is the size of a military field and the palace itself is huge, ostentatious, ornate. I wander from golden room to golden room, watched by the servants. A fraud, they judge us, Republican imposters.

We won't be here long, I hope.

September 10.
Mail from Paris. Trouble again. I'm even more confused than before.

18 Fructidor, Luxembourg Palace, Paris
Chère amie,
    It is over; I am alive. So, it would seem, is the Republic.

*Headquarters had been moved to Passariano north-east of Venice in order to facilitate the peace talks.

At dawn I ordered the alarm gun fired. Over sixty Royalist deputies have been arrested. Soon they will all be deported. So be it, the Republic has been saved.

Again.

Again and again.

Directors Carnot and Barthélemy escaped—to Switzerland, it is suspected.*

My secretary, Botot, is on his way to Italy with instructions for Bonaparte. Please keep me informed.

You are right to suggest that we communicate in cipher. Next time.

Père Barras, Director—still

Note—Please disregard my last letter. I was, as they say, "in the cups." I vaguely recall writing something about horses.

September 9, Fontainebleau

Dear Rose,

Our government has arrested itself—and just when I was preparing for our move to Saint-Germain. I had to tell the carters to return the following week—at my expense, alas. But there was no way we could travel safely with the roads so agitated. Soldiers were everywhere, cart wheels rumbling over the cobblestones, dragging cannon. Almost two hundred of our elected—yes, elected!—representatives have been taken away in iron cages like wild beasts. Even that lovely General Pichegru, President of the Five Hundred.** Even two Directors! And just because they would not keep Décadi? The King was more just.

Your godmother Aunt Désirée

[Undated]

"Excellent, the Royalists have been kicked out," Bonaparte said, throwing down the *Moniteur.* "*Now* Austria will negotiate."

* Director Barras is reported to have thrown a writing desk into a mirror in his rage at discovering that Director Carnot had managed to escape so narrowly that his bed was still warm.

** General Pichegru was a Royalist agent.

September 20.

A surprising announcement from Bonaparte. Shortly after two he came into my suite of rooms, sat down across from me. "You've been saying you'd like to see Venice," he said.

I looked up from my embroidery. "We're going to Venice?" I was astonished he would even consider it. Ever since the Venetians had risen up against French soldiers, massacring them in their hospital beds, Bonaparte had conceived a burning hatred for them. An effeminate, treacherous race! he would rant. A city of scoundrels!

He drummed his fingers on the arm of the chair. "No, *you're* going."

And then he explained: the Venetian government, anxious about their fate in the negotiations, had invited him to visit Venice in order to prove their loyalty to the French Republic. He scoffed. "Stinking liars. Of course I won't go, but refusing outright would complicate things. So I'm sending you in my stead."

"But Bonaparte . . ." I paused, trying to take in what he was saying. "This is a job for a diplomat. I can't—"

"I'll tell my secretary to make all the arrangements," he said, standing. "You'll require a gown, something suitably impressive." He hesitated for a moment. "Three hundred francs? Four hundred should do it. Don't worry, the Army of Italy will pay."

"What has happened?" Lisette exclaimed, finding me in the wardrobe, gowns and shawls everywhere. It looked like a field of war.

"I've just learned I'm to go to Venice—"

"That's wonderful!"

"—on a *diplomatic* mission." I groaned. She looked at me with a blank expression. "And the problem is, I'm going to have to dress the part—but in a traditional style."

"So, you'll get gowns made?"

I sighed. Five hundred francs for each gown, three hundred for a cape, one hundred and fifty for hoops, six hundred . . .

Bonaparte insists that I will look sufficiently elegant in a four-hundred-franc gown. As if one gown would suffice! I'm to be fêted day and night for three days in only one ensemble? "My mother wears one gown for weeks at a time," Bonaparte pointed out. Wisely, I held my tongue.

Venice!

Coming to Venice has been like falling into a deliciously sensual dream. Everything conspires to make one feel that one is not on this earth, but in some watery magical realm.

My welcome has been overwhelming. A "parade"—in boats!—down the Grand Canal, the citizens hanging from the windows waving banners, showering me with flowers. I'm overwhelmed. And a bit ill, I confess, from so much rich food.

September 24.

I have returned to Passariano, to the land of Reality. At my suggestion, the President of the Venetian Republic returned with me in order to press the case for Venice. I regret it now, for Bonaparte was cold, unwelcoming. At dinner, I raised a glass in toast to Venice, spoke warmly of the Venetians, the Revolutionary zeal I saw in the citizens of this newly formed Republic. There was no warmth in Bonaparte's response.

"Murderer," he cursed as the Venetian President's carriage pulled away this morning.

I feel sad and defeated. A diplomat I am not. My heart is too easily engaged.

September 29.

I've been busy with official duties. Following my "diplomatic" mission to Venice, I've been called upon to write to the office of the Emperor of Austria, petitioning for the release of French prisoners. (I find these new duties hard to believe myself.) Now, if only I could do something to push the negotiations along. They're proceeding so slowly, and not at all helped, I suspect, by Bonaparte's ill humour. He's not an easy man to live with, and he becomes even more difficult when things are not going his way. "Je le veux!" is his favourite expression. I will it!

September 30.
Barras's secretary arrived covered with dust. "I'm too old to travel," Botot said, using his hat plume to brush himself off. "I had no idea the roads would be so rough."

"Did you have trouble from bandits?"

"My valet sent them scurrying." A smug smile.

"Bonaparte is in Udine this afternoon at the headquarters of the Austrian delegation," I told him. The meetings alternate. One day Bonaparte goes to Udine, the next day the Austrians come to Passariano. "He has been looking forward to your arrival." A lie. Bonaparte is convinced that Barras's secretary was being sent to spy on him.

Lisette came skipping down the wide stone steps, her skirts billowing out behind her. "A visitor from Paris! Is there news? Mail?" She came to an abrupt stop in front of us, flushed.

I smiled at her youthful exuberance. "First we must offer our guest refreshment, Lisette—and *then* we'll attack him for news."

News: Lazare Hoche is dead.

I excused myself and set out across the courtyard, alone. Eugène was in the riding arena, I knew, taking a lesson. Inside the stables it was dark, cool, smelling of dung. Two horses in box stalls watched me, munching. The stable boy jumped out of a pile of hay. "Signora!"

"Mi dispiace." I'm sorry. "Non importa." It doesn't matter.

I heard someone yelling from inside the arena. I pushed open the heavy door. Eugène was riding a black horse around the circumference, his face glistening, his horse foaming with sweat. The instructor was standing in the centre, yelling, "Keep your leg on him. Thumbs up. Outside rein!"

I took a seat in the stands. Eugène had turned his horse into the centre of the arena and was talking with his instructor. Then he looked up, saw me and grinned. The instructor turned, bowed deeply. "We are finished, Madame la Générale!"

"I am content to watch, Citoyen." I dreaded breaking the news to Eugène.

Eugène flung himself down beside me. "Did you see that turn on the forehand?" His face was flushed, his hair damp with sweat.

"Quite precise." I stood. "Let's walk in the garden."

He pulled at my arm. "Maman, what is it?"

I scanned the arena. It was empty now. "It's not good news," I said, sitting back down. "Your sister is fine, Aunt Désirée, the Marquis," I assured him, seeing the apprehension in his eyes. "It's about General Hoche, Eugène." I clasped my hands. "He is . . . He passed away." My chin began to quiver in spite of my resolve.

Eugène stared at me, not comprehending. "Dead, you mean? In battle?" With a hint of a stammer.

"No, in his bed. Of an infection in his lungs." I found a handkerchief. "Consumption." My voice was unsteady yet. I took a careful breath. It was inappropriate for *me* to weep.

Eugène leaned forward on his knees, blinking, hitting his riding crop on the bench in front of him. "He died in his *bed*?" He threw down his crop and stood, his face blotched.

"Eugène, I wanted you to—"

His footsteps down the wooden stairs echoed through the arena. I started to rise, to follow him, chase after him, but I stopped myself. He wanted to be alone.

It is late, dark but for a single candle, which is gradually lighting up the room. I am at a marble-topped table in the sitting room, wrapped in a patchwork counterpane. I can hear the hall porter snoring outside our bedchamber door, hear someone singing drunkenly in the courtyard.

The sound of frogs croaking is like a pulse throbbing, a night pulse. I cannot keep my thoughts from wandering, reaching for Lazare. I cannot believe what I have been told: that he is dead, that he died in his bed, robbed of a soldier's heroic death in battle.

My eyes well up, overflowing. When may I grieve? Where? I dare not. All this evening Bonaparte watched me, taking in my red-rimmed eyes, my sad smile.

A woman's truths, how secret they must be. Hidden, buried, only to emerge in the night.

I remember the rough surface of the cold stone walls as I climbed the stairs to Lazare's dank prison cell. I remember the taste of whisky on his tongue, the sputtering sound of a dirty taper burning, the silken texture of his skin. I remember, with wonder—and gratitude—the heat of his love . . . and my own, kindled from ashes.

I found the Saint Michael medal Lazare gave me, stashed away at the bottom of my box of gems. *La liberté ou la mort*, he'd had etched on the back. *Ou la mort.*

Should anything happen to me, he had written.

He died of galloping consumption, Botot explained again at dinner, his eyes fixed on his crystal glass of wine. At Wetzlar. He was buried there.

Should anything happen . . .

Something catches in my throat. It is bitter, foul, it makes me gag. It is a sudden thought: was Lazare murdered?

October 1.

A long talk with Botot this evening. This is what I understand:

The Royalists had changed tactics. Rather than attacking the Republic by force, they decided to try to topple it from within, and to that end succeeded in getting a number of Royalists elected to the Legislative Councils. The goal, of course, was to overthrow the Republic and reinstate a monarchy.

Barras, together with Directors Reubell and La Réveillière, decided to take action. Forming a majority in the Council of the five Directors, they decided to replace Royalist ministers with loyal Republicans (Lazare as Minister of War was one). Fearing that these changes would provoke a Royalist uprising, Barras persuaded Lazare to bring his troops close to Paris.

But here the story fades. Somehow the plan failed, the troops were discovered and Lazare ended up having to leave Paris under a cloud of suspicion, branded a traitor, an enemy of the Republic.

And then, a few weeks later, Barras made a second attempt to oust the Royalists and this time he succeeded. And then Lazare died.

There is more to this, I fear.

October 3.

Lisette set a tray down beside my bed. I could hear Eugène's voice in the stairwell, calling for his valet to bring down his riding jacket. I was glad he was going riding; he'd been morose, quiet. "Madame, remember when General Hoche called on you in Paris?" she asked, handing me a mug of frothy hot chocolate. "Just before we left for Italy. It was on your birthday, he brought you roses."

"I don't remember roses," I said, blowing on the steaming chocolate before taking a cautious sip. "Why?" Knowing even as I asked that I was going to regret the question.

"It's awful, Madame. It makes me want to cry. Everyone's saying he was murdered!"

October 1, La Chaumière
Darling,

I have just returned from the funeral for Lazare and am overcome with sorrow. The entire nation grieves, stunned by the loss of the Republic's golden boy. He died accused by his enemies, but the people have judged him a saint—a saint of the Revolution. It was a lovely procession of shepherds wearing cypress crowns, their staffs wrapped in black ribbon.

Lazare's young wife was there. She looked quite faint, tragic. I suspect she's with child. Lazare's father supported her as best he could, but then he himself was overcome by heart-wrenching sobs, a dreadful keening wail. I weep now even to think of it.

I am haunted by the memory of an evening at my salon. Bonaparte was reading everyone's palm, and he looked at Lazare's and predicted that he would die at a young age in his bed. Do you remember that night?

The rumours are vicious, of course. Everyone is convinced Lazare was poisoned—and by Barras, of course. (They blame him of every crime!) It's terrible, especially considering how Barras himself is so overcome with grief. He spends entire days in a darkened room, refusing to speak.

Tender caresses from Thermidor. And love from the Glories, of course. Will you ever return? Things are so sad here.

Your loving and very dearest friend, Thérèse
Note—I heard you've hired Vautier to renovate your house. A brilliant choice!

October 13.
The Austrian delegates dined here tonight. Bonaparte in a surly temper.

[Undated]
Damp today. I've ordered the fires lit. I'm in a melancholy mood. How does one set the stage for peace? I arrange cut flowers, ask the housekeeper to have the silver tea service polished and set out on the buffet, check the liqueur decanters, review the day's menu with the head chef. But despite my best efforts, the fires, the flowers, the succulent food, a gloomy chill pervades. There will be no peace today, I know.

October 15.
"The head of the Austrian delegation wishes to speak with you, Madame." Lisette opened her eyes wide.

"Comte de Cobenzl? Show him in, please!" One did not keep a man of such importance waiting.

As the Comte de Cobenzl entered, my impulse was to bow, but I refrained. As I am the wife of General Bonaparte, the victor, the Comte

Louis de Cobenzl should, in theory, bow to me. We solved the impasse by bowing at precisely the same moment, and with an equal degree of respect.

"I will not be long, Madame Bonaparte," he said, refusing my offer of a chair. "I requested a private audience with you because I am gravely concerned about the future of the negotiations. General Bonaparte has been treating us . . . *rudely*, to be frank. At the least request from us, his temper gives way to violence. No doubt you are aware that he destroyed my prized china tea set."

The day before, in a fit of temper, Bonaparte had thrown Cobenzl's tea set to the ground—the tea set the Comte was so proud of, the one that had been given to him personally by Catherine the Great—exclaiming, as he did so, "I'll break your monarchy like this china!"

"Comte de Cobenzl, please believe me," I said, "I was dismayed when I—"

The Comte put up his hand. "There is much more at stake than a tea service, Madame. If the General continues in this fashion, I'm afraid Austria will have to withdraw from the negotiations."

"Comte de Cobenzl—" Words escaped me. If the Austrian negotiators withdrew, there would be war again.

"My question to you is this: Would you speak to the General?"

Speak to Bonaparte? Was such a thing possible?

"We await the result." The Comte de Cobenzl bowed, I bowed lower, he bowed lower still.

October 16.

"You are not to interfere!" Bonaparte showered spittle in his fury.

"I am not interfering!"

Bonaparte had returned from Udine early, fuming; the negotiations had been broken off. War would be resumed in twenty-four hours, he'd threatened. "How can you say that? Yesterday you met with the Comte de Cobenzl privately. You call that not interfering?"

"Have you been spying on me, Bonaparte?"

"This palace is riddled with spies. We are all of us spied upon. Even the spies are spied upon."

I turned to face my husband. "The Comte de Cobenzl came to me of his own accord. He was seeking . . . advice." Was a direct approach wise? So much was at stake. "He feels you have been rude, Bonaparte, that you do not wish to make the peace."

Bonaparte laughed. "He's fortunate to be alive and he complains about niceties. How . . . how *aristocratic*. Cobenzl acts as if he were at a salon, an afternoon tea. And then he demands Mantua. *Mantua!* Mantua is the key. If I were to let the Austrians have Mantua back, they would control Italy again in a very short time. And he wants me to be *civil* in the face of such a demand?"

"Bonaparte . . ." I took his hands in mine. It always surprises me how soft his skin is, how fine his bones. I looked into his eyes. How did one persuade such a man? "There is something I must say."

"I do not hinder you."

"If you treated Cobenzl civilly, perhaps he would be more likely to accede to your wishes."

He looked incredulous. "You are suggesting that I be *nice*?"

"Bonaparte, really, you are so charming when you smile. Who could refuse you?"

October 17.

Bonaparte's carriage pulled into the courtyard quite late, almost midnight. I saw him jump down from the carriage, followed by Eugène and Louis. I opened the window. "Peace is signed,"* Eugène called out, holding a flambeau aloft. "Pack for Paris!"

---

* *Historically, the Treaty of Campo-Formio is regarded as both spectacular and shameful. Spectacular because, among other things, the French Republic gained Belgium and the Rhineland (including Mayence), getting back its "natural frontier," and shameful because of the sacrifice of the fledgling Republic of Venice to the Austrians.*

III

Profiteer

The scourge and leprosy of the services! Impudent thievery!
—*Napoleon, on military suppliers*

In which problems await me at home

December 16, 1797—France!

"I can understand what people are saying!" Lisette threw her arms in the air and twirled.

I knew her joy. The innkeeper in her crisp white bonnet had a familiar face. Did I not know her? Even the postillion seemed to have mounted his horse in a way that seemed mysteriously *right*.

"Look!" Lisette leapt about the cobblestones. "The sky is French, the mountains are French, the air is French. I bet that horse speaks French." The old nag turned its head. "See?"

December 17.

"Where did you learn to load a pistol, Madame?" Lisette looked up from mending the train on one of my gowns.

"In Paris, during the Terror. A friend of mine taught me." A friend now dead, along with so many others. I clicked the chamber shut, slipped on the safety lock. We were travelling with only two mounted escorts; at night, in the inns, I did not feel secure.* I'd sewn my jewels into a little velvet bag, which hung under my gown.

"I love hearing stories about the Revolution, about all the fights and riots. Forgive me, Madame," she said, seeing my stricken expression.

---

* *Napoleon had returned to Paris by way of Rastatt, Germany, where meetings continued regarding the peace accord. Josephine had left Milan at a later date, returning to Paris on her own.*

I handed her the pistol. "Never aim it at a person, even if it's empty."

"I know!"

I smiled. "Have I ever told you that you remind me of my daughter?"

"Many times, Madame."

"Except, of course, that you're a young woman now. Have you given any thought to marriage, Lisette?" She was nineteen. It was time. It was past time, frankly.

"I prefer to serve you, Madame," she said, hiding the pistol at the bottom of her mending basket.

"You may marry and continue to serve me."

"You would permit it, Madame?"* She picked up her mending.

"Do you think I would expect such a sacrifice from you?"

"Other ladies do." She shrugged. "And anyway, who would want to marry me?"

"You're lovely!" But without a dowry, true. "I will be happy to provide you with a dowry."

"Truly?" she asked with an incredulous look.

"On my honour."

December 19—Lyons.

There was a letter awaiting me at our inn in Lyons: embossed in gold, it was from Citoyen Louis Bodin of the Bodin Company, inviting me to call.

December 20, 4:30 P.M., a gloomy day.

I was, I confess, taken aback by the Bodin estate. I had not expected it to be so imposing. A wide driveway wound through a beautifully manicured park, opening onto enchanting vistas, before coming to the château.

I was guided by a silent footman in a white cravat through a series of elegant rooms to, at the last, a game room, where Louis Bodin (round as a pumpkin and quite pink) was shooting billiards. A sleepy one-eyed

---

* It was customary to fire servants who married or got pregnant.

maid with frizzled hair stood in attendance by the high table. In spite of the hour, all the shaded candles in the bronze chandelier had been lit.

"Welcome, Madame Bonaparte." Louis Bodin bowed from the waist. He was welcoming, sincere in manner, yet dignified in spite of his complexion and his youth. Old money, I thought, taking in the antlers over the fireplace, the worn, elegant furnishings, the family portraits, the hound curled by the fire with its chin on its hind paws.

We talked, pleasantries at first, and then of our mutual acquaintance, the irrepressible Captain Charles, our Masonic affiliations, spiritualism (carefully avoiding a discussion of religion), the Treaty of Campo-Formio (avoiding a discussion of politics), his brother Hugo, who ran the company's office in Paris. And then, retiring to a book-lined study where a light collation had been set (Seville oranges, little white boudins, pistachio nuts), we began at last to discuss that which had brought us together: the pursuit of wealth.

Louis Bodin explained that the Bodin Company had profited nicely from the purchase and sale of National Properties, but that due to the increasing scarcity of such "opportunities," the company wished to expand into the more lucrative area of military supplies—specifically, the supply of mounts to the Army of Italy. "We have everything in place to make a success of such a venture," he said. "Everything, that is, but the one essential element—approval by the Directors." He spoke softly, with an enormous orange cat purring on his lap. "As you are no doubt aware, the competition for these contracts is keen. It is perhaps no accident that those who do succeed are the personal acquaintances of one Director in particular." He smiled, displaying brilliantly white false teeth. "Director Barras, of course, with whom, I am given to understand, you have influence."

I considered how I should respond to such a statement. "Director Barras is a friend of mine," I said, a simple statement of fact.

Louis Bodin pushed the cat off his lap and sat forward, his hands on his plump knees. "Madame Bonaparte, would you be . . . That is, would you consider . . . ?" He scratched the end of his nose.

I knew what he wanted to ask. I waited.

He tugged on his shirt cuffs, revealing enormous emerald links.

"Would you consider acting on behalf of the Bodin Company? That is, discussing the merits of our company with Director Barras?" He sat back, his hands on the arms of his chair. "We'd be willing to discuss a partnership arrangement."

"That would depend—"

"On the terms, of course. I understand entirely. For that reason, I took the liberty of preparing a draft contract for you to look over." He retrieved a portfolio from a side table and handed it to me. "Please, at least take it, Madame. You may study it at your leisure."

I held the contract without looking through it. Once back in Paris, I would go over it with my lawyer and then I would decide. I knew that my answer—be it yes or no—would have significant consequences. If no, I would have to find a way to deal with my mounting debt. If yes, I stood to profit—enormously—but not without risk. "Could I presume, Citoyen Bodin, that my involvement would be kept confidential?"

"We fully understand, I can assure you, the sensitive nature of your position."

"Then yes," I said. "I am willing to consider."

December 28—one stop past Nevers.

This afternoon, as Lisette and I were airing out the linens, we were startled by four rhythmic raps. "Isn't that Captain Charles's knock?" Lisette asked. "I knew it was you," she said, on opening the door.

For there, drenched and mud-splattered, the plume of his hat broken at the stem and hanging sadly down his back like the tail of some unfortunate creature, was Captain Charles. Pugdog sat up on his cushion, his curled tail wiggling.

"Captain Charles!" I was astonished to see him. "What have you done to yourself?"

"I've been riding like a madman," he said, gallantly doffing his ruined hat, "in the hope of catching up with you."

I motioned to him to take the worn chair by the fireplace. "What an unexpected pleasure."

"I feared you might have reached Paris by now," he said, dusting off his leather breeches before lowering himself into the armchair. He reached down to tug Pugdog's tail, teasing.

"We've had a few breakdowns," I said.

"And ceremonies in every town," Lisette said. "Madame has been making speeches."

I opened my fan. I wanted to talk to the captain about my meeting with Citoyen Bodin—but in private. "Lisette, please bring us some midday collations. And a bottle of that good local wine." After she had left I said, "Captain Charles, we have only a moment. I wish you to know that in Lyons I met with your associate Citoyen Louis Bodin."

"He told me. I understand that you'll be meeting with his brother Hugo in Paris. I must tell you, Madame, we are—"

I put up my hand. "I only told him I would consider." In fact, I was beginning to have reservations. "I hope you understand how important it is that our discussions on this matter never be revealed."

"Of course, I would never—" He stopped abruptly, staring over my shoulder.

I turned. Lisette was standing in the open doorway with a tray in her hand. "Ah, there you are," I said.

New Year's Day, 1798, 1:00 A.M.

A day of unexpected twists and turns. I should know better than to try my hand at matchmaking. While Lisette was attending me at toilette this morning, I made a suggestion to her. "I have observed that you and Captain Charles have a companionable relationship, Lisette. Have you considered the possibility of a match?"

"You are serious, Madame?" was her initial response. "Me and Wide-Awake?" She giggled.

"The captain may not be wealthy, Lisette, but someday soon he will be a man of means. Do I have your permission to discuss this with him?"

We dined together, the three of us: Lisette, Captain Charles and I. The cook devised a simple but pleasing repast: a green pea soup (he keeps peas in mutton fat in the cellar over the winter), carp, pickled mushrooms and small onions, followed by cheeses and sweet chestnuts.

"Captain Charles," Lisette announced after our dishes had been taken away, "perhaps you could take my place at the trictrac board tonight. Madame has given me the night off to go to church." (In fact, *Madame* had told her that she needed to converse privately with the captain, and perhaps Lisette wouldn't mind going out for the evening.)

Captain Charles glanced at Lisette, then at me and then back at Lisette. "*You're* going to church?"

"There are many things about Lisette that are perhaps unknown to you, Captain Charles," I said, dunking a bit of Roquefort in the mulled claret punch (of which we'd all had quite a bit). "Under a gay and buoyant demeanour she hides a serious spiritual nature."

Captain Charles guffawed, and then ducked as Lisette hurled a hard bread roll at him. Was this a good sign? I wasn't sure.

After Lisette departed for church (a bit inebriated, I suspect), the captain and I adjourned to the front drawing room. The room was small, but warm, and it afforded a view of the square. "You may close the door behind you, Captain," I said, ceremoniously lighting three candles.

Captain Charles stood with his hands clasped, like a servant awaiting direction. His ensemble—wide Venetian velvet pantaloons and a silver-embroidered waistcoat—gave him the look of a royal courtier, someone of another time, out of place in our world of egalitarian linen and rough wool. "Please, make yourself comfortable." I poured us each from an opened bottle of still champagne. I handed the one good glass to the captain. "To the New Year."

He sat down on a wooden side chair. I sat on the sofa opposite him. (The down cushions smelled of ducks.) Why this lack of ease? We seemed like strangers to one another. "There are only two more years until the year 1800," I said, offering the captain from a plate of sausage puff pastries and then helping myself to one. "Imagine, a new century."

"Already, the fortune-tellers are making predictions. Have you read them?"

Ah, the predictions—how good of him to bring them up. "I *always* read the predictions, Captain," I said. "And I believe them, I confess."

Captain Charles leaned forward. "The indications are that it will be an excellent year for commercial endeavours."

"Excellent." I opened my ivory fan, then snapped it shut. The subject of marriage is not an easy one to broach. I had hoped that Captain Charles's customary levity would make it easier. I cleared my throat; Captain Charles did likewise. We smiled at this coincidence. "There is something I have been wanting to ask you, Captain," I said finally.

"Concerning the Bodin Company, Madame?"

"No—something to do with matters of the heart. Have you given any thought to taking a wife?"

A laugh escaped him, rather like a snort. I was not sure how to interpret his response. It seemed somehow ironic. Was it possible that my suspicions regarding the captain were true? "I amuse you?" I asked.

"On the contrary, Madame, you enchant me."

He was being silly. "Captain Charles, no jests. I beg you." I put up my hands, palms towards him. "Seriously, as a *friend*, as someone who is concerned with your welfare, I recommend that you marry, raise a family. You are young, but before you know it, your youth will have slipped away. Children give one immeasurable joy."

Captain Charles pushed the toe of his boot against the frayed carpet fringe. "Perhaps you have someone in mind, Madame?"

I nodded, smiling with my eyes. "Guess."

He pursed his lips, a perfect rosette. "Your daughter?"

I laughed, taken aback, I confess. Although I found Captain Charles a charming companion, I did not consider him a suitable match for Hortense. "Forgive me," I said, whisking a crumb off my lap—for his mortified expression made it clear that I had offended him. "It is just that she is so young, Captain, only fourteen. I have yet to consider a husband for her."

"You need not dissemble, mia belissima regina. I know my standing in this world."

I disregarded his statement; clearly, he'd had too much to drink. "I will tell you who I think would make a perfect wife for you," I persevered, tapping my fan against my palm. The bells began to ring, welcoming in the Christian New Year.

"You."

I sat back. "Captain Charles, do be serious!" Many bells were ringing now, a joyful tumult. Where had they come from, these bells?

"The clown, Madame, is always serious." Pulling down on his feathered jockey hat, he made a sloppy bow, kissed me lightly and staggered out the door.

I watched him from the window, weaving on the cobblestones. His hat fell off; he paid it no heed.

Late afternoon.

Lisette looked relieved when I told her that Captain Charles had been disinclined to discuss the subject of matrimony. And much to my relief, the captain doesn't remember a thing. My new year's vow: to give up matchmaking.

Tomorrow, Paris!

January 2—Paris!

"What took you so long!" Bonaparte crumpled a piece of paper and threw it against the wall. His hair hung down over his ears, giving the impression of a Florida Indian. I was alarmed by his sallow skin, his thin, almost emaciated frame. His health had clearly deteriorated in the six weeks since I'd last seen him. His temper, as well.

His rage had to do with money. The designer I'd hired to make over the house had demanded payment for the renovations—one hundred thousand francs! I sat down, stunned. That was an incomprehensible sum. "One hundred and thirty, in fact," Bonaparte ranted, kicking the flaming logs, making sparks fly. "The house itself is only worth forty, and you don't even own it. The frieze in the dining room isn't even painted by David. It's by one of his students."

There was a frieze in the dining room? "Most of the value is in furnishings, Bonaparte," I said in my defence.

"Most? Even seventy thousand in furniture would be outrageous—I don't care who made it, Jacob Brothers or not! There's no way I'm going to pay for half of this. I'll contribute thirty thousand, but not a sou more."

Leaving *me* with a bill for one hundred thousand? "No doubt there has been a mistake. I'll talk to Vautier." The renovations were the last thing I wanted to deal with, however, after an absence of almost two years. First I had to see Hortense. And then, of course, Aunt Désirée, the dear old Marquis. And then Thérèse—had she had her baby yet? And how was Père Barras? *And* the Glories, of course! Not to mention the business I needed to attend to, my lawyer to see.

"How can there be a mistake? Vautier produced your letters as evidence. You gave him total licence! One never gives total licence."

I removed my gloves, taking in the changes: the Pompeian frescoes, military trophies, chairs upholstered in striped fabric. The renovation was simple, yet elegant. I ran my hand over the surface of the new mahogany desk. The grain seemed to shimmer under my fingertips. I felt I could see deep into the heart of the wood. "Does *none* of it please you, Bonaparte?"

"Come see our beds," he said with a little grin.

Our bedroom had been designed to look like a military tent. "Watch." Bonaparte released a latch and our two beds sprang together with a noisy clatter.

"Clever!" I sat down on one of the stools, covered with chamois leather to resemble a drum. The beds were draped with a canopy of blue and white stripes, the bedposts forged from cannon.

Bonaparte tugged at my arm.

"Not now, Bonaparte," I pleaded, but smiling. "It's not even noon yet, and I need a bath."

"We'll bathe together," he said, pulling at my sleeve, "after."

Late now, almost 11:00 P.M., a very long day.
I'd bathed and was changing into an afternoon gown when I heard horses

in the courtyard. A slender young woman in a white riding frock was stepping down from a barouche. A mass of golden curls fell to her shoulders. I put my hands over my mouth. Mon Dieu. Hortense?

"Maman!" Hortense cried out when she saw me, all the airs of une élégante of Paris giving way to that of a girl. Her eyes were an extraordinary blue; how was it possible that that surprised me? She slipped off her cloak, chattering. "Where's Eugène? I saw his horse saddled by the stable. That's Louis Bonaparte's horse? The General's brother is staying here? But why isn't Eugène back yet? I've been telling all my friends he would be returning with you."

My daughter's long fingernails were painted red. And breasts—she had breasts! "Eugène is in Rome," I stuttered. "He'll be—"

"What took you so long? Where were you? Every day there have been notices in the journals that you'd arrived. Maman, what's wrong? Is something wrong?"

"No, nothing," I croaked, taking her in, this lovely young woman.

Aunt Désirée arrived shortly after, barking instructions at two valets who carried the old Marquis into the house by the garden entrance. They deposited him in the down armchair, where he looked about with a dazed expression. I asked my manservant to put on a fire and Lisette to set out the gifts I had brought back from Italy with me.

"Modern," Aunt Désirée said, looking around the drawing room, appraising the changes.

"Grecian is modern?" I stooped to kiss the old Marquis. His beard smelled of brilliantine.

"Bonne à Pare Té!" he said with vigour.

Hortense laughed. Aunt Désirée motioned to her to sit straight, keep her knees together, fold her hands in her lap, and not to laugh so loudly— all in one silent gesture known to all women and girls. Hortense made a prim face, but nevertheless did as instructed. Aunt Désirée gave me a triumphant look. "Hortense, that shawl looks lovely—did your mother bring it back from Italy for you? Where is our famous General, Rose? I bought a flower vase for three francs just because it had his image on it."

"Bonaparte is at the Luxembourg Palace right now, at a meeting with the Directors." I motioned to Louis Bonaparte to join us. "But I'd like to introduce you to Louis, Bonaparte's brother." Hoping that the presence of at least one Bonaparte might appease.

Aunt Désirée gave Louis what I knew to be the appraising look of a woman on the watch for a husband for her niece. "Charmed! How many brothers does General Bonaparte have? And sisters, of course."

"There are a great many of us, and soon to be more," Louis said, tugging at a budding moustache. He glanced at Hortense, a flush colouring his cheeks. My daughter lowered her eyes. "My oldest brother Joseph is in Rome with my sister Caroline—"

"And Eugène," I interjected, arranging gifts on the table—a Roman vase, a glass bowl from Venice, a length of embroidered silk brocade from Genoa as well as a number of pretty trinkets.

"My sister Pauline is in Milan," Louis went on. "She's married and in an interesting condition. And my other married sister who lives in Corsica is also in an interesting condition. And my brother Lucien is in the north, and *his* wife is in an interesting condition, as well. And then there is Jérôme, who is going to school here in Paris."

"Jérôme is only thirteen," I said, chagrined by the parade of fertile Bonaparte women—of which, it was clear, I was not one.

"How nice for Hortense and Eugène to have so many new brothers and sisters," Aunt Désirée exclaimed with too much enthusiasm, perhaps in an effort to display her Christian acceptance of so many Corsican relatives. "I mean aunts and uncles. And *so* many cousins to come," she added, acknowledging the fecundity of the Bonaparte clan.

Louis backed toward the door. He had an English lesson to attend, he explained, and therefore had to take his leave.

"It was a pleasure to meet you," Hortense told him in careful English.

"Thank you, miss. Goodbye," Louis answered in kind, tipping his hat in the English manner.

"What a charming boy," Aunt Désirée said as soon as he was out the door, turning the Roman vase in her hands. I explained to her that it was not "modern" but actually quite ancient. And then we talked of this and of that—the extraordinary welcome Paris had given Bonaparte on his return, Hortense's awards at school, how well Eugène was doing as an aide-de-camp—and then, of course, the gossip:

"Of course, you've heard the news regarding General Hoche." Aunt Désirée had the look of a cat depositing a dead mouse at the foot of its owner. "Regarding his *murder*."

I closed my fan. I opened my fan.

Aunt Désirée leaned forward. "You know what I heard? That it was your friend Director Barras who did it."

"Aunt Désirée," I interupted. I didn't want Hortense to hear false rumours.

"My theory," Aunt Désirée went on, disregarding me, "is that Director Barras, who is known to be greedy, was after the million francs General Hoche embezzled."

"Aunt Désirée, I don't think—"

"It was eight hundred thousand."

I looked at the Marquis in astonishment. He had slumped down so far into his armchair that he was practically doubled over, a dreamy expression in his half-closed eyes. "Did the Marquis speak just now?" I asked.

"He doesn't know what he's talking about," Aunt Désirée said. "It was well over one million."

They stayed for a light repast and then had to leave in order not to unduly tire the Marquis. Hortense is staying with them in town because, as Aunt Désirée informed me, it would be improper for an unmarried young lady to stay in the same house as an unmarried young man, even if that young man is actually her uncle. Tearfully I bade them all adieu and ordered my horses harnessed: I was anxious to see my lawyer about the Bodin Company contract. And then, after that, Thérèse, and after *that*, Barras.

"Thérèse is still in childbed," Tallien (civil, but not sober) informed me.

The baby had been born thirteen days earlier, on the solstice. "A girl," he shrugged. "She died at birth."

"I'm so sorry, Lambert!" I put down the parcel of infant gowns I'd brought from Italy and embraced him. How many times in the past had I done so, thinking him young, thinking he was not so much vulnerable as impressionable, in need of guidance. But now he had the weary fragility of age. Something in him had broken, had not mended. "How is Thérèse taking it?"

"I wouldn't know."

Thérèse was enthroned on the chaise longue in her bedroom. I leaned over to kiss her cheek.

"Did Tallien tell you I've locked him out? Did he tell you why? Of course not. He refused to call a priest! My baby died unbaptized. And then, a few days after, he expects 'service.' I've had it with these men of the people."

Her hand was icy cold. I pressed it between mine to warm it. I felt utterly miserable. I loved her with all my heart, but I loved Tallien too. I'd known him as an idealistic youth.

The maid appeared with a bottle of port, crystal stem glasses. Thérèse wiped her cheeks, embarrassed to be caught crying. "My midwife's orders," she said brightly, clinking the rim of my glass with her own. "I can't tell you how relieved I am to see you. We're all still in shock over Lazare's death. You should have seen his funeral. The streets were thronged—I've never seen anything like it. And now my midwife tells me his widow miscarried, the poor thing. She's only nineteen. A bit touched, though, they say." Thérèse downed her glass. "You're going to Talleyrand's ball tonight?"

"I'm so sorry you won't be there."

"I wasn't invited. It appears that I'm no longer wanted at any gathering that includes virtuous women," she said with obvious irony. "Did you hear what happened at the ball given by Pulchérie de Valence? As soon as I arrived, all the women left."

"I don't understand!" During the Terror Thérèse had saved the lives of many of these so-called virtuous women, often at the risk of her own life.

"I was apparently too public about threatening Tallien with a divorce. Women are supposed to suffer in silence, remember? And then I made the mistake of offering shelter to a young man who had rescued me from bandits one night. He was injured, but a woman of virtue would have sent him away regardless. And *then* there was a horrific scandal over a portrait of me that was hung in the annual Salon. The arbiters of good taste demanded that it be removed."

I smiled. "Were you clothed in this portrait?"

"I've never looked more chaste! No, they didn't approve that the painter portrayed me in my prison cell. Anything to do with the Terror is not to be mentioned in polite society, I gather. I'm not sure I care, frankly."

But she did. I could hear it in her voice.

The door was pushed open by a child in ruffled muslin. "Maman?" It was baby Thermidor—walking, and talking!

"Sweetie, do you remember Josephine, your godmother?"

"Yes," the two-year-old said doubtfully, her chubby fingers stuffed into her mouth.

I held out my arms. Would she come to me? She ran across the room and onto my lap. I felt her tiny fingers pat my neck, tap, tap. I glanced at Thérèse. *She's so beautiful,* I mouthed. But thinking, I confess, how the little girl's future would be ruined if Thérèse and Tallien were to divorce.

After my visit with Thérèse I instructed my coachman to take me to the Luxembourg Palace. The drive seemed to take forever, the streets were in such poor repair. And everywhere, signs of misery. Children in rags ran alongside my carriage, crying for alms. I threw them what coins I had. A boy in a moth-eaten English travelling cap, his ribs showing, beat the others away with a stick. I looked away, sickened, as I pulled through the palace gates and into the privileged realm.

"Damn the Royalists," Barras's parrot squawked as I was shown into the salon. Barras was sitting in an armchair by a roaring fire, petting his miniature greyhound. "Don't get up," I told him, stooping to kiss him.

"No, no, a gentleman must always rise for a lady," he said, lowering Toto onto a tasselled cushion, patting the dog's head apologetically and then pulling himself up out of the chair. "Grand Dieu, my friend, but you do look lovely," he said, his Provençal accent laconic, caressing. "As always."

"Oh, I've made a mess of you," I said, brushing powder from his velvet smoking jacket. He smelled pleasantly of cigars and spirit of ambergris.

"Sit, sit," he insisted.

There was a web of worry lines around his eyes. He seemed to have aged in the year and a half since I'd seen him last—or was it simply that I'd not noticed before? "How *are* you?" I asked, accepting the chair he indicated. He seemed weary, I thought. World-weary. Battle-weary, more likely.

"Oh . . ." He made a dismissive gesture, then let his hand drop. "The usual. I'm getting a new roof put on Grosbois, my modest country abode—now *that's* a job." He cleared his throat. "And now all this fuss over Talleyrand's ball. Too Ancien Régime, according to my fellow Directors, who have only reluctantly consented to go, but in plain dress. We're going to look as out of place as Quakers at a brawl."

The name Lazare Hoche hovered between us, impossible to ignore. "I noticed funeral wreaths at Saint-Roch," I said finally. "My coachman told me there'd been a service just recently in honour of Lazare."

"The official service was three months ago, but people just won't stop! Every time I turn around, I run into some damn procession carrying an effigy of him." He looked away, struggling, I suspected, for control.

I studied my hands, turning my betrothal ring round and round. "You know, ironically, the last time Bonaparte saw him, he predicted that Lazare would die at a young age in his bed. We were at Thérèse and Tallien's that night, before we were married, and Bonaparte was reading everyone's palm. I never told you this story?"

Barras shook his head, his hand over his mouth.

"It comforts me, I confess," I said, my voice quavering dangerously, "to think that maybe it was meant to be." If Death wants you, he will find you: every soldier's creed.

"*Merde.*" Barras buried his face in his hands.

January 3.

Oh, what a day, what a night. It began with my cook, who was frantic—Bonaparte would only eat hard-boiled eggs, he claimed. Callyot leaned toward me confidentially. "Because they cannot be tampered with, Madame."

Then the designer arrived; it was impossible to put him off. "I trust the work is pleasing?" Vautier said, handing me a scrap of paper on which the terrifying figure 130,000 francs had been written in a tiny script.

Oh, extraordinarily pleasing. Brilliant. But perhaps somewhat more . . . *costly* than I had anticipated. (By tenfold!)

"As you wrote, nothing but the best for the Liberator of Italy." He bowed.

I'd written him that? "I will have my banker contact you." Thinking, how was I going to come up with the money?

Lisette appeared at the door, one hand on the ivory knob. "The dressmaker, Madame."

I dispatched the designer with extravagant praise and equally extravagant promises. He politely gave way to my frenzied dressmaker. Every woman in Paris required a new gown for the ball, her staff of thirty-two seamstresses had been working day and night, she exclaimed, instructing her footman to display our creations. The gown for Hortense was exquisite, I thought, but the gown for me—a simple yellow tunic of a Grecian design—had an under-chemise made of muslin. "But English muslin is expressly forbidden," I said, dismayed. It had even been printed on the invitations.

Her eyes bulged; I feared she would be taken with apoplexy. "But Madame," she said, lowering her voice to a whisper, "Madame de Chevalley's underskirts are of muslin, as well as those of Madame de la Pinel."

"Neither Madame Chevalley nor Madame de la Pinel is the wife of General Bonaparte," I reminded her gently. As well—although I declined to tell her this—the design lacked elegance. (She'd ruffled the hem!) I repeated my request for simplicity.

"Madame Bonaparte—if I may be so bold—are you sure you want such a plain tunic? I have three girls in my employ devoted entirely to the application of sequins."

No ornaments, I insisted. And no muslin petticoat.

On account, Madame Bonaparte?

Yes, of course—on account.

And then the jeweller, who insisted on being shown in with his case of (I confess) irresistible wares. I selected a lovely strand of gold interlocking leaves. What else would look right with a Grecian tunic? "On account, Madame?"

And so, on it went. Lisette has just arrived with a jug of warm mulled wine. The carriages have been called for nine, she informs me.

"So early!"

It is time for my bath . . .

And perhaps just a bit of laudanum.

Bonaparte sat on a stool beside my toilette table, watching as Lisette made up my hair. He was pleased, he said, with the simplicity of my gown. "We must appear to live within my means."

I refrained from laughing. Even the bachelor generals weren't able to live on a general's salary of forty thousand francs a year, and as for my "simple" tunic—

"How's this?" Louis appeared in the doorway, pulling at the sleeves of a nankeen coat. He'd been ill earlier in the day and still looked pale. (Ever since Italy his health has been uncertain.)

"Ugly!" Jérôme called out from behind his older brother, jealous because he was too young to go to the ball.

Bonaparte jumped to his feet. "Who made that jacket for you?" The collar was of black velvet, the insignia of a Royalist.

"How about your blue one?" I suggested.

"Don't move, Madame!" Lisette sprayed lacquer over my hair. "You look lovely," she said, handing me the looking glass.

I looked hideous! The curls were stuck to my head with a substance that made me look as if I had just been drenched by rain.

Bonaparte pulled out his timepiece. "We're late."

We set out in a light snow, Bonaparte, Louis, Hortense and I. The jingling of the brass bells on the horses' harness made a festive sound. At the Rue de Grenelle we came to a stop. Equipages were backed up all the way to the Seine. Hortense made a peek-hole in the steamed-up glass. Where had all the carriages come from? For years only shabby hacks had been seen on the streets of Paris, and now suddenly the roadway was crowded with elegant landaus, phaetons, barouches and curricles.

It was half-past nine by the time we pulled into the courtyard of the Hôtel Gallifet. A bivouac scene had been created at the entrance—a campfire surrounded by men in uniform, tents. "The fields of Italy," Louis explained to Hortense, offering her his arm. "But for the snow, of course," he added and my daughter laughed.

As we headed up the steps, the double doors were flung open. Four hall porters jumped to take our cloaks. A butler with an operatic voice announced us. The musicians stopped playing and everyone turned to stare. Then a cheer went up and horns blazed out a welcome.

I was overwhelmed by the scene I saw before me. A profusion of candles in enormous hanging chandeliers revealed a crowd of men and women in glittering finery. A man with a shiny forehead was making his way toward us with the help of an ebony cane. He was slithering rather than walking, dragging a club foot, I realized. It was Talleyrand, the famous (infamous) Minister of Foreign Affairs.

He bowed deeply to Bonaparte and then to me, extending two fingers of his right hand as if in benediction. (He had been a bishop, I recalled.) "We have awaited your arrival, Madame la Générale." Only his eyes showed any sign of life. They filled with a fawning reverence whenever they happened to alight upon my husband. My husband, who was ignoring us, however, looking out over the crowd with a hawkish expression, his hands clasped behind his back.

"I am astonished by the beauty of the décor," I told Minister Talleyrand, introducing Hortense, who curtsied, and then Louis, who bowed.

"Delighted," Talleyrand said, his voice a drone.

The playwright Arnault appeared, greeting us shyly. Bonaparte clasped his arm. "Take me about the room, Arnault. We shall engage in discussion; that way no one will accost me." Louis offered to escort Hortense to the ballroom.

Which left me quite suddenly alone with our host. "For this entire evening," he informed me, "I will be your cavaliere servente. Is that not how it is done in Italy?" He smiled, an expression that made him look frightful. I heard the musicians warming up. "Come," he said, "you must see my quarrelsome dancers. In a misguided spirit of equality they insisted that if they were to perform for us, they should have the honour of eating with us."

The crowd parted for us as we approached. I moved slightly to one side in order to make room for each swing of his big foot. "And who was the victor in this debate?"

"I am always the victor, Madame."

The orchestra stuck up a chord. "Ah. They are about to perform a new dance from Germany. The waltz, I believe they call it." One corner of the Minister's thin lips curled. "It requires that the male and female grasp one another, and so of course the priests are endeavouring to have it condemned."

The ballroom was crowded with musicians, dancers, men standing behind women who were seated, watching. The waltz was a swirling of couples holding each other's arms. I saw Hortense in an alcove with Louis, showing him how it was done.

"Ah, there's Bonaparte." I spotted him in a far corner.

"In my humble estimation, all five Directors together are not worth the General's little finger. Twenty victories are becoming in so young a man. General Bonaparte *is* the Republic." The Minister's toneless drone was at odds with the impassioned nature of his words.

Yes, I nodded, feigning to listen. Bonaparte was heading toward us, arm-in-arm with Arnault. A cluster of men and women were following behind him—like a king's entourage, I thought, a dazed feeling coming over me.

In which I become involved in intrigues

January 4, 1798.

"Where to, Madame?" my coachman asked, tipping his sheepskin cap. Feeling poorly, I suspected. The drivers and postillions had hob-nobbed and glass-jingled last night, while their masters were enjoying the ball.

"One hundred Rue Honoré," I told Antoine, reading the card on which was printed the Paris address of the Bodin Company. I'd told Bonaparte I was going to call on Thérèse—which was true, in part. After I called in at one hundred Rue Honoré.

A butler in tails opened the oak door. I was shown into a salon so large it required two fireplaces. In a window alcove was a desk covered with files and a counting device.

I heard the even thump, thump, thump of a wooden leg. "Madame Bonaparte?" Hugo Bodin was younger than his brother, but every bit as round, and his complexion even pinker. He pulled on the bell rope. "Captain Charles," he instructed the butler, pushing forward a shield-back chair for me. "I have been anticipating your call, Madame. We are honoured. The fervour of the people for your husband is *electric*, to use a modern word." He lowered himself onto a crimson sofa, his stump stick-ing out to one side like the oar of a boat. "That was quite a fête last night in his honour, I am told. Even we plebeians who were not invited were all 'in a twitter,' as the English say."

"It was an extraordinary display." A ball in the style of the Ancien Régime: a full orchestra, dancers, a feast. "And quite cleverly done. The

Minister of Foreign Affairs transformed his residence to look like the backstage of the opera."

"I was told that that dance the clergy wish to have banned was performed. Wallace? No, valse."

From somewhere in the building, I heard a dog bark. "The captain said to tell you that he will be a moment," the butler announced.

As if on cue the captain appeared, buttoning the top button of a corded white vest figured in gold. "Madame Bonaparte! I hope this means . . . ?"

"I'm not sure," I told them both. "My lawyer and I have gone over the contract carefully, and considering the amount of the investment, I'm afraid that the—"

Hugo held up his hands. "Before you say anything, Madame, you should know that we'd be willing to up your share to twelve per cent."

They'd doubled it. "I appreciate your offer, Citoyen Bodin, but I'm afraid I'd require at least fifteen."

"Done," Hugo said.

Done? I looked from one man to the other. Then I smiled at the captain and said, "Captain Charles, it would appear that we are now business associates."

"Hooray!" Hugo exclaimed in a burst of undignified enthusiasm. We toasted our partnership with thimble-glasses of Chartreuse.

After, in the privacy of my carriage, I laughed at my audacity. Fifteen per cent: a small fortune. A fortune I urgently needed.

Thérèse was thrilled. "You're actually going to do it? You're going to be a partner in a military supply company? That's so daring! You're the only woman I know who has done that."

"But you're the one who told me I should."

"I just can't believe it. You'll be making *millions.*"

"Borrowing millions is more like it."

January 6.

"It's a large sum," I warned Barras. The leather chair creaked as I shifted my weight. "Four hundred thousand." I was conscious of blinking—once, twice, three times.

Barras sat back, examining his fingernails. Then he grinned. "Welcome to the world of high finance."

High finance, high debt: high profit.

January 8.

"There's a Negress outside demanding to see you," Lisette informed me this afternoon. "I told her to go around to the back entrance, but she just stood there."

I fumbled with the window latch and looked out. A Negro woman was standing in the courtyard—a tall, older woman, shivering in a worn wool cloak over a long calico gown. "Mimi?" She looked up, squinting against the sun. "Mimi!"

I did not know how to greet her. It had been over seven years. We'd parted in a difficult time, in a world torn by Revolution, a world divided. It seemed a lifetime ago. "I thought I would never see you again," I said, my eyes filling. She'd been like a sister to me in my youth—a sister, a mother, a friend. It was Mimi who'd taught me to dance, read the cards, make charms, Mimi who had nursed me through childhood fevers, helped birth my babies, Mimi who had been their nanny.

"Yeyette," she said, calling me by my baby name, her warm Island accent music to my ears, "still always weeping." And then she smiled, that big-toothed, big-hearted grin.

We've been talking for hours. I'm *starved* for news of home. "And how is Maman?" was one of my first questions.

Mimi pushed out her big lower lip, the inside pink as an oyster shell. "She can't walk or use her hands."

"How awful!" My mother is a proud woman, independent. She had run the family sugar plantation without any help from my hapless father. After his death she'd worked hard to pay off his debts.

"She says you've married a Jacobin, the Devil himself."

I smiled. I was not surprised. My mother believes in God and the King. "I miss her!"

Mimi touched my hand. "She told me to look after you for her."

My throat tightened. Oh, *Maman*.

January 9.

I was reviewing procedures with Mimi when Hortense stuck her head into the room. She started, surprised by the presence of a dark-skinned woman.

"Hortense, do you remember Mimi?"

"My nanny, you mean?" Hortense asked, putting down her portfolio.

"Oh, my Lord." Mimi slapped her hands over her cheeks.

[Undated]

News of an uprising in Rome. Lieutenant Duphot, Eugène's friend who was to be married, was killed the night before his wedding. How awful! No word yet from Eugène. I can't sleep.

January 22.

It was past midnight when I was awakened by a tap on the door, the sound of the door creaking open. "Madame?" Lisette's candle threw ghostly shadows onto the walls.

I slipped out of bed, my heart aflutter. Bonaparte, asleep, did not stir. "What is it?" My teeth chattering, I pulled on a robe.

"Your son, Madame."

I put my hand over my mouth, fearing the worst.

"He's downstairs!"

"Maman!" Eugène pulled off a boot and lumbered to his feet.

"You're back!" I wept. "I've been frantic with worry."

He held his lantern high, letting out an appreciative whistle. "Is this the right house, Maman? The street name isn't even the same.* And a porter at the gate! He almost didn't let me in."

We talked late into the night, whispering by the fire. So many adventures!

Twenty-four days of storm at sea . . .

"I was so sick, I thought I was going to die."

"I get like that too."

Murderers waking him in the night in Naples . . .

"Murderers?"

"With these tiny rusty daggers." Laughing about it now.

The gift of a jewelled sword from the Municipality of Corfu, which he proudly unsheathed for me . . .

"Are those real rubies? It must be worth a fortune."

"I was thinking of selling it and buying a horse, but Uncle Joseph says I can't—that it was really intended as a gift to the General, and that therefore it belongs to the Bonaparte family."

"He said that?"

And then, at the last, what happened in Rome, the uprising . . .

"Is it true—was Lieutenant Duphot . . . ?"

"The night before his wedding, Maman! We were giving a dinner for him when the trouble started. He grabbed his sword and went charging out into the mob. I *tried* to stop him. He fancied himself a hero, and now—" Eugène stopped, a stricken look in his eyes.

February 9.

I had planned to meet with Hugo Bodin and Captain Charles today, but it proved to be too difficult. Bonaparte insists on knowing every move I make.

* *Rue de la Chantereine had been changed to Rue de la Victoire in honour of Napoleon's victories.*

February 10.
Bonaparte departed this morning with Eugène and Louis for an inspection tour of the coast. I stood waving until the carriage was out of sight. Bonaparte will be gone for three weeks—time enough.

[Undated]
Barras has agreed to one per cent, but the Minister of War will expect more, he warned me. "And what about General Berthier?" Bonaparte's former chief of staff was now Commander-in-Chief of the Army of Italy.

"Him, too," he said.

Everyone expects a piece of the pie. *Bien.* So long as there is a piece for me.

February 18.
I was preparing to go to the Luxembourg Palace to meet with Barras when Bonaparte's carriage pulled up the narrow laneway, the horses steaming in the chilly air. He leapt out while the carriage was still moving.

"You're back early," I said, embracing him—but thinking, I confess, that I had a meeting to get to, and now . . .

"I saw what I needed to see."

"It was not a good trip?" He smelled of the sea.

"The Directors are dreaming. We're in no position to attack England."

His new secretary, Fauvelet Bourrienne, stumbled as he climbed down out of the coach. Then young Louis Bonaparte emerged, yawning and blinking, followed by Eugène, his hair sticking up like a haystack.

"Welcome home!" I said, kissing my son's cheek (stubble?), but worrying about how I would get word to Barras. The Bodin Company business would have to wait.

February 23.
Every afternoon Citoyen Talleyrand, the poker-faced Minister of Foreign Affairs, calls and he and Bonaparte disappear into the study. Then I

disappear as well—to go to the riding school, I tell my husband. Or to the dressmaker's. Or to visit Thérèse.

All lies. It is "to work" I go—to the Bodin Company office on Rue Honoré. There, over a table covered with parchment and counting machines, we—Captain Charles, Hugo Bodin and I—work out the final details of the proposal: the suppliers, transportation, delivery schedules, but most important, the finances.

I confess that I enjoy this vocation, in spite of my sex. I feel a certain thrill, as if I were visiting a lover. But it is money I court, money that woos me, and the intoxicating power to earn a very great deal.

February 24.
I put down the draft of the proposal. Captain Charles's eyes seemed huge in the lantern light, black ink spots. "It's clear, well documented. I think it's ready."

He stood behind me, leafed through to the third page. He smelled of water of roses. "What about this?" He pointed at a paragraph.

"It's fine." His hand was only inches from my breast. He gathered up the papers with exaggerated, busy movements and put them in his blotting book.

I pulled on my gloves, my heart skittering like a leaf in a tempest.

Late afternoon, around 4:00.
At last, the Bodin Company proposal is finished. Captain Charles copied it out two times in his neat and tiny script. I'm to deliver it to Barras in the morning. "Wait," the captain called out as I was leaving. He did a handspring and landed on his feet in front of me.

"Yes?" I asked, amused.

He wiggled his fingers over the envelope as if casting a spell.

February 25.
"Voilà, the Bodin Company proposal," I told Barras, presenting the portfolio.

Barras pointed his gold-braided hat at the stack of papers on a side table. "Put it there, along with all the others." With a weary, long-suffering look.

I put it on top of the pile and smiled my persuasive best. "The first to be considered, Père Barras?"

Now all we can do is wait. Everything depends on the approval of Schérer, the Minister of War.

Late afternoon (just before 5:00), still raining.
"Does the Minister of War ever attend your salon, Fortunée?" I asked, dealing out the cards.

"Citoyen Schérer? Every week."

"Oh, there she goes bragging again," Thérèse said.

"I thought you knew him, Josephine."

"I've conversed with him at Barras's, and I know his wife, but he has yet to come to my salon."

"The Minister of the Interior came to my salon last week. *And* four deputies," Madame de Crény said, swinging her feet.

"Deputies will go to anything."

"I've been trying for months to get the Minister of Foreign Affairs to come to mine and at last I succeeded."

"So I heard."

"You mean you actually lured Talleyrand away from Josephine's salon?"

"All the important men go to *her* salon."

All but Schérer, the Minister of War, I thought—the one man who mattered.

"Invite Geneviève Payan," Fortunée Hamelin told me later, as she was leaving.

The opera singer? "I'm in your debt," I said, embracing her.

February 26.
At noon Lisette brought me the calling cards that had been dropped off

over the course of the morning. I sorted through the names, placing them in three piles—those to whom I would send a card, those who required a call, those I would invite to return.

The last card gave me pause. Bordered in black, it was of common design. *La veuve Hoche.* Lazare's widow.

After 10:00 P.M. (a guess).
It was dark, the narrow streets muddy. "Are you sure, Madame?" My coachman let down the step, gave me his hand. The house was small, without a courtyard. I nodded. "I won't be long."

"Citoyenne Beauharnais," the widow Hoche said, addressing me by the name of my first husband, by the name Lazare would have called me. Her dark eyes, hidden under the fluted ruffle of a plain linen cap, had a frightened look. She dropped a dutiful curtsy, much as a schoolgirl might greet a teacher, lifting the hem of her stained white apron at each corner. She seemed a wounded bird, a foundling, her shoulders painfully thin. I could not imagine her in Lazare's arms, could not imagine that *this* was the woman he'd loved, the wife he'd betrayed. I had imagined Lazare's wife as a well-made farmgirl, blushing and buxom, with apple cheeks and a hearty laugh. Not this ethereal creature with thin fingers more suited to lace work than to pulling on a cow's teat.

"My profound condolences," I said.

She pushed a wisp of hair back under her cap, blinking. I followed her upstairs to a small sitting room at the end of a dark and narrow passage. A portrait of Lazare hung over a coal fireplace—it made him appear stern. I was surprised to see a crucifix on the wall next to it. I accepted the offer of a chair, clearly the best chair in the room, the place of honour. His young widow took the seat opposite, her hands clasped in her lap. I heard a child's laugh, then little footsteps, hard leather shoes on a bare wooden floor. "Your daughter?" I asked.

The door creaked on its hinges. "This lady was a friend of your father's." Adélaïde Hoche's voice quavered.

The child poked one finger in her ear, and then pointed to the portrait. She was not yet three, I estimated, but a big girl for her age. "She has her father's eyes," I said. And his mouth.

An old woman appeared, scooped up the child. The door closed with a slam that shook the thin walls. I wondered if she was the aunt who had raised Lazare, the peddler of vegetables who went without vegetables in order to save every sou, so determined was she that Lazare would learn to read and write.

We sat for a moment in silence, Adélaïde Hoche sitting on her hands, staring at the floor. From somewhere I could hear a cat meowing plaintively. I was about to make a comment on the indifferent weather when she blurted out, "He said you would help me if I ever needed it."

"General Hoche?" *Should anything happen to me, please, I beg you, help my wife and child.*

"He said I could trust you."

I nodded, yes!

In the other room the child began to cry; the widow tilted her head, assessing the degree of distress. The crying stopped, turned to chatter. "It has to do with Père Hoche . . ." The knuckles of her clasped hands were white.

"General Hoche's father?"

"He's gone back to Thionville to look after things, so I took the chance to talk to you. I'm glad you came. He's coming back tomorrow." She stared at a blue crockery urn on the mantel. "He's in a bad way," she said finally, her chin trembling.

I looked away. I feared she might begin to weep and then we would both be crying, I knew. "It must be terribly hard. Is there anything I can do?"

She paused before saying, "If you could just get the report. Père Hoche tried, but they won't let him see it."

"I don't understand." The autopsy report?

"Père Hoche has become—" She twisted her fingers together. "Maybe if he could just see the report on how his son died, maybe it would help."

"But is there any doubt? Were you not with your husband?"

"He died in my arms," she said with pride.

A sob burst from me. "Forgive me," I said, wiping my cheeks. I'd vowed I would not let it happen.

"I do forgive you," she said with a look of ancient wisdom.

"I understand why he loved you so very much," I said, my eyes brimming.

Immediately after I called on Barras. I was relieved to find him alone. "I've just been to see the widow Hoche," I told him, attempting a casual tone.

He pulled out his lorgnon, looked at me with surprise. "*You* went to see her?"

"She initiated it. She is concerned about her father-in-law."

"Hoche's father? He broke down at the funeral, did you know? It was terrible."

Yes, I'd heard. "The widow feels that Père Hoche has become obsessed, I guess one would say, with his son's death, with trying to find out how he died."

"He knows perfectly well how Lazare died—of consumption. The autopsy made it perfectly clear. It was in all the journals. I don't understand what the problem is."

"Perhaps if he could just see the report."

"That's classified information."

"Paul, you know the rumours," I said softly. "If the autopsy report states that Lazare died of consumption, then why not make it public? It would help—"

"I'll tell you why!" he said, his hands gripping the arms of his chair. "Because there is nothing to hide. I've *had* it with these ignorant, suspicious . . ." He sputtered, seeking yet another invective.

February 27.

The door to chez Hoche was ajar. I pulled the bell rope, waited. I heard the child chattering. A tall white-haired man in a heavy wool coat and ribbed stockings came to the door. Lazare's father, Père Hoche—it was easy to see from his bushy eyebrows, the set of his jutting jaw, his proud stance. The child peeked out from between his legs. I introduced myself, handing him my card. "Citoyenne Bonaparte."

"The wife of General Bonaparte?" Père Hoche asked with respect in his voice.

"I knew your son, in the Carmes prison."

"Yes, he told me." With an appraising look.

I flushed. "My profound condolences, Citoyen Hoche."

"Hoche is *my* name," the child said from between her grandpapa's legs.

"Yes, I believe we have been introduced." I smiled.

Squealing, she ran back into the depths of the house.

The old man waved me into the house. "You're here to see Adélaïde?"

"She is expecting me, I believe."

"She told me she was expecting somebody, but she didn't tell me it was the wife of that rascal Bonaparte," he said, lighting a candle enclosed in oiled paper.

I followed his slow progression up the narrow stairs to the dark sitting room. "Sit. I'll tell her you're here." I waited in the spare little room, feeling Lazare's eyes staring down at me. A silk flower had been placed under the portrait, next to the blue urn. I heard a door, footsteps. Adélaïde Hoche appeared, dressed entirely in black, a widow's veil draped around her shoulders. "Père Hoche, please join us. I believe it regards Lazare," she said over her shoulder. She touched the urn on the mantelpiece, crossed herself and sat down.

The old man appeared in the door, filling it. "Oh?"

I glanced from one to the other uneasily. "I'm sorry, but I'm afraid I wasn't able to obtain the report. I was told that the law prevents making it public and—"

"The autopsy report?" Père Hoche asked, stepping into the room.

"But Director Barras assured me himself that the results are clear—your son died of consumption."

Père Hoche slammed his fist against the wall. "Don't you dare speak the name Barras in this house!"

I started, my heart pounding.

"Père Hoche, please," the young widow hissed, but her father-in-law ignored her.

"Yes, my son had consumption, but that wasn't what killed him. You don't get convulsions from consumption. Lazare was *poisoned*."

With the appearance of calm the widow stood, straightened Lazare's portrait. "It is not a good likeness," she said.

In which I am accused

February 28, 1798.
Bonaparte is in a meeting with Talleyrand again. They closet themselves in the study every afternoon. It has become a bit mysterious, for now Bonaparte has forbidden anyone from entering that room. "Even the servants, Bonaparte?" I asked, perplexed. For the study was in shambles.

"Even *you*," he said, tweaking my ear.

[Undated]
Books stacked by Bonaparte's bedside—Ossian, Plutarch, the Koran.

[Undated]
I felt like a thief in my own house. I lit a candle, looked about. Bonaparte's study was in that familiar state of disarray, that look of volcanic activity. Every surface was covered with papers, journals, scrolls. I picked up a plate with chicken bones on it, to clear it, then put it back exactly where I found it. I held the candle down over the map that was spread out over the carpet—*Egypt*.

March 1.
Minister Schérer has yet to even read the Bodin Company proposal. "Why is he taking so long?" I asked Barras. We were standing in an

alcove of his palatial salon, ostensibly to admire a painting that had recently been hung there.

"Because he spends every minute of every day dealing with your husband's proposals, that's why."

I glanced toward the people gathered at the far end of the salon. Joseph was hunched over talking to Bonaparte—lecturing him, I gathered, from the expression on Bonaparte's face. In spite of his retiring nature Joseph took his position as head of the Bonaparte clan seriously. According to Corsican custom his younger siblings were all under his care. Indeed, whatever glory accrued to Bonaparte, Joseph took credit for it; whatever profit, he managed. We're Corsican, Bonaparte would tell me, as if that explained everything.

"Does your husband never sleep?" Barras went on. "We receive at least one memo from him a day, and this in addition to all the meetings he keeps calling."

"Regarding Egypt?" I asked, my eyes on his, watching to see what his reaction would be.

Barras made a sputtering sound. "It's insane, this plan of his," he hissed, grasping my elbow.

"People said the Italian campaign was insane," I said, rising to my husband's defence. But noting—Barras did not deny an Egyptian plan.

He waved his arms through the air in the Provençal manner. "Maybe he's right, who knows? Maybe this *is* the only way to get at England, to cut her off from Asia, her source of wealth."

England: the enemy. For as long as I could remember, it had been thus. We would have peace, were it not for England. We would have prosperity, were it not for England. Almost every man I had ever loved—my hapless father, my dissipated first husband, my honourable Lazare and now even my brilliant and driven second husband—had been consumed by one thought and one thought only: defeating England. "I take it you're not in support," I said.

Barras ran his fingers through his thinning hair. "Officially, yes, of course I'm in support. But privately—and I've told Bonaparte this myself—I have serious reservations. His proposal is based on three assumptions, three *false* assumptions, in my view. First, that it is possible to conquer Egypt, which is doubtful. Second, that he would then be able to establish a connection with India, which is unlikely. And third, that India would then join forces with us to conquer England, which is ludicrous.

"But you know what's *really* mad? My fellow Directors might just go along with it. Personally, I think they'd agree to anything if it meant getting your husband out of the country. His popularity is making them uneasy. Have you seen the Bonaparte dolls the vendors are selling down on the quays?"

"India?" I asked, confused. What did India have to do with it?

Barras regarded me for a long moment. "You didn't know anything about this, did you? You were just guessing."

[Undated]
"You might as well tell me about Egypt," I told Bonaparte, putting down my glass of watered wine.

He turned to me with an enigmatic smile.

March 2.
Captain Charles did three handsprings in the Bodin Company courtyard. "It's been approved!" he whooped.

At last—the Bodin Company is now the official supplier of horses to the Army of Italy.

"We did it," Hugo Bodin called out from the top step. He clasped his pudgy fists together and raised them in victory.

Captain Charles twirled me. I felt light in his hands. He danced me off my feet, singing, "We're going to be rich, we're going to be rich, we're going to be *stinking* rich!"

March 5.
Bonaparte slammed the door behind him. "The Directors gave their consent." He threw his hat at an armchair; it missed and sent a lantern toppling.

"To what?" I asked, righting the lantern, checking to see whether any oil had spilled.

"The invasion of Portugal." *Portugal?* He grinned like a schoolboy. "At least, that's the official story."

March 10.

It was our anniversary yesterday—our second. We'd planned a quiet evening, but at four in the afternoon, Bonaparte informed me that Admiral Bruyes and two aides would be joining us for dinner. "I thought we were dining alone, Bonaparte. It's our anniversary."

"It is?"

"We discussed this yesterday."

"Do you have any idea what I do in a week?" he exploded, storming out of our bedchamber.

Later, much later, he returned, repentant. He'd been drinking, which was unusual. "I want to make a baby," he said, fumbling with the bed spring. Our beds flew together with a crash—a sound that could be heard throughout the house, I knew. A sound that set the servants tittering, no doubt.

"I am beginning to despair of ever having another child," I confessed. It had been some time since I'd had the monthly sickness.

"Sterility in a woman is decided in the first three years of married life." He sat down, pulling at his boots. "For a woman over the age of twenty-five, the interval is lengthened."

"You've been studying?" Bonaparte believed anything could be achieved by knowledge—and by will, *his* will.

He planted his hand purposely on my breast. "The womb and the breasts are in sympathy. To excite the womb, one need merely excite the breast."

"Then I should have been with child long ago," I said with a smile.

He tugged at my nightdress, pulling it up over my head. "Queen Anne of Austria brought Louis XIV into the world after twenty-two years of sterility."

Twenty-one years of fidelity was how I understood it. But did not say.

[Undated]
From Madame Campan's book, chapter twenty-six, "Of Sterility": *Sterility is a Want of Conception in a Woman of requisite Age who duly suffers the Approaches of Man.*

I don't know what to think. I'm of "requisite age" and I certainly "duly suffer" (!) the approach of a man. I don't understand why I'm not pregnant. For that matter, I don't understand why I no longer have the flowers, in spite of the bitter rue tea Mimi has persuaded me to try.*

March 13.
I am . . . yes, *shattered* is the word—betrayed. Bitterness fills my heart. Disbelief. Lisette is gone. Her tears failed to move me.

What happened:

After my morning toilette I took a quick repast in the upstairs drawing room. Lisette, claiming vapours, had gone to her room in the basement. Bonaparte was in the study with Fauvelet, Junot and several other of his aides. Or so I thought.

It was as I was finishing a cup of coffee that Bonaparte came upstairs, asking after Junot. "I thought he was with you," I said.

"I haven't seen him all morning." Perplexed. "Perhaps he went riding."

"Perhaps," I said, standing, suddenly uneasy.

The steep stairs that led down to the servants' quarters in the basement were dark. At the landing I paused. I thought I heard a man's voice. Perhaps it was the cook, or my manservant. But I didn't think so.

At the bottom I stopped, suddenly unsure. The air was colder than above, but stale and smelling of flat-irons. I could simply open the door to Lisette's room—was that not how it was done in plays? Instead, I knocked.

"Tell her I'll be up in a moment," I heard Lisette call out with an irritated tone. The door was thin; I could hear quite clearly.

I knocked again, harder this time, more insistent.

* *Tea made of rue, an evergreen shrub, was commonly used by women wishing to abort.*

"Tell her to hold her horses!" A man's voice: Junot!

"I'll hold *your* horses," I heard Lisette say, giggling, and then, "That woman's going to drive me mad."

That woman. I turned the metal latch. The door swung open with a complaining creak. There, nude on a narrow trundle bed under the high dirty window, were Lisette and Junot, Lisette straddling. Both of them turned their faces toward me in a curiously co-ordinated motion.

"Bonaparte is looking for you, Colonel Junot," I said, backing out of the room and closing the door behind me. I went back up the stairs, pushing against both walls for support, my legs unsteady beneath me.

Mimi was in my bedchamber, gathering soiled linen. "I'm fine," I reassured her. "But I'd like to be alone." Her look of tender concern would make me weep, I feared. I heard heavy footsteps downstairs, heard a door open, slam shut, the low rumble of men's voices. I sat down on one of the hard stools by the bed. I'd never seen a man with a woman before, not like that, *en flagrante*. A man with a girl.

I was sipping a second glass of hysteric water when I heard the floorboards creak outside my door and then three light raps. I did not answer.

Three raps again. The latch turned, the door swung open. "Forgive me, Madame," Lisette said, her hands clasped in front of her, her head bowed.

I didn't know what to say. I did not have it in me to forgive her. It was not the deed so much as those words she had spoken: *that woman.* Was that all I was to her? I had come to believe that we shared an affection, one for the other. We'd been through so much together. But clearly, I'd been mistaken. "Gather your things, Lisette."

"Madame, please—!" She pressed her hands to her face.

Was she crying? I doubted it. She reached out to touch my hand as I passed by her, heading out the door. I was not mistaken. Her eyes were clear.

"It was just once, Madame. I promise . . ."

I closed the door behind me, short of breath.

"You'll be sorry," I heard her cry.

"You dismissed your maid?" Bonaparte asked, pulling on his jacket, preparing to go to the Luxembourg Palace for a meeting with the Directors. "But why?"

Junot, leaning against the mantel, observed me, his cold blue eyes unflinching.

"It was a personal matter," I told my husband evenly, avoiding Junot's gaze. There was no point telling Bonaparte. Junot was one of his oldest friends.

"You allowed her too many familiarities. It spoils a maid."

"Yes," I said.

"Next time, you'll know better."

I heard Junot's knuckles crack.

March 14, midday.

"Everyone knew," Mimi told me.

"Why didn't you tell me?"

"That's not my way."

"Will you be my lady's maid?"

"An upstairs maid?" Mimi paused, considering.

I touched her hand. "Please, Mimi—I need someone I know I can trust." I felt like a ship without a rudder. I no longer believed in my own judgement.

She made a doubtful face. "I'd have to learn manners."

"But you'll do it?"

She grinned. "I promised your mother I'd look after you, didn't I?"

March 16.

Bonaparte's older brother Joseph has taken to dropping in every day for the midday meal. Today he asked for a private consultation with Bonaparte, so I excused myself. They were sequestered for some time. Then Bonaparte's secretary appeared. "The General and his brother wish to speak with you, Madame," Fauvelet Bourrienne informed me, his look uneasy.

Bonaparte had his feet up on his desk and was tapping the desktop with a riding crop. "Leave, Fauvelet," he told his secretary. "And close the door!"

Joseph was slouched in the chair by the fire examining his fingernails. He looked up at me and smiled. It was then that I knew I was in trouble.

"Joseph has just informed me that you have had dealings with a military supply company." Bonaparte glanced over at his brother, who nodded. "The Bodin Company, to be specific, which was recently awarded a contract to provide horses to the Army of Italy."

I glanced from Bonaparte to Joseph and back again. "What are you talking about?" I demanded, my heart pounding.

"Perhaps this will refresh your memory." Joseph withdrew a sheet of paper from his waistcoat pocket and read, "Twenty-one Rue Honoré." He smiled.

Hugo Bodin lived at one hundred Rue Honoré, not twenty-one. "I've never been there."

"Curious," Joseph said, still smiling. "You were seen entering at twenty to eleven on fifteen Ventôse and did not emerge until three that afternoon. You were seen there again on the twenty-second, and then again on the twenty-third."

"Am I being followed?"

"Confess, Josephine!" Bonaparte exploded. "Is that not where you go every day—when you tell me that you go to the riding school to watch your son?"

It was a violent exchange. (I'm trembling still.) "Go ahead, divorce me, if that's what you want!" I ended up screaming. All the while Joseph Bonaparte smiled.

March 17, late morning, exhausted.
A sleepless night. Joseph knew everything—the details about the contracts, the finances! How did he find out? Somebody must be informing him. I suspect it might be Jubié, the banker Hugo Bodin has been dealing with. I've dispatched a letter to Captain Charles to warn him, warn Hugo Bodin.

I feel trapped, enraged. What right has Joseph to interfere in my dealings? What right has he to spy on me? For that matter, what right has

Bonaparte to treat me with such contempt! They self-righteously accuse me of crimes of which they themselves are guilty. I'm not married to Bonaparte, I'm married to a Corsican clan—and I despise them.

11:30 P.M. (can't sleep).
Bonaparte sat down on his bed. I was on my own, stretched out stiffly in my dressing gown. "You know I am right in this matter," he said coldly, as if from on high.

I did not answer.

"Answer me!" His hands fists.

"You are always *right,* Bonaparte," I said, turning my betrothal ring on my finger. I could have it melted down, I was thinking, made into earrings.

"Admit it—you've been dabbling in military supplies."

Dabbling. The word irked me. Did men "dabble"? The fact was, I'd "dabbled" long before we were married, long before we'd met. And I happened to be good at it. The profits paid my rent, enabled me to send my children to school—enabled me to survive. "Yes, Bonaparte, I *dabble.* As do your brothers, as does your Uncle Fesch." As he himself had in Italy. As did virtually all the officers in the army. As did all the *bon ton* of Paris, for that matter.

"It is unseemly for women to mingle in business."

He was talking like an old-fashioned country friar. "Things have changed. Many women—"

"Not my wife!"

"We have an agreement, Bonaparte: you pay for your expenses and I pay for mine." I clenched my hands, digging my nails into my palms. "I'm the one who must pay for Hortense's schooling. I'm the one who must raise a considerable sum for her dowry, who must provide uniforms for my son. How do you expect me to do this, I ask you? I'd be on the street, frankly, if it weren't for my so-called dabbling." (Well, perhaps I was exaggerating a little.)

He stomped out of the room. He is sleeping in the study tonight. *Bien.* He can stay there, for all I care.

March 18.

Mimi helped me on with my wool cloak. "Not your fur?" she asked, giving my shoulder a motherly squeeze. "It's cold out."

"I'll be fine." To Mimi, it was always cold. "Should Bonaparte ask, tell him I've gone to the stay-maker's."

She looked at me for a long moment. "But the stay-maker is coming here tomorrow."

"I mean the milliner's," I said, my cheeks heated. I'd never lied to Mimi before. I was becoming a person who did not trust—a person who was not trustworthy. At the door I looked back. "Forgive me?"

In a reckless clatter my coachman drove the horses out the gate. Approaching Monceau Park, I pulled my black shawl from my basket, draped it over my head. My coachman helped me down, cautioning me against the mud. Fortunately, it was no longer raining. An army of beggars cried out, holding out their hands. I gave them a bag of crusts. Where was Captain Charles? I wondered, opening my parasol in spite of the clouds. I'd sent him word to meet me at ten. I felt uneasy entering Monceau Park unescorted. I was relieved, finally, to see a man approaching on a black horse, trotting smartly down the central path. He waved a white plumed hat. I headed for a bench by some Roman columns.

"I meant to get here before you," Captain Charles said, dismounting East Wind with a graceful leap, "but I got tied up making arrangements for Milan." He looped the reins over a branch. Then he pitched two empty wine bottles into the bushes. "Here," he said, taking a silk tasselled scarf out of his saddlebag and spreading it over the stone bench.

I sat down at the far edge in order to give him room—more than he needed. I pulled my cloak tight. It was a damp and miserable day; now I regretted not wearing my fur.

"I talked to Hugo," he said, sitting forward, looking out over the pond. His full lips grazed the edge of his blue neck scarf, tied so that it completely covered his chin. He cleared his throat. "You were right. It was the banker Jubié. It turns out he knows your husband's brother."

"So." I crossed my arms across my chest. I didn't like it when I felt this way—so distant. "And Jubié told Joseph I was involved in the company?" Captain Charles nodded. "But how did *he* come to know? Hugo vowed to keep it confidential."

Captain Charles threw a pebble into the pond. "Hugo said he had to tell him. Otherwise he wouldn't have advanced us the money."

Of course, of course, I thought angrily. I watched the rings of water opening. I wanted to throw something into the pond too, but I felt too old for such games, and that thought made me sad.

"Jubié and your brother-in-law went out on the town, apparently." Captain Charles grinned. "To three taverns, a gambling establishment and a brothel."

I shrugged. I'd heard stories of Joseph's debauchery before, usually from his tearful wife.

"Are you going to quit the company?" he asked.

"No." I couldn't—even if I wanted to. I'd borrowed a small fortune in order to join. If I pulled out now, I'd be ruined. "I'd sooner get a divorce," I lied.

"That would please your brother-in-law. Apparently he told Jubié that he would not rest until he'd succeeded in getting his brother to divorce you," the captain said, tapping a stick against the toe of his boot.

"Oh?" That helped explain why Joseph had been spying on me, his mean little smile. Yet even so, it surprised me. I knew Joseph didn't care for me, but I didn't think he'd go so far as to try to get Bonaparte to divorce me.

"He told the banker that you married his brother for his money."

I laughed, I confess. When we'd married, Bonaparte had had no money. "That's amusing. What *else* did he say?"

"That you have Bonaparte under your spell." I smiled. Well. . . . "And that you're a witch." He made an apologetic shrug.

A witch? What had I ever done to Joseph to deserve such a hateful slur?

"I'm sorry, Madame Bonaparte, but I thought you should know. It helps, I think, knowing who you can trust—"

"And who you can't," I said, kicking a pebble. It skittered across the path and into the water. I watched the rings opening, one upon the other. How far did it go, the deceit?

After, I went to Thérèse's. I was in a state. "Look," I told her, pacing, "I can't quit the Bodin Company even if I wanted to." I owed almost half a million francs to Barras alone. The only way to get out was to stay in long enough to pay off my debts.

"May I make a suggestion?" Thérèse said, trying to calm me. "Talk to Bonaparte. Tell him he's been a cheap tightwad—impossible to live with!—that he's put you in an untenable position, that you didn't intend to compromise him by doing what *everybody* in Paris is doing, including all the members of his avaricious family, and then tell him you intend to withdraw. So, maybe extricating yourself will take a little longer than you let on, and maybe he's better off not knowing. From the apoplectic fits he throws over the purchase of a hat, I can guarantee you that he doesn't want to know the extent of your debts. Frankly, all he really wants to hear is that you love him. So why don't you just tell him?" She laughed at my cross expression. "Well, you do, you know. Why don't you just admit it?"

[Undated]
"Yeyette?" Mimi set a tray down on the table beside the bed. "I got the cook to make some plantain bread for you." She handed me a piece.

"Oh Mimi, I'm so miserable," I confessed. I'd slept alone for three nights, tossing and turning.

"The General is unhappy, as well."

"Oh?" I bit into the heavenly smelling loaf, my childhood welling up around me in my mind.

"I've never in my life seen a more miserable man."

"Good!" I said, but blinking back tears.

"I think it's time we talked," she said, handing me a flannel to dry my face.

And so we did. I told her how confused I was about Bonaparte, how angry he made me, how exasperating he was. And then I told her how brilliant I believed him to be, how his mind was volcanic, always thinking—and how it frightened me sometimes, knowing the thoughts in his mind, knowing his dreams. I told her how different we were, how hard it was to live with him. And then I told her how alike we were, how we'd both grown up on islands, far from France, how we knew what it was like to be an outsider. And then I told her how he loved me more than anyone had ever loved me, and how he needed me, how I was his good luck star, and how sometimes I felt we were fated.

"Do you think he is your spirit friend?"

"I fear so," I cried, weeping anew.

March 19, Feast of Saint Joseph.

I was combing my hair at my dressing table when I heard footsteps in the bedchamber. "Bonaparte?" I called out, standing.

He stuck his head in my dressing room, his hat still on. "There you are."

"I'm . . ." Sorry, I started to say.

Solemnly, he held out a brass-plated chain. "It's your name day today."

The nineteenth of March, of course—feast of Saint Joseph. I was surprised he remembered, surprised he even knew. "How kind of you." I slipped it on. "It's lovely," I lied.

"Josephine, I . . ."

I looked into his great grey eyes, his melancholy eyes so full of dreams. "I know, Bonaparte."

"The Sultan of Turkey has over a hundred wives," Bonaparte told me, "beauties awaiting their turn, devoted to pleasing, to the art of pleasing." He stroked my breast, my hip. "Like my wife." For I please this man, my husband.

"I want to go with you," I told him.

"To Egypt?" he whispered.

"Wherever you go."

In which I must stay behind

March 20, 1798.

The Black Land—it haunts my thoughts. I have been reading about it, hiding the text under my mattress. We will arrive in June, after the simoon, a suffocating wind that blows across the desert. The temperature will be hot. "I'm a créole," I reassure Bonaparte. "I will be able to take the heat."

There is no rain in Egypt. Every year the Nile River overflows and inundates the land with a slimy substance. But for this, nothing would grow.

A land without water! Even the names of the oases sound dry on my tongue: *Khârgeh, Dâkhel, Farâfra, Sîwa, Bahrîyeh.*

Diseases flourish in that land—plague, cholera, ophthalmia, dysentery . . . even boils so deadly that they can kill a man.

A land of crystalline rock, covered by shifting sand.

A land without trees. It is impossible to imagine such a place. I am curious to see a papyrus plant, from which the paper used throughout the ancient world was made. The lotus is a water lily that grows on the Nile.

Oxen, horses, asses, sheep, goats—familiar creatures. But camels! And cats without tails. (Fortunately, crocodiles are seldom seen.) The pelican, the beloved bird of my youth, abides in the north.

The cities are inhabited by white vultures, which are worshipped—as are certain beasts, reptiles and even vegetables. The sun god is Ra, a hawk-headed man, the moon god is Thoth. Seth is the power of evil, a spirit with a gentle, seductive name.

"Egypt is the first nation known to man," Bonaparte told me with awe in his voice. He works by candlelight on the floor of our bedchamber, studying the maps, tracing the footsteps of Alexandre the Great, Julius Caesar. He dreams of desert sands.

April 2.
Meetings here all day preparing for "the expedition"—the *mysterious* expedition. Eugène emerged from the smoke-filled study, laughing with the men. "We're going to Portugal," he told me confidentially.

"Oh?" It is all I can do not to tell him the true destination.

April 3.
The widow Hoche called on me today, her worry about Père Hoche over-coming her timidity. Her father-in-law was suffering, rage and grief were burning him up. "Is there nothing you can do?"

April 4.
"There's a strange man to see you," Mimi said, crinkling her nose.

It was my old friend Fouché,* looking like a beggar. "How kind of you to come so soon." For I had sent for him only this morning. I offered him a glass of orange water—Fouché did not partake of spirits, I knew. His hooded eyes, his disordered clothes, his stale odour, all brought on a feeling of affection in me. He was an eccentric, this slovenly man, this ardent Revolutionary with bad breath. This man who was devoted to his ugly red-haired wife and all their ugly red-haired children. This man who was making a fortune (I'd heard) as a partner in Company Ouen, a military supply company. This man, the extraordinary spy. "There is a document I need to obtain," I ventured. "Might you be available?"

---

* *Joseph Fouché was a radical Revolutionary with a reputation for violence (even atrocities) and a penchant for conspiracy.*

He opened his snuffbox. "For a price," he said, sniffing a pinch. I flushed. "You mistake me, Citoyenne. It is information I trade in. I give you what you want, you repay me in kind."

He made it sound so innocent, a simple exchange. But I knew what he meant, in truth. In exchange for whatever answers he might deliver, I would become a spy on his behalf. "I would never compromise a friend," I said.

"That would hardly be necessary. You are no doubt aware that you have a number of enemies who could provide you with numerous opportunities to fulfill such an obligation."

"Perhaps you could begin by telling me who they might be?" I smiled behind my fan.

"It does not take a clairvoyant to see that the Bonapartes wish you dead, but given the inconvenience of being caught with blood on their collective hands, would settle for ruin, no doubt. And in their midst, of late, a rather lovely young woman has been seen—a girl who was, at one time, your lady's maid." He took a small, careful sip of his glass of orange water. "It is a wisdom well understood by our ci-devant nobility that one should never reveal oneself to a man or woman who is in one's pay. Servants thus taken into confidence come to know a great deal, putting them in a position to profit from the sale of such. And profit, even a Revolutionary will tell you, is an irresistible force of Nature. Perhaps it is this young woman who concerns you."

Lisette had been seen with the Bonapartes? I went to the window, my cheeks burning. "No, it is not Citoyenne Compoint."

"Perhaps it has to do with your present state of"—he paused—"embarrassment."

My debts, he meant. "It has nothing to do with that." Appalled, I confess, by how much Fouché knew.

"Then no doubt it regards the somewhat suspect practices of your business associates, the brothers Bodin."

Suspect practices? "The name Bodin is unfamiliar to me, Citoyen Fouché," I told him with splendid calm.

Fouché unbuttoned his jacket, revealing a dapper silver-trimmed waistcoat underneath. "Citoyenne, you are an effective liar, a quality I have always admired in you. Tell me, then—what is it you wish to know?"

"General Hoche's widow has solicited my help." Fouché sat back, surprised. It pleased me, I confess, to startle a man such as Fouché, a professional in the matter of knowing. "Her father-in-law, Père Hoche, the late General Hoche's father, is subject to morbid dreams, rages that have weakened his constitution. He has become obsessed with finding out how his son died."

"Case closed, Citoyenne. It is common knowledge General Hoche died of consumption."

"Specifically, the elder Hoche has tried, without success, to obtain a copy of the autopsy report—"

"Which, being a military matter, is confidential, of course."

I nodded. "So I was told. The fact that no one is permitted to see it has inflamed Père Hoche's imagination further."

"But no doubt Director Barras could obtain a copy for you."

"I'm afraid not." I paused, unsure whether I should tell Fouché how emotional Barras had become at the very mention of it. "The problem is, Père Hoche is convinced his son was poisoned."

"Père Hoche and the rest of Paris." Fouché made a dismissive gesture. "Does he have cause? Or is he feeding off rumours like the rest of us?"

"He claims his son suffered convulsions in his dying moments." I swallowed, a wave of tears rising dangerously within me. "Apparently, convulsions are not symptomatic of consumption."

Fouché bit the inside of one cheek, considering.

"I'm of the view that the father's grief is driving him mad. If he could just see the autopsy report, it might put his imaginings to rest. But after talking to Director Barras, I have come to the conclusion that obtaining a copy of the report will not be easy. Indeed, that it might require a certain degree of, well—"

"Sleuthing?"

I smiled apologetically. "Not to mention discretion. For I'm sure you can understand, Citoyen Fouché, how important it is that my own involvement in this matter be kept strictly confidential."

"Secrecy is my passion, Citoyenne."

April 6.

At Barras's salon last night Fouché sidled up to me. "The autopsy report appears to be missing from the Ministry of War's files," he whispered, widening his eyes.

I motioned to him to be silent. Talleyrand had just entered the room.

"I have a contact at the School of Medicine," he went on. "He should be able to give me the name of the surgeon who performed the autopsy."

"How good to see you this evening, Citoyen Talleyrand," I said, giving the Minister of Foreign Affairs my hand.

April 7.

"I located the surgeon who performed the autopsy, but he demands one hundred francs," Fouché informed me tonight in the corridor at the Luxembourg Palace. "Are you willing?"

"To pay one hundred francs? Just for a copy of the report?"

Fouché shrugged. "I was surprised he didn't ask for more."

April 8, Easter Sunday.

"You got it?" I asked Fouché, my voice thick. I did not care for this, did not care for any of it, neither the seeking nor the finding. I wanted it to be over. Were it not for my promise to help the widow Hoche, I would wash my hands of this business completely.

Fouché arched his thin red eyebrows, his hand on his coat pocket. "I did. But it will not appease the father," he warned, unfolding the single yellowed sheet. "According to the autopsy report, the cause of General Hoche's death is"—he paused for effect—"unknown."

It was not at all what I had expected. Barras himself had told me that the autopsy had determined that Lazare had died of consumption. "So General Hoche did not die of consumption?" I scanned the document and then folded it. I did not want to read it.

"Possibly—because if he had died of consumption, it seems to me that the surgeon would have clearly stated so. But if one were to die of poisoning—let us say, just for the purpose of inquiry—the effects being subtle and therefore mysterious, then the cause of death would, most likely, be reported as—"

"Unknown!" Père Hoche shook the report in the air, as if at the gods. "My son was poisoned. There's nothing unknown about that. And I'll tell you who did it—Director Barras."

I glanced at the widow, dismayed. She was standing by the fireplace, her hand on the blue urn on the mantel. I wanted to speak out in Barras's defence, but I knew that it would only enrage the old man further.

"And I'll tell you why," he ranted on. "Director Barras murdered my son because Lazare had integrity. Speak that word around Director Barras and see if he even knows it. Integrity, honesty, bravery—they're all foreign words to that traitor."

"Can't sleep?" Mimi asked, discovering me in the downstairs drawing room, curled up on the sofa, staring into the embers.

"What time is it?" I asked.

"Two," she said.

I sighed. Would I ever sleep? "I have worries, Mimi."

"I know."

I smiled. Mimi knew everything.

"Want to talk?"

"Not yet," I told her, standing.

"Always remember, we're looking over you," she said, "your mother and I."

I turned at the landing. "Thank you."

April 9.
Bonaparte and I have just returned from an evening at Barras's salon. I'm in turmoil over a conversation with Fouché. He informed me that the man who had performed the autopsy had come to his home offering

more information—in exchange for more money, of course. "I took it upon myself to pay on your behalf."

"Oh," I said weakly. I thought the matter was finished. He'd obtained the report. The business was done.

"It seems that after the autopsy, General Hoche's doctor asked that the heart be put aside."

Lazare's heart? Why? I sat down, sickened. I could not bear to think of Lazare's body in this way, as a collection of so many parts.

"Furthermore," Fouché said, sitting down beside me and hunching forward, his elbows on his knees, "there were specks in the lining of the stomach—sufficient to cause suspicion, but insufficient to prove anything."

"Suspicion of what?" I heard a clock chime, followed by another, and then another.

"Of poisoning." He turned to me and smiled. "May I make a suggestion, Citoyenne? Over the years I have learned that success depends on one thing and one thing only—the courage to ask the true question. And with respect, the true question may not be how General Hoche died, but rather who, in fact, killed him."

"Citoyen Fouché, I would like this investigation dropped."

He looked puzzled. "But Citoyenne—"

"I insist!"

April 10.

Bonaparte is frantic. There is so much to do, and everything made difficult by the necessity of raising the funds for the expedition—an expedition whose actual destination must remain unknown (to prevent the English from finding out). To that end we have been entertaining every evening—last night the banker Perrégaus; tonight Collot, the munitioner. Those evenings we do not entertain, Bonaparte and I attend Barras's salon at the Luxembourg Palace, where the talk is invariably of what everyone is now calling "Bonaparte's crusade."

April 11.

Every evening we receive members of the Académie: engineers, chemists, zoologists, cartographers, antiquarians. Bonaparte is determined to take over one hundred savants with him. He must be persuasive, for the destination remains secret.*

April 12.

"*Basta!*" Bonaparte threw his hat onto the carpet, pulled off his boots. "You know the song and dance about Louis being too ill to join the expedition?" He made a sputtering noise. "I just found out the true reason."

"Louis is going to Barèges, for a cure." Ever since we'd returned from Italy, Bonaparte's younger brother had often been unwell. "Isn't he?"

"That's just an excuse." Bonaparte hit a table with his fist. I steadied the clock just before it toppled. "No, it's because he's in love, of all things."

I took Pugdog onto my lap, stroked his silky fur. "Why that's—"

Bonaparte glared. "With Émilie."

"*My* Émilie?" I was astonished.

"The daughter of an émigré," he said, his cheek twitching. "And her parents divorced. And her mother remarried to a mulatto!" He pulled the servant rope. Mimi appeared, tying her apron strings. "Get Louis."

"What do you intend to tell him, Bonaparte?"

"To begin packing for Egypt." Bonaparte glowered into the embers. "And that he's never to see her again. And that she is betrothed."

"But Bonaparte—"

"And that she's to be married in a matter of weeks."

"Married?" I'd seen Émilie a few days ago, and she'd said nothing of the matter. "To whom?"

"That's for you to determine." He strode to the door. "Louis!" I heard him stomping up the stairs.

---

* *Ultimately 167 scholars were persuaded to go, forming a Commission of Arts and Science that would, in turn, be called the Institute of Egypt. Out of this campaign, a twenty-four volume* Déscription de l'Égypte *was published, upon which the science of Egyptology is founded.*

April 13.

Both Bonaparte's brothers Lucien and Joseph have been elected to the Council of Five Hundred. (Lucien is only twenty-three!) At this rate, the Republic will be ruled by Bonapartes. *Bien*—so long as they don't rule me.

April 18.

Eugène waved a paper in the air, Lavalette hovering behind him. "We're leaving in four days!"

Four days? "Why so soon?" Bonaparte and I wouldn't be leaving for at least a month—or so he'd told me.

"At four in the morning," Eugène said, puzzling over the paper. "Lieutenant Lavalette, Louis and I. We're to go in civilian clothes. We're not allowed to tell anyone that we're aides, and if asked where we're headed, we're to say we're going to Brest." He looked at Lavalette. "*Brest?*"

"That's likely to keep the English confused," I said.

"If they're only half as confused as we are, they'll be confused," Lavalette said.

I heard footsteps on the stairs, light hurried steps punctuated by clicking spurs—Bonaparte.

"One word before you go, Bonaparte." I stood in the door to stop him.

"I'm late. What is it?" he demanded, buttoning up his grey uniform jacket. No matter how many fashionable new jackets I had the tailor make for him, Bonaparte invariably chose to wear his plain grey one with the frayed epaulettes.

"Lavalette might be the man we're—"

He squinted at me, confused.

"For Émilie." I nodded toward the front door. "He's in the courtyard."

"Lieutenant Lavalette? You want me to talk to him? *Now?*"

"He's to leave in four days!"

Lavalette stood in the dining room door, his green felt hat in his hand.

"The General has spoken to you?" I asked, standing to greet him.

"Madame Bonaparte, I am . . . I must confess, she is an angel, everything I could ever . . . but"—he ran his hand over his balding head—"but she is a girl, and I'm already twenty-nine."

"Twenty-nine is not so very old, Lieutenant." I'd thought he was older, in fact.

"The General said that the wedding must be held in one week."

One week! Was Émilie to be introduced at the altar? "In that case we should go out to the school tomorrow." Lavalette, Bonaparte, Eugène and I would go. "I will introduce you, and you will make your proposal."

"T-t-tomorrow?"

April 19.

Bonaparte had a report to dispatch to the Directory, so it was noon by the time we arrived at the school. Caroline (who has only recently been enrolled) and Hortense came bounding out to join us, Émilie following. "It's such a lovely day, I thought a picnic might be nice," I said, embracing each in turn. Émilie looked charming in her broad-brimmed bonnet: a good omen, I thought.

"I already ate," Caroline said.

I glanced at Lavalette. He was standing with his hands clasped in front of him, gripping a bouquet of wilted violets. "Lieutenant Lavalette, do you know everyone here?" I introduced the girls, but they were more interested in Eugène's new uniform. "Perhaps Eugène will carry the basket," I suggested, taking Bonaparte's arm. I knew a spot under some oak trees.

We proceeded down the wide gravel path. Now and again Caroline cast a glance at Lavalette, at the curious bouquet of wilted flowers he was clutching. She whispered something to Hortense, who burst into giggles. I caught Lavalette's eye. "I know a girl who happens to love violets," I said, nudging Émilie. Wordlessly, Lavalette pushed the bouquet at her. Suddenly the girls fell silent.

We came to the spot I had in mind. Caroline, Émilie and Hortense rushed to help me unpack the basket. Eugène busied himself folding the napkins in cocked-hat fashion. We spread the hemp picnic cloth, laid out the food: flat bread, a mild cheese, roasted hare.

We ate quickly, in silence. Bonaparte threw his bones into the woods. I asked Eugène to entertain us with his imitations. Then the time came to pack the basket. I took Bonaparte's arm. "I'd like to see the pond before we go."

Eugène grabbed Caroline and Hortense by the hand and began running down the path. Émilie made a few steps to follow them. "No!" Eugène called back to her. "You stay."

"Oh, I can't bear it," I told Bonaparte, walking briskly to keep up with him. I glanced over my shoulder. I saw Lavalette bend down and kiss Émilie on top of her head. "I think we can go back now," I said.

[Undated]
Louis looked surprised that Émilie is to be married, but other than that he showed no emotion. He was not happy, however, about having to go on the expedition. His health concerns me.

April 22, Sunday.
Eugène has been packing. Slipping something into his leather valise (a song Hortense had written for him), I saw his scrapbooks on the shelf. The house was silent: safe. I took down the one about Hoche, opened the glue-stiff pages. It was all there: Lazare's glory, his final disgrace.

What followed were the eulogies: the profound outpouring of a nation's grief over the death of a true Republican, a passionate defender of la liberté. In the words spoken following his death, I could read a lament not so much for Lazare, but for the freedom he had fought for, died for: *la liberté ou la mort.*

Had Lazare been poisoned? Had he died defending la liberté? I closed the scrapbook, put it back on the shelf exactly as I had found it.

May 4.

It was on the way home from the theatre that Bonaparte informed me, "We leave tonight."

I put my hand on his wrist. "You don't really mean tonight . . . do you?"

He held his watch fob to the light of the moon. "As soon as we get home. We'll pick up Louis and Eugène in Lyons."

"But . . ." We weren't packed. "But what about Hortense? I can't just leave without—"

May 9—Toulon.

It was early when we pulled into the port of Toulon, in spite of a mishap on the road.

"Look," Bonaparte's secretary Fauvelet exclaimed.

Looking out over the harbour I saw the French fleet at anchor, a forest of masts. "Is that *La Pomone*?" I asked. Seventeen years before I'd come to France on *La Pomone*. "How many ships are there?" I'd never seen so many.

"Three hundred and ten," Louis said.

"The greatest fleet in history since the Crusades," Eugène said in an awed whisper.

10:30 A.M.

In the market the talk is only of the fleet, where it may be heading. "There is even a booth for placing bets," Eugène said.

"I bet a sou there on Portugal," Mimi said, looking up from her mending.

"Oh?"

"And then there was a rush of bets on Portugal. Everyone thought I knew."

"Which is the favoured destination?" Bonaparte asked, looking up from the volume of poetry he was reading, his beloved Ossian. (*"A tale of the times of old! The deeds of days of other years!"*)

"The Crimea," Mimi said.

Eugène and Louis snickered, imagining that they knew the true destination.

May 12.

Bonaparte has been in a flurry of activity, organizing provisions, going over the lists, the ships, the artillery. Going over the maps. Now, he is ready, and impatient. He waits on the wind.

Evening.

A wind has risen, but not in the right direction. Bonaparte watches the sky. Hourly, from the widow's walk, he scans the horizon with a spyglass, searching for signs of the enemy.

May 14.

This morning, bringing my cup of hot chocolate himself, Bonaparte informed me I would not be going.

A breeze billowed the curtains, filling the room with the rancid smell of the harbour. "Going where?" I asked, confused, pulling the covering sheet over me. I was naked, my sleeping gown tangled somewhere in the sheets. Since reaching Toulon Bonaparte had become even more ardent than usual. Being back in active command had brought out a vigorous energy in him.

He sat down on the bed. I moved over to make room for him. He put his hand on my shoulder, as if to console me, and it was then that I knew what he was going to say. "Bonaparte, no. *Please* don't leave me behind." I felt tears pressing. Stupid tears.

"It's too dangerous—the English are out there. They'll likely attack."

It was silent in the room but for the ticking of a clock. "You never told me that."

He took my hand, kissed it. "When we get to Egypt, I'll send a ship back for you. *La Pomone,* if you like."

I pressed my head against his shoulder. "It frightens me to be separated from you, Bonaparte."

"What is there to be afraid of?"

His family, I thought.

May 15.

I sit idle as everyone scurries about, preparing for the "crusade." They are filled with excitement, and I, with a feeling of sadness . . . and dread.

May 18.

The flags are blowing to the east. Eugène came running up the stairs to my suite. "We're leaving at dawn," he cried out breathlessly, his cheeks rosy.

May 19.

All night I could not sleep. At the first hint of light, the first crow of a cock, I slipped out of bed, went to the window. The masts in the harbour were bobbing in the breeze. The weather vane pointed east.

"Where's Fauvelet?" Bonaparte jumped out of bed, fully alert. I helped him into his uniform. He had been shaved the night before, in anticipation of the morning. A knock, three knocks. "There he is."

"General, they're—"

Bonaparte bolted out the door, buttoning his long linen trousers.

I sat down at my toilette table and regarded myself in the glass. The morning light was cruel, the worry lines clear.

Another knock. Fauvelet again, apologetic. "Twenty minutes, Madame."

Twenty! Mimi performed a small miracle, transforming me from an anxious woman who had had no sleep into the elegant wife of General Bonaparte.

Eugène burst in and struck a heroic pose. "Ready?"

There was a call from the first floor. "Coming!" He leapt down the stairs, his hat flying off behind him.

As we came out into the morning sun, a great cry went up. People were waving flags, dressed in a colourful assortment of feast-day clothes. A cluster of people surrounded a man with a board hanging from his shoulders that proclaimed, "Final bets here." The locations were listed along with the odds. I dared not look for fear my expression might give the true destination away. *Portugal,* I kept telling myself. They are sailing to Portugal. The crowd cheered, began singing "Chant du départ."

The moment I'd been dreading came. I took Eugène's hands, examined his face, his soft eyes, the freckles across his nose, thinking: I will always remember him thus, *if...*

"How does one tell a soldier to be careful?" I asked, choking up.

"Maman." Squirming, uncomfortable in front of Louis and all his shipmates.

I kissed him quickly, before he could escape. "I'll be joining you." *Soon.*

Bonaparte met me on the railing. I held my handkerchief to my nose. Everyone was watching us, I knew.

"Stay in Toulon until it's clear that we have made it," he said.

"There's a chance you might turn back?"

He stroked a lock of hair out of my eyes. "If we're forced to."

By the English. "Oh, Bonaparte, I hate this." I pressed my cheek against the rough wool of his jacket—that same frayed jacket he'd worn in Italy.

"If you need anything, ask Joseph," he said, his voice thick. "I've told him to give you forty thousand a year."

"But I will be joining you in a few months." Why this talk of a year?

"You'll go to Plombières for the treatment?"

I nodded. The treatment for infertile women.

"When it's safe, I'll send *La Pomone* for you." He kissed me lightly on the cheek. "And then we'll get on with our project."

"General Bonaparte?"

"One moment, Fauvelet." A gust of wind blew hair in my eyes. I held onto my hat. Bonaparte put his hand on my shoulder. "If I should—"

"No, Bonaparte!" The angels watched over him; I had to believe that.

He stopped, his eyes glistening. I pressed my face into his neck. *Please:* "Take care."

I was escorted to a balcony of the Marine Intendancy building, where a number of women were sitting, officers' wives. They shifted so that I might have the best chair. The paymaster came out, carrying a tray of spyglasses. "Oh," we all exclaimed in unison. And then laughed.

I took a spyglass, searched the decks of *L'Orient.* "I see your husband," I told Madame Marmont, a young bride of only sixteen. But no Eugène, no Bonaparte. "By the helm." I showed her how to adjust the glass, so that the focus might be clear.

She put her glass down, blinded by tears. "It's hopeless."

Gunshot! The crowd on the shore began singing *La Marseillaise,* and we all began to sing along. I pressed my glass to my eyes. Finally I spotted Bonaparte in a cluster of men at the helm. I recognized him by his hat. My heart surged with pride to see him. I searched the faces for Louis and Eugène.

"I put my money on Sicily," one of the women said.

"I'm sure it's Africa," Madame Marmont said. "Else why would they take so much water?"

"Even I don't know," I lied.

As the ships weighed anchor, the cannons in the fort were fired and a military band on the shore broke into a brassy hymn. The warships and the fort exchanged salutes. The smell of gunpowder filled the air.

"They're raising the sails!" The wind pulled *L'Orient* forward. A cheer went up on the shore.

"Oh," I cried out. For the huge ship had listed sharply.

"Something's wrong." Madame Marmont jumped to her feet.

"It's dragging bottom!"

"It will right itself," I assured them—Madame *Bonaparte* assured them. But inwardly I was trembling.

"It's righting now."

Yes. The huge ship bobbed on the water like a toy. The crowd cheered. Wind filled its gigantic sails, pulled it forward. A lone trumpeter blasted out a note. I waved my soggy handkerchief, but I could no longer see through my tears.

IV

Lobbyist

"... women are politics."
—*Talleyrand*

In which I very nearly die

June 14, 1798—Plombières-les-Bains.
A harrowing voyage, but I'm here at last in the charming mountain spa of Plombières-les-Bains—slate grey houses crammed into a narrow valley as if they had tumbled into a crevice and were too weary to rise. A beautiful setting, cliffs rising to the sky, thick forests all around, the air bracing and clean. But such a small village! (I walked its length in seventeen minutes.) And so much more isolated than I'd expected.

June 15.
I met this morning with Dr. Martinet, the water doctor. He is a short man with a trim build and a businesslike air. He wore thick spectacles and a white canvas coat. His hair, which is thinning, was unpowdered, braided at the back into one very long tail, looped and caught up with a white cord. All along one wall of his study were framed testimonials.

"Letters from happy patients," he said with a sweep of his hand. He had moist lips (as if he had been licking them), and moist eyes too, I noticed, as one might expect in a water doctor. "I like to begin by pointing out that our program enjoys a high rate of success." He closed his eyes when he talked. "It is important that the patient begin with this knowledge, for faith—or rather the obedience that faith makes possible—is essential to its successful completion." He opened his eyes.

I sat forward on my chair. The possibility that there might in fact be a cure encouraged me. I had come with prayers in my heart, but little hope, I confess. "I intend to be a model patient, Dr. Martinet."

He leaned back in his cracked leather chair, his hands gripping a board onto which papers had been clipped. "The program is not for those lacking in courage. It requires some degree of both physical and mental strength to successfully complete. But"—he held up an index finger— "nature rewards those who endure. Now, Madame Bonaparte, if you will begin by telling me your history." He peered at me over his spectacles. His eyebrows are thick, bushy (in contrast to his thinning hair), giving him a somewhat diabolical look.

This is what I told him:

I first conceived at the age of sixteen, after only a few months of marriage, but miscarried. My son, Eugène, was then conceived and brought to term. Less than two years later I conceived a daughter. It was a difficult pregnancy and she was born several weeks early.

"But otherwise normal?"

"I had difficulty producing milk." I cleared my throat. "And then—" Did he need to know that Alexandre and I had separated? "Years later my husband died . . . and two years after his death I married General Bonaparte. That was just over two years ago."

"And you have conceived by this union, but miscarried?"

"My doctor thought it might have been a mole."

"Interesting! And then did the flux resume?"

"For a time it was sporadic."

"And the last one was . . . ?"

I wasn't sure exactly. I'd been in Milan. "Over a year ago." Although possibly a year and a half.

"Did you take anything to re-establish the flow?"

I pushed forward the list of herbals (linden blossom, wormwood, coltsfoot) that a doctor in Milan had prescribed, the tea of aloe, gentian root and jalappa. "I also consulted a midwife, who gave me uterus powder." I declined to tell him about the Gypsy I'd gone to in Italy—the one with a well-picked savin bush in her vegetable garden—and the rue tea Mimi had persuaded me to try.*

"But no results?"

"The powder made me ill."

"And your relationship with the General is . . . ?" He licked his upper lip.

I nodded, flushed.

Dr. Martinet tapped his pencil on the desk. "Madame Bonaparte, during the Terror you were held, were you not?"

Imprisoned, he meant. "Yes, I was in the Carmes for four months."

The doctor leaned forward, resting his elbows on the desk. "I must tell you, I have had a significant number of patients who were likewise 'held' during the Terror—women who likewise seem to be suffering from an inexplicable infertility."

I felt a tightening in my chest. "It's true that the flux became unpredictable during that time."

"The effect of shock on the female constitution is proven to be disruptive. If nourishment is lacking, the air oppressive, exercise restricted—any one of these factors is known to affect a woman's capacity to be that which Nature intended her to be, a mother."

"Are you saying that the cessation of my periodic sickness may have been caused by my being in prison?"

"I am suggesting that it may be a very strong possibility. According to my observations, a number of women who have been detained in this way have suffered a cessation of the flow and have plunged, regardless of age, into a condition curiously resembling that of a woman long past the age of reproduction. They have difficulty sleeping, experience an overwhelming anxiety, melancholia—insanity in some cases. And, needless to say, all of them are barren."

"Dr. Martinet, do you mean *menopause?*"

---

* All of these were popular abortive measures. Uterus powder is likely ergot, a black, hard fungus that grows on stalks of rye, an abortive widely used for "bringing on the flowers." Powder made from the leaves of a savin bush, which was often to be seen in the garden of a village midwife, was commonly used. Tea made from rue was considered just as powerful and more reliable than savin, however.

From a book Dr. Martinet loaned me:

First, one grows stout at the back of the neck, where two prominences form at the lowest cervical vertebrae.

The breasts become flat and hard, less spongy.

The legs and arms dry up, resembling those of a man.

The abdomen enlarges to the extent that the woman may appear to be pregnant.

A beard often manifests itself.

I am at the desk in my sparely furnished room overlooking the main street of Plombières. It is warm. I've opened the double doors wide onto the balcony. I can hear the sounds of horses, carriages, people talking, walking. Somewhere, someone is playing a violin beautifully.

I am shaken, I confess, by my conversation with Dr. Martinet. It had never occurred to me that I might be past the age of fertility. I think of old women, stooped and withered, whiskered and dour, and despair overwhelms me.

June 16.

This afternoon I experienced the showers—"the torture chamber" the women here call it. Now I know why.

In an outer chamber I was asked by an attendant to remove my clothes—all of them. In this state of Eve I went into a small steam-filled room occupied by another woman standing in front of a drawn curtain of white canvas.

I was alarmed to hear a man say, "Madame Bonaparte." The voice was coming from behind the curtain. "This is Dr. Martinet speaking. Do not be alarmed; your privacy will be respected. Are you ready?"

The steam was already so thick I felt I might suffocate for want of air. The attendant, a thin woman with a massive nose, was fiddling with a hose and a series of valves. In front of her was a pit, into which she aimed a powerful flow of steaming water. "Get on the mark," she said, holding the pulsating hose to one side. I stood on a faded green circle in the middle of the pit. "Turn around."

"My assistant will aim the flow of the water on the base of the neck." Dr. Martinet's voice seemed ghostly, detached. "She will proceed slowly down the spine. The sensation may be uncomfortable, but be assured that in spite of the stinging sensation, you are not, in fact, being burned. Support bars are provided in case you require support."

I clasped hold of the bars.

"The nape of the neck is the centre of your being, the centre of vitality. The nurse will begin the descent."

The stream of boiling water began to burn its way slowly down my spine. *Uncomfortable!* I would kill him, I vowed, but not quickly. Quickly would be too kind.

At the end of this torture I was so weak that the attendant had to help me into the accompanying room, where I was laid out on a bed and left to sweat in great quantities. A cure, I am told. If I survive.

---

2 Prairial, Luxembourg Palace
My friend,

Paris is seething yet again. Last year we were attacked from the right; this year it's from the left. As feared, the elections resulted in a number of radical Revolutionaries taking seats in the legislature, all of them united in one cause: to bring down the Directors. The committee we set up to review the election results disqualified one in four. You can imagine the reaction.

Tallien, unfortunately, was one of those disqualified, and there is nothing I can do to reverse the decision. Thérèse has appealed to me to get him a position with Bonaparte in Egypt. Frankly, I think she just wants him out of the country.

Père Barras

June 4, Paris
Honoured sister,

As manager of the Bonaparte Family Trust,* I have been instructed by my

---

* *The Trust would be made up almost in its entirety of the estimated eight million francs Bonaparte is thought to have brought back from Italy.*

younger brother to provide you with three thousand francs on the first of each month. I have forwarded a bank note to Citoyen Emmery, your banker. I advise you to manage it responsibly.

In answer to your query, the cost of a cure at Plombières is not the responsibility of the Bonaparte Family Trust. A wife's lack of fecundity is a problem to be borne by the wife. The estate of the husband's family should not be encumbered.

Familial regards, Joseph Bonaparte

Rue de Thrévenot, Paris
Dear Rose,

Émilie is now married; I dissolved in tears. You were missed—our little party seemed sadly lacking without you. The bride looked lovely in the dress you had made for her, although mute, which I attributed to a virginal apprehension. But later, on discovering the bride and Hortense in the powder room in tears, I learned that there is more to the story. The bride had apparently confessed to your daughter that she loved another.

I lectured the girls on duty, and spilled milk, and how fate had intended Émilie to marry Lieutenant Lavalette since that is how it turned out—then I left to look after my guests. Eventually the girls appeared, Émilie red-faced and mournful. The groom—a dear man, if a bit of a simpleton—was fortunately oblivious to his young wife's sorrow.

I warned you about allowing the girls to read romantic novels. Now you see the result.

Remember your prayers,
Your godmother, Aunt Désirée

Note—I read in the Publiciste *that the fleet is headed for Spain. And I thought they were going to Africa! I'm relieved, I confess. At least in Spain Eugène can go to church.*

And another—Madame Campan asked me to remind you about Hortense's and Émilie's tuition. *

---

* It wasn't unusual for a young married woman to go to a boarding school when her husband was away.

Chère Maman,

I have a terrible confession to make. Émilie is unhappy and it is all my fault. It began in the early spring. Louis Bonaparte had taken to visiting our school, and I told Émilie it was because he fancied her. But the truth, the terrible truth, was that I feared he fancied me and I didn't want anyone to guess! And so then she fell in love with him! And because of that, poor Louis had to go on the crusade and poor Émilie is miserably married. Oh, my dear Maman, I want to die for shame.

Your daughter, Hortense

[Undated]

I don't know what to make of Hortense's letter. It dismays me to think that Émilie is unhappy, but at the same time I confess I'm charmed by the admission that Louis may fancy my daughter—my daughter who is so terrified of boys! How am I ever to marry her?

Corsica

Honoured sister,

This letter is to inform you that my husband is available to take over the command of the fort in Marseille. Please inform Director Barras that General Bonaparte's brother-in-law is the only suitable candidate for the post. We will move to Marseille in July.

Elisa Bonaparte Bacchiocchi

[Undated]

After posting my letters, I took a long walk up the mountain to a little chapel perched at the top of a steep hill, a charming stone structure overlooking the valley. I had to pry open the door. It was musty and damp inside. The silence was heavy, comforting. I sat for a time thus, alone with my thoughts. On impulse, I knelt.

So many prayers tumbled out of my heart! I prayed for the safety of the fleet, for Bonaparte and the boys. I prayed that Émilie would come to love her husband and that my daughter's heart would calm. I prayed for the health of Aunt Désirée and the old Marquis, and for the success of my treatment here. I prayed that the Bodin Company would prosper and that I would soon be able to pay off my debts and provide for my children's future. But above all, I prayed for patience in dealing with Bonaparte's family.

June 18.
A day at the baths—huge, steaming pools dotted with heads, women in bright scarves. The cavernous chamber echoed the sounds of laughter, whispered gossip. Shoulders immersed, toes emerging, a knee, two. Floating languorously, a woman laughs, another blows bubbles. A dream world, this.

[Undated]
I've had an accident.* Hortense is with me now, thank God. Great pain, despair.

June 23, Rue de Thrévenot, Paris
Dear Rose,
    To think that you almost died! I am enclosing an ounce of licorice and

---

* *On June 20, Josephine and three acquaintances were on her balcony when it collapsed. Josephine's injuries were critical. She was immediately wrapped in the skin of a newly slaughtered lamb. For a time it was not known whether she would live, and Hortense was sent for. Josephine's treatment, which was published in a medical journal, consisted of a punishing regime of enemas and douches.*
    Dr. Martinet's initial report stated: "Citoyenne Bonaparte was the most seriously injured of the group. She was given a drink of infusion of arnica to stop the bleeding and an enema, which she evacuated, urinating as well. She was immediately put in a warm bath, after which leeches were applied to the most severely bruised parts of her body, as well as to her haemorrhoids, which were swollen. Warm topical remedies and emollients were put on her bruises (apples cooked in water had a good effect). This was followed by compresses soaked in camphor."

coriander seeds your girl could make up into an excellent purge. Scrape the licorice and slice it thin, bruise the seeds and put these both in a pint of water and boil it a little. Strain this water into an ounce of senna and let it sit for six hours. Strain from the senna and drink it while fasting.

Remember your prayers, now more than ever.

Your godmother, Aunt Désirée

Note—My neighbour informed me that the fleet is headed to Spain. She read it in the Messager des Relations Extérieures. But an article in the Postillon de Calais said your husband intended to seize the island of Malta. Isn't that in the other direction?

June 23, La Chaumière
Darling,

The Glories wept to hear of your terrible fall. It's shocking to think that such a thing could happen at a health spa. Barras informs me that the doctor insists you will recover. I'm sending a parcel of remedies. I was comforted to learn that Hortense is with you.

Your loving friend, Thérèse

June 24, Luxembourg Palace
Chère amie,

Dr. Martinet assures me you are out of danger. You must be his only patient; the memos he sends would take hours to prepare, not to mention the reports he has been publishing in a medical journal in which he describes in fulsome detail each and every enema he administers. (Are you aware of this?)

I wrote to General Brune* as you requested. I will let you know as soon as I hear. The last thing you need to worry about right now is the fate of the Bodin Company. Don't worry, my dear, "Papa will fix it."

Père Barras

* The command of the Army of Italy passed from Napoleon to General Berthier, Napoleon's former chief of staff, and then to General Brune. Berthier had favoured the Bodin Company (it is possible he was in on the financial rewards), but General Brune did not and was threatening to cancel the contract.

July 8.
It has been eighteen days now. My arms, although still horribly bruised and painful to move, are out of the bandages. At least I am able to feed myself again, and to write, although my script is feeble, like that of an old woman. I am both comforted and plagued by a constant stream of well-wishers.

I can remember very little of the actual fall. The first thing I recall is lying on the street with men standing over me, everything dreamlike. And then the sharp pain of being turned—I'm told I cried out horribly—and then the sickening comfort of something warm and moist on my skin, the woollish smell of blood (for a quick-witted servant had slaughtered a lamb and wrapped me in its still-warm hide). Then the treatments began—the enemas and douches, the baths, the leeches, the bleeding and the infusions. I am determined to get better if only to end the "cure"!

Hortense is doting and sweet (but bored, I fear). "I love you," I told her this morning, as she wheeled me around in my invalid chair. "Whatever happens to me, I don't want to be a burden to you."

She stooped down under my sunshade and kissed me on the cheek. "You *will* walk again, Maman."

This tenderness between us almost makes my suffering worthwhile.

July 10.
Again, terrible pain—just when I thought I was getting better. I am overcome with a feeling of hopelessness. It has been twenty days and I still can't stand.

9 Messidor, Luxembourg Palace
Chère amie,
I want you to be the first to know. Bonaparte has dodged Nelson's ships and taken Malta—a stroke of incredible good fortune.

Père Barras

July 16.
I walked for three minutes. Shooting pain.

22 Messidor, Luxembourg Palace
Chère amie,

    No doubt you are recovering, judging from the constant stream of petitioners you have been sending my way. Regarding your requests, please note that I have:

    1. Found employment for the nephew of the former Abbess of the Convent of Panthémont.

    2. Seen to it that Bonaparte's doctor's wife, Citoyenne Yvan, was sent her bonus. (She asked me to tell you that Pugdog is content and has even grown plump.)

    3. Named Citoyen Félix Bacchiocchi, the General's esteemed (sic) brother-in-law, commander of Fort Saint-Nicolas in Marseille. I pray to God that the citizens of that town are never in need of his protection.

    4. Succeeded (finally—it wasn't easy) in getting the names of three of the five citizens you requested erased from the List.

    5. And last, but certainly not least, regarding that spirited dancer who was run out of Milan for her so-called convictions (for coquetting with French soldiers is more to the point), I've succeeded in finding a placement for her with the Opéra-Comique. (She has offered to "repay" me. If only all acts of mercy were so rewarding.)

    But my question to you, my friend, is this—how do all these strange and rather pathetic characters find their way to you? Do take care, chérie. Your last letter rather alarmed me.

Père Barras

July 17, Paris
Honoured sister:

    I am aware that forty thousand per annum translates into three thousand three hundred and thirty-three francs a month. One must, however, take the cost of administration into account.

    I am returning to Dr. Martinet the bills submitted for your treatment since your fall. I have informed him that all expenses incurred in the course of a cure of infertility, however unexpected and unusual, are your responsibility. The Bonaparte Family Trust cannot be held accountable.

Familial regards, Joseph Bonaparte

July 18, La Chaumière
Darling,

You would have loved to see the parade here yesterday: eighty wagons loaded with the finest art of Italy were carted with great éclat to the Louvre. Over each enormous case there was a banner proclaiming the contents— Raphael, Titian, Domenichino, Guerchino. It was enough to make even the most uncultured among us swoon. But the triumph, of course, were the four horses of Saint Mark from Venice.

Naturally, the Directors neglected to give your husband the credit for bringing all this wonderful loot to Paris. Oh, forgive me, I forget myself—for "liberating works of genius." In Paris, at least, the statue of Apollo may be viewed without his silly fig leaf. If that isn't liberation, what is?

Your loving friend, Thérèse

August 4, Luxembourg Palace
Chère amie,

Victories in Egypt! One at El-Ramanyeh, another at Chebreis and then, the coup de grâce, a decisive victory over the Mamelouks near Cairo. "The Battle of the Pyramids" we have named it.

I know as heartening as this news is that you will be disappointed over the lack of letters from that land. Unfortunately, the English are high-jacking whatever ships Bonaparte sends in our direction. It has a certain charm, this relationship. We capture their ships, read their mail; they capture our ships, read ours. If only their letters were more interesting.

Regarding more mundane matters, you will be amused to know that General Brune came all the way back to Paris from Milan just to complain about the chicanery of certain of our government officials there, including the "shameless plundering" of your charming sister-in-law Pauline Bonaparte *and her accomplice in greed, her husband General Victor Leclerc.*

However, before General Brune returned to Milan (stomped back, I should say), I managed to have "a word" with him about the Bodin Company contract. The merest hint of a payback put him in an agreeable disposition. Ah, but these virtuous Republicans are the easiest to bribe.

Père Barras

Note—Forgive me, my dear, but I simply cannot and will not promote Citoyen Lahorie. As a director of this Republic, I must, from time to time, act responsibly. I understand that he was a friend of your first husband and that therefore you wish to help the man, but frankly, he's an idiot. *

August 9.
I walked for ten minutes. I am determined to join Bonaparte in Egypt.

---

* *Lahorie blamed Josephine for Barras's rejection. Consequently, in 1812, he joined a conspiracy to overthrow Napoleon and was shot for treason.*

In which victories are followed by defeat

September 16, 1798—Paris.

I arrived home to devastating news. Buried in a massive stack of calling cards, parcels, letters of congratulation and the usual demands from bill collectors, there was a note from Barras: *Come see me as soon as you arrive. Urgent.*

I put my hat back on. "What is it, Maman?" Hortense has become sensitive to my moods.

"Director Barras wishes to see me." No doubt it had to do with news from the East regarding Bonaparte. Or perhaps Eugène! I didn't like the word *urgent.*

It took some time to get to the palace—the streets were congested, and everywhere there were signs of festivity, preparations for the Republican Year VII celebrations. On Rue Honoré, an enormous banner depicting Bonaparte with palm trees and pyramids in the background had been hung from the bell tower of a church.

"Madame Bonaparte!" Barras's elderly valet bounded to his feet. "Director Barras has been most anxious for your arrival." Bruno pulled the big oak doors open.

Barras was playing the violin when I entered. He stopped abruptly when he saw me, his gold-rimmed lorgnon falling, swinging on a pink cord, his eyes tender and sad. "I'm so relieved to see you. You've survived the journey? You look thin." His voice sweet, bell-like.

I embraced him, inhaling his familiar scent, spirit of ambergris. How was I? Fine, fine, I lied. In fact, the journey had been painful, but I didn't want to list my aches and pains. "I received your note." Gingerly, I took a seat, for my hip was inflamed after two days in a jolting carriage. "I confess I'm anxious."

"Of course! Of course!" Barras took the chair near mine, shifted uncomfortably. "We've had . . . news," he said, clearing his throat, his Adam's apple bobbing.

"Paul, please tell me—are they all right?" Nothing could be worse than what I imagined.

"Bonaparte, you mean?" Crossing his legs at the ankle.

"Yes—and the boys." Eugène, Louis.

"Of course, yes. They're fine, I assure you, but there has been . . . How should I put it? There's been a bit of a setback. But I assure you, yes, Bonaparte and the boys are safe," he repeated, raising his left hand as if making a vow, "as are most of the men."

Most? I tilted my head to one side, my dangling earrings tinkling.

"But the fleet is . . . sunk," he said in a whisper.

Sunk? I listened in a daze as Barras explained. After Admiral Brueys anchored the fleet at Aboukir, the English swooped down and destroyed all but four of our ships. The commander of the *Timoléon* set his ship on fire rather than surrender. He died, standing on the deck. Admiral Brueys was cut in two standing at the helm of *L'Orient*. The explosion of the gunpowder in the hold could be heard in Alexandria, twenty-five miles away. The battle went on for three days, the bloodiest ever fought at sea. And yet the English did not lose a single ship.

I put my fist to my lips, overwhelmed by the enormity of the loss. The greatest fleet in history since the Crusades—*gone?* Over three thousand men killed or wounded. All the supplies—including the gold needed to buy provisions—lost.

Barras refilled his glass, spilling spirits onto the carpet. "And, of course, the unfortunate thing is that now the troops are . . ." He cleared his throat again. "Stranded."

My heart began to pound. "But surely we'll rescue them," I said, twisting my handkerchief.

"I can't see how! The English are now in control of the sea. It's doubtful that we'll even be able to get a mail boat through."

A feeling of panic came over me. I had to get home, before I was over-come.

"You understand, we're keeping this confidential," he went on.

"But Paul, an entire fleet, how can you—?"

"The exhibition opens tomorrow! We've planned the most spectacular New Year fête imaginable, to celebrate Bonaparte's victories. And now *this*. The people laugh at us as it is. I'm already accused of every vice, of committing every crime, every petty thievery. To hear people talk, I'm a very busy man. Have you heard the latest epigram? 'If only the Republic could be disem*barras*sed.' Charming, don't you think? And what about that poster of a lance, a lettuce leaf and a rat? It's everywhere; you'll see it. I finally figured it out: *the seventh year will kill them.** And, you know, I'm starting to think maybe they're—"

"Paul, please, tell me. What does this mean?"

Barras's glass missed the fireplace and shattered against the wall. Toto jumped up, cowering. "What it means is that the *goddamned* English have downed the entire French fleet." He sank back into his chair, his hands over his eyes. "Grand Dieu, I'm going mad."

September 17.

Hortense was hopping up and down with excitement. "There are ribbons and bouquets on all the posts."

"And colourful silk banners fluttering in the breeze," Émilie (Madame *Lavalette* now) said.

"That's wonderful," I said, trying to put some enthusiasm in my voice.

Hortense became concerned. "We *are* going to the exhibition, Maman—aren't we?"

It was easier than I thought it would be, accepting congratulations on behalf of my husband's victories, smiling, bowing, nodding—not letting on. I watched as if from a distance the people dancing, singing, stagger-ing in the glow of their country's glory, in the illusion of victory. The

---

* *Lancette (lance), laitue (lettuce), rat: a play on the words* l'an sept les tuera.

realization of defeat would come soon enough. Perhaps it is always thus. Perhaps all victories are false, defeat the inevitable reality.

Or perhaps, more truly, I too did not want to think about what I knew to be true, that the greatest of victories had been followed by the greatest of defeats.

I felt a gentle touch on my shoulder. Barras, looking ill—from last night's tippling, no doubt. "How are you managing?" he asked, his soft voice very nearly drowned out by all the commotion. He was wearing the ceremonial robe of a director, an enormous crimson cashmere cape and a velvet toque with a tricolour plume.

"Not too bad," I said, keeping an eye on Hortense, Caroline, Émilie and Jérôme, who were over by a lemonade vendor. An enclave of Bonapartes sat in a roped-off cluster directly in front of the stage. "It's not as hard as I thought it would be." During the day, that is. During the night it was another matter. "Do *they* know?" I tilted my head in the direction of the Bonapartes—Joseph and his wife Julie, Lucien (back from Corsica), Pauline and Victor Leclerc (recently arrived from Milan). All of them were curiously sullen in the midst of so much festivity.

"Certainly not. That hot-headed Lucien would leak it to the *Moniteur* in a minute, along with accusations that it is the fault of the Directors— my fault, to be specific. Did you know that he's been made Secretary of the Five Hundred?"

"But he was only elected a deputy three months ago."

"He's become quite popular on the strength of his rather vocal opposition to the Directors—on the strength of his opposition to *me*, I should say. And as for that smiling jackal of a man, that mild-mannered—" He raised one bushy eyebrow. "I wouldn't walk a dark alley with Joseph Bonaparte, let's put it that way."

"But why do they all look so glum?"

Barras snorted. "They don't like their seats, they should be up on the stage, the posters should have their faces on them, there should be more posters, the posters aren't big enough." He threw up his hands. "In short, it's not enough. It's never enough for a Bonaparte, apparently. Your husband excepted, of course."

"Of course," I echoed—not paying attention, I confess. An attractive young woman had stooped to exchange a word with Joseph. There was something familiar about her.

"Ready, Director Barras?" It was Director Neufchâteau, the newest member of the council of five Directors, and as Minister of the Interior the mastermind behind the exhibition. I wanted an opportunity to thank him personally for responding to my request that funding to the Vosges municipalities be increased. As well, I had a number of other requests to make. But most important, Bonaparte was going to be in need of allies—especially now.

I gave Director Neufchâteau my hand. "A brilliant display, Director, quite inspiring. I congratulate you." The woman talking to Joseph stood, turned—Lisette! She headed toward a door, the gems in her headdress glittering in the torchlight. Fouché had warned me she'd been consorting with the Bonapartes. Why had she been talking with Joseph? I wondered with apprehension, recalling her words: *You will be sorry!*

The military band began to warm up. I felt a stir in the crowd, craning heads. "Ah, there she is," Barras said, speaking in the Provençal dialect, "our lovely Amazon." I looked toward the entry. It was Thérèse, in shimmering silver and mauve, towering above the crowd. She was followed at a distance by her footman and nanny, carrying Thermidor in petticoats. Thérèse caught my eye, made a look of surprise, waved wildly.

Director Neufchâteau put his gloved hand on Barras's shoulder. "We're being summoned, Director," he said. The two men headed toward the stage.

"I didn't even know you were back," Thérèse exclaimed, folding me in her arms.

I took her hand, feeling suddenly, unaccountably, choked up. It was so good to see her.

Thérèse held me at arm's length. "And how *are* you?"

"I'm going to be all right." I think. "I'm walking, that's the important thing."

"And what do you make of all this?" Thérèse asked before I could tell her about Lisette. "Everyone's gone crazy over your husband. Maybe it's true, what he says—maybe you *are* his Lady of Luck."

I turned away. It was impossible to lie to Thérèse. Fortunately, the nanny appeared with Thermidor, her thumb in her mouth, her big eyes transfixed. "This little one is sleepy," Thérèse said.

"I'm not little," Thermidor said, taking her thumb out of her mouth. "I'm—"

"Three! I know." I took her in my arms. "My, you *are* a big girl now." She smelled of soap. I pressed her silken cheek to mine.

"You will make a wonderful grandmother," Thérèse said.

She hadn't said, *a wonderful mother.*

September 19.

A sleepless night. One year ago Lazare died, yet even still he is often in my thoughts. I am no Lady of Luck. Every man I have ever loved has fallen. I am ill at the thought that harm might come to Bonaparte and to Eugène. I have mourned too many loved ones. I plead with my guardian angels: fly, fly! Go to them. Keep them from harm.

September 21.

Ah, my dear Glories . . .

"Darling, we're so *relieved* to see you. What have you done with your hair?"

"I love that gown. Turn, turn, let me see."

"Oh, *that's* different, I like the way the sash comes up over the shoulders."

"All of Paris has been singing your husband's praise."

"The French Caesar, my cook calls him."

"Everyone."

"Hail, Caesar!" Fortunée Hamelin was wearing a blue wig. She'd dyed one of Thérèse's blonde ones. "My, but this champagne is excellent," she said, shrugging her shoulders to lower her bodice. "Better get your girl to bring up a few more bottles, *Josephine.* There, you see? I remembered."

"Is it true? Citoyenne Marmont told me that you're going to Egypt with her, that the General is sending *La Pomone* back from Malta just to fetch you."

"That's so romantic. I'd love to have a ship sent for me."

"But are you well enough to travel, darling? I noticed you walking with a bit of a limp."

"We read *all* about your treatment in that medical journal—how ghastly."

"It's a wonder you survived the cure."

"All those enemas—mon Dieu." The bright silk flowers piled high onto the crown of Madame de Crény's ruffled bonnet made her seem even shorter than she was.

"That's one thing I simply can't abide."

"Enemas? Some women actually like them." Minerva giggled.

"And some *men* like giving them."

"Parbleu!" Fortunée Hamelin guffawed.

"It's true. Madame Mercier constantly complains that her husband wants to physic her too much."

"Why, that scamp."

"*Not* that I want to change the subject, *Josephine*, but the big house down the road, the one at the corner of Rue du Mont Blanc—is that the one your sister-in-law and her husband bought?"

"The Leclercs?" I nodded, playing a card. On their return from Milan, Pauline and Victor had purchased (with cash, it was rumoured) the property three houses down. Every time I passed, I saw Pauline's face at a window. My personal spy, I was coming to think of her.

"I think it's nice to have family close by," Madame de Crény said.

Thérèse caught my eye. "Not always," I confessed.

"Oh?" They looked at me expectantly.

"You know you can always trust a Glory," Minerva said, sensing my hesitation.

And then I broke down, told all: how Joseph had vowed to break up my marriage; how Bonaparte's mother called me "the old woman" (and worse!); how Pauline spied on me; how I'd finally come to understand that to Corsicans a wife was nothing, that it was the husband's family that truly mattered, and that my husband's love for me and my children had provoked a profoundly jealous hatred in them.

"Mon Dieu, I've heard about vendettas, but . . . I had no idea," Madame de Crény exclaimed, swinging her feet.

"I'm rather surprised by the fuss over your business dealings. I thought your husband's uncle was an army supplier."

Fesch? I nodded. As well as Joseph. *And* Lucien.

"And not Pauline and Victor Leclerc?"

I rolled my eyes, well, yes . . . them too.

"Is it true they were *recalled* from Milan?"

"For filling their pockets, I heard."

"I heard they bought an estate in Italy."

"*And* are looking to buy a property up near Senlis."

"I thought it was the other brother who was looking for a property near Senlis. What's his name? Lucien. The young one with the thick spectacles."

"But didn't he just buy that big town house on Grand-Rue Vert?"

"On a deputy's salary?"

Fortunée Hamelin whistled. "I *love* this champagne."

"Did you hear about Fortunée's adventure, Josephine?"

"She walked down the Champs-Élysées—*naked* to her waist."

"They dared me." Fortunée Hamelin looked smug.

"She practically started a riot."

"I still don't understand why," Fortunée said. "It's not as if people haven't seen a woman before."

"You should have read all the articles in the journals."

"Speaking of journals." Minerva put down her cards. "Did any of you read that article in *La Révélateur*? Something about the Directors having known for a week about the defeat of our fleet?"

"*What* defeat?"

"That's what I wanted to know."

They turned to me. Tears filled my eyes. Please, no, I didn't want to be the one to tell them.

November 4.

Rumours that Alexandria has been burned, that Bonaparte is in retreat.

November 16.
Rumours that Bonaparte's army is faltering, that he's surrounded.

December 12.
My manservant returned from the market in tears. "General Bonaparte has been killed in Cairo!"

Immediately, I set out for the palace to see Barras. I had resolved not to read the journals, much less to believe them, but this account was impossible to ignore—I *had* to know.

The journey to the palace was a slow one. There were signs of disturbance, more so as I neared the market. Several times my carriage was recognized. One man doffed his hat as if for a funeral procession. I sat back, out of view.

What if Bonaparte *had* been killed?

I burst into tears the moment I saw Barras—in spite of the presence of his guests—for I saw the answer in his eyes. My knees gave way.

As if from a distance I could hear Barras giving out orders for cold cloths and salts. He felt my pulse, pulled back my eyelids. "Please," I said, struggling to sit up. I felt bile in my throat. A circle of faces was looking down on me, men's faces.

"Help me get her onto the bed in the next room," I heard Barras say. He pulled me up. My feet were comically disobedient, my legs like those of a rag doll. Inexplicably, I began to giggle.

"She'll be all right in a moment," Barras said. "She's stronger than she looks."

I was laid out on the bed, my ties loosened, a comforter pulled over me.

I closed my eyes, turned my head. "Tell me," I said. "Tell me what you know."

His name meant "Desert Lion," he'd told his men.

"I didn't know that," I said. Bonaparte had dreamt of riding an elephant, of wearing a turban. "Go on."

Soldiers! he'd called out. *From these pyramids, forty centuries of history look down upon you!*

"That's beautiful. He had a way of putting things."

He'd entered Cairo with the Koran in one hand, Thomas Paine's *The Rights of Man* in the other. Triumphant.

"He had a great sense of theatre," I said, closing my eyes, imagining his feeling of exultation at such a moment, what it must have been like for him, his soul infused with the spirit of destiny, walking in the footsteps of Alexandre the Great, of Caesar.

He believed himself chosen. I opened my eyes. "Barras, he can't be dead."

[Undated]

Every day, rumours—Bonaparte lives, Bonaparte has perished. I grieve, I rejoice, I grieve again. I begin each day with a prayer, and a conviction that Bonaparte will survive, that he will endure, that he will overcome— but by nightfall, doubt and fear have come into my heart like evil demons.

I have been reading through the letters Bonaparte sent me when we first were married. I read his burning words of love and I want to weep. I have not loved him as I should, have not given him my heart. There are so many things I want to tell him—and now I fear it may be too late.

[Undated]

People watch me for clues. "She's not smiling. He must be dead," I overheard a market woman say.

December 23.

I've not been out for two weeks, unable to face the looks of mourning, of exultation. Everywhere I go, I feel eyes.

January 1, 1799, New Year's Day.

The bottle of ink in my escritoire was empty. I went upstairs. There were writing supplies in the guest room.

It took an effort to push open the door. I stood for a moment, waited for something to shape itself in the dark. It was light out still, yet with the drapes drawn, no light penetrated. I pulled back the curtains, opened the windows.

What was to become of him? I thought. And what of my son?

A breeze swept into the room, fluttering papers to the floor. The clock under the glass bell struck. Bonaparte had wanted the room made into a second study—but there had been no time, in the end, to even discuss such matters. A desk, I recalled, shelves, and a desk in the corner for his secretary.

Yes, I thought, it will be done. I will get to work now, call in the architects, the furnishers, the drapers—prepare for his return. For he *will* return.

In which I have enemies everywhere

January 3, 1799.

"It's the damned ague again," Barras said from under a mountain of comforters. "A family tradition." His face, surrounded by cambric, looked like an old woman's.

I dislodged Toto from the little chair beside Barras's massive bed, took a seat. It alarmed me to see Barras so weakened.

"It comes, it goes. Don't look so worried." He took a sip of the quinine water his chambermaid brought for him, then spat it out. "You could at least put some brandy in it." She slammed the door behind her.

"My father swore by rum," I said. The room smelled unpleasantly of parrot.

"And *he's* dead." Barras thumped the side of the mattress. Toto jumped up beside him, sniffed around before curling up beside his master.

"So tell me, is there news?" I always felt anxious when summoned.

"I just want you to be assured that all these rumours of Bonaparte's defeat are false. We've had a report that he has assembled an army of one hundred thousand and is going to head into Syria."

"That's wonderful news!" I said, wondering where Syria was. I would look it up on my map when I got home.

"In England they shot cannon from the Tower of London, thinking that he'd been killed. There's even a play running in London called *Death of Bonaparte*, I'm told. Now they're going to have to shoot cannon to announce his resurrection." He laughed. "But there was something in this morning's *London Morning Chronicle* I thought I should show you."

"The English paper?"

He nodded, fishing around in a stack of journals on his bedside table. "My secretary's working on a translation right now. Where are my spectacles? Damn, I can't find anything any more."

"It concerns Bonaparte?" I found his spectacles on the side table and handed them to him. Whenever there was news, I assumed it would be bad.

"I wish I could read English." Barras squinted at the journal, holding it at arm's length. "I wish I could *see.*"

"The name Beauharnais is in there," I said, looking over his shoulder. Something about Eugène?

"Ah, there's Botot."

"You're not going to like it," Barras's secretary warned us, a paper in his hand. He read out loud, *"The publication of the letters confidential to be written—"*

"*To be written?* Or *written?*"

"Written. Excuse me. Yes . . . *of the letters confidential* written *by Bonaparte and his men to friends and family in France (letters by our navy intercepted) does a little honour to the morality of our cabinet. Such scandal cannot serve to make good our national to ennoble—"*

"Wait a minute, slow down, Botot. That doesn't make any sense."

"Maybe it's my translation."*

"Go on." I sat forward on my chair. Something about publishing letters?

"One of these letters confiscated is from Bonaparte to his brother, a song on his wife's debauchery—"

My *debauchery?*

Botot shrugged. *"Another, from young Beauharnais—"*

Eugène? "One of the letters is from my son?"

---

* *The article in the* London Morning Chronicle *read: "It is not very creditable ... that the private letters ... which were intercepted, should be published. It derogates from the character of a nation to descend to such gossiping. One of these letters is from Bonaparte to his brother, complaining of the profligacy of his wife; another from young Beauharnais, expressing his hopes that his dear Mama is not so wicked as she is represented! Such are the precious secrets which, to breed mischief in private families, is to be published in French and English."*

"... *the hope expresses that his chère maman is less evil than she was represented.*"

"I don't understand." Evil? The air in the room was close, the fire blazing.

"The English intend to *publish* these letters?" Barras demanded, his teeth chattering. "But that's unethical. There are international agreements that apply."

"Damn the Royalists," the parrot suddenly squawked.

28 Nivôse, Luxembourg Palace
Chère amie,

We've finally obtained copies of the two letters referred to in the London Morning Chronicle. *I don't think it wise to send them to you by courier. I will be in this afternoon, if you would care to come by.*

Père Barras

January 17, late afternoon.

"You'll be comforted to know I intend to have them banned," Barras said, searching through the stacks on his desk.

"Are they that bad?"

"Ah, here's one." He handed it to me. "It's a copy of the letter Bonaparte wrote his brother Joseph. But where's that other one, the one from your son?"

I glanced at the words, *I am undergoing acute domestic distress, for the veil is now entirely rent.*

"The one from Eugène will explain."

Chère Maman,

I have so many things to tell you that I do not know where to begin. For five days Bonaparte has looked very sad, ever since a conversation he had with Junot. From what little I could overhear, it had to do with Captain Charles—that he returned from Italy in your carriage, that he gave you your little dog, even that he is with you now.

You know, Maman, that I do not believe a word of it. I am convinced that all this gossip has been made up by your enemies. I love you no less, no less long to embrace you.

A million kisses, Eugène

"This letter is going to be published in England?" I asked.

"*And* the one from Bonaparte to Joseph, apparently. The bastards—the English are totally immoral. We have an unwritten agreement with them to respect private correspondence. Of course, we'll see what we can do to prevent them from making the letters public. My dear, are you all right?"

I tried to swallow. "I think so." I felt so exposed, my life on display. I felt mortified—but angry, as well. What had I done to be ashamed of? Yes, Captain Charles gave me Pugdog; yes, he accompanied me on the return from Italy; and *yes*, he is a friend and I enjoy his company—and why not? "Paul, you understand, don't you, the captain is just a friend."

"Of course! Is our pretty captain even interested in women? But don't worry about rumours, darling, no one will know." He twirled his thumbs, frowning. "I just can't understand why Junot would go out of his way to upset Bonaparte."

"I think I know why," I whispered, remembering Lisette's words: You will be sorry.

January 24.

The dressmaker arrived at eleven, her three assistants carrying enormous bolts of fabric samples, boxes of laces and ribbons, books of drawings. I selected a particularly lovely creation. "I do not recommend that one," Henriette said. "Your sister-in-law, Madame Leclerc, has one very like it."

"Pauline Leclerc is one of your clients?"

"And such a curious little thing. Every time we have a fitting—quite often, for she requires a new gown every week—she wants only news of you, Madame."

"She asks you questions about *me*?"

"Indeed, Madame. All about you."

January 25, afternoon.

My milliner arrived at three. I showed her the sketch of the gown I had chosen, the fabric samples. "Lola, we've known each other a long time."

"A *very* long time, Madame."

"If I asked you a question, would you tell me the truth?"

"Madame, if I didn't know you better, I would think you had offended me," she said, her eyes bulging out.

"You must forgive me, I am not myself." I wasn't sure how I was going to ask. But I had to know. "Have you made hats for Madame Leclerc?"

"Oh yes, Madame, she has kept my girls quite busy—a new hat each week, sometimes two," she said, a straw form in her hand.

"Does she ever . . . *inquire* of me? I am just curious, that's all."

"She does like to talk, that one." Lola wrapped a length of gauze around the crown of the straw form, fashioning a turban in the manner of the East.

"She *says* things about me?" I asked, looking into the glass, adjusting the plume. The hat didn't suit me.

"Of course, I don't believe a word of it." Lola pulled the hat off me. "If I didn't have my girls to look out for, I would have told her long ago that I wouldn't be making any more hats for her. She's fussy and she's never on time, always keeping me and the girls waiting. And her with *three* lovers."

"Oh?" It was common knowledge that Pauline was having affairs with Generals Moreau, Macdonald and Beurnonville now that her husband had been posted to Lyons.

"And a valet she gets to lift her out of her bath and carry her to her bed. It's not a sin because he's Negro and not really human, *she* says, but still, one can't help but wonder. Really, Madame, she is making a bad name for the General, may God bless him in his trial. And as for you, what she told my girl Doré was that she has seduced all your lovers, one by one, and asked each one who was better, you or she, and what were your—" She flushed, tongue-tied.

"Go on, Lola. I'm finding this amusing."

"Your *tricks* is how she puts it." Lola grinned. Her two front teeth were missing. "You know, Madame—female ways with a man, special things you might do when he's in a heat, things that make him mad for you. I have a few myself. Drives my Lugger crazy—" I liked to think of Lola driving her crippled husband mad with pleasure. "But *then* she says that your lovers say she's just as good, that the only difference is experience. Which I don't believe for even a moment, Madame."

I wasn't sure exactly what Lola didn't believe. "Please inform your girls, Lola, that I have no lovers."

Lola looked at me with an expression of incredulity. "But Madame, even *I* have lovers."

[Undated]
I've received three Bodin Company bank notes, but I sent them all directly to Barras to pay off that debt. Others will have to wait. Joseph Bonaparte has cut me off entirely.

February 1.
The Seine flooded. Poor Thérèse—her lovely home is waist-high in mud. Barras has taken her in—Thérèse, the little girl, the nanny and eleven servants. I suspect he'll find accommodations for them quickly.

February 6.
The Glories met at Thérèse's (beautiful) new house on Rue de Baby-lone—a "gift" from Barras. After admiring the décor, after debating whether to play commerce, casino or loo, after exchanging news of our children and grandchildren, lovers and spouses, we settled down to what has, of late, become our main topic of conversation—gossip about the Bonaparte clan.

"I finally met the hiccupper," Madame de Crény announced.

"Elisa Bonaparte?"

"She introduced herself to me as a *femme savante*."

"She's here in Paris?" I asked, playing a card. "I thought she and her husband were in Marseille." Sadly, their child had recently died, I knew.

"She left her husband in Marseille and is now living in Paris with her brother Lucien."

"I hear she's started a salon."

"I went. The entire time she reclined on a sofa fanning herself." Thérèse flicked her scarf in an imitation of a woman putting on airs. "Pauline Leclerc was there, as well—*alone*, I might add."

"Serves her right. I heard her three lovers discovered each other—"

"—and all agreed to abandon her!"

But the big news was that Joseph had just purchased Mortefontaine, one of the most regal estates in the country.

"I hear he's pouring millions into it—a lake, an orangery, a theatre."

"Where does the money come from?"

"His wife's dowry?"

I shrugged, pulling in my winnings (eleven francs). Julie's dowry of 100,000 francs was substantial, true, but it was not enough to buy and renovate an estate like Mortefontaine. It just didn't add up.

"*Every* gentleman requires a country seat, Joseph told me."

"And every gentlewoman, I should think," Minerva said, nudging me.

"Poor Josephine. She's the only Bonaparte without a country estate."

I rolled my eyes. *Poor* Josephine indeed.

"I thought you and Bonaparte make an offer on a country château?"

I nodded. "We did, for a place on the Saint-Germain road." Malmaison—a property I'd fallen madly in love with. "But the offer was refused. And then Bonaparte left for Egypt." I'd asked a land agent to look into the purchase again, but I'd yet to hear back.

"Now's the time to buy."

"Prices aren't going to go much lower."

February 8—at Aunt Désirée and the Marquis's small but lovely new house in Saint-Germain.
The Marquis is eighty-five today. "I could go at any time," he told me,

making an attempt to snap his fingers. Aunt Désirée had dressed him up in his blue velvet smoking jacket.

I smiled. "I think you will live to one hundred."

"I am content to die now but for one thing."

I tucked the comforter around his legs and moved his invalid chair closer to the fire. I knew what it was, this "one thing." He stilled my hand. "Before I die, I must see François," he said, his little rheumy eyes filling. François, his émigré son.

"Marquis, I've tried, but I—" *Can't*, I started to say, but the words, "I'll keep trying" came out instead.

11 Ventôse—Croissy.
Chère Madame Bonaparte,

This morning, I spent four hours at Malmaison. If you were as wealthy as is commonly believed, I would tell you only of the charm of the estate—but you require an income property and I am happy to report that Malmaison is just that.

The owner suggested 300,000 francs for the grounds (which she claims General Bonaparte offered her last summer) and an additional 25,000 for the furniture. Add to that 15,000 for the agricultural equipment and about 15,000 in taxes would mean that you would have to pay approximately 360,000 francs. If property had not gone down in value, Malmaison would normally sell for 500,000 francs.

The land has been in the care of a steward for the last thirty years. He told me that there are 387 arpents of grain, vines, woods and open meadows. The park, which is excellent, consists of 75 arpents, with 312 arpents additional for renting. Letting these out for only 30 francs brings in over 9,000 francs, which added to the 3,000 income from the park brings the total to 12,000. This should reassure you. This year alone they made 120 barrels of wine selling at 50 francs each. The twenty-five farm people who live on the grounds are entirely self-sufficient.

The property, which has the advantage of being both practical and pleasant, is one of the nicest I've yet seen.

Citoyen Chanorier

March 3.
I've instructed Chanorier to make an offer of 325,000 francs for Malmaison—an excellent value, if I get it.

March 4.
Offer accepted! Now all I have to do is come up with the money.

March 7, Paris
Honoured sister,
  With respect to the purchase of a country property, I refuse to advance any funds from the Bonaparte Family Trust without direct instruction from my brother. Therefore, if you are to proceed, you will have to do so entirely under your own name.

  Familial regards, Joseph Bonaparte

March 9.
Citoyen l'Huillier, the estate steward, has agreed to loan fifteen thousand in exchange for a guarantee on his job.

March 10.
Twenty-two thousand from Ouvrard (thanks to Thérèse, with whom Ouvrard has been "keeping company") but it's still not enough.

March 16.
I just found out that Louis Bonaparte (ill apparently) returned to Paris five days ago with Signora Letizia. Why have they not contacted me? Louis will have news of Bonaparte, of Eugène—I am desperate to talk to him.

March 17, late morning.

I've invited all the Bonapartes to a dinner party in Signora Letizia's honour this coming Décadi. My coachman left a few moments ago to deliver invitations. I'm praying this will work.

Shortly after 4:00.

"If one had disturbing news about a friend's husband, do you think one should tell the friend?" Minerva fanned herself so vigorously the feathers in her hat fluttered.

"It would depend on the nature of the news, I would think," Madame de Crény said, playing a card.

"Friendship requires honesty, however painful," Thérèse said.

"Do you have *news* regarding a friend's husband?" I asked Minerva, picking up my cards.

"Oh, no."

We played in uncomfortable silence. When the clocks chimed four, I put down my cards. "Minerva, please . . ."

"It's false. Just a rumour."

"Told to you by . . . ?"

She winced. "Your sister-in-law, Pauline Leclerc."

"Oh?" I slapped down a card. "You might as well tell me. I'm bound to hear it eventually, and I'd rather hear it from friends."

"It's just the usual sort of rumour, you know, that the General has taken a mistress, that kind of thing."

The General: my *husband.* I looked around the table. There was more to it, I knew. "And?"

"And the thing is . . ." Madame de Crény stammered.

"He's apparently told her he will *marry* her . . ."

". . . if she gets pregnant."

I threw down my cards.

March 19.

The Bonapartes send their regrets—each and every one.

March 24, Easter.

I've been three days abed. "Melancholy," the doctor said, insisting that I
be bled twice a day from the foot.

April 9.

This afternoon, shortly after the midday meal, Mimi announced a caller.
"Captain Charles?" Returned from Milan!

But before I could even put down my embroidery hoop, he'd come
into the room, twirling like a dancer. "Buon giorno, Signora." He curtsied, holding out his wide Venetian trousers as if he were wearing a skirt.

"If you could bring us some port, Mimi," I said, laughing, "and something to eat. Are you hungry, Captain?" I removed my embroidery basket
from a chair.

"As a bear. You have a new maid?"

"Lisette is no longer with me, Captain."

"Oh!" He gave me a sly smile. "Might it have something to do with
Colonel Junot?"

"That was part of it," I said, flushing angrily. Had everyone known
but me?

"Ah, there's my monster!" Pugdog appeared at the door. "Have we
been good?" the captain asked, stroking the dog's head. "Been keeping
the lurchers away?"

"He's been sick, in fact." I motioned to Mimi to put the collations on
the table beside me.

"Well, my good fellow," Captain Charles said, addressing the dog as if
it were a man, "you are in the hands of the kindest woman in all of
Europe. Many a man would envy you."

"I regret to say that an international incident has occurred on Pugdog's account."

"Oh?" he said, pulling away as the eager dog tried to lick his chin.

I explained to him what had happened, the letters that had been intercepted by the British. I told him what Eugène had said in his letter, some
of the things Junot had told Bonaparte.

"But how did Junot know I gave you Pugdog?"

"Lisette must have told him, of course."

"Ah, so she told Junot, who in turn told your husband."

"Insinuating to him that you and I are . . ." I flushed.

"I confess I find it flattering to be accused of cuckolding the great General Bonaparte." He grinned. "I could go down in history for this."

How young he was, how ignorant in the ways of the world! "I wish I shared your buoyant humour, Captain, but I fear my husband will demand a divorce."

"Over the gift of a dog?" he sputtered.

"Please understand, Bonaparte is an exceedingly jealous man. His emotions are volcanic. The least suspicion grows in his imagination until it rules his reason."

"So, I guess an evening at the Opéra-Comique with your cavaliere servente is out of the question?"

"I go nowhere. I am a prisoner of suspicion. Pauline Leclerc is now my neighbour and she reports to her brothers every move I make. No doubt they will soon be informed of your call. Frankly, if I don't get out of Paris, I'll go mad. I've been looking into purchasing a country property on the Saint-Germain road, but despair of even raising the down payment."

"This may help." Captain Charles withdrew a fat packet from his inside pocket. He twirled it in the air and caught it, presenting it to me formally. "We did rather well on the last delivery."

I felt its substantial weight. *Fifty* thousand livres, he said.

April 21.
I've signed. Malmaison is mine.

In which I retreat

April 23, 1799—Malmaison!

It is late afternoon. I'm writing these words at my little desk in the boudoir of my country château. A spirit of rebelliousness has come over me. I've not dressed my hair, not painted my face, I'm wearing old "rags"—a cosy déshabillé. A feeling of peace fills me as I look out over the hills, my four hundred acres of woodland and fields dotted with grazing sheep, cows, a few horses. A bull with a ring through its nose is lowing plaintively next to the cowshed. This morning I'll ride the bay mare over every dell and glen, and in the afternoon the gardener and I will lay out an herb garden.

And this evening? This evening I'll listen to the night silence. This evening, I'll sleep content.

This is my home. I will grow old here, die here.

April 24, morning.

I have just had a report from my steward. With his face turning red as a turkey-cock and his battered straw hat clutched in his hands, he informed me that the chickens haven't been laying, the clover in the far field is overgrown with hemlock and the winnowing machine is in need of a part (forty francs). Such "problems" are a balm to my battered spirit.

April 27.

More and more I retreat from the civilized world. I rise with the sun, spend my day in the company of the servants, the peasants, the animals. In the early morning I work in the kitchen garden, planting, pulling up weeds, thinning. I think of Paris, of the ferment that is always there, the glitter and wit, with something akin to revulsion.

[Undated]
Twice I have set out to go to Paris; twice I have turned back. I have become a country savage.

May 20.
Frustrated by my absence, the Glories have descended!

"Ah, darling, now you have everything: a harp, a coach and a château. What more is there?"

"My harp lacks three strings, my coach needs a new shaft and as for my château . . . !" I laughed.

"Don't despair, you can have it repaired," Minerva said to comfort me.

"I confess I love it just as it is," I said, checking under the table to make sure that Pugdog was getting along with my guests' pets. We were five women, four pugs—a zoo.

"The grounds *are* lovely."

"It's perfect," Thérèse said, embracing me. She looked a little plump, I thought. "You might as well know. I'm going to have a baby," she announced sheepishly to the group.

"Oh!"

"Oh?" And Tallien, her husband, in Egypt. And Ouvrard, her lover, married.

"Don't look at me like that!"

We played cards and talked all afternoon, catching up on the news: the assassination of the French envoys in Germany; the depressing military losses in Italy; how one of the Directors had accused Fesch, Lucien and Joseph Bonaparte of pilfering public funds. But most important, the wonderful news that an attempt was going to be made for an Egyptian rescue.

May 24.

The rescue attempt failed. Our ships were unable to get through the English blockade. I've been all day in bed.

June 16.

A courier came cantering into the courtyard this morning. A letter from Bonaparte? I thought hopefully, recalling the early days of the Italian campaign. But no, of course not. The envelope contained a current issue of the journal *La Feuille du Jour*. Attached to it was a note, unsigned, but in Captain Charles's tidy script—*page 4, top left. I must see you.* On page four there was an article reporting the delivery of unsound horses to the Army of Italy—by the Bodin Company. Apparently, the soldiers had been forced to cross the Alps on lame and feeble mounts, cursing the name Bodin.

Captain Charles's basement rooms at one hundred Rue Honoré are dark. The porter squinted to make out the printing on my card. "Madame Tascher?"

I nodded, giving him my cloak. I was asked to wait in a small drawing room. (I remember wondering whether I heard barking.) I made myself comfortable, taking in the tasteful simplicity of the furnishings—the paintings on the walls, the bouquets of flowers, a side table covered with books (Montesquieu's *Persian Letters* open, face down), a bronze sculpture of a horse—the pleasing clutter of a room much lived in.

"He's receiving," the porter informed me, then led me down a dark passage. We stopped before an antique oak door with a brass knob. I heard a dog barking again. The porter rapped three times.

"Come on in, Claude," I heard a voice call out—Captain Charles.

The porter swung the door open. There, in the centre of a mass of dogs was Captain Charles wearing an artist's frock coat of coarse linen. In his arms was a beagle with one ear missing. "Madame—"

"*Tascher.*"

Gently he lowered the beagle onto the floor and stepped over a long-haired mutt, wiping his hands on his frock coat. His braids had been tied back with a scarlet and black striped ribbon. "You've discovered my secret life," he said shyly, glancing down at his flock.

"Where did they all come from?" How many were there? Eight? Ten?

"I claim them from the streets," he said, removing his coat and ushering me out the door. Underneath he was wearing a scarlet wool cutaway coat with white satin lapels. He closed the door behind him, muffling the yelping.

"And then what do you do with them?" I asked, following him back into the drawing room.

"And then I can't bear to part with them!" he said, pushing forward an upholstered chair. "You've come about the article in *La Feuille du Jour*?"

"It alarmed me."

"The horses that the Bodin Company bought were sound, I assure you. But the horses that were shipped were apparently slaughterhouse animals. The problem appears to be with the dealer."

"Louis and Hugo Bodin are both in Lyons?"

The captain nodded. "I just received a letter from them. There is talk of an inquiry."

This could be the end of us, I thought—the end of *me*. "There's only one person who can help us."

"Grand Dieu," Barras exclaimed when he saw me. "I was beginning to think we'd never see you in Paris again. You're just in time for the celebration." He did a little dance and then winced, his hand on the small of his back. "At last, that braggart Director Treilhard's out—his election as director has been disqualified."

"Ha, ha." The parrot, chuckling like Barras.

"Oh?" Trying to remember who Director Treilhard was. I'd been living in another world. "Why?"

"He's four days too young to be eligible."

"Only four days?"

"Four, four hundred, what does it matter? The law is the law," intoned Barras in a mock deep voice. "The irony is that it was your brother-in-law Lucien Bonaparte who discovered the discrepancy and demanded justice. He himself is four hundred days short of being eligible to be a deputy, and he started screaming about Treilhard's four days. All this at one in the morning. It's a good thing I have a sense of humour."

"Barras, please, have you read that article about the Bodin Company in the—"

"*La Feuille du Jour?* Ah yes, the latest little scandal. The Legislative Councils are outraged, calling for an investigation, of course." He held his hands up, as if under arrest. "And they're just dying to pin it on me. This place is as explosive as a powder keg."

Barras's secretary Botot appeared at the door. "Another deputation to see you, Director."

"That's the third group already today." Barras took me by the elbow, ushering me out.

"Paul, what's going on?"

He kissed me on both cheeks. "Just another coup d'état, a little milk-and-water revolution." He waved gaily, disappearing from view, his words echoing in the vast chamber—*coup d'état, coup d'état, coup d'état.*

"So he can't do anything?" Captain Charles asked, keeping his eyes on the six balls he was juggling.

"I never had a chance to ask him. Things are . . . tense. The last thing he'll want to align himself with right now is the Bodin Company. Maybe later."

"Later will be too late," the captain said, letting the balls drop.

June 21.
With a sinking heart, I have written to Barras, begging him to defend the interests of the Bodin Company.

June 29.
I was working in the herb garden with Mimi when a hired fiacre pulled through the gates. I squinted to see who it might be. "I think it's that

funny man," Mimi said, for her eyesight is better than mine.

Captain Charles? I untied my apron.

"And a mess of dogs, sounds like," she said.

"We've been turned out," the captain explained as his porter picked the dog hairs off his red shooting jacket. The beagle and a spotted dog pressed their damp, black noses out the carriage window, sniffing. From the variety of barks, I suspected he had brought them all.

"Because of the investigation?" Government payments to the Bodin Company had been withheld until the investigation was complete.

He nodded. "I put all the office files in safe keeping, but as for the dogs—I know it is a lot to ask, but . . . ?"

I started to turn him away, thinking of what might be said, fearing the consequences. But then I thought: how can I let down a friend in such desperate need? Were it not for Captain Charles, I wouldn't even own Malmaison. And who would ever know he was there? I lived in such isolation. "There's a suite of rooms empty in the farmhouse," I told him, wondering as I said the words if I were doing the right thing. "My daughter comes only on the weekends. I'll tell the servants you are my accountant." In fact, I could use his help.

"It won't be for long," he assured me, opening the carriage door and standing back as all the barking, bounding dogs leapt out.

July 7—Paris.
Although the Bodin Company contract is still under review, at least we will not be charged. "That's the best I can do," Barras told me. He seemed distant, harassed. I dared not ask him for yet another loan, as I'd intended.

July 10.
What a night. Now all is topsy-turvy. Where do I begin? I suppose it was inevitable that the captain and I would become . . . well, perhaps I am being misleading.

It began with inviting the captain to join me in sampling the first bottle of our Malmaison wine. It was, after all, an occasion. We'd learned that the investigation had been dropped. The Bodin Company was going to survive. And besides, the pheasants that a neighbour had been kind enough to give me had been splendidly prepared by my cook and required a "full-bodied" (the captain's words) red.

The first bottle revealed that the wine was, indeed, ready. The captain and I settled into the game room, where, after I noisily beat him at backgammon* (three times!), we propped our stockinged feet up on the big leather hassock and talked: of his family and their need; of his ambition (to own a stud farm, raise horses). I asked him once again why he had never married.

"The woman I love is spoken for," he confessed.

"You won't tell me who she is?" I asked, wondering, I confess, if he was telling the truth. Wondering if the rumours about the captain were true. I took my wineglass in my hand, holding it by the stem. I looked at the captain, held his eye as I raised my glass, emptied it. It is an old-fashioned ritual, this "taking a glass"; I doubted whether he was even familiar with it, young as he is. But gamely he followed suit, holding my eye, downing his glass. I leaned over and filled his glass again. I was conscious of the revealing cut of my gown.

"I'll give you a hint," he said, standing abruptly and propping his hands on the arms of my chair. I could smell the sweet scent of pistachio on his breath. Before I could protest, his lips were upon mine, his tongue soft, seeking. I pulled away. "Why did you do that!" (Shocked, I confess, by his ardour. I'd always considered the captain to be "safe.")

Captain Charles fell back on his haunches. "*Why* is not the question a lady usually asks when she is kissed," he said, rising to his feet, pulling at his coat to try to disguise the rather obvious fact that he was in the manly state. I looked away, a flush heating my cheeks. Perhaps I should take a lover, I thought, thinking of my husband in the arms of another. But was that lover funny little Captain Charles?

* *Backgammon dice were initially tumbled in a noisy iron container and for that reason (some claim) the game was considered ideal by men wishing an opportunity to converse privately with a married woman without arousing suspicion. During the noisy game for two, they would not be overheard.*

The night was foggy. I felt my way cautiously, holding onto Captain Charles's arm for support. We were both of us giggling like schoolchildren, stumbling in the dark, starting at the slightest sound. A snort and low rumble made me jump. "It's just my manservant snoring," he whispered, leading me up the narrow path to the old farmhouse. Inside, two dogs began to bark. "Quiet," Captain Charles hissed through the open window.

I put my hand on his shoulder to keep from swaying. Then he hiccupped and I fell against the wall, trying not to laugh. I remember thinking, I'm in a state, I'm going to regret this.

Captain Charles opened the creaky door to his bedchamber. The room smelled of dog. He lit a lantern and stumbled about the room making it tidy, throwing a woven cloth over the bed. "There." Then he kissed me, pulling me against him. "Please don't change your mind," he whispered, sensing that I might. He pulled at my bodice strings, his fingertips on my breast, his lips, his tongue. I moaned, my hands in his hair. We fell onto the bed. Kiss him, I thought—before you think better of it.

He stood and untied his pantaloons, pulling down his breeches, his drawers. Demurely, I looked away. He stepped towards the bed, and I believe he must have lost his balance, for he began to hop about the room, his ankles tangled in his breeches, the light of the single lantern gleaming off his exposed buttocks, his rather large and bouncing manhood.

And then, I could not help it—I began to laugh. And then the dogs began to bark. Captain Charles pulled up his breeches and ran downstairs to silence them. When he returned I was sitting cross-legged on his bed, drying my cheeks, laughing still but contained, my sides aching. He sat down beside me, confused and shy. "My valet's still snoring," he said.

"Oh, Captain Charles!" I put one hand on his shoulder. I felt him begin to laugh himself. And then we were both of us convulsed.

He kissed me tenderly and helped me to my feet. The moment of danger had passed.

July 11.

The captain came to my door this morning with a bouquet of wild flowers. I looked at him for what seemed like a very long time, but was probably little more than a heartbeat or two. I kissed his smooth cheek. "I'm sorry, Captain Charles, I don't know what to say," I said, accepting his kind offering.

July 13.

I was awakened by a courier cantering up the drive. Bonaparte had been injured in Egypt, I was solemnly informed, in an attack at Saint-Jean d'Acre.

"A general's wife becomes accustomed to false reports," I reassured the servants, but ordered the carriage harnessed none the less.

"I'm coming with you," Mimi said, running back into the house for her hat.

I stood waiting as my coachman hitched the second horse, a grey gelding. It laid back its ears at the bay, swishing its tail.

"Josephine?" It was Captain Charles, standing by the gate. "I heard the bad news."

A stinging sensation came into my eyes. "No doubt it's just another false report. I'm going into Paris to Luxembourg Palace. Director Barras will know." I jumped at the sudden sound of muskets going off. Bastille Day tomorrow—of course.

Mimi came running, blue hat ribbons aflutter. The carriage leaned as my coachman climbed onto the driver's seat.

Director Barras wasn't receiving, his aide informed me. "His doctor has forbidden any visitors."

"But surely he'll receive me."

"No exceptions." He is a young man, new at the job, fearful of misstep.

"Perhaps you could help me then," I said, the tremor in my voice betraying me.

"It's true. They've been injured," I told Mimi. I felt numb. The enormity of the news was just sinking in. "Both Bonaparte and Eugène."

"Badly?"

"I fear so!" With a shaky breath, I told her what I'd learned. During an attack on Saint-Jean d'Acre, a shell had exploded in the midst of headquarters. A fragment struck Eugène in the head. Bonaparte, himself wounded, risked his life to come to Eugène's aid. A sergeant had thrown himself upon Bonaparte to protect him, but was hit and died.

Mimi put her arm around me. I began to cry.

The horses bent their heads against the wind, heading back to Malmaison. My heart reached for Egypt, for a hot desert land. Fear inflamed my imagination.

Captain Charles was in the game room, sitting by the fire reading a volume of Voltaire's tragedies, his slippers on the leather hassock. He put down the book when he saw me. I took off my hat, my gloves. In a few hours Hortense would arrive. She would be buoyant, excited about the Bastille Day ceremonies tomorrow in our little village of Rueil. And then I would have to tell her—that her beloved brother had a head injury, had not woken. "I'm going to have to ask you to leave," I told Captain Charles.

"I know, your daughter will be arriving soon. I was just going back to the farmhouse in any case." His tone tender. "The news is not . . . ?"

"No. I mean, it's not that."

"What happened?" he asked. "Was General Bonaparte injured?"

Captain Charles spoke my husband's name with reverence. "Yes. They don't know how badly. And Eugène, as well. He was struck unconscious from a head injury, so there's a chance that he might be . . ." I thought of the village idiot.

I felt Captain Charles's hand on my shoulder. "I'm so sorry."

I pulled away, out of his reach.

"You don't want me to comfort you?"

I shook my head. He looked like a boy to me, not so very much older than my son. My relationship with the captain was not sinful, but it was not innocent, either. The gods were punishing me, surely! "Captain Charles, I'm . . . I must ask you to leave Malmaison."

"Now?" He looked confused.

"Yes please." How could I pray for my husband and son, with the captain by my side? "I'm sorry!" I fled the room before I could do more harm.

July 14, Bastille Day.
Fire rockets, trumpets, a steady drumbeat. I fastened the latch on the leaded window, drew the brocade curtains, muffling the sounds of festivity. I am keeping Hortense with me for a few days.

July 15, early evening.
Twice today Hortense and I walked the dusty road to Rueil to light candles in the village church. We have each of us set up a prie-dieu in our bedrooms. Mimi walks in the moonlight, chanting to the voodoo mystères. We have all returned to the gods of our youth.

July 22—Malmaison.
Good news—Bonaparte has recovered. But no news yet about Eugène— I'm sick with apprehension.

Close to midnight—Paris.
"Director Barras is expecting me," I lied to the aide.

The young man looked at the clock on the mantel. "I guess," he said, still unsure.

I followed him up the grand spiral staircase and through a series of elegant chambers to the last, the smallest and most intimate—the bedchamber of Director Barras. There I found Barras in an alarming condition—pale, too weak to stand. "I'm sorry for keeping you out the other day," he said, waving his hand through the air, then letting it fall

onto the bed sheet. "If my enemies were to find out how weak I am—"
He made a pistol of his index finger and thumb and aimed it at his temple. "I'm not even letting Talleyrand in. You know he's resigned? Everything's falling to pieces. But at least I was able to get Fouché named Minister of Police. He should be back in Paris in a few weeks. The sooner the better. You wouldn't believe the plots that are brewing. I should be flattered, I guess. Everyone wants to depose me. Even your charming brothers-in-law are circulating the story that I sent Bonaparte into the desert just to get rid of him, that the entire fiasco is my fault."

He was babbling incoherently. I put the palm of my hand on his forehead. "You have a fever. Have you seen your doctor? Have you been bled?"

"Yes, yes, but not bled—not today, in any case. I haven't any blood left." He smiled weakly, his eyes fever bright. "That was good news about Bonaparte. You must be relieved."

"Yes! But I've heard nothing yet about Eugène—"

"My aide didn't tell you? Merde. It's so frustrating. I told him to let you know. These young people are incompetent."

"Tell me what, Paul?" My heart was pounding.

"That your son has fully recovered!"

I put my hand to my chest, put down my head and gave thanks to my son's guardian angels.

July 23—still in Paris.
Thérèse told me Captain Charles is staying in old Madame Montaniser's suite in the Palace Égalité. I've sent him a message, asking him to meet me in Monceau Park tomorrow at eleven. I dare not invite him here, not with Pauline Bonaparte watching every move I make.

July 24.
The captain was at Monceau Park when I arrived, sitting on the shady bench by the Roman columns. He smiled at my blonde ringlets, for I was wearing one of Thérèse's wigs.

"Would you care to sit, Madame Bonaparte?" he asked, as if we were in a parlour. He'd spread a cloth over the bench.

"Thank you for meeting me," I said, closing my sun parasol. I balanced it against the bench. "I want to apologize." I swallowed. I didn't want to give the wrong impression. He looked so sadly hopeful. "I'm sorry, Captain Charles. I behaved poorly."

"I have an apology to make as well, a confession of sorts." He glanced at me, his eyes the colour of sea-water shallows. "I courted you for what you could give me, for the advantages that you offered, the connections."

I looked away, out over the pond. Two ducks were swimming in the middle. On the far side a girl was pushing a baby in a pram. The captain's words hurt. I had used him—I knew that—but even so they hurt.

"And then I came to love you," he said.

Tears filled my eyes. It all seemed so pathetic, somehow, these little dramas of the heart. I thought of Bonaparte, of Eugène, their struggle for life on far desert sands. "Captain Charles, you are a dear man." I did love him, but as a friend.

We parted with tenderness. The captain agreed to take Pugdog back. I dare not have any reminders of my follies when Bonaparte returns, as I pray he will—*soon*.

July 27—Malmaison, a glorious summer day.
Émilie and Hortense are coming for the weekend. I've been all morning in the kitchen with Callyot, helping him with the baking—mille-feuilles, cherry comfits and a delectable apple flan. I miss Pugdog. I keep expecting to see him at my feet, eagerly waiting for a scrap. I am thankful he is in the captain's care.

July 28.
Émilie swooned at the dinner table, slumping over into Hortense's arms. A cup fell onto the floor. "I'm sorry," she moaned, her teeth chattering.

Mimi and I carried the shivering girl upstairs, laid her out on the bed.

The chill changed abruptly to a flush of heat, and she begged me to open the windows, which I had just closed.

I told Mimi to run for the doctor in town.

Hortense came to the door. "Is Émilie all right?"

"I don't want you near this room, Hortense." She'd been inoculated as a child, but I wasn't taking any chances.

"Maman!"

"I mean it." I stroked a damp strand of Émilie's hair out of her eyes. I had had a mild case of the pox as a child; it had slightly scarred me, but now I was protected.

6:00 P.M., waiting for supper.
The doctor clothed himself completely in a gown, gloves and mask. Émilie took fright when she saw him. I watched his face for some indication. He cleared his throat, stood back, his hands clasped behind his back. "I will return in four days, when the poison has emerged." He paused, his hand on the door handle. "Pity," he said.

August 1.
As if by magic, as if by evil, spots have appeared on Émilie's face and neck, exactly as the doctor predicted.

"Give me a looking glass," Émilie demanded. I could not refuse her. "They're little," she said, touching them. "And pointed." Almost with tenderness.

The worst is yet to come.

August 4.
I have removed the looking glasses from Émilie's room, but nothing can remove the nauseating smell that thickens the air, the scent of the poison that seeks to kill her.

[Undated]

"It's just me, Émilie." I put down the tray of medications. Her eyes had been sealed shut by fever blisters. Her face was unrecognizable now, a monster face.

"Papa?" she cried out.

Tears came to my eyes. She was dreaming of her father François de Beauharnais—her émigré father who had fled France during the Revolution, who could never return. The father she'd not seen since she was a girl of twelve. I sat down on the bed beside her. "No, Émilie, it's me, Auntie Rose."

"Papa!"

Did it matter who she thought I was? "I'm going to put a medication on your face." I dipped a scrap of clean flannel into the glass jar. "It might sting a little," I warned her.

She flinched, then stilled. "I've been waiting for you," she whispered.

21 Thermidor, Luxembourg Palace
Chère amie,

Very well, very well. I'll see what I can do about getting François de Beauharnais's name erased. I wouldn't be too hopeful, however. There is a murderous mood in the Councils these days.

Speaking of which, opposition against your husband is growing. I'd advise you to give up the life of retirement. I can't fight this battle alone.

Père Barras

August 29.

Émilie emerged from sickbed this morning. She lifted her veil and one by one we embraced her, trying our best to conceal the distress in our eyes. Her face is a mass of scars. Thank God she is married already.

In which I am forgiven (& forgive)

September 4, 1799.
Émilie's trials have awakened me from self-pity. If that frail girl can win against Death, surely I can find the strength to take on the Bonaparte clan. I'm moving back to Paris, preparing for battle.

September 10.
Today, calls on the Minister of War, Director Gohier (who is now President of the Council of Directors), Barras—trying to revive interest in an Egyptian rescue. It's shocking how indifferent everyone has become to Bonaparte's fate, to the fate of our stranded men.

September 11.
I am overcome with frustration. I've been all this week making calls, trying in vain, I fear. Opposition has strengthened against Bonaparte. They, the smug men in power, busy themselves with details, oblivious to the obvious fact that the Republic is falling.

Bonaparte will return (I tell myself, I tell myself), that I cannot doubt. I am resolved not to give up. As a woman, my voice is weak. As a woman, my strength lies in persuading men to act. I will sleep, and then tomorrow I will rise, begin again, make my way back to the offices and homes of the deputies and Ministers and Directors, and with my woman's heart—persistent and nagging, persuasive and flattering, cajoling and flirtatious—I will harry the men who would do my husband ill. Using all the weapons in my arsenal, I will win them to his side.

September 22, the first day of the Republican Year VIII.
I've been exhausting myself on Bonaparte's behalf, but today was the hardest. Today I swallowed my pride and called on Joseph Bonaparte. "Madame," he greeted me, bowing neatly from the waist. A smile flickered at the corners of his thin lips. "Forgive me for keeping you waiting. I was with my dancing master," he said, pushing a door open to a tiny room that was more of an antechamber than a drawing room. "My porter informs me that you wish to speak to me about Napoleon," he said, pronouncing his brother's name in the French manner. He checked his timepiece and sat, his hands perched on the knees of his white leather breeches, smiling his unctuous little grin. "I can't be long, I regret to say."

"I won't incommode you, Joseph. As you are aware, the Ministry of War has become indifferent to Bonaparte's plight. Another rescue must be attempted." I laced my fingers together. "If we united, we might have an impact. For your brother's sake . . ."

Joseph shrugged. "It's useless. I've done all that I can."

October 5.
Glorious news. Bonaparte has had a victory over the Turks at Aboukir. Maybe now men will listen, maybe now they will work for his return.

October 13—dusk.
The windows of the palace glimmered with the light of a thousand candles, illuminating the faces of the beggars camped by the Palace gate. "Citoyenne Bonaparte," they called out to me in chorus, and then began singing "Chant du départ," which they knew I would reward with a shower of coins.

Director Gohier's valet announced me with dignity. I stood only for a moment, aware of the heads turning, the stares. There were about twenty or thirty present, a select group. Barras, his scarlet cloak draped dramatically over one shoulder, was on the window seat, conversing with a woman (an opera singer) who regarded him with a bored, voluptuous look. Talleyrand, distinct in black, was standing by the fireplace, leaning on his ebony cane. He looked up, grimaced, his broad forehead glistening. Seated nearby, the assistant to the Minister of War was talking with the Minister of the Interior. Good, I thought, assessing the crowd. Many of the key people I needed to talk to were here.

Director Gohier's wife greeted me with arms outstretched. "I love your hat," she whispered. "A Lola creation? I knew it. I adore those gigantic silk flowers." I enjoyed the Director's wife, but in befriending her I was not blind to the importance of her husband in my cause. The powerful Director Gohier had been vehement in his opposition to Bonaparte. By degrees, I had succeeded in softening him.

After civilities, I joined the group at the hazard table. The dice felt loose and smooth in my hands. I'd won over two hundred francs when I heard Barras say, "Well, look who's here."

I looked toward the big double doors. There, standing without introduction, was the Minister of Police, my friend and spy, Citoyen Fouché. He came straight up to me.

"Citoyen Fouché, how good to see you." But there was something alarming in his expression.

"May I speak to you in private, Citoyenne?" But even before we'd reached the antechamber, he handed me a scrap of paper.

I turned it over in my hand. "What is this? I don't understand."

"Your son sent it. It came by semaphore."*

"Eugène?"

Director Gohier was sitting at the silent whist table, oblivious to all but his cards. "President Director." I leaned to whisper into his ear. "There's something you should know. Bonaparte is back; he's in the south."

Gohier put his cards face down. "If you'll excuse me a moment,

* A message relayed from one vantage point to another by means of flags.

Citoyens, Citoyenne," he said, addressing his guests. He signalled to Barras as he hurried me out of the room.

"With respect, Director Barras, from a legal perspective General Bonaparte has deserted his army." Director Gohier crossed his arms, as if bracing himself against some invisible force. "I ask you, in all honesty, how can we *not* arrest him?"

"Arrest Bonaparte and the nation will rise up against us, I guarantee it," Barras said.

I stood. "Directors Gohier, Barras—please, if you will excuse me. I must go." Both men looked at me as if they'd forgotten I was present. "I'm going to try to meet Bonaparte on the road, before he gets to Paris." Before his brothers get to him.

"Now?" Director Gohier asked, astonished.

"But the roads aren't safe," Gohier's wife exclaimed. "And it's so frightfully cold."

"And the fog," Barras objected.

I felt dazed, a strange combination of both joy and fear. It was true, the fog was thick—too thick to travel, especially at night. "I'll leave at dawn."

"In that little coach of yours?" Director Gohier pulled the bell rope. His valet appeared, scratching his ear. "Tell Philip to ready the government travelling coach." He put up his hand. "I *insist*. It can be made into a sleeping compartment." He grinned at Barras. "Handy that way."

My manservant met me at the door holding up a lantern, which threw a ghostly light. "General Bonaparte is back," the coachman called out to him before I could say anything.

Gontier looked at me, not comprehending. A gust of chill wind blew dead leaves into the foyer. "The General's back from Egypt?" he asked, pulling the door shut against the cold.

I nodded, shivering. "He's in the south. Eugène sent a message, by semaphore."

Hortense appeared in her nightclothes, a red woollen shawl draped over her shoulders. "What's going on?" Yawning and then sneezing.

"General Bonaparte is back," Gontier exclaimed.

"And Eugène is with him," I cried out, my self-control giving way.

Hortense put down her candle. *"Eugène* is back?"

"They landed in the south, two days ago. They're on their way to Paris. I'm going to meet them." I would need linens, provisions, blankets, I thought.

"I'm coming too," Hortense said, her teeth chattering. It was freezing, even in the foyer.

I paused, considered. "But you have a cold, sweetheart."

"I'm better now!"

"I won't be stopping," I cautioned her. "I'll even be sleeping in the coach."

"I don't care."

Her golden curls framed her big blue eyes—her irresistible blue eyes. Bonaparte was fond of Hortense; it might help to have her with me. And I was in need of help. "You'll wear your fur bonnet?"

"Anything!" Even that.

It was still dark when the enormous government travelling coach came rumbling down the narrow little laneway, harnessed to four strong carriage horses. It did not take long to ready it: a charcoal heater, down pillows, fur coverlets, bedpans, medications (laudanum for my nerves and back pain, spirits of hartshorn and Gascoigne's powder for Hortense's cold). We took an enormous basket of provisions: bread, eggs cooked hard, comfits and bonbons for Hortense, wine and brandy for us both.

The sun was just rising when finally we started out, the big coach scraping twice against the garden wall. I waved to the porter, yawning in the door of his shack. The morning felt hopeful.

We careened toward the south. I had thought that we would sleep, but we could not. Hortense was effervescent with excitement. Her beloved brother was alive, he was safe, he was coming home. And myself? I was going to meet my husband.

October 15 (I think)—Auxerre.

We have stopped briefly in a posting-station in Auxerre. We have requested a private room while a wheel is being repaired. The response of the people to the news of Bonaparte's return has been overwhelming. All along the route arches of triumph are being built in his honour. Men, women and children line the road in hopes of seeing him pass. Last night the lights from all the torches made a magical effect. "The road to heaven," Hortense said, awed.

Such outpouring of enthusiasm is akin to madness, surely. Whenever we stop, we are mobbed, people crying out, "Is it true? Is the Saviour coming?"

Savage,* I thought I heard the first time. Is the *savage* coming. "Pardon?"

"The Saviour!" a cobbler exclaimed. "*Our* saviour."

October 16—Châlon-sur-Saône, dawn.

We've missed him. At Lyons, he took the Bourbon route, west through Nevers, his brothers in close pursuit.

"Ah, they'll get there first," Hortense said, as if this were a game.

"Back to Paris," I told the coachman, my anxiety rising. "Fast."

October 19—Paris, late morning.

It was after midnight when our coach pulled up at my gate, the horses steaming. There was a light in the porter's shack, illuminating the sleeping forms of the beggars. The coachman jumped down and pounded on the door. "Chandler, wake up, open the gate."

I nudged Hortense. We were exhausted from five days of travel, eating and sleeping in the coach. Violently jolting over the rough roads had inflamed my back, my hip. The night before I'd been unable to sleep at all. A dreamlike daze possessed me, a curious tingling in my skin. Approaching the dark streets of Paris—the smell of garbage, even in the cold fall air; the mud hardened into ruts; the taste of smoke; the shadows of beggars and ruffians huddled around fires in the alleyways—I felt a sense of doom come over me.

*Sauveur *means saviour;* sauvage *means savage.*

"Are we here?" Hortense asked, sneezing and blowing her nose. "It's so cold. What time is it?"

"We're here." I gathered up my basket, sorting through the travel clutter. I put my hand to my hair; I'd braided it, fastened it with a tortoiseshell comb, but some strands had worked loose. Why didn't the porter open the gate? I took off my gloves so that I could do up the laces of my boots.

The coachman came to the carriage door, holding a torch. "There's a problem," he said, his breath making mist. A freezing blast of air came in the open door.

I pulled the musty fur coverlet around my shoulders. "Is the General not here?" And Eugène!

The coachman nodded. "But the porter—" He stopped.

"What is it, Antoine?" One of our horses whinnied. The porter was standing in the door of his shack, looking out. The shadows from a lantern gave his face a diabolic look.

"He can't open the gate," the coachman said finally.

"Can't open it?" Hortense giggled, tying her hat ribbons.

"What do you mean, he *can't*?"

"General's orders, Citoyenne."

"Bonaparte's ordered the gate locked?" Perhaps it was a security measure.

"The porter said to tell you that your belongings are in his shack, all trunked up."

Hortense looked at me, puzzled.

"I—I don't understand," I said. Trunked up?

"The General, he . . ." The coachman looked up at the night sky, shifting his weight from foot to foot. "He moved your belongings out."

And then I understood—Bonaparte had dared to move me out of my own house, dared to lock my own gate against me, dared to instruct *my* porter to forbid me entrance!

I was furious. I started to get out.

"So we're walking?" Hortense asked, fastening the top button of her cape. "From here?"

It was dark in the verandah antechamber. Hortense pulled the bell rope. I leaned against one of the posts, panting from the effort to keep up with my daughter. "Here comes somebody." Hortense jumped up and down so that she could see in through the little window in the door. "Oh, it's Mimi." Then she shrieked and burst into giggles. "Maman, I see Eugène! I see Eugène!"

"You see him?"

"Oh, he's dark as an Arab!" she hissed, spinning, her hands on her cheeks in mock horror.

The door swung open. "At last—you're back." Mimi rolled her eyes as if to say, You would not believe what's been going on here. "It's your mother and sister," she said over her shoulder.

Eugène was standing in front of the dining room fireplace with a wool blanket draped around his shoulders. He put down the candle, held his arms open wide, the blanket falling.

Hortense threw herself into her brother's arms, bursting into sobs. He held her shyly, blinking. He looked like a young man—thin, tall . . . and so dark.

"Maman," he said, his voice breaking. His voice told me so much—that he loved me, that I was in serious trouble, that he had tried.

He stooped to embrace me. He smelled of cigar smoke, the smell of a man, not a boy. The smell of a soldier, I thought, not without regret. I put my hand on his cheek, surprised by the stubble of beard. He was smiling, yet there was something amiss, a tremor around his eyes, a slight convulsive twitch.

"I can't tell you—" I took a sharp breath. "I love you so much! We . . ." But I could not speak for a choking feeling welled up in me.

"We thought you had died!" Hortense sobbed, all the nights of cold-sweat dreams breaking loose in her. She took a shuddering breath and laughed at herself, and then at the three of us, for we were all weeping.

Sniffing, my breath coming in little gasps, I pulled away. There was so much I wanted to ask him—about Egypt, his injury, how they'd managed to return*—but now was not the time. "Bonaparte—is he . . . ?"

* On August 22, four ships slipped out of Alexandria harbour. By staying close to the coast, they luckily managed to evade the British for six weeks.

"He's in the study," Eugène said.

"Upstairs?" In the room I had had made over for him. I took up a candle.

"Maman, you know . . . ?"

"I know."

As I turned the narrow stairs onto the half-storey landing, a cry escaped me. In the dark at the top of the stairs, a black man had leapt to his feet in front of the door to the study. The light of my candle caught the curved edge of a scimitar, the whites of his eyes, his teeth. "You gave me a fright," I said, catching my breath. He was young, more than a boy, but not quite a man.

He said something to me in a foreign tongue. "I don't understand," I said, stuttering a little. "I am Madame Bonaparte. I must speak to my husband. Is the General in there?" I spoke slowly and simply, so that he might understand. But I kept my distance.

"Bonaparte!" He clasped the pommel of his scimitar.

The name Bonaparte he understood. "Me," I said, pointing at my chest, "me *wife* of Bonaparte." I paused, for effect, then said, "Go!" with a sweep of my free hand.

With relief I saw that he understood and, sweetly obedient, slipped past me down the stairs. I went to the study door, knocked. There was no answer, although I heard movement within. "Bonaparte?" I turned the handle, pushed. "It's me, Josephine!" The door was locked. "Please, open the door." I knocked again, called out. I pressed my ear to the wood. I shook at the handle, turned it, rattled it. "Bonaparte!" Louder this time. "I know you're in there. Please!"

Silence.

It was cold in the corridor. My thoughts were in disorder, slowed by exhaustion, anticipation. And now, I was stumped. I hit the door with my palm. "Bonaparte, let me in! I can explain. It's not what you think." I pressed my forehead against the door. "I love you," I said, but too softly for him to hear. Then I banged on the door, violently, more violently than I'd intended. "I love you," I cried out, weeping now. You *bastard.*

After a long and terrible time, my children came to my aid. Hortense looked distraught. Eugène was standing behind her with a look of pained concern, his cheek twitching. I felt humiliated; how much did they know? I pulled my shawl around my shoulders. Why was it so cold? What season were we in?

Hortense stooped down beside me, caressed a lock of hair out of my eyes, as if I were her child and she my mother. By the light of the single guttering candle she had an ethereal look. "Oh, Maman, please don't cry," she said, handing me a handkerchief.

Her tenderness made me weep all the harder. "He won't open the door."

"We know," Eugène said.

Of course. The house was small. "There must be a key somewhere," I said. Or an *axe*.

"Maman." Eugène looked uncomfortable. "You can't just—"

"There is no key," Mimi hissed up from the ground floor. "I looked. He must have it."

He—General Bonaparte. My husband. Hortense and Eugène's step-father. Barricaded on the other side of a small oak door. "This must be what a siege is like," I said. A shadow of pain crossed my son's face.

"Eugène, maybe you could say something to the General," Hortense said in a conspiratorial tone.

"There is something you should know, Hortense." I glanced at Eugène. "Bonaparte believes I have been—"

"It's all right, Maman." Hortense gave me a knowing look, an expression curiously woman-to-woman.

"Just keep trying, Maman," Eugène whispered.

Tears filled my eyes. What had I done to deserve such children? I felt I had somehow tarnished them.

Eugène helped me to my feet. I pressed my forehead against the door. Bonaparte, *please!* Listen to me!

How much can a man take? Now I know: a very great deal. Bonaparte, in any case.

Yet when he finally lifted the latch, it was a shockingly frail man I saw before me. He'd wound grey flannel strips around his head in the manner of a turban. His skin, like Eugène's, was bronzed by the sun. Although his face was in shadow, it was clear that he, too, had been weeping.

We three, my children and I, froze in surprise. After hours of crying, pleading, praying—*cursing*—we'd come to accept the fact of that locked door.

I don't recall the children leaving, only the silence, the sudden awareness that Bonaparte and I were alone. I'd been talking to myself for days, imagining this moment, imagining what I would say. But now, words seemed foreign. "It's cold out here in the corridor," I said finally, starting to shiver.

I followed him into the study and sat down in the leather chair by the fire. The room smelled of cinnamon and ginger. A snuffbox decorated with an Egyptian motif lay open on a side table. A single lantern burned on the desk, which was already covered with papers and reports, books and maps.

Bonaparte pulled the door shut, not so much for privacy, but for warmth, I suspected. "Well? Are you not going to speak?" he said, holding his hands out over the fire. He'd put several waistcoats on over a linen shirt, and over that a heavy woollen smoking jacket. The layers of clothing made him look thin. He grabbed a chair and sat down, leaning on one arm with the air of an indulgent monarch. "You've been *wailing* to be let in, and now that I've opened the door to you, you have nothing to say."

I sat watching him, fighting the anger that was growing in me. "It is you who say nothing."

"I am speaking."

"Without truth, Bonaparte—without heart."

"*You* have the nerve to talk to *me* of heart?"

My self-control gave way. "You claim to love me, yet you are prepared to divorce me based on the gossip of soldiers! It is you who should explain, Bonaparte."

"You *dare* to imply that you are innocent, that you have not—" He hit the arm of his chair with his fist, hard.

I took a breath, held it, held it longer, held it as long as I could stand. "And what about your mistress, Bonaparte—your 'Cleopatra,' as the soldiers called her. You told her you would marry her if she were to bear your child." Blinking, my eyes stinging, trying not to sniff.

"How do you know this?"

"Your brothers and sisters went out of their way to make sure I found out."

He sat back. It was not the answer he'd expected.

"They're so intent on destroying me, they don't care what it might do to you in the process." Caution, I told myself. One wrong word, and forgiveness would be impossible. "They tell you I do not love you."

The light of the lantern shimmered in his eyes. I had found his vulnerable spot, I realized sadly. "I do love you," I said, knowing the truth of those words. I do love this man, this intense, haunted, driven soul. Why, I cannot explain. "And I long for you," I said—meeting his gaze, holding it. Bonaparte is not easily fooled.

It was almost four in the morning when I blew out the candles. We'd crossed the desert and returned, wounded but walking. We had made our confessions (yes), both of sin and of pain. We'd confessed to weakness, to the power of grief. We'd confessed to the desperation of loneliness. I told him I'd not managed well, that weakened by constant attack, I'd fallen.

"Were you unfaithful?" he asked bluntly.

I paused. The time had come to be truthful—but what was the truth? "Not in the sense that you mean." I touched his hand; it was so cold. "Not carnally." Not quite. "But almost." I took a breath. "And you?"

"She got on my nerves."

It felt good to laugh . . . and cry. He told me of the despair he'd felt in that country, convinced that I'd betrayed him, convinced that the Angel of Luck was no longer with him. "Without you . . ."

He made love to me, and then again. "I am with you now," I said.

V

Conspirator

We are sowing today in tears and blood.
Liberty will be our harvest.
—*Napoleon, to Josephine*

In which Eugène is healed

October 20, 1799.

I woke with a start. Fauvelet, Bonaparte's secretary, was shaking him, trying to rouse him. I stuck my hand out from under the fur coverlet. An enormous fire was raging in the fireplace, yet even so, I could see my breath. "Greetings, Fauvelet." Groggily. "What time is it?" A sliver of light showed through the drawn curtains. "Is something wrong?"

"No, Madame, the General is always hard to wake—as you know," he added. By the dim light Fauvelet's face looked dark, like Eugène's, like Bonaparte's. "It is seven. I allowed the General to sleep in this morning, but now his brother Deputy Lucien is here to see him." A shy smile. "We have been missing you, Madame," he whispered.

Lucien Bonaparte? I put my hand on my husband's shoulder. He was like a man dead. Everything he did, he did with profound intensity, I thought—work, love, even sleep.

He stirred, then rolled over and embraced me, his eyes closed shut. He smelled like a baby, sweaty and sweet. "Fauvelet, have I introduced you to my lovely wife?" Talking into my nightcap.

Fauvelet pulled back the drapes and morning light filled the room. I was taken aback by how sallow Bonaparte's skin was—his face, although darkened by the sun, had a sickly hue. "Your brother is here to see you," I said, kissing my husband, stilling his roving hands. "Lucien."

Bonaparte rolled over onto his back. "I know, I sent for him," he said, stretching and yawning and talking all at once.

Sent for him—when? I started to get up, but Bonaparte put his hand on my shoulder. "Bonaparte!" I did not want to be in the room when Lucien was shown in.

"Remember what I said last night—about the transition to the offensive?"

I fell back against the pillows. *The transition from the defensive to the offensive is a delicate operation, one of the most delicate in war.* "This isn't war."

"No?" Bonaparte smiled. I followed his gaze. Lucien was standing in the door looking rumpled and aged, stooped over like a man of eighty, not like the young man of twenty-four that he is.* His gangling arms hung down out of his coat sleeves. He is a talented young man, fiery and ambitious. I would admire him but for one glaring flaw: he wishes me dead.

"Good morning, Lucien," I said, pulling the comforter under my chin. I wanted to grin—*gloat.* "How nice to see you." Overdoing it, I knew.

He peered at me through his thick spectacles, disbelieving. Then he remembered to bow, lower than was called for, an exaggerated show of subservience—a degree of subservience that signified treachery, to my mind. "I'm leaving, Napoleone," he announced, pronouncing Bonaparte's name in the Italian way. He looked like a disgruntled spider, all long legs and arms. His brother, to whom he clearly felt himself superior, had had the gall to disregard his advice and forgive his wife.

"No, you're not." Bonaparte swung his feet onto the floor. Then, with a mischievous smile, he turned and whacked my bottom. I buried myself under the comforter. If I looked at Lucien, I would burst out laughing, I feared.

At the door, suddenly, carrying a clattering tray, appeared the black-skinned youth I'd encountered the night before. Dressed exotically in bright silks and fur, he looked like a vision out of a storybook. A jewel-encrusted scimitar dangled from a thick silken cord at his waist.

---

* *The young considered it fashionable to look old as well as rumpled: shirts were slept in to give the right effect, servants given new clothes to "break in."*

"Roustam!" my husband said, knotting the sash of his winter robe. The youth bowed, put the tray down on the table beside the bed. "This . . . is . . . my . . . wife," Bonaparte said slowly, pointing at me. "He's a Mameluke, but a good boy," he told me. "A great favourite with the ladies, however. I have to keep an eye on him."

"Good morning, Roustam," I said, reaching for a mug of steaming chocolate.

"And . . . this . . . is . . . my . . . brother . . . but . . . he . . . is . . . furious," Bonaparte said, tugging on Lucien's ear.

The black youth bowed and slipped backward through the door, his scarlet silk slippers making a sliding sound on the parquet floor.

"It's so cold in this country." Bonaparte threw on one of my cashmere shawls, stomping his feet. He took a tiny cup of coffee, gulped it down. A roll disappeared as quickly, crumbs covering the front of his robe. He poked at the fire with the iron, chewing, then threw on two more logs. "There," he said, standing back to watch the flames. He pulled one of the little drum stools over beside the fire and sat down.

"The General fancies himself at camp," I said to the glowering Lucien, attempting to leaven the mood.

Lucien crossed his arms. "Noi dobbiamo parlare, Napoleone." We must talk.

"So talk."

"Privatamente."

"My wife is to be included in all discussions."

"You are a fool!" This with the voice of a man addressing an inferior. "Your wife has played you false. She defames our good name."

I was relieved to hear Bonaparte laugh. "Our good name, you say? And our charming sister Pauline with three lovers? And Elisa throwing herself at the feet of poets one month after the death of her child? And Joseph in a mercury treatment again? And *you,* Lucien, making a fool of yourself over Madame Recamier while your wife languishes in childbed?"

I regarded Bonaparte with astonishment. He had only been back in Paris a short while and yet had managed to discover everything.

"I did not come with the intention of debating family matters," Lucien said, his eyes half-closed.

"Correct. You came because I summoned you."

"Bonaparte, I can—" I put my cup down on the side table.

Bonaparte glared at me as if to say, Don't move. "And sit down, for God's sake," he barked at his brother.

With haughty obedience, Lucien lowered himself onto one of the little stools, his ankles and wrists showing long and bony.

"General? The journals have arrived." I was relieved to see Fauvelet at the door. "But I could come back at another time."

"Now, Fauvelet." Bonaparte motioned to his secretary to take the remaining stool. I sat back against the pillows, resigned. There would be no escape.

Fauvelet ruffled through the stack of journals perched on his knees. "Ah, here's one you should know about. Director Moulins claims you broke quarantine when you landed, that you're bringing the plague to the Republic." His voice was nervous, high.

"Bah! We were forty-seven days at sea, for God's sake, and not one man ill. Is that not sufficient proof?" (I listened to this rebuttal with some relief, I confess.) "And?"

"This one regards Citoyen Bernadotte." Fauvelet cleared his throat.

"Ah, yes, my charming new relative."*

"He sent a letter to the Directors suggesting that you be court-martialled."

"That sounds like something a relation would do." Bonaparte smiled, but I couldn't tell whether he was amused or not. "Like something a *coward* would do."

"He's going around calling you 'The Deserter,'" Lucien informed Bonaparte with unseemly relish. "For abandoning your post."

"*Basta!* I left this country at peace and I return to find it at war. I left it crowned with victories, and I return to find it defeated, impoverished and in great misery. And who, I would ask the good Bernadotte—our once-upon-a-very-short-time Minister of War—who is to blame? That's

* *Bernadotte had married Eugenie-Désirée Clary, Joseph's wife's sister (and Napoleon's former fiancée). Bernadotte will be crowned King of Sweden, and their son will marry one of Eugène's daughters.*

my question to him." Bonaparte hit the mantel with his fist. "Anything else?"

Fauvelet and I exchanged glances. Bonaparte was back.

October 22, early evening.

Each day, more soldiers return, bronzed and bearing gifts. Paris is aglow with celebration, abuzz with stories. Wives and daughters parade scarves of exotic silks, fathers and sons proudly wear bejewelled scimitars. Our meals have suddenly become hot with spice. We've been invaded by the East—seduced.

October 23.

It's only four in the afternoon and already my little house is bursting with soldiers. "My Egyptians," Bonaparte calls them. Hortense, home from school, powders her nose and studies her reflection in the looking glass before descending the stairs.

Loud and boisterous, the soldiers celebrate their return "to civilization," consuming with great gusto, as if they had been starved. (They were.)

Fearless Murat, swarthy, jewelled and plumed, struts from room to room displaying his battle scars to every servant, the wounds still fresh, barely healed, two holes, one in each cheek. "But not my tongue," he says, sticking it out for examination. The pistol shot went in one cheek beside his ear and exited the other, "without even breaking a tooth," he told me, pulling his thick lips with his fingers.

"You were lucky," I said, stepping back.

"And Junot?" I asked Fauvelet, trying to sound offhand. "Did he not return with Bonaparte?" A number had yet to return, including Tallien (much to Thérèse's relief).*

"Andoche Junot, I regret to say, had to be left behind in the desert"—

* In Egypt Tallien became blinded in one eye, possibly due to untreated syphilis. On his return he is captured by the English. He does not arrive back in France until 1801, only to discover that his wife Thérèse is living openly with Ouvrard. They divorce and he ends his days in poverty.

a sly smile—"with *Othello*," he whispered, "the child he had by an Abyssinian slave."

With liquor the men begin to talk—uneasily at first—of the killing heat, the flies, the dysentery. Stories of an ocean of sand, and of thirst. Stories of soldiers blinded by fever. Stories of the Black Plague.

It is the whispered stories that I listen for, and hear—stories of a sea of white turbans, barbaric tortures, French soldiers left in the desert to die of thirst, murdering one another for a cup of water.

"How horrifying!"

"It was different there, Maman," Eugène said, his cheek quivering.

Close to midnight, a cold evening.

"So, the domestic spat is resolved? All is well?" Barras greeted me with a bone-crushing embrace. "You'll not join me for a cup of chocolate? My cook has made the most glorious Brussels biscuits. I must say, Eugène looks like a strapping young man. But a bit uneasy? I don't know how to put it, but I see it sometimes in young soldiers." He made a face. "Has he said anything to you? The conventional wisdom is that it's best not to dwell on their experiences, but I'm not so sure. Sometimes it helps to talk. Call me an old woman! But tell me, how is my protégé? I hardly ever see Bonaparte."

"He's working on a paper for the Institut National."

"Ah, yes, something about a stone, I've been told.* How charming. The military man returneth and taketh up the mantle of an academic hermit. A wise posture. One I myself would have recommended, had I been consulted."

"It's not a posture." Although Bonaparte had indeed decided that he should remain out of the public eye to weaken rumours of ambition. And to consider his next move. *At the beginning of a campaign, to advance or not to advance must be carefully considered.* "Won't you come see us?" I asked. Something in Barras's voice suggested that he'd been offended. As well, I was concerned. The Directors had been treating Bonaparte with a

* *The stone slab found near the city of Rosetta provided the key to scholars on how to translate Egyptian hieroglyphics. The Rosetta Stone is now in the British Museum.*

conspicuous lack of respect. Jealousy, I suspected. And perhaps fear.

"Is that an invitation from you, or from the General?"

"From us both, of course."

"Of course," Barras said, lowering himself into a chair, his hand on the small of his back. Toto leapt onto his lap. "Have you heard what Director Sieyès said, when he learned that Bonaparte was back?"

"Sieyès was dining with Lucien Bonaparte, was he not?"

"Yes, those two are cosy, I've noticed. When Sieyès was given the news of Bonaparte's return, he is said to have exclaimed, 'The Republic is saved.' Curious, don't you think? I've been wondering about that, wondering what exactly he meant."

"*Sieyès* said that? Are you sure?" Director Sieyès is said to detest Bonaparte—and the feeling is mutual, certainly. I leaned forward in my chair, my eye on the door. "Do you think there is any truth to the rumour that Director Sieyès is plotting?"

"A conspiracy? Every man of politics in Paris is plotting something." Barras carefully lifted Toto back down onto the carpet and tugged the dog's tail playfully. "Rousseau warned that if one were foolish enough to found a Republic, one must be careful not to fill it with malcontents. Malcontents! The French Republic is a nation of malcontents. I've been telling you for years—we're doomed."

October 24.

"Bonaparte, there is something I have to ask you." I'd been reading to him from *Carthon*, his favourite poem by Ossian. *Who comes from the land of strangers, with his thousands around him? His face is settled from war.* "It's about Eugène."

Bonaparte looked at me, his eyes glazed, as if in a reverie.

"What happened in Egypt? I mean, what happened to Eugène. I've asked him, but he won't talk." It was more than that. At any inquiry, my openhearted son closed down, his voice became guarded, he looked away, his cheek muscle quivering.

"He fought in battles, he killed men, he was injured." Bonaparte shrugged. "He returned victorious. What more is there?"

Afternoon.

I discovered Mimi in the larder, sitting in the dark on the stone-flagged floor. "Are you all right?" I asked, alarmed.

"I overheard the soldiers talking. I found out what happened to Eugène."

I slid down on the floor beside her. "Oh?" Pheasants ripe with maggots were hanging above the slate shelves.

She examined the palm of her left hand, tracing the lines with her fingers. "I don't want to tell you."

I put my hand on her arm. Her skin was smooth and cool. "Please?"

She took a breath: Eugène and another aide, the two youngest, had captured a town of Turks.

"An entire town?"

The men had surrendered, pleading for their lives. Proudly, my son and his companion returned with their prisoners. But Bonaparte could not feed his own men, much less all these Turks. So the prisoners—thousands of them—were driven into the sea to drown. The next day Eugène's partner shot himself.

"Oh no," I whispered.

"There is more," Mimi cautioned me. Eugène was commanded to cross the desert. "He was to deliver a parcel to the Pasha—a warning." I leaned my head back against the wall, closed my eyes. Mimi's voice in the dark closet was low, musical. "A sack of heads."

Sickened, I imagined the shimmering heat, the stench. I imagined the flies, the ghosts. "But that can't be!" Bonaparte would not do such a barbaric thing—and he certainly wouldn't have commanded a boy to do it for him.

Bonaparte was tied up in meetings. I lay down, trying to decide what to do. Finally I got up and went out to the stable, where I found Eugène helping the coachman with a harness. He looked at me expectantly.

"May I talk with you for a moment?" I led us to the bench under the lime tree in the garden. "I've learned what happened with your prisoners—and the warning you had to deliver, to the Pasha." He turned away, biting his cheeks. "I wish you had told me!"

"I couldn't, Maman."

"Why?"

"You wouldn't have understood! You would have wanted to talk to the General about it." He looked at me directly, as if to challenge me. "You would have held it against him."

"Oh, Eugène . . ." But what could I say? He was right.

"Maman, please, *promise* me," he said, blinking back tears. "The General did what he had to do; we all did. You must not say a thing to him about it."

"Maybe Eugène would heal if his head spirits were soothed," Mimi suggested to me later.

Head spirits? And then I remembered. According to voodoo beliefs, head spirits imparted ancient wisdom—without them, one was at the mercy of life, a boat without a rudder.

"A ritual headwashing—to cleanse him, appease the spirits."

"Yes," I said. *Anything.*

"No," Eugène said, his cheek muscle twitching.

"But what would be the harm? It's no different from getting your hair washed."

"It's stupid, that's why."

"Perhaps, but . . . I'll buy you that horse you've been wanting."

"The black thoroughbred?" His mouth fell open. "*Really?* But it's four thousand francs."

I shrugged. *Somehow.* "Tonight?" A deal.

Gathering the ingredients proved easier than I expected. The stall in the market Mimi knew about had everything we needed.

At two in the afternoon I corralled Eugène. "Quiet," I commanded whenever he protested. Mimi mixed the ingredients, chanting, the words coming back to her slowly. She worked her strong fingers into his scalp. I poured buckets upon buckets of clear water over my son's head, murmuring, *I baptize thee, I baptize thee, I baptize thee.*

"That's it?" Eugène asked, rubbing his hair dry.

October 25.
One full day, and still no twitch.

3:00 P.M., a quiet moment.
Hortense, although polite toward Bonaparte, continues to regard him as a stranger. "I am fine, General Bonaparte," she'll say, or, "Good morning, General Bonaparte." Will he ever be Papa to her?

Eugène also calls Bonaparte "General," but with warmth in his voice. They shared a tent in Egypt, and it is easy to see that they've become close. He's started a new scrapbook, I've noticed, this one on Bonaparte's battles—his victories. Already it is thick. It sits on the shelf next to his childhood books, his scrapbooks on his father and Lazare. "You need room," I told him. "Perhaps you should store these ones in the basement."

He ran his fingers over the old scrapbooks, considering. "No, Maman, there is room for them all," he said, putting them back on the shelf.

This pleased me, I confess.

Early evening.
"The Directors had the *nerve* to put me on half-pay," Bonaparte exploded, coming in the door. I was in the drawing room with Hortense, trying to make conversation with Fouché and Bonaparte's brothers, Joseph and Lucien. "They treat me like a civil servant."

I suggested to Hortense that she go.

"Did you talk to Director Sieyès?" Lucien demanded.

I took up my embroidery hoop, my needle. Why would Bonaparte want to talk to Sieyès? And why would Lucien want him to?

"Uff. How anyone can stand the man is beyond me," Bonaparte said, scratching. He'd broken out in boils and was irritated to distraction by a rash.

Joseph noisily sipped his tea. "He would be useful, however."

"Essential," Lucien echoed.

Bonaparte scowled. In Egypt he'd been a king. In Paris he was merely a civil servant, a penitent begging favours at the feet of the five Directors—a cabal of old fools, he called them. "Although he is right about the constitution. It *is* unwieldy," Bonaparte went on, talking to himself, thinking out loud. "Five directors is too many. A three-man executive would be more efficient, one person in charge, the other two advising." Bonaparte paced back and forth in front of the fireplace, his hands behind his back. "And the constant change-over is only creating chaos. We've been reduced to a parliamentary comedy. There is such a thing as overdoing it—holding elections every year has exhausted the population. But the trick will be to change the constitution within the law."

"To do that," Fouché said evenly, "you must have the support of both the Revolutionaries and the Royalists." He'd powdered his hair in an unsuccessful attempt to disguise its ugly red colour.

The three Bonaparte brothers turned to Fouché, as if surprised to discover that he was in the room.

"And do I have that support, Citoyen Fouché, Minister of Police?" Bonaparte asked.

Fouché took out a battered tin snuffbox, tapped it, then pried it open with his thumbnail, which was long, pointed and yellowed. "Yes, General, I believe that you do," he said slowly, taking a sniff of snuff without offering any. "Or, to be more precise—I believe that you will."

October 26.

Bonaparte and I set out at seven this evening to see Diderot's *Le Père de famille.* I was looking forward to an evening of entertainment.

Now it is only one hour later and we are already back home, frustrated and dejected—and a little overwhelmed, for as soon as the people recognized Bonaparte they started to cheer and scream, drowning out the voices of the actors. We had to leave in order that the performance could go on. We are prisoners of their adulation.

In which I must make a choice

October 27, 1799.

Lieutenant Lavalette gazed around our drawing room. He looked lost, somehow, one of the world's innocents. He clasped my hand, his fat cheeks flushed pink from the cold. "Please tell me, how is Émilie? How is my wife? I did not know! Oh, but I would not have been able to live had I lost her."

"You've not seen her yet? You've not been out to Saint-Germain?"

"I understand you and the General will be going out tomorrow morning."

"And Hortense, and Eugène. Do you wish . . . ? Would you like to come with us?"

"Oh, yes," he exclaimed, clearly terrified to go by himself.

October 28.

We set out for Saint-Germain early, Bonaparte, Lavalette, Hortense and I in the carriage, Eugène riding beside us on Pegasus, his splendid new horse. The road was a bit heavy in spots, so it was noon by the time we pulled into the school courtyard.

"General Bonaparte, we are honoured." Madame Campan, wrapped in a black cape, dipped her head. We were ushered into her office—all but Hortense, that is, who went running to find Émilie (to warn her). A bell sounded; the ceiling shook with the sound of stampeding girls. "I'm to fetch your wife, Lieutenant Lavalette?" Madame Campan asked.

"Madame Campan, if you don't mind, I'd like to tell Émilie myself," I said, moving toward the door.

It had been over a year since I'd been in the upper storey of the school. The air was heavy with the smell of pomade and starch. Two girls in the green hats of second-year students were gliding down the hall, arms linked, giggling as they slid on the waxed parquet.

"Hortense is in that room," the girl with golden ringlets said, pointing across the hall.

The door creaked open. "She refuses to go downstairs," Hortense whispered, stepping aside. Émilie was huddled on a narrow bed in the corner, her scars inflamed.

I sat down at the foot of the bed. "Are you afraid, Émilie?" Her husband certainly was.

"No!"

"What is it then?"

"I don't want to be married." (I thought, If you only knew, poor girl, how lucky you are.) And then, her voice low, "To him."

Lieutenant Lavalette's eyes filled with tears when he saw his wife's scarred face. I'd prepared him as best I could, but even so, the sight could only have been a shock, she is so terribly disfigured.

"Ah, so it is true. You've been poxed," Bonaparte said.

Émilie stood in the doorway, her reddened eyes fixed on the toes of her lace-up boots. "Yes, General Bonaparte. Sir." She glanced at Eugène, nodded a furtive, shy greeting. Eugène went up to her, pressed his cousin to his heart. I was touched by my son's tenderness. He'd so comforted Émilie when she was a child of four, and he not much older. "Your husband saved my life," he told her. "More than once."

Lavalette flushed modestly, clutching his hat.

And now perhaps this gentle man might save the heart of this girl, I thought—if only she would let him.

October 29, early morning.

"You paid 325,000 for it?" Bonaparte regarded the château of Malmaison, its crumbling façade, the roof in need of repair, the cracked glass on a second-storey window.

"But Bonaparte—" I started to remind him that he himself had offered 300,000, but thought better of it. "It's less than one hour from Paris and the grounds are superb. Plus, the winery alone brings in an income of eight thousand francs annually." Well, seven. "The agent felt it was an exceptional value."

"The chicken coop has more prestige."

But by the end of the day, after riding the property on horseback, looking over the sheep herd and talking with the estate-steward about the sugar content of this year's grape harvest, even Bonaparte had begun to succumb to the charm of the place. At nightfall we sat by the roaring fire playing backgammon, while Hortense played a new composition she had written on the piano and Eugène mended fishing gear.

At nine Bonaparte and I retired, taking candles up to our drafty little bedroom ourselves. We slid between the frigid bed sheets, our teeth chattering, our feet seeking the hot brick wrapped in flannel. Then, in our little cocoon of warmth, we talked and loved, talked and loved.

Evening—Paris.

We're back in the city. This afternoon I've meetings with tradesmen. Bonaparte wishes work done on Malmaison—renovations, furnishings, gardens! He loves it there.

October 30.

"What are you thinking?" I nudged Bonaparte with my toe. He was sitting on the edge of the bed, motionless as a statue.

"That I should talk to Director Gohier," he said finally, as if waking from a trance.

"Concerning . . . ?"

Fauvelet came to the door, a stack of journals under his arm. "The General's bath awaits," he said grandly.

Bonaparte stood, took the tiny cup of Turkish coffee his secretary handed him, downed it in one swallow. "Concerning getting elected director."

3:00 P.M.

"*Basta.*" Bonaparte pulled at his boots, kicking one free. It went flying across the foyer and hit the door.

"Director Gohier wasn't helpful?" I followed him, retrieving his boots. They were filthy, in need of a polish.

Bonaparte threw himself down on a chair and glared into the fire. He was wearing the pair of leather breeches that the actor Talma had lent him, so that he would have something presentable to wear to meetings with the Directors. They should have been returned. I tugged at his toe to get his attention.

"I told him I wanted to be a director."

"And what was his response?" Both in Italy and in Egypt Bonaparte had proved his genius for administration. If he were one of the five Directors, perhaps the Republic would—

"He laughed at me! 'You're too young, the constitution doesn't allow it, it wouldn't be legal.'" Bonaparte's voice was mocking. "Legal! The constitution is strangling this country and they refuse to do anything about it. They pray at the altar of the law, as if it were the word of God, this thing, this constitution they serve. They forget that it is the other way around—*we* made the laws, *we* created the constitution and *we* can change it." Pacing, his hands behind his back. "And if they won't, I will!"

October 31.

A hectic but exciting day at Malmaison, planning gardens, supervising improvements. Hortense's new horse was delivered, a lovely bay cob mare. It raced around the paddock, whinnying to Pegasus. "Thank you for the horse, General Bonaparte," Hortense said, addressing her stepfather as if he were a guest—an honoured guest, but a guest none the less.

In the late afternoon the four of us—Bonaparte, Eugène, Hortense and I—surveyed the grounds on horseback, talking with the workers. Then Eugène and Bonaparte raced their horses back to the château.

"You know, Hortense, it would please Bonaparte if you called him Papa," I said to her, our horses walking lazily.

"Yes, Maman," she said, her eyes welling up with tears.

[Undated]
This evening I noticed Bonaparte standing in front of the pianoforte, studying a sheet of music—*Partant pour la Syrie*, a marching song Hortense wrote when she was sick with worry about her brother in Egypt.

"That's one of Hortense's compositions," I said.

"It's good," he said thoughtfully, flicking one corner with his fingernail.

November 1—back in Paris.
"Do you know what Minister Fouché told me?" Fortunée Hamelin asked, stooping to tie the leather thong of her Roman-style sandal. "He suspects someone fairly high up in the government may be in league with the Royalists." She sat up, demurely tucking a breast back into her bodice.

"How high up?" Madame de Crény asked, playing a card.

"A director."

"Can't get any higher than that."

"*That's* interesting. I heard that one of the directors was sending copies of all the minutes and correspondence to England."

"What an awful thought!"

"And so, of course, everyone suspects Barras."

"Ah, poor Père Barras, everybody's favourite bad boy."

"My linen maid is convinced the Royalists gave Director Barras five million."

"I heard two million."

"Rumours!"

"But that's not the worst of it."

"Oh?"

"The worst of it, is they're saying that General Hoche found out, and so Barras had him—"

No! *Don't* say it.

"—poisoned."

And now, alone in my dressing room, I prepare for bed. I've bathed, powdered, done up my hair in a pretty lace nightcap. Waiting for Bonaparte, who is in meetings still. It is a peaceful picture I see in the glass, a woman writing in her journal. The candlelight throws a soft halo of light. Yet within me there is no peace, for I am disturbed by some of the things that the Glories said this afternoon. Gossip, I know, but even so, an evil seed of doubt has been planted in my heart. I think I know Barras—but do I? I thought I knew Lisette.

November 2, late.

Thérèse looked like a goddess of fertility, comfortably enthroned in Ouvrard's opulent box at the Opéra-Comique. At six months, her belly prominent, her bosom abundant, she was a vision of voluptuous femininity.

"I feel I haven't seen you for a decade," I said, kissing her. "Sorry I'm late." The three hammer strokes had sounded as I'd entered the lobby, but then there had been greetings to exchange with Fortunée Hamelin and Madame de Crény.

On stage two actors were engaged in a heated debate, two ladies under a "tree" looking on, bemused, fluttering enormous feather fans. "You haven't missed anything." Thérèse took my hand and didn't let it go.

The two men began chasing the two women around a bush. The people in the pit stood up and started yelling, waving their arms. "Is Ouvrard not here?" I asked.

"He detests opéra bouffe." Thérèse leaned forward into the glare of the gaslights. "Oh, there he is—with Talleyrand. Ah, and look—" She nodded to the left. "Our newly elected President of the Five Hundred." She stuck her nose in the air, a mocking gesture.

Lucien Bonaparte? I ducked back out of view. "I told Bonaparte I was at the riding school. He doesn't approve of the Opéra-Comique. He thinks I should only go to the Théâtre de la République." But the truth was, I didn't want him to know I was meeting Thérèse.

"He's getting to be such a snob." But smiling. "How *is* our darling boy?"

Thérèse considered Bonaparte a friend, but a history of favours and affection did not hold much credit in his eyes, I'd discovered—especially now, with her illicit pregnancy so visible. "Busy."

"I hear you've started your evenings again. From what I gather, all of Paris comes to your salon." She poured a glass of champagne, handed it to me. "Don't worry, darling, I won't embarrass you. I've been a social outcast for so long it doesn't even bother me."

A big man in the pit stood up and shook his fist at the stage. Others were pulling at him, trying to get him to sit down.

"Well! I knew the loveliest ladies would be in Ouvrard's box." Barras, his legendary hat askew, appeared with Toto tucked under one arm, wrapped in a red cashmere scarf. "So the General let you out tonight, Madame Bonaparte?"

"You brought Toto to the theatre?" I put out my hands.

"He's not feeling well. The two of us actually."

"He's cold," I said, tightening the scarf around the quivering creature. The miniature greyhound resembled a rat more than a dog.

"You'll join us, darling?" Thérèse asked.

"Is the General among us?" Barras looked behind the curtain. A stone on his little finger caught the light—an enormous ruby. "Or is he still in hiding?"

Barras had been drinking, I suspected. There was something dangerous in his manner. "I couldn't induce Bonaparte to venture out," I said. The public's enthusiasm for my husband made appearances difficult. But I couldn't say that to Barras.

"A wise move. We've had reports that his army want to kill him—for deserting them in that godforsaken land." He smirked. "For leaving them to die."

Thérèse threw me a look of caution.

"Forgive me, ladies! We are enjoying an evening of light opera, are we not? Certainly not tragedy, of which the much-applauded General does not approve." In fact, Bonaparte enjoyed tragedy, loved classical theatre, but I didn't think it wise to correct him. "Of course not," he ranted on. "The General understands Parisians. They want only victory, glory, a glittery show. But caution, Citoyennes—for they weary quickly. Indeed, one must ask, does such a fickle people even deserve democracy? Perhaps there is something to be said for the stability of a monarchy. The French are a feminine people—they *long* to be dominated." He smiled. "What a shocking thing to say! How fortunate to be among friends."

November 3.

Shortly after eleven I heard the sound of a horse galloping down the lane. Only Bonaparte galloped into the courtyard—he knew no other pace. Then I heard the front door slam.

"How did it go?" I'd been waiting for him to return.

"How did *what* go?" Tossing his hat onto a table.

"Your meeting with Barras," I said, taking up his hat, wiping the rain from the brim.

Bonaparte threw himself into a chair by the fire. "Well, you were right about one thing—Barras agrees that a change is in order." He jumped back to his feet. "Indeed, he even told me the Republic is in need of someone to take the helm, a man with vision, a military man who enjoys the confidence of the people."

Yes, I nodded, almost fearfully. It was obvious to everyone who that man was.

"He even informed me that he has the man picked out." Bonaparte paused for effect. "General Hedouville."

Hedouville? Who was Hedouville?

Bonaparte hit the wall with this fist. "Exactly! Hedouville is a nobody. Barras insults me by making such a suggestion. Wasting—my—time." He enunciated each word with spite.

I took a breath, not moving. "No doubt there has been a misunderstanding."

Bonaparte stomped out of the room, knocking an ancient Egyptian vase to the floor as he went by.

November 4.

"I've decided to go with Director Sieyès," Bonaparte informed me at breakfast.

"But—" Sieyès and Bonaparte detested each other!

"The romance of the Revolution is finished; it's time to begin its history." He downed his scalding coffee in one gulp and wiped his mouth with the back of his hand. "Can I count on you?"

"I don't understand." Count on me for what?

"To help out, talk to people, be persuasive. You're good at that. But you'll have to keep quiet about the plan. No talking to your Glories."

"There's a plan?"

"Director Sieyès has had one worked out for some time, as it turns out."

Ah, I thought, so the rumours are true—Director Sieyès has been plotting something.

"First, the five Directors resign. Second, Directors Sieyès and Ducos and I form a new executive council. Third, we craft a workable constitution. Sieyès assumes it will be the one he has been working on, of course." He scoffed. "But everything within the law."

It sounded so logical—so easy. "And Barras will agree to resign?"

Bonaparte poured himself a second cup of coffee, scooped in four heaping spoons of sugar. "He'll have no choice."

I paused before asking, "What do you mean?"

"I mean he'll be powerless, we'll be stronger."

Suddenly I understood what Bonaparte was saying. He was going to overthrow Barras—by force, if need be. "But Bonaparte, Barras has helped you so much. If it weren't for him . . ." I started to say, If it weren't for Barras, we wouldn't be married. If it weren't for Barras, Bonaparte would be nobody. But these were not words one could say to a man like Bonaparte. "Why can't Barras be included? You said yourself he believes something needs to be done."

"He'd want to be in charge. The people are not going to support a new effort if they see him at the helm. They'll think it's just another money grab on his part, just another way to milk the Treasury for his personal gain."

"There's no evidence to support those rumours! All we really know for *certain* is that Barras has been your most loyal supporter."

"That's not a factor any longer. There are more important issues."

"This is heartless." I threw down my embroidery.

"You'd likely not say that if you knew that your so-called friend is conspiring with the Royalists."

"That's a terrible thing to say!"

"Correction—it's a terrible thing to do."

I stared out the window, unseeing. War times are not moral times, Barras had once told me. But there were things I preferred not to know.

"The Royalists have long been seeking someone inside the French Republic to help put a king back on the throne—someone high up, someone powerful and someone who could be swayed by their gold. Your friend—"

"Our friend, *your* friend, Bonaparte. This is just conjecture. You don't have proof."

"Look at Grosbois, look at the way Barras throws money around. Do you think one can live like that on a director's salary, on gambling wins?"

I swallowed with difficulty. "Just because Barras is wealthy doesn't mean he's in league with the Royalists. Barras voted for the death of the King. He believes in the Republic."

"Barras believes in himself! Open your eyes, Josephine—he has been bought. This is no longer a personal matter. Too much is at stake. Do you think I make these decisions lightly?" He paused before saying, almost sadly, "There *is* evidence. Fouché has being going through General Hoche's papers."

I felt a strange sense of detachment, as if this were a story I had already heard. Barras was in league with the Royalists. If this were true, as I feared it must be, then what of the rest? What of all the other rumours—that Lazare had found out, that Barras had had him poisoned?

I felt weakened, sick at heart. I thought of the man I knew—big-hearted, generous Père Barras, a dedicated Republican, an ardent anti-Royalist. I thought of the tears I'd seen in his eyes when he spoke of Lazare. *This* was the Barras I knew in my heart. The other Barras seemed a fiction, a character in a play. "Are you sure, Bonaparte?"

Bonaparte put his arm around me. He saw that I was shaken, heard the dismay in my voice. "Josephine, my angel, we must be brave. We can't afford to fool ourselves. The Republic—and all that it stands for—will either survive, or it will perish."

"I know, Bonaparte, but—"

"Please, listen to me." He held my face in his hands. His skin felt soft and cool, soothing against my hot cheeks. "If you're with me, you can't be with Barras. It's as simple as that."

"You would ask me to betray a friend?"

"I am asking you to help save the Republic," Bonaparte told me gently, wiping my cheek with his thumb.

I laid my head on his shoulder. "What do you want me to do?" If I could not trust my heart, what could I trust?

"Just be your charming self. Don't let on. Barras must suspect nothing."

I nodded slowly. Very well then. "Can you promise me one thing?"

He kissed me lightly.

"Barras must be spared."

"I told you, this will be bloodless."

"There are other ways to ruin a man."

In which we have "a day" (or two)

November 4, 1799, evening, around 9:00 P.M.

Barras greeted us with open arms. "I've opened a bottle of excellent Clos-Vougeot. Did I tell you about the string quartet I've hired for later? I'm determined to conquer that German dance—what is it called? *Valse?* Un. Deux. Trois. Un. Deux. Trois. You see, it is not in the least bit complex, just a triangle, but somehow, by this means, one must move about the room. There's a trick to it. Un. Deux. Trois. Un. Deux. Trois. Ta la! You see, I've got it." He danced ahead of us into a salon where a small table had been laid with three covers, the fine crystal and golden flatware glittering in the candlelight. Gold-plated serving dishes had been placed on a side table. The air was sweet with the smell of juniper. "General? You will have a glass?" Barras pulled hard on the cork, sniffed it.

"I have my own, thank you," Bonaparte said, signalling to Roustam to step forward.

Barras looked with astonishment at the bottle of wine Roustam was uncorking. "A health measure," I rushed to explain.

"You have not been well, General? You must talk to my doctor. He'll be joining us later. He is oh-so-very wicked with the enemas." A peal of laughter. "Pardi! But I am full of animal spirits tonight. I must be getting sick. It is always the first sign."

The footman pulled out a seat for me. He started to pull one out for Bonaparte, but Roustam stepped in. A maid removed three golden lids: thrushes in a juniper dressing, rice with saffron, fat white asparagus with purple tips.

Two maids rolled in a trolley. Barras lifted a silver cover. "Ah, a most excellent tunny, esteemed for its beneficial effects on a troubled digestion, you'll be happy to know, General. You'll not be offended if I do the honours?" He scooped asparagus onto my plate. "We are, after all, like family here. I've been in the kitchen all morning, coaching my new chef on how a court bouillon is to be properly rendered—how it must be coaxed into being," he said, dipping and licking his index finger. "Grand Dieu, I believe he has a knack for it. General? May I have the honour of . . . No?"

Roustam had placed a hard-boiled egg on Bonaparte's plate. It rolled around the brim. Bonaparte cracked it against the edge of the table.

My hand jerked, nearly toppling my glass. What could I say? "Barras, have you seen that play that just opened at that little theatre on Rue du Bac? *Les Femmes Politiques,* I think it is."

"The play Thérèse is so upset about?* No, I've been too damn busy with Grosbois renovations. This new roof—what a mess. I haven't been out at all. Fortunately, watching Director Sieyès taking horseback riding lessons from my window here is entertainment enough. Every morning he manages to fall off. It's getting so a crowd turns out just to watch. I'm starting to think we could charge for admission. The last time I was so amused was watching Robespierre learn to ride."

"Sieyès is a little old to be taking up horseback riding, isn't he?" I could feel the heat in my cheeks. I knew that Director Sieyès was intent on riding beside Bonaparte—when the time came.

"What is it they teach in military school, General: when a politician begins to ride, prepare for battle?"

Bonaparte wiped the egg from his lips with his lap cloth and handed his plate and glass to Roustam. "No. When a politician betrays the people"— Bonaparte pushed back his chair—"that's when the battle begins."

[Undated]
"Just so you know, we're saying Director Barras is aware of the plan, that he's with us." Bonaparte tapped a stack of correspondence with his silver-tipped riding whip.

---

* *Thérèse believed that the play was about her.*

I nodded yes. Yet another deceit.

I have become a person I do not care for.

November 5.

President Director Gohier arrived punctually at four, as is his custom, carrying a bouquet of roses. "For the loveliest lady in Paris," he said, giving me a rather wet kiss.

Shortly after, Minister of Police Fouché arrived, skulking into the room in a dishevelled state, smelling of garlic and fish. I was on the settee by the fire, sitting with Director Gohier, enjoying a conversation about theatre. I moved over to make room for Fouché.

"What's the news, Citoyen Minister of Police?" Director Gohier asked.

"There is no news," Fouché said, feigning weariness.

"But surely there is something," Gohier said.

"Only rumours," Fouché said, catching my eye.

"About?"

"Just the usual about a conspiracy."

"Conspiracy," I exclaimed, shocked that he would so boldly speak the truth.

Fortunately, my shock gave the impression of ignorance, for Director Gohier, spilling his tea, echoed, "Conspiracy?"

"Yes, conspiracy," Fouché repeated without a trace of emotion. "But trust me, Citoyen Director, I know what's going on. If there were truth to the rumour, heads would be rolling by now, don't you think?" He laughed.

"Citoyen Fouché, how can you laugh about such a thing?" I pressed my hands to my heart.

Director Gohier put his arm about my shoulder. "Don't worry, my dear," he said to reassure me. "The Minister of Police knows what he is talking about."

All the while Bonaparte was leaning against the fireplace mantel watching—watching and smiling.

November 6, just after 1:00 P.M.

Bonaparte has just left for the banquet in honour of the Republic's military victories. I could tell by his embrace, his damp hand, that he was uneasy—as well as by the basket of provisions Roustam was carrying: a bottle of Malmaison wine, three hard-boiled eggs.

9:20 P.M.

Bonaparte didn't return home until almost eight. I took his wet hat. "Where have you been?" I demanded, keeping my voice low so that our guests would not overhear. I'd been in knots worrying.

He glanced over my shoulder into the drawing room, which was crowded with savants, politicians, military men, all talking politics, tense and conspiratorial. "I went to Lucien's after the banquet to make the final arrangements."

The *final* arrangements? "How was the banquet?"

"A dismal affair." I helped him off with his greatcoat. One of the boils on his neck was inflamed again. "The place was freezing," he said.

The playwright Arnault came up behind me. "General," he said under his breath, "Talleyrand sent me to find out what time tomorrow we—"

"Day *after* tomorrow," Bonaparte told him.

"But General, a day's delay, is that not . . . ?"

Dangerous, he started to say.

Our guests fell silent as Bonaparte entered the drawing room. Throughout the evening they watched to see who he invited back into his study—for whom the door was closed and for whom it was kept open. All the while I entertained gaily as if nothing was going on, as if I knew nothing.

Which may be the case, in fact. I calm and I charm, I amuse and I placate, but increasingly I have the sense that a great deal more is at stake than I realize, that the game has changed and I do not know the rules.

November 7, morning.

I woke to the sound of Bonaparte's tuneless singing. I remembered that it was Septidi, the second Septidi in Brumaire, and that the Glories would be gathering at Thérèse's for a coffee party. I decided to send word I wouldn't be able to come. Ill, I would be.

Ill I am, in fact—in spirit, in soul. I can't face Thérèse right now, can't bring myself to lie to her, to say, No, nothing's going on, there is no plan, no conspiracy to overthrow Père Barras.

Bonaparte just stuck his head in the room and told me to send Hortense and Caroline back to school in Saint-Germain—*today*. I protested that they had been looking forward to a ball that was going to be held tomorrow. Couldn't they stay one day longer? His answer worries me: "I don't want them anywhere near Paris," he said.

There is more to this than what I've been told, I fear.

Darling,

The Glories were sad to hear that you're not well. Perhaps you are suffering from the same ague Barras seems to be afflicted with right now—of all times, the poor dear, what with his cousin from Avignon visiting with all five of her girls. The palace is swarming with little Barrases—it's like a girls' school there!

Get well. Soon it will be the turn of the century. Imagine! We are all of us already planning our gowns.

Your loving and dearest friend, Thérèse
Note—Good news. Barras promised to get that odious play closed down.

November 8.

Bonaparte returned from the palace shortly before noon. "You saw Barras? How is he?" I asked anxiously.

"He doesn't suspect a thing. I told him I'd like to see him tonight, at eleven, so that we might talk privately."

"And will you?"

"Of course not."

Lie, detract, deflect. So this is what it is like to be a conspirator, I thought—to put on the face of a friend, to plan that friend's undoing. I can only pray that it will be over soon, and that after I will become, once again, a person who speaks truly.

I heard a curse, the sound of a horse prancing. I opened the sash windows, leaned out. The coachman, Antoine, had an enormous black horse by the reins and was trying with difficulty to control it. "Whose horse is that?" It wasn't Pegasus, Eugène's new mount. This horse was bigger—and fiery.

Bonaparte joined me at the window. "Admiral Bruix has lent me his stallion for tomorrow."

"*You're* going to ride that horse?"

Bonaparte looked at me, amused. "You don't believe I can?"

[Undated]

Bonaparte is happy, industrious, cheerful even: writing dispatches, speeches, preparing for what's to come—preparing for a victory. "How does this sound?" he asked, reading out loud: *"Nothing in history resembles the end of the eighteenth century, and nothing at the end of the eighteenth century resembles the present moment."*

"Perfect," I said, frightened.

7:20 P.M.

"This jacket suits you," I told Eugène, picking a hair off his lapel. It is a becoming dark green, cut away in the front, tails in the back, and a high turned-over collar.

"It's too new, too pressed," he complained.

"You're going out?"

"I'm going to the Recamier ball at Bagatelle—I told you last week. Don't you remember?"

I groaned. Everything was happening so fast, it was impossible to keep track. Every evening there had been meetings late into the night.

"Why aren't the girls here? I thought they were all excited about it.

And oh, about tomorrow," he said, heading out the door, "I think I'll invite that juggler I told you about—the one I met at the Palais Égalité. And maybe his friend the mime artist."

Mon Dieu—his breakfast party. I'd forgotten. "Eugène, I'm sorry, but I'm afraid I'm going to have to ask you to cancel it," I called after him.

"Maman!" He gave an exasperated groan.

"It's just that we have so many coming as it is."

"So I gather! What's going on?"

November 9.

I woke to the smell of smoke. I pushed back the bed curtain, alarmed. The fire in the fireplace illuminated Mimi's face, her white morning gown. "Oh, it's you," I said, whispering so as not to waken Bonaparte. "What time is it?"

"Just past six." She pushed open the heavy drapes.

"Six!" I swung my feet onto the cold floor. Thinking: day one, day two, and then it will be over. That is the plan. Thinking: today is day one. Today it begins.

Mimi draped a cashmere shawl over my nightclothes. "There's frost on the ground," she said, giving my shoulder a squeeze. "And men in the courtyard."

"Already?" I pushed my feet into a pair of fur slippers and shuffled to the alcove window.

"I invited them in, but they said they preferred to stay outside." She rolled her eyes. "Soldiers."

"What time is it? Is Fauvelet here yet?" Bonaparte asked, abruptly opening his eyes. "Where's Roustam? Roustam!"

Roustam, wearing a thick turban of wool for warmth, looked in at the door. "Master?" He bowed, putting down the tray of shaving implements on the dressing table, the crockery bowl of steaming hot water.

"Get Gontier up here, and the groom," Bonaparte commanded Mimi. He sat down in the hard leather chair, pulling a fur throw from the bed and draping it over his knees. He tilted back his head, exposing his throat. "And Antoine!" he ordered, causing Roustam's brush of thick lather to catch his ear.

I went downstairs to the kitchen to see how the cook was managing. Breakfast invitations had been sent out to over one hundred military officers. Did we even have china for that many?

Callyot, unfortunately, was about to have an apoplectic fit. The yeast dough for the bread had not risen due to the unseasonable frost. We contrived to cover the pans with a comforter, lining them up near the ovens. Then Eugène came tumbling down the narrow stairs, groggy from not enough sleep, and starving, he said. "Why is everyone in uniform? What's going on?"

"I suggest you get in uniform as well," I said, handing him a roll which he consumed in one gulp. "And best saddle your horse."

It was still dark when Talleyrand arrived. "I didn't think you rose before noon," I said, serving him the beer soup I knew he favoured.

"I haven't been to bed yet."

"You won't have a coffee?" The smell of beans roasting filled the house.

"My brain does not require nourishment," he said without expression.

"You are so calm, Citoyen." Unlike the rest of us!

"Perhaps you forget, Madame, I am always the victor."

Immediately he was joined by Bonaparte and the two moved slowly toward the door, Talleyrand's big boot making a scraping noise on the parquet floor. "Be respectful," I overheard Bonaparte telling him, "but make sure he understands that he has no choice."

"Is Talleyrand going to see Director Barras?" I asked Fauvelet, my voice low so that the men in the drawing room would not overhear. "To persuade him to resign?"

"With the help of two million francs," Fauvelet said, biting the nail of his thumb.

Two *million?* I mouthed the words, made frog eyes. "That *is* persuasive."

"Yes, if Talleyrand doesn't pocket it for himself."*

I went the rounds of the drawing room, making light conversation, but it wasn't easy: everyone was tense, sipping champagne, all the while watching the door to the study. I heard the sound of trumpets.

Two messengers of state stooped as they came through the door, careful not to crush the plumes on their hats. "An official message for General Bonaparte," one announced, sniffing from the cold. "From the Council of the Ancients."** Pox scars, enflamed by the chill air, gave him a feverish look.

Everyone in the drawing room parted as I led the two men through to the study. "Get Eugène," Bonaparte's secretary told me. "The General wants him."

Eugène leapt to his feet when I summoned him. Flustered, he disappeared into Bonaparte's study, then reappeared shortly after smelling of cigar smoke. "I have to go," he told me, strapping on his father's sword.

"You'll be needing this," I said, handing him his hat. "What's going on?" Not that a mere mother had any right to know.

"I have to make an announcement—to the Council of the Ancients! I'm to tell them the General is coming." He made a nervous face, chewing at his nails in mock terror.

I smiled at his charming antics. He is eighteen now, but often acts like a boy. "You'll be fine," I assured him. Although, in fact, when it came to theatre Eugène had always been one to forget his lines.

The courtyard was crowded with men in uniform, all waiting—for what, they didn't know. They watched with interest as Eugène mounted his horse. He tipped his hat—proud, I knew, to be riding such a fine creature in the uniform of an aide-de-camp—and cantered down the

It's not known whether Barras ever received this money; it is possible Talleyrand did in fact keep it.

** *Napoleon was expecting a decree from the Council of the Ancients giving him control of the troops in Paris. This was the first step in the plan.*

laneway. I went back into the house where I discovered Bonaparte in the dining room, talking to Fauvelet. He gave me a quick kiss. "It's time."

The men in the courtyard cheered when Bonaparte emerged. *The king of mighty deeds,* I thought, recalling a line from Ossian. He addressed them from the top step as if he were on campaign. Suddenly—magically!—the sun came out and there was a clashing of swords and a jubilant tossing of hats. *The sunbeam pours its bright stream before him, a thousand spears glitter around.*

Antoine, the coachman, emerged from the stable with the black stallion, the horse rearing in spite of the stud chain over its nose. Someone held the stirrup as Bonaparte mounted. The stallion shied, very nearly unhorsing Bonaparte. He yelled to his men, pulling back on the reins. The horse reared, then bolted down the narrow lane, shaking its head and bucking, the men in pursuit.

Suddenly it seemed so quiet. I turned, surprised to discover Fauvelet behind me. "You're not going with him?" Except for the servants, the house was empty now. Empty for the first time in what seemed like months.

"Madame," he said, observing the distress in my eyes, "be assured that the plan is a good one—"

"I know, Fauvelet." Today the Directors would resign. Tomorrow a temporary committee would be formed to craft a workable constitution. All within the law—a bloodless coup. "I guess I'm not very good at this, at being a conspirator."

"Madame, I beg to differ. I believe you are very good at it."

A day in history does not have any special weather; there is nothing unusual about the way it unfolds. The cow must be milked, linens freshened, bread baked. But for the skipping of my heart, my silent prayers, but for my anxious watching at the window, listening for the sound of horses in the laneway—a day like any other.

It was shortly after noon when Bonaparte's courier Moustache came trotting into the courtyard with the news that General Moreau had agreed to take command of the troops guarding the Luxembourg Palace.

Fauvelet jumped up. "That's the key!" He confessed that he had, in truth, been a little bit worried—more worried than he'd let on, in any case.

"But why must the palace be kept under guard?" I asked.

"Directors Gohier and Moulins are being kept prisoner there," Moustache said.

Prisoner! "What about Director Barras?"

"He's gone to his country estate, under escort."

Under guard, he meant. Mon Dieu.

A night of betrayal, a night of prayer. Mimi helped me into bed, gave me hysteric water and laudanum, piled me high with comforters. Yet even so, warmth eluded me. I waited, clutching Lazare's Saint Michael's medal, startling at the slightest movement, the shadows. Full of fear, remorse. Waiting for my husband, my son. Waiting. And praying. *La liberté ou la mort.*

It was very nearly midnight when I heard the sound of horses in the courtyard. I met Bonaparte and Eugène at the door. "Thank God, you're safe!" I cried out, embracing them both. I was so relieved to see them. My son yawned, indifferent to danger, and stumbled up the stairs to bed.

"You were worried? Why?" Bonaparte asked, unbuckling his sword. "Everything's going smoothly, according to plan."

"I'm . . . frightened." *Terrified.* "I'm worried that Barras might try something, send some of his ruffians to—* Is there enough of a guard outside, do you think?" We seemed so exposed.

"There's no need. Roustam will sleep outside our door," Bonaparte said, but he nevertheless pulled out a brace of pistols, cocking them to see

* In his memoirs—published one hundred years later—Barras confessed that he had in fact arranged for assassins to kill Bonaparte, but had called them off at the last minute.

if they were loaded. He came around to my side of the bed and put one on the table beside me. "Just in case," he said, tugging my ear.

Bonaparte, accustomed to battle and battle nerves, made feverish love and then immediately fell asleep. I lay beside him for what seemed like hours, my heart's blood pounding: *la liberté ou la mort, ou la mort, ou la mort.*

November 10.
Day two. I woke with a start, pulled the bell rope. What time was it? I could hear commotion out in the courtyard. Bonaparte wasn't in bed— why hadn't he wakened me?

"They're almost ready to leave," Mimi said, rushing in with a lantern. She went to the window, pulled back the curtain. "The General is in the courtyard now."

By the light of the flambeau, I could see Bonaparte adjusting his saddle. "Quick, tell him I must see him."

"Now?"

I grabbed her elbow. "Insist on it."

Bonaparte ran up the stairs, his spurs jingling. I pulled him to me, kissed him. "For luck," I said, my eyes filling. He pressed his forehead against mine, his eyes closed as if in prayer. Everything depended on this day.

Just after 6:00 P.M.
Still no word. It's so quiet I can hear the candles dripping.

8:15 P.M.
A crowd has gathered at the gate. I sent my manservant to inquire. He returned with a hangdog look. "They think there's been an attempt on the General's life, Madame."

"An attempt?" I repeated, imagining the words *wound, injure, cripple, maim*. Imagining the word *killed*.

Shortly after the clocks struck ten—in unison, a rare and almost mystical occurrence—a carriage pulled into the courtyard. I recognized the white horses, the Leclercs' ornate carriage. Pauline fell into her valet's arms and was carried to the house, followed by a woman in black, Signora Letizia! I rushed to the door, opened it myself. Pauline was sobbing hysterically. "What happened?" I cried out, panic rising in me.

"It's just a mother fit," Signora Letizia said, stomping into the house.

I asked Mimi to fetch hysteric water and whisky.

"Brandy," Pauline said between gasps for air.

Signora Letizia took a chair by the roaring fire. "We went to the theatre," she said, looking about the room with obvious disapproval. She thinks my taste too expensive, I've been told, but at the same time lacking sufficient display. "We were in act two—"

"What does it matter which act?" Pauline cried out, pulling at her handkerchief. "The comedian Eleviou stopped the performance—" She was interrupted by Mimi's entrance into the room with a tray of glasses and bottles containing hysteric water, laudanum, salts and brandy. Pauline pushed the hysteric water aside and poured herself a brandy, dousing it liberally with laudanum and downing it in one choking gulp. "He stopped the performance to announce that the traitors of the Republic—"

"She made a scene." Signora Letizia imitated the sound of loud weeping.

"—had tried to assassinate my brother."

I gripped the arms of my chair. Assassinated? "Bonaparte has been . . . ?" A sob rose in my throat.

"No. At the gate a lady told me my son was *king*," Signora Letizia said.

I stood up, went to the window, pulled back the drape. A chill came off the glass. King?

"The General has saved the Republic!" Bonaparte's courier Moustache smelled of liquor. "The spirit of the Republic has saved the General!"

"What did he say?" Signora Letizia demanded. "The spirit saves who?"

"He said Bonaparte has had a victory," I said slowly, so that my mother-in-law would understand.

"Ah, victory," she said, flashing her even teeth.

Almost midnight.

A cold pouring rain. Signora Letizia and Pauline left about a half-hour ago, thank God. I am alone again, alone with my thoughts, my prayers—keeping vigil. I think of the men on horseback in the rain, of Bonaparte and Eugène. I think of Barras out at Grosbois, alone like myself. I see him walking the cold and empty halls—drunk, likely, weaving and raging. Betrayed.

Fouché just came and went, bringing the news that victory had not been as easy as they had hoped. In the end, force had been required.

Force? "But everything was to be done within the law."

"It's law now," he smirked.

Almost 2:00 in the morning, still raining.

Eugène is home—at last!—soaking wet, but exhilarated by battle, a battle won. "Deputies were running all over the place, holding up their togas like ladies. Their red capes are everywhere—on the bushes, in the trees."

"And Bonaparte?"

He laughed. "That black stallion very nearly threw him. He looked a fright. His face was covered with blood—"

"Blood!"

"—from scratching that boil," he assured me.

Dawn.

Bonaparte and Fauvelet didn't return until four in the morning. I was sitting up in the dark when they came into the bedchamber, Fauvelet carrying a lantern, teasing Bonaparte about "talking foolishness."

I threw my arms around my husband. "What foolishness?" Examining his face in the dim lantern light, I could see traces of something dark. As Eugène had said, it looked as if Bonaparte had scratched his boil. I would treat it with plantain water in the morning, I thought. I made a mental note to talk to my cook.

Bonaparte threw his jacket over a chair. "I guess I got *a bit* carried away," he confessed.

"Tell me!"

Fauvelet let out a little giggle. "The General announced to the Five Hundred that he was the God of War and the God of Fortune," he said, setting the lantern down on a drum stool.

I looked at Bonaparte, amused. "Both?"

"I didn't say I *was* God," Bonaparte protested, putting out a foot so that Fauvelet could pull off his boot. "It just sounded as if I did."

"So tell me, what happened? How did it go?" I crawled back into the bed and pulled the comforters up to my chin, like a child eager to hear a bedtime story. And so I was told:

How Lucien had been the hero of the day—

"Lucien?"

Bonaparte shrugged as if to say, Who would have guessed?

How Lucien had publicly threatened to stab Bonaparte if he were ever a traitor to Liberty—

"He told them he'd stab you?"

"With his dagger drawn," Fauvelet exclaimed, demonstrating.

How Lucien had thrown down his toga and jumped on it—

"At the Tribunal?" Incredulous.

"Like this." Fauvelet jumped up and down.

"But he put it back on." Bonaparte was drinking cognac—something I'd never seen him do.

How fearless Murat had led the charge—

"There was a charge?" Alarmed.

"They were rising up against me!" Bonaparte pulled a flannel night-shirt over his head.

And how, confronted by a pressing crowd, Bonaparte had started to faint.

"Really?" How awful.

Fauvelet rolled his eyes as if to say, Yes, *really.*

"I hate that feeling," Bonaparte said.

And how it had been Lucien who had chased after the fleeing deputies in the dark, and had gathered together a sufficient number to pass a decree establishing a new government.

"So there are no longer directors?"

"Gone," Fauvelet said, yawning. "Instead, there are three consuls who have full executive—"

"Three *provisional* consuls," Bonaparte corrected him.

"Yes. General Bonaparte, together with Sieyès and Ducos, who—"

"Good night, Fauvelet." Bonaparte cut him short, slipping under the covers and burrowing close to me for warmth. I wrapped my arms and legs around him, kissed him. "And oh, don't forget—" Bonaparte lifted his head just as his secretary was about to shut the door. "Tomorrow we sleep in the palace."

VI

Angel of Mercy

The Age of Fable is over;
the Reign of History has begun.
—*Josephine, to Thérèse Tallien*

In which I must live in a haunted palace

November 11, 1799.
Hortense and Caroline arrived shortly before the evening meal. "Maman, it was so exciting!" Hortense exclaimed.

"I want to tell it." Caroline pressed her hands to her heart. "Joachim sent four grenadiers of the guard—"

"Commander Murat, you mean?"

"Yes . . . Joachim Murat sent four grenadiers to our school to tell me that the Republic had been saved by my brother." She fell back onto the sofa, as if in a swoon.

"Well, they weren't sent just to tell you," Hortense said.

"They were!"

"They came out to the school in the middle of the night?"

"Yes, and pounded on the door with the pommels of their swords!" Hortense said.

"No—with their muskets."

"Madame Campan must have been terrified." Those of us who had survived the Terror knew only too well the horror of that sound—the pounding on a door in the dead of night.

"We all were," Caroline exclaimed. "It was so romantic!"

The children are thrilled that we will be moving into the Luxembourg Palace.

"I wonder if it's haunted," Hortense said.

"Of course it's haunted," Bonaparte told her.

We crowded into our little carriage: Bonaparte and I, Caroline, Hortense, Eugène and Fauvelet. "Will we get a bigger carriage?" I asked. Ours was too small for us and inclined to break down—something that worried me on the isolated road to Malmaison. There were rumoured to be bandits in the quarry.

Bonaparte scowled. "The coaches at the palace seem to have disappeared. *And* the horses." He glanced at Fauvelet. "Make a note to check the crown jewels."

"But we'll have our very own riding arena," Eugène said.

"Is there a piano?" Hortense asked.

"I'm afraid all we have acquired are debts," Bonaparte said, drumming his fingers. And a broken country to mend. And a hungry people to feed.

The Gohiers' suite was very much unchanged. Their bed linens were rumpled, a mug of cold chocolate sat on the windowsill. I felt like an interloper, a thief.

"It will do," Bonaparte said, looking around. "We'll live in this suite, I'll work in the one below."

The salon was darker than I remembered, sombre and pretentious. Every few years a new director had moved in. The result was a nightmare hodgepodge of styles, all of them pompous. I did not want to live here, but I'd entered a realm in which personal choice was no longer relevant. "Could we redecorate?"

"We won't be here long," Bonaparte said.

"No?" I asked, hopeful. Hortense, Caroline and Eugène were racing up and down the marble staircase, yelling to make echoes. I wondered if my children remembered coming to see their father here, during the Terror, when the palace had been used as a prison.

Bonaparte circled the room, his hands clasped behind his back. "As soon as a new constitution is ratified, we'll move into the Tuileries."

The *Tuileries?* My heart sank. The Palace of Kings. The palace of beggars was more accurate. That dank, depressing structure had stood empty for almost a decade, home to vagrants and rats, no doubt—home to rest-less spirits.

"What about Barras's suite?" I asked. "Have you looked at it?"

"Haven't had a chance."

"Maybe I will," I said, suddenly anxious.

4:00 P.M.

Bruno leapt to open the door to Barras's former suite for me. "You're still here?" I said, shocked to see him.

"Madame, I was born here," he said with dignity.

I understood. He'd served first the King, then the Revolutionaries, then Director Barras, and now Bonaparte. It didn't really matter whom. It was the building he was loyal to, the palace itself. "I'm glad to see you, Bruno. I'm going to need your help."

He opened the wood shutters to let some light in and busied him-self building a fire. I sat down in the chair by the window. A red velvet throw had been draped over one side of it, giving off a strong scent of spirit of ambergris. I'd never seen this room so bright, I realized. Bar-ras liked it dark. The afternoon sun sparkled in the tiny crystal beads of the huge candelabra. I bent down to smooth a corner of the carpet. The parrot cage was still there, I noticed, the wire door open. There was a china cup half-filled with cold coffee on the table, beside a stack of journals. A violin case was open on the floor, Barras's violin laid on the upholstered bench. The music stand had been knocked over. I stood, righted it, put the music sheet back on the stand. Everything seemed familiar, yet strange. I thought I knew Barras so well, but now I wasn't sure. Was he a Royalist? Was he a murderer? I could not say for sure that he *wasn't*. All the rules had been broken. Now, anything seemed possible.

My reflection in the gilded bronze mirror startled me. I saw an elegant woman in a classical gown of fine muslin, her short curls veiled. She pulls her red cashmere shawl around her, for warmth. This was the home of her friend, but he no longer lives here. Her own home sits empty and she lives in the rooms of a stranger.

The fire roared, catching. "There," Bruno said, pleased, jumping back to admire the blaze.

"Is Barras's study open?" I asked.

"The office or the cabinet? I have the keys to all the rooms, Madame."

"The cabinet." Where Barras worked each morning, where he attended to his private correspondence.

I followed Bruno through two rooms to a small door off Barras's bed-chamber. It resembled the door of a confessional. Bruno knocked before inserting the key. "Habit," he explained with a sheepish grin. He opened the door, lit a lantern and bounded back into position against the wain-scotting, his eyes fixed on the ceiling.

Entering Barras's cabinet was like entering a cave: dark and remote from the world. I inhaled the scent of old wood. The furnishings were of plain design—which surprised me, for Barras loved opulence. I took in the shelves of books, the hourglass, the compass next to the marble quill holder on the desk, the globe, the oil portrait of a woman—his mother, I suspected, from the set of her eyes. I straightened it. The safe door hung open, the contents emptied. I ran my finger over the desktop. I wanted to look through the drawers, but I felt uneasy with Bruno watching. "Thank you, Bruno," I said, emerging. "No, don't lock it," I added. I would come back.

After midnight.

I don't know what I was looking for. I don't know what I expected to find. I knew Barras would be clever enough to empty the drawers and files of anything incriminating. And I was right, so I knew that the three letters I found had been left there intentionally—for Bonaparte's eyes. I recognized Lazare's loopy script right away. The letters were addressed to me. Three letters of love.

Now it is the dead of night. Bonaparte is fast asleep. I've read the let-ters, burned them. (Oh, my heart!) Lazare had written them to me at the end of 1795, when Bonaparte had been courting me—and Barras had been urging me to consider marrying him. I loved Lazare against all reason, and so was blind to Bonaparte. But then Lazare had stopped writing—or so I had thought. Assuming that I'd been forgotten, I gave in to Bonaparte's attentions.

And now, with a feeling of helpless anger and dismay, I understand. Barras had intentionally withheld Lazare's letters from me in the hope that I would marry Bonaparte. Bien. I can live with that, for I have come to believe that fate, however convoluted, however indirect, had intended for me to meet and marry Bonaparte.

But what I find truly shattering is the realization of why he'd held onto them. There is only one explanation: as long as Barras had those letters, he had the power to ruin me.

November 21.
Our first evening entertaining at "home": a long sober game of whist with the Consuls: Bonaparte, Sieyès (dry, taciturn, wrinkled beyond his years) and Ducos (nervously watching Sieyès and Bonaparte, imitating each by turn). After the game, the men took out their snuffboxes and discussed constitutional law. Yawning behind my fan I excused myself and went to the window, "for air."

It was a beautiful night, clear but cold. It smelled as if it might snow.

"A constitution should be short and obscure," I heard Bonaparte say.

"Yes, short," Ducos echoed, clearing his throat.

I heard a duck call outside. On the street side of the metal gates stood a man and three women—Fortunée Hamelin, Minerva and Madame de Crény! The man did a handspring: Captain Charles! I waved, threw them a kiss. Come out, come out, they gestured. I shook my head: I can't, sorry. (Oh, *so* sorry!) They began to sing an aria from *Don Giovanni.*

"The rabble are noisy tonight," Sieyès observed.

I closed the window, the drapes.

November 22.
"I'm sorry, Madame Bonaparte, Madame Tallien is not receiving."

"Still? Please, I must see her."

Thérèse's butler closed the door.

[Undated]

Every morning Bonaparte begins work at eight, whistling tunelessly. He reappears every few hours, kisses me, exchanges pleasantries, an amusing story, has a quick collation, a coffee or a sip of watered wine (usually a coffee), advises me on my toilette and disappears again, singing.

He is full of optimism. "My government will be a government of spirit and of youth." He says this in the face of the hordes of beggars on the streets, the robber bands everywhere, the nation's staggering debt. No detail is overlooked. This morning he ordered bulls imported from Switzerland to give strength to French herds, trees to be planted along all our roads. The Ministers are exhausted trying to keep up with him, for he requires daily reports.

And nightly, when a normal man would be entirely depleted by the events of the day, he attacks with the same zeal "our project." I'm not married to a man, I'm married to a whirlwind!

November 29.

"I'm sorry, Madame Bonaparte, Madame Tallien is not receiving."

Not receiving *me*.

[Undated]

Bonaparte is going mad working out a new constitution with Sieyès, who is both slow and illogical. For a price (a high one) Sieyès has at last agreed to step aside. Now, I pray, things will begin to move.

December 24, Christmas Eve.

There is great celebrating in the streets. The new constitution has been announced. "The Revolution is over!" people cry out, tears streaming.

Over? I want to believe this. I want to believe these words.

December 25, Christmas Day.
A lovely family gathering here this morning: Aunt Désirée, Hortense and Eugène. (It was too chilly for the Marquis to travel.) The children and I enjoyed taking Aunt Désirée on a tour. Aunt Désirée admired the black "Eagle" cooking range with a coal grate in the kitchen, and the elaborate network of bells and cords for summoning servants. The children insisted on showing her the secret passages. (I kept thinking I could hear Barras laughing.) Aunt Désirée left me with careful instructions on the use of Goddard's powder to polish silver and the proper way to clean walls lined with brocade (brush down and then rub with tissue followed by a soft silk duster).

Now, a quiet moment before preparing for the Bonapartes tonight. Bonaparte is busy drafting a letter to the King of England, proposing peace. Peace! A spirit of optimism has come over us all.

December 31.
Today is the last day of the eighteenth century. It seems that everyone in Paris (except me) is festive, gay, *drunk*—openly celebrating, for mercifully Bonaparte has allowed the Christian holidays to be observed. Wisely, rather, for it would have been impossible to ignore this significant turning.

January 1, 1800!
This is the first day of a new century. Just imagine! Everything I do, every move I make, has a careful yet excited feeling of beginning anew. This morning Bonaparte and I lingered long in our big feather bed, laughing and whispering, teasing and coquetting, working on "our project" (as he so solemnly puts it). I had a hint of the flowers two weeks ago. I am filled with hope.

Later.
One hundred and fifty-seven hackney cabs lined up outside the Palais Egalité to buy sugared almonds and marrons glacés. "Just like in the days

of the Ancien Régime," Eugène said, chewing a sugared almond, his chin dusted with powdered sugar. "I guess it wasn't all bad," he added, licking his lips.

[Undated]
I have been reading to Bonaparte every evening before he drops off to sleep.* This is a quiet time for us, a precious moment. He makes love to me, and then we talk, of our astonishing life, the challenges we each face, the exciting possibilities that lie ahead. And then I read to him, usually from his beloved Ossian. This evening the worn leather volume was not in its usual spot beside the bed. "I've burned it," he said, more in sorrow than in anger.

"Why?" I was shocked. Bonaparte took that book with him everywhere.

"It was a fake," he said. "I found out they're looking into it in Scotland."

"They weren't the words of Ossian?" I found that impossible to believe.

"No, someone made them up, and then claimed that Ossian had written them. Fooled us all." Embittered. "It just shows, doesn't it, that nothing can be trusted."

"But Bonaparte, the beauty in the words—nothing can take that away. Certain things one can trust absolutely." I put my hand against his cheek.

January 2.
It's official now. "We're moving to the Tuileries," Bonaparte has informed me.

The palace of the Bourbon kings.

The palace of our dead King.

And Queen.

---

* *Josephine was said to have a low, musical voice. When she read to Napoleon, the servants would hover outside the door to listen.*

January 3.

Mimi stood on the dirty cobblestones, looking up at the façade of the Tuileries Palace. Obscene messages, revolutionary emblems and slogans had been painted all over the walls. There were dark stains on the cobblestones—bloodstains, I feared. "What a mess," Mimi said, frowning.

The doors were stuck; it had been a long time since they'd been opened. Two men together (the architect and a journalist) were unable to loosen the seal. Then Bonaparte threw himself against it and the doors fell open. We laughed to see him fly.

"How easy for *you* to enter this Palace of Kings, Consul," the journalist said. "One would think you were expected."

"Palace of the *Government*, we're calling it now," Bonaparte corrected him.

"Yes, Consul!" He took out a paper, lead pencil.

I peered into the vast depths. The windows were high, dirty, some boarded over. It was cold, too, colder than outside. And musty. It smelled of old air.

"The hard part will not be moving in," Bonaparte said, brushing off his shoulders. "The hard part will be staying. Antoine, get the torches," he ordered our coachman. "I've a country to run."

"And the shawls!" I called after him.

"I'll get them," Mimi said, sprinting down the steps two at a time.

We were like a medieval procession in that place, some ancient doomsday rite. Antoine, torch held high, bravely took the lead, hitting a stick against the walls to scare off rats.

"Oh," Mimi said, clasping my hand.

"This must have been the King's suite," Bonaparte said, studying a plan. He looked up, around, paced off the room. "This will be my office. I'll receive in that room there." The room with the throne.

We descended to a lower level, darker, mustier and colder: the Queen's rooms.

"This place is gloomy, Consul General," the journalist said, his deep voice echoing in the empty rooms.

"Gloomy like all grandeur," Bonaparte said.

"The Committee of General Security met in this room," the architect said, examining the fireplace façade. "I recognize the detail on the chimney face. The Queen could not bear monotony—everything had to be ornate."

"Yes," the journalist said, his voice a whisper. We were in that forbidden realm: the realm of the past.

"Then that room over there, the reception area, must have been where Robespierre—" I put my hand to my eyes and pressed until I saw stars, but the image remained: of the tyrant, wounded, stretched out on top of a table with Blount, his faithful Great Dane, whimpering, licking his hand. Had Robespierre not died that day, I would not be . . .

It was then that I saw her, the figure of a woman in white, standing by the wardrobe.

They laid me out on the cold floor, my shawl under my head. Mimi fanned me, stirring up dust. I coughed, struggled to sit up. All of them were standing over me with worried expressions. "I'm fine," I assured them.

"She'll be fine," Bonaparte said, tugging at my hand.

"I'll get her, General," Mimi said, her hand supporting my head.

I leaned on Mimi for support. She was steady, not trembling. "Oh Mimi, wasn't she a fright!" I whispered. The men were examining the windows. I put my hand to my chest. A shakiness had come over me, and a chill; it seemed to come from within me, from inside my very bones.

Mimi frowned. "Who?"

"That woman by the wardrobe." Breathing in, out, in, out.

She had been mannish, her jaw firmly set, her hair cropped short, ill-covered by a ruffled cap. She'd been wearing a white gown with long sleeves, plain. "You must have seen her. She was standing by the wardrobe door. How could you not have seen her?" She was so clear.

"Oh-oh," Mimi said, screwing up her face.

Then I remembered where I'd seen that face, the jaw clenched against adversity. At Citoyen David's studio—his rough pen portrait of Queen Marie Antoinette, on her way to the scaffold.

January 7.

Too busy to write: working day and night getting the Tuileries Palace in condition to live in. It is ten o'clock in the morning and already I have selected fabric for all the drapes, met with my frantic cook about what the Tuileries kitchen will need (everything had been stolen: there's not even a stockpot) and met with Madame Campan about protocol and staff. (Madame Campan's experience as lady-in-waiting to the Queen makes her invaluable to me now. It's so overwhelming: my cook alone will require three assistant chefs in the kitchen. No wonder he's having fits.)

Tomorrow I'll attend to my wardrobe.

I'm hearing Barras's chuckle from somewhere in this palace. We are all of us going mad.

January 17.

Bonaparte came into my drawing room at noon. He sat down, staring into the fire. "Murat just asked for Caroline's hand."

"Oh?" Relieved, I confess. A week before I'd discovered Murat and Caroline sprawled on a sofa.

"Murat's the thirteenth child of an innkeeper; I don't want to mingle my blood with his. I was thinking more of General Moreau."

"But Bonaparte—"

"Perhaps it would be wisest to wait. In a short time it's possible I could marry her into royalty." He smiled. "Now that's a thought."

"Murat is brave," I persisted. A swearing swashbuckler so much the fashion now. A swashbuckler in peacock plumes. "He served you well at the Battle of Aboukir, and at Saint-Cloud."

"Brave isn't enough. He's not intelligent, he's uneducated and he's of lowly birth—"

"He suits Caroline perfectly."

Waiting to be called to supper.

An amusing exchange. "Are you sure this is what you want?" Bonaparte demanded of his young sister.

Caroline sat primly on the sofa, muslin ruffles everywhere. "I love him."

"That's easy to say now, but as your brother I must warn you, when he's naked, a big brute of a man like that, and in a state of desire, you're not going to find him so very—"

She burst into a peal of delighted giggles.

January 18.

It's done, the contract has been signed in the presence of every Bonaparte in Paris: Signora Letizia, the five brothers, two sisters, Uncle Fesch. And, as well, a tiny trio of Beauharnais: myself, Hortense and Eugène.

The house-poor brothers were scarcely able to scrape together a dowry of thirty thousand francs, ten thousand less than Elisa and Pauline each received when they were married, so at the last moment Bonaparte added a lovely pearl necklace. I frowned when I saw it. It looked familiar. It was familiar: it was my own.

January 20.

The iridescent pearls, loose on a black satin cloth, reflected the candle-light. "I've never seen pearls so . . ." So *pure.*

"Indeed, Madame, these are that rarest of gems, the round saltwater pink pearl." Monsieur Lamarck spoke in a reverent hush. "It is *impossible* to find pearls of this size and perfection: look at these ugly baroque pearls, Madame, to compare: covered with blisters. They resemble potatoes. Or look at this set of freshwater pearls, shaped like little wine barrels. But *these* pearls—" He handed me a magnifying glass, pulled a lantern closer. "These pearls have lustre." He murmured the word "lustre" confidentially, as if he were imparting dangerous information. "And *iridescence.* Observe: rainbows. *Captured* within. Indeed, Madame, it is an exceptionally thick layer of nacre that makes them so"—he rolled his eyes erotically—"*hypnotic.* Some claim that the nacre has healing powers—but that is strictly conjecture and as you know, Madame, we deal *only* in fact. Observe, Madame, a fact: they are imperfect. A *perfect* pearl is an imperfect pearl. Did you know, the Queen of Spain wears green pearls?" Whispering now. "Her jeweller should be hanged. But these pearls, Madame, these pearls are without question the finest in the world. Even a queen could wear them with confidence. Oh, forgive me." Withdrawing an enormous handkerchief from his gold-embroidered waistcoat pocket. "Excuse me, Madame." Sniffing. "I got carried away. Now, where was I—yes, the price. The price is five hundred thousand francs."

I swallowed, my mouth suddenly dry.

"Y-y-yes?" Monsieur Lamarck slipped off his spectacles, cleaned them with a corner of his handkerchief, put them back on. "Did I hear you correctly, Madame? Was it *yes* that you said?"

What has come over me, what have I done? I am made breathless by my daring, shaken by my foolishness—giddy by my gall! Such money! The price of a vast estate contained in a necklace. I look upon them entranced; it's as if they have cast a spell over me. I am transformed, bewitched! How am I to pay? I'll find a way, for I cannot be parted from them. I put on these gems, and I *am* a queen. Grand Dieu.

In which I must sleep in
Marie Antoinette's bed

January 21, 1800.
This evening Bonaparte handed me a thick file.

"What is this?" But I knew: it was the List—the names of the French aristocrats who were forbidden from returning to the Republic. For years Thérèse and I had lobbied to get names removed. Each small success had been a battle won.

"I'd like you to determine who should be taken off," Bonaparte said, opening his battered tin snuffbox.

I stared at him, not comprehending. "You want me to decide?" To name who was innocent, who guilty—rule whose life would be ruined, whose life saved?

"If you prefer, I could get Duroc to do it."

Duroc, the most heartless of Bonaparte's aides. "No, I'll do it!"

Now, alone in my boudoir, I look through the thick file, the names of so many thousands of men and women, and I am overwhelmed. Can I do this? I pray for strength.

February 5.
"Don't blame your hall porter," I told Thérèse. "I pushed my way past

him. May I come in?" I stepped boldly into the room. "I heard you had your baby, a girl."

Thérèse regarded me without a smile. Swaddled at her side was the infant, only a few days old. I stood for a moment in uncomfortable silence, remembering Thérèse as I'd first met her, her eyes so dark, so seeking. Eyes of wisdom, of innocence. And now, tired eyes. "I need your help going over the List. I've been asked to name the émigrés who should be allowed to return."

"Back to the Republic?"

I nodded. "But it's a big job, too big for me." One of Thérèse's canaries broke into song.

"Come in then," she said finally. "And take off your coat," she added in an exasperated tone, as if it was too difficult to maintain, this chill, an unnatural thing.

I put down the basket of comfits and toys I'd brought and leaned over the bed. "She's beautiful. She looks just like Thermidor when she was born. What's her name?"

"Clémence."

Mercy. Forgiveness. "Yes."

Thérèse touched my hand. "How are you doing, Rose?" Addressing me by my former name. My old self. Not my new self.

"Surviving." I shrugged.

"You and I, we'd hoped for more," she said, gesturing to a chair beside the bed.

Before long we were sharing confessions. I spilled out my heart to her, telling her how dismal it was to live in the palace, about all the boring fêtes, the tedious ceremonies, the Queen's ghost. "Forgive me," I said when the clock chimed three. "I promised myself I wouldn't stay long." It was unfair of me to unburden myself to this woman in childbed. I pulled my shawl around my shoulders and stood—but there was more, we both knew, a name not yet spoken. "How is he doing?" I asked finally.

"You care?" Yet her tone was curiously gentle.

Yes, I nodded. I cared. In spite of everything.

"He's drinking too much, gambling recklessly, his health is not good—but then all that's to be expected, I think, under the circumstances."

I felt the weight of her accusation. "You don't understand."

"Then enlighten me, please." Her huge eyes swimming.

"I had reason. That's all I can say."

She stared at me for a long moment. "I know Barras was taking Royalist money, but that was no reason to betray him. He was playing all sides. That's his way—he makes no secret of it. He was taking their money and using it against them." The baby made a chirping noise.

"Is that what he told you?"

"You don't believe it?" Thérèse asked, putting the infant to breast.

I felt a familiar tingling in my own breasts. "It's more complex than that, Thérèse." More deadly.

"He didn't poison Lazare, if that's what you're thinking. He broke down one night, told me everything."

"Oh?" Wine talking, no doubt—wine and tears, a potent mix. Wine and tears and rage. I knew Barras so well. But not well enough, as it turned out. I sat back down on the little upholstered chair by her toilette table. "But Lazare *was* poisoned?"

She nodded. "By a Royalist agent."

I propped my elbow on the table and rested my chin in the palm of my hand. Trying to take this in. "The Royalist agent Barras was taking money from?" My words hung in the silence.

She paused before saying, "One of them."

I glanced at my friend in the looking glass. Then I turned to face her. "But why?"

"Do you really want to know?"

I nodded, but fearful.

"Lazare found out what Barras was doing. So then he knew too much. The agent was worried he might talk."

So. A Royalist agent poisoned Lazare to silence him, to protect his dirty secret that Director Barras, the most powerful man in the French Republic, was in his pay.

"Barras went mad when he found out," Thérèse said, switching the baby to her other breast. "He wanted to strangle the man."

When did this happen? I wondered, thinking back. I was stunned by the realization that Thérèse had known and had kept it from me. "You knew all along." We had all been deceiving each other—a thought that did not comfort me in the least.

"We're all guilty," she said with a sweet-sad smile.

Except Lazare, I thought.

"*And so you see,*" Thérèse sang to her baby, quoting a line from *Candide,* "*the new world is no better than the old.*"

8:30 P.M.

Adélaïde Hoche sat upright in her chair like a schoolgirl, her hands folded neatly in her lap. Her eyes look frightened. Père Hoche stood behind her.

"I just want you both to know I found out what happened. At least, what likely happened," I said.

Père Hoche leaned forward, one hand on the back of Adélaïde's wooden chair, the other hand on his cane, a thick oak cudgel. One could kill with such a stick, I thought.

I began: "Director Barras had been taking money from the Royalists." Père Hoche cursed. "It's hard to know for sure what his intention was," I persisted. He'd been taking money from the Pretender faction as well as from the Orléanists, I explained. He'd been dealing with all parties, as was his way, but holding his cards close, playing his own game. Then, when he learned that evidence had been found exposing the Pretender agents, he decided to jump ship. To cover himself, he attacked the Pretender group—but the plan failed (at least the first time) and Lazare took the blame.

"They called my son a traitor."

"He had to go along with it, Père Hoche," I told him, as gently as I could. Lazare would have preferred musketfire to such a slur, I knew. Traitors were scum in his eyes. The scar on his face was testimony to the passion of his creed: as a youth of sixteen, he'd challenged a grenadier in his barracks who was spying for bribes. They'd duelled on Mont-Martre on a cold winter's day. The spy had scarred him, a badge Lazare had worn proudly. "If Director Barras had been accused, the Republic would have fallen. The agents knew that, so they tried to expose Barras. The agent for the Pretender must have shown your son proof that Director Barras had accepted their bribe money."

I could imagine the depth of Lazare's disillusionment, his disgust. "The Royalists were trying to get your son to turn against the Director, but it didn't work," I went on. "He knew what was at stake. Then the agent must have panicked, because General Hoche, their worst enemy, knew too much—knew everything."

"And so the agent poisoned him," Adélaïde said, her voice clear and strong. She was standing with one hand on the mantel—on the blue urn.

The urn. Mon Dieu, I thought, suddenly remembering what Fouché had said, about Lazare's heart. "Yes," I said, sickened, my throat tight. I heard the child laughing. I glanced up at Lazare's portrait, for strength. "Director Barras had nothing to do with it." The truth was not so simple, however. The truth was that Lazare, the brave innocent, had fallen victim to one of Barras's greedy intrigues.

February 6.
The final vote on the new constitution has been tallied. Bonaparte is now First Consul. Three million voted in favour—and less than two thousand voted against.* It's a miracle.

[Undated]
I knew by Fauvelet's flustered look that he had something to say to me, something I wasn't going to like. "It's about your debts, Madame. The First Consul wishes to have them settled."

"And so Bonaparte sent you?" Coward!

Fauvelet nodded. "I'm to ask you the total sum." He scratched his chin. "He will pay them. He only asks that you withdraw from all speculative endeavours now and in the future, Madame."

I paced around him as he talked. In truth, there was no other way. My debts were beyond my ability to settle. It wasn't all hats! (Although

* *The actual vote was 3,009,445 in favour, 1,562 against. Sieyès and Ducos stepped down to be replaced by Cambacérès as Second Consul and Lebrun as Third.*

I did owe for thirty-eight—how did that happen?) The big bills were substantial: Bodin Company debts, a National Property I'd invested in and Malmaison alone accounted for over one million. And the pearls, mon Dieu.

It is done: I've withdrawn from the Bodin Company. Bonaparte settled my debts. There were tears.

February 7.
"Damn, Washington died," Bonaparte said, throwing down a dispatch.
"The American?"
"Of all times. Now I'll have to show mourning." He looked over a calendar. "How many days left?"
How many days until we moved to the Tuileries Palace, he meant. "Eleven," I said, examining the calendar. Just thinking about the move induced a panic in me. There was so much to do, so much that had to be accomplished in so little time. The walls were not yet plastered. And the floors—the workers were *supposed* to have begun work on them three days ago.
"Perfect, ten days of mourning: and *then* the move."

February 14.
A good meeting with Thérèse. We're making progress going over the List. It's so much easier with the two of us.

February 16.
"You sent for me, Citoyenne?" Émilie's husband Lavalette stood before me at attention, as if for a military review.
I begged him to be seated. "I have a favour to ask of you, Lieutenant Lavalette. However, I am hesitant, as it entails a certain degree of personal danger. I need someone to go into Austria—"

Lavalette registered surprise.

"—in order to locate a certain individual, an emigré whose name has finally been removed from the List. I need you to help that individual cross the border back into France." No easy task.

"May I ask who?"

"Certainly, but you must vow not to tell a soul, not even your wife." I paused, smiled. "François Beauharnais." Émilie's father, the Marquis's son.

February 17—Tuileries Palace.
I am writing this at my escritoire in what will soon be my new drawing room—the yellow room, I call it. I feel uneasy, at odds with the taste of the Queen, who occupied these rooms before me. Every surface—the walls, the ceiling, even the floor—is covered with ornament.

Will I ever be happy here? Was she? I wonder. (I doubt it.)

I'm exhausted, I remind myself. Even now, there are trunks to be unpacked, put away. But the dining and reception rooms are finally presentable, the heavy brocade drapes hung only an hour ago. Day after tomorrow . . .

February 18.
Everything should be ready for tomorrow's move—the grand parade, the reception, the dinner. Ready in *theory*, anyway. In reality, every time I go to look over the work, something is amiss. The workers were only this afternoon laying the carpets. And now, my cook is ill with an ague.

February 19.
Eugène's uniform has been mended and Hortense has finally determined the right shade of ribbon (a lovely blue-green) to go with her gown. Bonaparte just rushed in and we went through the order of events one last time. "Make sure Hortense is watching just after the cavalry," he whispered to me. But he wouldn't say why.

Shortly after 5:00—a quiet moment.

"I hate all this." Bonaparte tore at his sash.

"Be still."

"You look majestic, General," Fauvelet said, helping Bonaparte on with his jacket.

"I've never seen you looking so . . . pressed," I said with a smile. Bonaparte was most comfortable in old, worn clothes.

"Is that supposed to be a compliment?" He did not smile. "Fauvelet, you're lucky. You don't have to make a fool of yourself in public, as I do."

"Madame Bonaparte?" One of the movers gestured toward a mountain of trunks. "Do these *all* go?"

I nodded. Moving, on top of everything else. Any minute, I would collapse. "As you have said yourself, Bonaparte, the people need to see you, they need a spectacle."

"So you do listen to me."

"Bonaparte, I'm always listening." Tweaking *his* ear.

Hortense, Émilie and Caroline came gliding into the room, twirled for inspection. I fixed Hortense's hair ribbon. Caroline's dress was tight on her, but there was nothing to be done. (Is she in an interesting condition? I wondered. Already?) "You should see Joachim's new plume for his hat," Caroline said. "It cost three hundred francs."

"What's that terrible racket?" I looked toward the door.

Eugène appeared, straddling a chair, rocking and jumping it into the room as if it were a horse. The girls and I burst into laughter. He jumped off, tamed his "steed," saluted. "Well?" Grinning. Showing off his new uniform, the uniform of the Consular Guards.

"Oh," said Hortense, breathlessly, "all the girls will be throwing their bouquets at you."

"So long as they don't throw them at my husband." Caroline crimped the bow in her hair, so that it would stand better. "See how it droops?"

Our coachman appeared at the door wearing tails. "Your coach is ready, Madame."

I looked at the clock on the mantelpiece. We were on time—miraculously. I glanced in the glass: I felt I had too much make-up on, like an actress preparing to go on stage. And then I realized that I was an actress, and this was a stage.

"Come, darling. It's time!" Caroline said to Hortense and Émilie, putting on an exaggerated air of grandeur as she swept into the corridor.

I caught Bonaparte's eye, smiled—children!—but he was preoccupied. The valet was helping him on with his boots. "I'll see you later then—after the revue?" And before the dinner, I thought, which reminded me: had the silver been packed? Worrying: should I take my new pug dogs with me now?

Bonaparte stood, pulling at the bootstrap. "I can't get my foot in." The boot went flying.

I touched his shoulder. He turned, as if startled. Addressing soldiers, Bonaparte was at ease; addressing civilians terrified him. Every Royalist country in Europe would be praying for a stumble. "It's going to be splendid," I said, giving him a kiss.

The parade *was* splendid. Eugène looked wonderful (as did his new horse Pegasus), and of course the crowds went wild for Bonaparte. It was a moving moment when the tattered flags of the Army of Italy went by. Bonaparte removed his hat and bowed his head; the crowd suddenly became hushed, reverent. This little man with such big dreams has filled all our hearts with hope. If there are angels (and there must be, surely), they are with him now.

Indeed, even my daughter is falling under his spell. As soon as the cavalry went by she, Émilie and Caroline excused themselves to go to the powder room. I remembered Bonaparte's instruction just in time. "Wait, Hortense." The military band was marching into the courtyard, the brass instruments bright in the sun. "Just one moment, *please.*"

"Why?" Caroline demanded as Hortense slipped back into her chair overlooking the palace courtyard. The members of the band were in position and an orderly was running across the courtyard with a stool for the conductor to stand on.

"I don't really know." The conductor mounted the stool and lifted his baton. The musicians raised their instruments and the opening

Partant pour la Syrie

chords were struck. The piece sounded familiar, yet I could not place it.

Hortense sat forward, her hands on her knees.

"Can we go now?" Caroline asked, standing by the door. Hortense raised her index finger.

"Hortense, isn't that your song, the marching song you wrote?" I asked. "*Partant pour la Syrie?*"

"Hush," she cried out. "I want to hear it!"

Evening.

"What did you think?" Bonaparte asked, bursting into my dressing room. "I thought it went rather well."

"It was brilliant," I said. He hadn't noticed Hortense sitting by the door.

"Why is it so dark in here? Where are the children? What did your daughter think?"

I looked at Hortense in the looking glass, smiled. Bonaparte followed my gaze. "Oh!" he said, taken aback.

Hortense stood, her hands clasped in front of her. "I was so honoured."

Bonaparte smiled and tugged her ear. (Gently, for once!) "You were surprised? Good. The musicians want to know if you would write another for them."

Hortense nodded, tongue-tied, a flush covering her pale cheeks. "Caroline is expecting me!" she cried and bolted out the door.

"Is she pleased, do you think?" Bonaparte asked, puzzled.

"She's overcome." I pressed his hand to my cheek. "That was a very nice thing for you to do."

"It's a good piece," he said, shrugging, sitting down so that the valet could pull off his riding boots. "Why do you have the drapes drawn?"

"People look in." I'd had a fright earlier when I saw a man's face pressed against the iron grill. "But it's dark in here even when the drapes are pulled back." The rooms are set below ground level; the windows are high on the wall. Sitting, one cannot look out. "Your new breeches are on top of the trunk with your sash."

In moments he reappeared, his valet following him like a shadow.

"Excellent," I said, although the fit wasn't perfect. There hadn't been time.

Mimi came to the door, lovely in a new muslin gown. "Third Consul Lebrun and his wife are—"

"Already?" I looked at the clock. It was only five! We weren't expecting guests to arrive until six.

"Good," Bonaparte said, pulling on his dress shoes. "I need to talk to him about the deficit."

"I'll only be a moment." I stood in front of the large looking glass as Mimi fastened my pearls. The Queen had studied her image in this very glass, I thought.

After dinner with the Consuls (boring!), I went on ahead to the bedroom, to prepare for my husband. I dismissed Mimi. Alone, I bathed, changed into a simple flannel gown. I was weary of lace and pageantry. Wrapped in a comforter, I sat by the fire thinking of the woman who had once sat thus, in this room, by this fireplace, also waiting for her husband to join her. Her husband: King Louis XVI. I recalled the day he was guillotined, the slow, steady roll of the drums. And then I recalled the day of the Queen's death less than a year later, a ghost of a woman already, widowed, her children taken from her. She was thirty-eight when she died, only a few years older than I am now.

Queen Marie-Antoinette. How curious it is for me to be living here, writing at her escritoire. How curious, and how very unreal.

Bonaparte arrived as the clocks chimed midnight. "I'll ring for the valet," he said.

"No, don't." I helped him out of his coat.

In his nightshirt, his head wrapped in one of my madras scarves, he regarded the room thoughtfully. "Well." He took in the bronze-trimmed mahogany bed, a monument of (ugly) ornate ormolu.

"I still can't believe we live here." I did not say, I can't accept that this horrible place is now my home.

Bonaparte went to the grandiose bed, pulled out the little step. "Come, little créole." Smiling, he bowed at the waist, arms wide, like a courtier. "Step into the bed of kings."

"Bonaparte, don't you feel as if you're in a dream?" The centre of the enormous bed was like a valley; we kept rolling into it. (I'll have a new mattress made.)

Bonaparte grunted, on the verge of sleep, and pulled me closer, his arms around my waist. "Yes," he said a moment later, "a dream of my creation."

I lacked the courage to ask him what that dream entailed. "I keep thinking of all the things that happened in this room, the kings and the queens who have slept in this bed." The kings and the queens who have lost their lives.

"And I keep thinking how lovely you are, how I'm luckier than any of those kings." His hands were roving again.

"Bonaparte, I'm serious. It frightens me, being here, living here. I don't belong."

"You're questioning God when you make such a statement." He propped himself up on his elbow.

I rolled over onto my back, looked into his sad-serious eyes. "What do you mean?" There was no limit to Bonaparte's energy, to his dreams, to what he aimed to achieve. Was it faith that gave him courage?

"Remember the fortune you were told, that you would be Queen?"

Tears came to my eyes. "I don't want to be a queen, Bonaparte."

"But I'll need you beside me," he said, joking gently.

I put my hand on his cheek. "I love you."

I lay beside my husband for what seemed like hours, listening to the sounds of the night. I could hear the prostitutes laughing in the gardens, whisperings outside our windows. I lay listening to my heart, and to the strange, silent dark of the cold marble corridors.

The bells had just rung out one note when I felt it again, that chill. Bonaparte, often so deep in sleep I fear him dead, murmured and turned, pulling the comforters around him, as if he too could feel it. I sat up, watchful. I saw a light approaching.

"Mimi?" I hissed. My heart began to pound. Only bad news came thus, in the night. I pulled the comforter around me. Why was it suddenly so very cold? And then I saw her again: that plain white gown, that plain white cap. The Queen—in prison clothes. A cry escaped me, I reached out for Bonaparte. The moment I touched him, she began to recede, fade. And then the room was dark again, and silent, but for the pounding of my heart.

In which I am called Angel of Mercy

February 22, 1800.

"Twenty-seven already this morning," Mimi told me, her eyes wide.

Twenty-seven petitioners? Yesterday there had been twelve, and nineteen the day before. Proud, starving aristocrats, trembling beggars. Weeping women, tongue-tied men, stuttering children: all desperate, all needing help.

"Madame Bonaparte." The girl bowed. The elderly woman accompanying her was dressed in the uncomfortable style of the Ancien Régime. With the help of a walking stick she struggled to stand.

"Oh, please, do sit," I insisted. Her bustle had slipped sideways, giving her a deformed look.

"M-M-Madame B-B-Bonne . . ." the old woman stuttered, but she could get no further.

"Bon à Parté, Grandmaman." The girl threw me an embarrassed look.

"Mademoiselle de Malesherbes, is it not?" The girl had come to me weeks earlier. I guessed her to be twelve years in age, thirteen perhaps.

"You remember!" She flushed.

What I remembered was the charm of her devotion to her grandmother, whose name had been put on the List during the Revolution and who was destined to die in Germany, alone, far from her family, her loved ones.

I took the elderly woman's hand. "Then you must be Countess de Malesherbes."

"In Germany they call you the Angel of Mercy," the old woman said, her voice clear now. She had a vise-like grip on my hand. "I want you to come to my funeral."

I smiled. "I trust it will not be soon."

"It will be a splendid fête. My daughters have promised."

"We have come to say thank you," the girl said.

"And God bless!"

Over twenty petitioners later, I was growing fatigued. No wonder thrones are cushioned. "Only one more," the hall porter informed me. "Mademoiselle Compoint."

I tilted my head to one side. "Pardon?"

He squinted at the card. "Mademoiselle Louise Compoint."

Lisette?

"I could tell her to return tomorrow, Madame."

I drummed the arm of my chair—as Bonaparte so often does, I realized. Soon I would have all his nervous mannerisms—his twitches, his tics. Soon I might even have his short temper. If only I had his judgement, I thought. Should I refuse to receive Lisette? "Send her in," I said finally, putting back my shoulders.

She looked older than I expected. There were frown creases between her eyes that her heavy make-up could not hide. She looked like a grisette,* I thought, with an unexpected feeling of sympathy . . . and guilt. I knew what happened to maids who were let go without a reference, knew what choices they had.

"Madame," she said, standing nervously before me as she had stood only four years before. "I have come to beg your forgiveness." She dropped her head, a subservient gesture as superficial as her words.

"Forgiveness is a great deal to ask." I didn't like the feeling that had come over me, the realization that I had power and she had none. "Tell me why you have come," I said finally.

* Grisette: a lady of easy virtue.

"I wish to marry, Madame—but I am in need of a dowry."

Ah, of course: she had come for money. Once upon a time, in a more trusting time, I had promised her a dowry. "You are betrothed?" I asked, both angry and repentant. None of us was innocent, if the truth were to be told.

"Almost, Madame. If I had a dowry, an English jockey would marry me, he said."

"Would you be moving to England then?"

"Yes, Madame."

"Very well then."*

Evening.

Fouché slumped into the chair by the fire. "Discouraged, Citoyen?" I asked. The Minister of Police had just had a meeting with Bonaparte.

"I confess to defeat. It appears I've been unsuccessful in my attempt to dissuade the First Consul from going ahead with his plan to resurrect the odious custom of the masked ball." He made a wry face. "The Laundresses Guild won out, I regret to say."**

"You will get no support from me on that score, I'm afraid." It had been over seven years since the last masked ball. All of Paris was in a state of excited anticipation, the shops displaying costumes, fanciful creations. It was impossible to buy bright silk. Everyone, it seemed, wanted to go as an Egyptian god, a Mameluke, a Turk or a harem dancer. I myself was going as a butterfly. And Bonaparte—whom I had finally persuaded to attend—as Caesar.

"That surprises me not in the least," Fouché said, tapping his snuff-box. Made of black and gold enamel, it matched his jacket exactly—a fashionable detail curiously out of place in a slovenly man. "But then, the safety of the good citizens of Paris is not your responsibility."

He offered me a pinch of snuff. I refused. "Am I being reprimanded, Citoyen Minister of Police?"

* *The marriage ended poorly and Lisette died in misery.*

** *The Laundresses Guild, one of the most powerful in Paris, had been lobbying for the return of Mardi Gras because of all the laundry work the festivities generated.*

Fouché snapped closed his pretty little box and slipped it into his pocket. "Put masks on the good citizens of Paris and give them, for one night, the freedom to act without consequences?" He shrugged. "Nous verrons."

Sunday.
"You haven't told Émilie? She doesn't know?" Aunt Désirée was dusting her china figurines for the third time in ten minutes.

"Do you think I should have?" I asked, looking out the window into the courtyard. Why were they late? It was quarter-past three. Lavalette and his *very* special charge—Émilie's father and *my* former brother-in-law, Vicomte François de Beauharnais—were supposed to have been here fifteen minutes earlier, one full hour before Émilie herself was due to arrive. The anticipation was unendurable.

"When I told the Marquis that his son was coming, the shock almost killed him. Imagine if François had walked in without any warning? Émilie is frail, she might . . ." Aunt Désirée blinked, sniffed. "Oh dear, François is not even here and already I'm weeping!"

I helped her to the sofa and rang for her maid to bring hysteric water. "*And* the salts," Aunt Désirée exclaimed, fanning herself. "I sent the scullery maid to the apothecary this morning just to make sure we had them on hand. Oh!" she shrieked when the doorbell sounded. "It's them." With a terrified expression.

"Sit down, sit down," I said soothingly, but practically pushing her back onto the sofa. "You stay here."

"Is my hair all right?"

"You've never looked lovelier," I assured her, hurrying into the foyer where I found Lavalette helping a middle-aged man off with his jacket. It was François, looking heavier, true, and curiously old-fashioned in his powdered periwig, but distinguished, gentle François nonetheless. Without ceremony I rushed to him and took his hands in mine, blinking back tears; he looked so very much like Alexandre.

"Rose?" He folded me in his arms. It had been . . . how long? Seven years since he'd fled? In those terrible seven years his brother had been guillotined; the King and Queen had been beheaded; we'd endured a Reign of Terror and established not one but three Republics (trying to get it right). And I had remarried, a man who had saved the nation, and the Palace of Kings was now my home. "You haven't changed a bit," he said, drying his eyes.

"Fou-Fou?" Aunt Désirée exclaimed the moment François entered the drawing room, calling him by his baby name. François stooped to give the woman who had been a mother to him a tender kiss. "You look so old!" she exclaimed, crossing herself. And then she started to bawl. "I'm going to be fine, don't worry, don't worry!" she cried out, honking into an enormous kerchief.

François helped her to her feet and took her in his arms, his chin resting on the top of her coiffured hair, blinking and blinking, shyly patting her heaving back.

"That's enough!" Aunt Désirée said, standing back, sniffling. "So. There. I've wept and now I'm finished. Let's go see your father, lest he die before you even get up the stairs. Did you know that we're married now? You may call me Maman."

"Maman," François echoed obediently, smiling with tender affection.

I caught Lavalette's eye. "Émilie will be here at four," I whispered to him, glancing at the clock. Only fifteen more minutes.

"I'll wait for her down here," he said, taking off his silly round hat and running his hand across his balding head. "Does she know?"

I rolled my eyes, shook my head and ran up the stairs.

François was standing on the landing outside his father's door, his hand on the crystal knob. "Désirée—*Maman*—told me to wait out here," he said, his voice nervous.

"Go, go," I said, taking hold of his elbow, urging him in.

The room smelled of aromatic vinegar and roses.

"Father?" François said, with a hint of disbelief in his voice. The shrunken man in the feather bed was not the stern patriarch he'd known.

"Let's wait downstairs," I whispered to my aunt.

The Marquis held out his trembling hand. François pressed his father's fingers to his lips. His face was glistening with tears and his lower lip was quivering uncontrollably.

I tugged at my aunt's sleeve. "Let's leave them alone together," I repeated. Frankly, I didn't know how much more my heart could take. But just as I said that, I heard light footsteps on the stairs—Émilie?

She appeared in the door, her veil covering her face.

"François, there's someone here to see you," Aunt Désirée said.

Émilie began backing out of the room, but her husband was behind her—she couldn't. "Don't be frightened, sweetheart," I said, reaching for her hand.

"Émilie?" Her father's voice was thick with emotion.

"Don't be silly," Aunt Désirée said. "This is your father."

With aristocratic gentility, François bowed. Émilie slowly raised her veil.

"Very well, that's enough tears for today!" Aunt Désirée said, opening the window and taking a deep breath of cold air. "Whew!" she exclaimed, fanning herself. "Whew."

[Undated]

A blissful day at Malmaison. Rollicking games of Prisoner's Base with the children on the lawn, Bonaparte laughing. We debated (noisily!) who would play what parts in the play we've decided to put on (Corneille's *Mélite*). And then, chess in the evening in front of the fire, Bonaparte cheating (or trying to), the children teasing, in an uproar! "You can't do that, Papa," Hortense blurted out, objecting.

Papa. Bonaparte smiled, caught my eye. He looked as if he'd just been blessed.

February 25.

"Why are you laughing?" Bonaparte stood before us in a badly draped white toga, a haphazard crown of gold leaves circling his brow.

I tried to control the laughter that was welling up in me, but it kept overflowing, sending first Hortense and then Eugène into a fit. Bonaparte looked so serious.

"That's it. I'm not going," he said, pulling off the crown. Four golden leaves fluttered to the floor.

"Bonaparte, no!" We all jumped up in protest. "It's perfect," I assured him, and then Hortense and Eugène joined in. "With your Roman features, your profile, it gives you a heroic look."

He regarded us without expression. "Then what, may I ask, do you find so amusing?"

"*We* know you are Bonaparte," Hortense said, sweetly taking his arm.

"Nobody else will," Eugène joined in.

"You'll be in disguise," I assured him.

Of course Bonaparte was recognized immediately. The ballroom was thronged, yet the crowd parted reverently when he approached. (Fortunately, no laughs.)

I clasped his hand—it was clammy. Crowds made him uneasy, I knew. Perhaps he was right, perhaps this had been a mistake, I thought. I looked over my shoulder. Roustam, dressed as himself, was not far behind.

"Is that Émilie?" I asked Hortense, nodding toward a young woman in a medieval gown, a veil covering her face. She was standing with her husband Lavalette (a knight) and another man I could not place at first. Her father François, I realized suddenly, dressed as a Revolutionary in long pants, short jacket and bonnet rouge.

"And isn't that Aunt Désirée?" Eugène asked.

"I don't believe it," I said. Aunt Désirée, dressed incongruously as a Gypsy, was seated beside the dear old Marquis, who was wearing his old (*very* old) Commander-of-the-Navy hat.

"There's Caroline, with Murat," Hortense said.

"Ah!" The Viking and the belly dancer—staring into each other's eyes. (Who would have thought that a rough soldier like Murat would fall so deeply in love, and with a girl like Caroline—his *wife?*)

A man in a black hood appeared before us: Fouché, dressed as Death. "I'll stay close by," he assured us.

"How comforting," I said.

Suddenly there was a flurry of excitement by the door, raucous cheers, rude hoots. Four women had made a rather dramatic entrance dressed as wood nymphs, their brief tunics (transparent over flesh-coloured shifts, so they looked naked) ending at their knees.

"Maman!" Hortense hissed. "It's Citoyenne Tallien—with her legs showing." She looked away, horrified.

My Glories! Followed by Fortunée's blinking husband Hamelin (dressed as a Venetian gondoliere) and a pretty little man dressed as a jester—Captain Charles? An old woman dressed as a harlot clung to his arm: Madame Montaniser. Rich old Madame Montaniser.

Bonaparte turned to Fouché. "Those women are half-naked. It's unacceptable."

"I'll take care of it," Fouché said.

The contredanse was about to begin. "No, wait." I grabbed Fouché's sleeve. "I'll talk to them."

Thérèse embraced me with open arms. "I have to tell you something." I pulled her into an alcove. How was I going to put it? "There's a bit of a problem." I took a breath. "Bonaparte is concerned about . . . dress." *Un*dress. "So." I swallowed. "So it might be best if you left, you and the others."

"But we just got here." She had to raise her voice to be heard.

I grimaced. "I'm afraid you will be asked to go—by the police—unless you leave." A tall man appeared at the edge of the dance floor, his hand on the small of his back. He was wearing a mask—the face of Lazare Hoche. I put my hand to my heart.

"We haven't done anything wrong," Thérèse said.

The man in the mask turned to face me and then disappeared into the crowd.

"It has to do with . . . changes," I said, my heart pounding violently against my ribs. Was it who I feared it might be? "Setting new standards." And personal sacrifice. I felt my eyes filling. I swallowed, took a careful breath. I didn't want my make-up to smear. "Thérèse, please, don't you see?" The musicians began to play. "The Age of Fable is over, and the Reign of—" I blinked back tears. The Reign of History, I'd started to say.

"Look," she said, taking my hand, "I do understand. I know it can't be easy." She kissed my cheeks. "I'll tell the—"

But she was interrupted by Fortunée Hamelin, her forehead glistening, her bare breasts heaving. "Isn't this wonderful? Parbleu, what a fête. Thérèse, Ouvrard wants you. We need one more to make a set. *Love* your costume, Josephine." Fortunée grabbed Thérèse's hand, swirled her off into the sea of revellers.

I stood for a moment, my back against a pillar, watching the revelry. I felt dizzy from the press of the crowd, the unsettling costumes, the masked eyes without warmth.

"Madame Bonaparte, do not disappear on me again."

"Oh, it's you, Fouché." He always approached so silently.

"There is something you should be aware of." He was, perhaps, the only sober person in the room—except for my husband. "Paul Barras is here. I recommend caution."

I nodded. I knew.

"He's wearing a mask that resembles the face of General Lazare Hoche."

Fouché led me back to the head table. "Ah, there you are." Bonaparte was irked: young Jérôme, already drunk, had challenged one of Pauline's lovers to a duel. He took my hand. His sad, serious expression was a welcome contrast, somehow, to the crazed gaiety all around me. "Why are you trembling?" he asked. I heard a woman laughing loudly. I looked back over my shoulder. Captain Charles was juggling balls for old Madame Montaniser. "Did you talk to Thérèse?" Bonaparte pressed my fingers to his lips.

I nodded, blinking back tears. We had only each other, I realized. But it was enough. Indeed, it was a very great deal.

"What did you tell her?"

"I told her things had changed." Things *had* changed.

"Consul General," Fouché interrupted, "I've just been informed that the musicians intend to play Chant au départ. I think you should—" But he'd no sooner said the words than the opening chords were struck. Suddenly, everyone was cheering: *Vive Bonaparte! Peace with Bonaparte!*

"I think you would be safer on the platform, Consul General."

Bonaparte clasped my hand and tilted his head toward the platform. "Me?"

"I want you beside me."

Fouché pushed his way through to the steps, Bonaparte and I following in his wake. When we emerged onto the platform, a cheer went up. *Vive Bonaparte!*

Over the heads of the crowd, I saw a scuffle at the back by the big double doors. Four gendarmes were escorting out the man in the Hoche mask: Père Barras. My throat tightened.

The noise was getting louder and wilder. Some had started to sing the *Marseillaise.* The ballroom walls seemed to shake with a roar of cheers: *Vive Bonaparte! Vive la République! The Revolution is over!*

I saw Joseph and Lucien Bonaparte, dressed as pirates, standing by a pillar. I bowed to them. (Gloating: Yes! I confess it.) Then I felt a tugging at my hem. It was Mademoiselle Malesherbes, my sweet young petitioner, dressed as a violet. Her grandmother, Countess de Malesherbes (with a jester's hat on), was slumped into an invalid's chair beside her. "Consulesse Bon à Parté." The girl had to yell in order to be heard. "My grandmother wants me to tell you: *Long live the Angel of Mercy.*"

I smiled and made a little wave at the countess, who clapped, grinning toothlessly.

"The Revolution is over!" a man yelled nearby, his tears ghoulishly streaking his black and white harlequin make-up.

I saw François Beauharnais in the crowd, standing by a statue of Venus, one arm clasped around his daughter's shoulders. Lieutenant Lavalette was standing behind them, hovering. He bent down to say something to his wife. Émilie lifted her veil and smiled.

It was then that I noticed Thérèse at the back of the ballroom, following Fortunée Hamelin, Minerva and Madame de Crény out the big double doors. My Glories! Thérèse threw me a kiss, waved goodbye. "Ahr-ree-veh-dayr-chee!" I heard Fortunée's husband Hamelin yell as the doors closed behind them.

The Age of Fable is over . . .

Then, strangely, I could see the cheering faces, but I couldn't hear the shouts. And it was then that I saw her again, in the shadow behind the two pillars: that face, set jaw, the ruffled white cap.

I touched Bonaparte's arm and I could hear again. The roaring in my ears mingled with the cheers. *The Revolution is over! over! over!*

"Long live the Angel of Mercy!" The girl tipped back her grand-mother's chair, spun it around, the old woman cackling.

"Bow," Bonaparte whispered, squeezing my hand.

I bowed and a great cheer went up. I glanced at Bonaparte. Was that for *me?*

"They love you," he said.

Us, I realized.

He held up my hand. We bowed to the cheering crowd.

The Age of Fable is over . . . the Reign of History has begun.

Chronology

YEAR	DATE	
1796	March 9	Napoleon and Josephine marry.
	March 11	Napoleon leaves Paris to take command of the Army of Italy.
	April 12-22	Napoleon opens his Italian campaign: six victories.
	May	Barras buys Grosbois.
	June 20	Désirée Renaudin and Marquis de Beauharnais marry.
	June 26	Josephine leaves Paris to join Napoleon in Italy.
	July 13	Josephine joins Napoleon in Milan.
	July 31	Josephine comes under cannon fire.
	November 15-17	Napoleon is victorious at the Battle of Arcole.
	late December	Napoleon's sister Pauline arrives in Milan.
1797	March 8	Thérèse sues Tallien for divorce, followed by a reconciliation that results in conception.
	April 18	Victorious, Napoleon forces the Austrians to agree to a peace agreement.
	May	Josephine and Napoleon move to the château of Mombello for the hot summer months.
	May 20	General Pichegru, a suspected Royalist agent, is elected President of the Council of Five Hundred.
	June 1	Napoleon's mother, two sisters and a brother come to Mombello, where Pauline and Elisa are married.

July 18-22	Barras persuades Lazare Hoche to bring troops close to Paris. When discovered, Hoche is accused and leaves Paris under a cloud of suspicion.
summer	Eugène joins Napoleon's staff in Italy.
September 4	"Journée du 18 Fructidor," led by Barras. Fifty-three deputies, suspected Royalists, are arrested.
September 19	Hoche dies at Wetzlar, Germany.
October 17	Napoleon and the Austrians sign the Treaty of Campo-Formio. Eugène takes news of the treaty to Venice, Corfu and Rome.
November 16	Napoleon leaves Milan for Paris by way of Rastadt, where the treaty will be ratified.
December 20	Thérèse and Tallien's baby dies at birth.

1798	January 2	Josephine returns to Paris.
	January 3	Talleyrand gives a ball in Napoleon's honour.
	January 22	Eugène arrives back in Paris.
	March 5	The Directors approve Napoleon's plan to invade Egypt.
	March 16	Napoleon and Joseph accuse Josephine of being involved in the Bodin Company.
	May 4	Josephine and Napoleon leave for Toulon, where the fleet will depart for Egypt.
	May 18	Émilie marries Lavelette.
	May 19	The fleet sets sail from Toulon without Josephine.
	June 14	Josephine arrives in the mountain spa of Plombières, where she undertakes a treatment for infertility.
	June 20	Josephine falls from a balcony and is seriously injured.
	July 21	Napoleon is victorious at the Battle of the Pyramids.
	July 24	Napoleon enters Cairo in triumph.
	July 27	Eugène writes from Egypt that Napoleon had been told suspicious details concerning Captain Charles and Josephine. Napoleon writes similarly to Joseph. Both letters are intercepted by the British.
	August 1	The French fleet is destroyed by the British in the Battle of the Nile at Abukir.

	September 16	Josephine arrives back in Paris.
	November 24	The contents of Eugène's and Napoleon's letters are alluded to in the *London Morning Chronicle*.
	December	Rumours of Napoleon's death.
1799	March 19	Both Napoleon and Eugène are wounded during the siege of St. John d'Acre, Eugène seriously.
	April 21	Josephine buys Malmaison.
	June	The Bodin Company comes under investigation.
	October 9	Napoleon sails into Fréjus harbour on the French Riviera.
	October 13	Josephine and Hortense leave at dawn to meet Napoleon on the road. (They miss.)
	October 16	Napoleon and Eugène arrive in Paris.
	October 18	Josephine and Hortense arrive back in Paris. Bonaparte has locked Josephine out. Reconciliation.
	November 9-10	"Coup d'État du 18 Brumaire." Napoleon becomes First Consul.
	November 12	Napoleon and Josephine move to the Luxembourg Palace.
1800	February 1	Thérèse gives birth to a girl, fathered by Ouvrard.
	February 18	Results of the vote on the new constitution announced: 3,011,007 in favour, 1,526 opposed.
	February 19	With ceremony, Napoleon and Josephine move into the Tuileries Palace.

Characters

Adélaïde Hoche: Lazare Hoche's young wife

Agathe: Josephine's scullery maid

Alexandre Beauharnais: Josephine's first husband; guillotined during the Terror

Antoine: the coachman

Barras, Paul: a director; Josephine's friend and mentor

Botot, François: Barras's secretary

Bruno: Barras's hall porter

Callyot: Josephine's cook

Caroline (Maria-Anunziata) Bonaparte: Napoleon's youngest sister

Charles, Captain Hippolyte ("Wide-Awake"): Josephine's intimate friend and business partner

Crény, Madame de: one of the Glories

Désirée Renaudin: Josephine's godmother and aunt; she lives with the Marquis

Elisa (Maria-Anna) Bonaparte: the oldest of Napoleon's sisters; married to Félix Bacchiochi

Émilie Beauharnais: Josephine's niece

Eugène Beauharnais: Josephine's son

Fauvelet Bourrienne: Napoleon's secretary

Fesch: Bonaparte's uncle (by marriage)

Fortuné: Josephine's first pug dog

Fortunée Hamelin: one of the Glories

Fouché, Joseph: Josephine's friend, talented in undercover work

Gontier: Josephine's manservant

Hortense Beauharnais: Josephine's daughter

Hugo and Louis Bodin: Josephine's business partners

Igor: Barras's parrot

Jérôme (Girolamo, Fifi) Bonaparte: Napoleon's brother, his youngest sibling

Joseph (Giuseppe) Bonaparte: Napoleon's older brother, married to Julie Clary

Julie Clary: Joseph's quiet wife

Junot Andoche: one of Napoleon's aides

Lazare (Lazarro) Hoche: Josephine's former lover

Lavalette: one of Bonaparte's aides-de-camp

Letizia Bonaparte: Napoleon's mother

Lisette (Louise) Compoint: Josephine's lady's maid

Louis (Luigi) Bonaparte: Napoleon's younger brother whom he raised like a son

Lucien (Lucciano) Bonaparte: Napoleon's fiery younger brother

Marquis de Beauharnais: the father of Alexandre, Josephine's first husband, and François, Émilie's father

Mimi: Josephine's childhood maid, a mulatto from Martinique

Minerva (Madame de Châteaurenaud): one of the Glories

Moustache: Napoleon's courier

Napoleon (Napoleone, in Italian) Bonaparte: Josephine's husband.

Ouvrard: a financial genius

Pauline (Maria-Paola, Paganetta) Bonaparte: Napoleon's beautiful and spirited younger sister

Pegasus: Eugène's horse

Père Hoche: Lazare Hoche's father

Pugdog: Josephine's second pug dog

Talleyrand, Charles-Maurice: a former bishop, sometimes Minister of Foreign Affairs, always influential

Tallien, Lambert: Thérèse's husband

Thérèse (Tallita, "Amazon") Tallien: Josephine's closest friend, one of the Glories

Toto: Barras's miniature greyhound

Genealogies

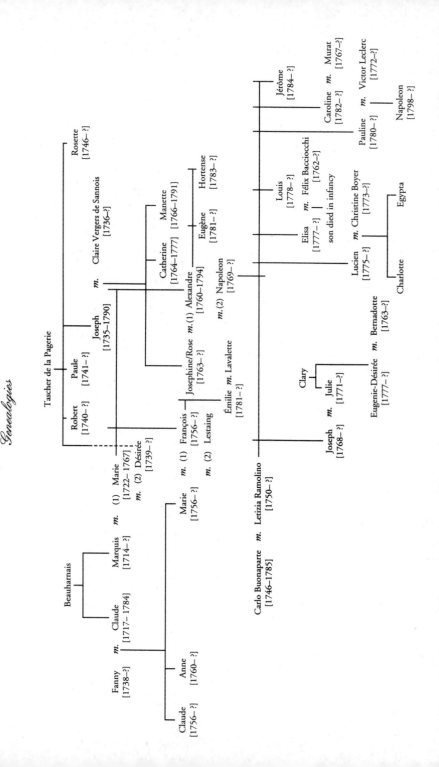

Selected Bibliography

In addition to several hundred reference and general texts, I largely depended on the following books in writing *Tales of Passion, Tales of Woe.* I've starred the titles I recommend to readers who wish to read more about Josephine and the Napoleonic era.

Allinson, Alfred. *The Days of the Directoire.* New York: John Lane, The Bodley Company, 1910.

Aulard, A. *Paris pendant la Réaction Thermidorienne.* Vol. 3–5. Paris: Maison Quantin, 1902.

———. *Paris sous le Consulat.* Vol. 1. Paris: Maison Quantin, 1903.

Barras, Paul. *Memoirs of Barras, Member of the Directorate.* Vol. 1–4. Edited, with a general introduction, prefaces and appendices by George Duruy. Translated by Charles E. Roche. London: Harper & Brothers, 1895.

Bernard, J. F. *Talleyrand, A Biography.* New York: G.P. Putnam's Sons, 1973.

Bonaparte, Napoleon. *Letters and documents of Napoleon.* Vol. 1, *The Rise to Power.* Selected and translated by John Eldred Howard. London: The Cresset Press, 1961.

Bonnechose, Emile de. *Lazare Hoche.* Translated by Emile Pernet. Toronto: Willing & Williamson, 1881.

Bourrienne, Louis Antoine Fauvelet de. *Memoirs of Napoleon Bonaparte.* Vol. 1– 4. Edited by R.W. Phipps. New York: Charles Scribner's Sons, 1892.

*Bruce, Evangeline. *Napoleon and Josephine: The Improbable Marriage.* New York: Scribner, 1995.

*Catinat, Maurice, Bernard Chevallier and Christophe Pincemaille, editors. *Impératrice Joséphine: Correspondance, 1782-1814.* Paris: Histoire Payot, 1996.

Cerf, Léon, ed. *Letters of Napoleon to Josephine.* New York: Brentano's, 1931.

*Chevallier, Bernard, and Christophe Pincemaille. *L'impératrice Joséphine.* Presses de la Renaissance. 37 rue du Four, Paris 75006. 1988.

Cole, Hubert. *Fouché: The Unprincipled Patriot.* London: Eyre & Spottiswoode, 1971.

*———. *Joséphine.* London: Heinemann, 1962.

———. *The Betrayers: Joachim and Caroline Murat.* London: Eyre Methuen, 1972.

*Cronin, Vincent. *Napoleon.* London: Collins, 1971.

Dupre, Huntley. *Lazare Carnot: Republican Patriot.* Philadelphia: Porcupine Press, 1975.

Goodspeed, D. J. *Bayonets at St Cloud; the Story of the 18th Brumaire.* Toronto: Macmillan, 1965.

*Hortense, Queen. *The Memoirs of Queen Hortense*. Published by arrangement with Prince Napoleon. Edited by Jean Hanoteau. Translated by Arthur K. Griggs. Vol. 1 and 2. New York: Cosmopolitan Book Corporation, 1927.

Hubert, Gérard. *Malmaison*. Translated by C. de Chabannes. Paris: Editions de la Réunion des musées nationaux, 1989.

*Knapton, Ernest John. *Empress Josephine*. Cambridge, MA: Harvard University Press, 1963.

Markham, Felix. *Napoleon*. New York: New American Library, 1963.

Mossiker, Frances. *Napoleon and Josephine: The Biography of a Marriage*. New York: Simon and Schuster, 1964.

*Oman, Carola. *Napoleon's Viceroy: Eugène de Beauharnais*. New York: Funk and Wagnalls, 1966.

Saint-Amand, Imbert de. *Citizeness Bonaparte*. New York: Charles Scribner's Sons, 1899.

Sorel, Albert. *Bonaparte et Hoche en 1797*. Paris: Librairie Plon, 1896.

Tourtier-Bonazzi, Chantal de, ed. *Napoléon Lettres d'Amour à Joséphine*. Paris: Fayard, 1981.

Woronoff, Denis. *The Thermidorean Regime and the Directory, 1794-1799*. Translated by Julian Jackson. Cambridge: Cambridge University Press, 1984.

Notes

This novel spans the most controversial years of Josephine's life. If she has what one would call a bad reputation, it arises largely out of her actions during these four and a half years—or rather, her actions as described by a number of historians. When I began my work on Josephine, I assumed that these scandalous stories about her were true. Through years of research and consultation, however, I came to change my view. I am well aware of the accepted version of Josephine's life, well aware that this novel presents a view of her that is unique in the literature. It is my hope that a study of Josephine will someday be undertaken reexamining primary sources, and that the rumours surrounding her will then be reassessed.

The following have been excerpted from authentic documents: the letters from Napoleon throughout; Director Barras's dinner menu on page 53; the Hoche letter that Eugène quotes on page 91; Dr. Martinet's medical report on page 216; the article from *London Morning Chronicle* on page 234; the letter Eugène writes Josephine on page 235; Citoyen Chanorier's letter regarding Malmaison on page 240; the musical score written by Hortense on page 338; the various passages quoted from Jean Astruc's *A Treatise on All the Diseases Incident to Women* and other medical books. Note, as well, that the prediction that Josephine would become Queen of France is referred to as early as 1797, well before she is crowned in 1804.

Some readers may have noticed that the Hoche child was a boy in the early printings of *The Many Lives & Secret Sorrows of Josephine B.*, and a girl in *Tales of Passion, Tales of Woe*. In researching this novel I discovered my error.

Regarding currency: It is difficult to determine the value of a franc at this period in French history. Before the Revolution, estimates place the value of the franc (then called a "livre") somewhere between $1.25 and $4.50 U.S. In the period after the Terror, the economy was unstable and inflation soared. In 1795, for example, the year before Napoleon and Josephine married, a loaf of bread could cost as much as 1,400 francs, and a barrel of potatoes, 17,000.

Acknowledgements

At times the creation of this novel resembled a team effort. Although solitary in my work, I could feel the collective goodwill of a number of people. First and foremost I'd like to credit my editor and publisher, Iris Tupholme, for the hours of creative think-sessions, her ebullient good humour, sound advice and inspired suggestions. Thanks also to Karen Hanson at Harper-Collins Canada for her careful scrutiny, Valerie Applebee, who volunteered to be part of the editorial team, Becky Vogan for her sensitive final polish, and Maya Mavjee, for her editorial feedback in the early stages. Warm thanks to Carol Shields, who was closely involved in the first draft, for her encouragement and wisdom. Both Peggy Bridgland and Fiona Foster were perceptive and supportive editors.

A number of readers gave invaluable feedback at various stages: Janet Calcaterra, Thea Caplan, Dorothy Goodman, Marnie MacKay, Jenifer McVaugh, Carmen Mullins, Sharon and Bob Zentner. Two book clubs took the time to read a draft of this novel and meet to discuss it. I'd like to thank the members of the Scarborough Book Club IV in Calgary, Alberta, and the Chapters 110 Bloor St. Book Club in Toronto, Ontario, for their insights.

A number of men and women helped me in my travel research. Prof. Egmont Lee provided the information I needed to locate Mombello north of Milan. Maurice Moncet was kind enough to open up Grosbois (now a museum) after closing hours and give me a private tour. As well, I'd like to credit the many individuals whose names I do not know who went out of their way to help: the caretaker who showed me around

Mombello (now a school); the housekeeper who showed me Josephine's rooms in the Serbelloni Palace (now government offices) in Milan; the men and women at Plombière-les-Bains who enthusiastically subjected me to a variety of water treatments.

I'd like also to thank Marc Sebanc for his help with Latin translations, Simone Lee and her mother, Prof. Valeria Lee, for help with Italian, and Translingua at the University of Ottawa (especially Christine Hug) for help with French.

A very special thanks to my two historical consultants, Dr. Margaret Chrishawn and Dr. Maurice Catinat, who gave generously of their time and knowledge. And thanks as well to Tony Kenny for passing on his extensive Napoleonic library to me: it is a daily blessing.

Story ideas come from far and near. In my community, specifically, I'd like to thank Christina Anderman for her ghost story and Fran Murphy for her parrot tales. Jim and Tish Smith put aside a stack of old medical books for me that inspired me to delve further. Chaz Este showed up at my door with a beautiful book on eighteenth-century interiors that he was willing to lend "indefinitely."

I'd also like to thank my readers, especially Lady Corry, who kept asking, "When is it coming out?" For emotional support, thanks to WWW (Wilno Women Writers), my Humber group, and to Internet writing cronies. But most of all I give a heartfelt thanks to my family: my son Chet, my daughter Carrie, and especially, my husband Richard. I could not have written this book without their support, both tangible and emotional.

Tales of Passion, Tales of Woe

*"Sandra Gulland's second installment of her history of Josephine, Empress
of France, is that rare phenomenon: a second novel even better than the
first. Gulland casts a strong spell, weaving reality and myth . . . seductive."*
—Nancy Wigston, *The Toronto Star*

Following the bestselling *The Many Lives & Secret Sorrows of Josephine B.,*
the first volume in the trilogy depicting the life of Josephine Bonaparte,
wife of Napoleon Bonaparte, the first Emperor of France, author Sandra
Gulland continues her narrative with *Tales of Passion, Tales of Woe.* As
previously, Ms. Gulland creates her historical novel in the form of
Josephine's private journals, filling pages with her unguarded thoughts,
fears, joys and sorrows. Imagining Josephine's voice, Gulland provides a
unique portrait of a clever and charming woman who married a man of
great passion and power and who suffered the consequences of the
union.

Beginning on the day after her marriage to the "Corsican" Napoleon,
we meet a mournful woman, beset by doubts, fearful of her children's
reaction to her marriage and what the future may hold for all of them.
For France is in a state of flux. Though the dreaded Reign of Terror
was ended and its architect Robespierre was dead, political intrigue is a
plague on the land. Only two days after their marriage, Napoleon
leaves Paris to take command of the Army of Italy; a month later in
April 1796, he opens his Italian campaign and ultimately proclaims six
victories.

Josephine writes of her husband's triumphs and defeats, but it is the
stresses of daily life that occupy her: the welfare of her children, aiding
friends who plead for the benefit of her political contacts, the running
of the household and the constant need for money to support the life
that is appropriate to a woman of her station. Her marriage was little
help in this regard; though Napoleon provided some funds for the running of the household, Josephine was expected to contribute the rest
from her own pocket. She is further cursed with Napoleon's family: a
mother-in-law who despises her, three selfish sisters-in-law and four
greedy brothers-in-law. Though she attempts at first to charm them, it
is quickly evident that nothing can defang this nest of vipers with their
thinly veiled insults regarding the six-year difference in age between
Josephine and Napoleon, he being twenty-six and she thirty-two at the

time of their marriage. Perhaps most cruel of all is her inability to conceive a child, an issue that will eventually threaten her marriage.

One of the most startling aspects of *Tales of Passion, Tales of Woe* is its many parallels to late-twentieth-century life. The manners and morals of the time, the political machinations and intrigues, the profligate spending without thought of tomorrow are all mirrored in the events we see today. Here are moralists and the licentious side by side; here friendships are cast aside in favor of political power; here true friends of the republic fall as opportunists rise. But beyond politics and at its core, *Tales of Passion, Tales of Woe* recalls the extraordinary love story of the remarkable woman who captivated the man destined to change the world.

DISCUSSION QUESTIONS

1. In *Tales of Passion, Tales of Woe,* Sandra Gulland explores one of the most volatile periods of French history. What were some of the most pressing issues of the time? What is the most interesting aspect of the period?

2. Josephine and Napoleon are generally depicted as among the great romantic/tragic couples in history. But here we meet a Josephine who often seems conflicted regarding her feelings toward her husband. She speaks of her love for him but also admits in her diary that he is, in many ways, a stranger to her. What may have been her reasons for the marriage? How did Josephine's feelings for Napoleon change over time?

3. Josephine initially kept the fact of her marriage to Napoleon hidden from her two young children, twelve-year-old Hortense and fourteen-year-old Eugène. While Eugène looked forward to the benefits of a masculine presence in his life, Hortense was decidedly unhappy with her mother's marriage. From a modern perspective, how might Josephine have eased the situation for both her children and her new husband?

4. Napoleon's family appears to be a venal lot at best—his sisters, greedy and grasping, his brothers, power-hungry—all of them plotted continually against outsiders and even each other. Many modern marriages are similarly assaulted by family members with varying agendas. What differences do you perceive between the late eighteenth century and the late twentieth century in this regard?

5. Despite Napoleon's passion and Josephine's growing love for her husband, their marriage seems to have no hope of succeeding. Discuss the pressures—family, duplicitous friends, politicians, each

with a particular axe to grind—that beset their union from the beginning. Given their respective characters, what might a meeting between the couple and a modern marriage counselor have been like?

6. Josephine and Napoleon agreed to share living expenses; even the purchase price of a country property was to be shared equally between them. Additionally, Josephine was required to pay for whatever expenses her children incurred. In this respect they had a somewhat modern marriage, but without the benefit, to Josephine, of any means of earning an income. What position did this put Josephine in? What options were open to her? Was she irresponsible in going so deeply into debt? Were her financial involvements ethically questionable? Was her spending frivolous, or might it be considered a legitimate business investment? Was it unusual for a woman to get involved in large-scale business ventures in the late eighteenth century? How unusual would it be today? Would Josephine's financial situation and dealings be viewed differently if she had been a man?

7. Napoleon announces that "the Romance of the Revolution is finished; it's time to begin its history." This will entail the overthrow of Barras, one of the five Directors of the governing council and considered to be the most powerful, "by force, if need be." Was it justified? Were Napoleon and Josephine right to turn against Barras?

8. Sandra Gulland offers an array of remarkable historical characters, some known to us from our history books, others more obscure. Which characters intrigued you and made you want to learn more about them?

9. How do Napoleon and Josephine seem as people? More or less as history has depicted them? Or did you discover elements unknown to you before reading *Tales of Passion, Tales of Woe*? Which characteristics do you admire? Which do you deplore?

10. As we observe this period in history through Josephine's eyes, it seems that people's crimes, and sins, even their foibles and their affectations, have changed little in the two centuries that have passed. What differences do you see? What do you think we can learn through the distance of historical perspective?

11. Sandra Gulland has chosen to make her trilogy of the life of Josephine Bonaparte fictional. How would this work differ had the author chosen to turn her extensive research into a narrative of nonfiction? What kind of distance would this have created?

12. Written in the form of a diary, this work of fiction departs from the typical style of the historical novel. Did you feel it brought you closer to Josephine, in particular, as she wrote of the joys and trials

of her life? Would you be interested in other novels or historical fiction written in this format?

13. Josephine fulfilled many traditional roles: mother, wife, hostess. She also involved herself in politics and business. Did she wield power? If so, in what way, and to what end? What role did she play in Napoleon's rise to power? Of all her roles, which do you think was the most important to her?

14. In France, women's dress had changed radically after the Revolution: no corsets or hoops were worn, no high heels, fabrics were lighter, the cut revealing, following the natural contours of the body. In what ways did the style of dress reflect the changes that had taken place in France? What periods would you compare this to in this century? When Josephine traveled to Italy, she discovered that the Italians dressed more conservatively. Why did they do so? How did the two countries differ at that point in time?

15. Josephine helped form a syndicate to sell provisions to the army. Were other characters involved in such ventures? Was it unusual for a woman to be involved? What was Josephine's motivation? Did she understand the full import of what she was doing? Were her actions ethical? Foolish? Justified? If a woman was in need of money, what options were open to her in the late eighteenth century? What might Josephine have done instead?

16. How did Josephine feel about Napoleon when she married him? Why did she marry him? Did she come to love him? When? (And why?) Was love considered important to a marriage? Napoleon professed to love Josephine passionately. Did he, in fact, love her?

ABOUT THE AUTHOR

SANDRA GULLAND experienced the passionate politics of yet another famous period: the sixties in Berkeley, California, where she attended San Francisco State College and the University of California, Berkeley. She emigrated to Canada in 1970, where she taught school in a remote Inuit village in Labrador; Gulland later moved to Ontario, where she became involved in book publishing. A writer and book editor, she has worked on her Josephine trilogy for a number of years, traveling to the cities and homes in which Josephine had lived, learning to read French and corresponding with scholars. She now lives near Killaloe, Ontario, with her husband and two children.

Discover more reading group guides on-line! Browse our complete list of guides and download them for free at
www.SimonSays.com/reading_guides.html